Holy Orders

An Unholy Novel by Charles McKelvy

9/1/90

Bless you,
Dan & Marilyn!
Charley McKelvy

Other Books published by the Dunery Press:

Chicagoland , four novellas by Charles McKelvy (1988)
My California Friends and Other Stories, four novellas by Natalie
McKelvy (1988)

Holy Orders
Published in 1989 by
The Dunery Press
P.O. Box 116
Harbert, Michigan 49115-0116
Phone: 616/469-1278

Cover illustration by
David Bates Design
Evanston, Illinois

Library of Congress
Catalog Card Number: 89-050230

ISBN 0-944771-02-5

For the Dean

"Almighty God, giver of all good things, who by thy Holy Spirit hast appointed divers Orders of Ministers in thy Church; Mercifully behold these thy servants now called to the Office of Priesthood; and so replenish them with the truth of thy Doctrine, and adorn them with innocency of life, that, both by word and good example, they may faithfully serve thee in this Office, to the glory of thy Name, and the edification of thy Church; through the merits of our Saviour Jesus Christ, who liveth and reigneth with thee and the same Holy Spirit, world without end. Amen."

--The Form and Manner of Ordering Priests
THE BOOK OF COMMON PRAYER

Chapter One

The men of the Alpha Chi Lambda chapter at Penn State had no argument about what to watch that damp April 1970 night.

The Nixon Administration had decided the only fair way to settle the draft controversy was to draw birthdays of eligible young men from a rotating drum on national television. And despite the invasion of Cambodia and the daily bombing of North Vietnam, Hanoi and its legion of Charlies were not about to capitulate.

LIFE MAGAZINE would have to do a cover picturing the dead boys from next door before middle America demanded an end to the police action in someone else's precinct.

Aldo "Al" Salerno, chapter president and eldest brother, entered the chapter lounge wearing a red-on-yellow U. S. Marine Corps T-shirt and a satisfied smile.

The 27-year-old South Philadelphian had served two tours in Vietnam, had been wounded twice, and awarded four battle commendations. He was active in the Vets Club, led all Alpha Chi intramural teams, and majored in Business Administration. He worked out with weights in the house basement and wore a menacing scowl under his close-cropped black hair.

Salerno hated "peace freaks," having proclaimed at a chapter meeting that Alpha Chi "is 100 percent behind the war effort. One hundred percent!"

Old Glory, at his behest, flew night and day from the roof. It was, of course, properly lighted at night.

Mostly blue-collar boys from Pennsylvania's mill and mining towns, the brothers of Alpha Chi accepted Salerno's right-wing views without challenge and competed for his approval. He was more of a father than most had known at home.

It was one minute to show time, and the lounge filled with muscular young men in T-shirts, sweatpants, and Converse All Stars — the chapter uniform.

Wearing a pair of pressed chinos, penny loafers without socks, and an oxford button-down, James Gordon Clarke III slipped into the smoke-filled room and found an empty folding chair against the far wall. The handsome fourth-quarter senior smoothed his modishly long brown hair and fixed his blue eyes on the 23-inch RCA television screen. He was a drama major with a minor in comparative literature.

Salerno, who was ensconced in the chapter's La-Z-Boy, spotted the troubled triple legacy.

"Hey, Clarke," he said, "you ready to die for your country? Your sweet little 2-S is finally running out, and I got a feelin' this is gonna be your lucky night. I bet you got the same feelin', huh?"

Jimmy shrugged. "Yeah, as a matter of fact, I do feel kind of lucky. Like I did when I won that Louisville Slugger at the Little League banquet. Hell, this could be my big chance to break in as an actor. I can just see it now: Bob Hope and all those beautiful ladies will be up there dancing around on the back of some tank or aircraft carrier, and old Bob'll spot me. How can he miss – I'll be the most handsome guy there. Talent running out of my pores. So he'll have me do a couple of routines, and the next thing . . ."

"Yeah, and next thing, you'll be filling in for his microphone stand," said Brian Lauderbach, a burly ag major from Latrobe.

"I knew a guy like you in Vietnam, Clarke. Always babbled like that when he was scared shitless. Dumb fuck got wasted one night 'cause he couldn't keep his friggin' mouth shut. Same thing's gonna happen to you, Clarke. I can smell it a mile away," Salerno said.

The brothers made machine-gun noises with their mouths. Jimmy couldn't disappoint them, so he did the dying swan routine that won him the part of Eben Cabot in a recent production of O'Neill's DESIRE UNDER THE ELMS. He had done such a convincing job of being strangled during the third act that the director had nearly stopped the play to see if he was all right. Naturally, the brothers of Alpha Chi weren't there to see him. They never were.

But now they applauded Jimmy's performance with hoots and hollers. Then Salerno silenced them with a wave of his meaty fist.

"No, man, that ain't it. First of all, you won't see it comin'. Dudes never do. They always act like Santa Claus just showed up in July. They'd go down like somebody just slashed all their tires. Most of 'em'd start cryin' like babies."

"But not you, right, Al? You were a hard-ass when you got yours, weren't you?"

Salerno grimaced. No one had ever sassed him like that. And if he said he had taken his shrapnel like a man and waited four hours for Medi-vac without a peep, then that's what happened.

"We can't all be hard asses, Al," Jimmy continued. "Me, I'm gonna cry my fool head off if they even look at me the wrong way."

Salerno, who HAD cried his fool head off the night he took a bullet in the butt, shifted uncomfortably.

"Man, the VC are gonna make mincemeat outta you, Clarke. And just pray to God you don't meet up with any North Vietnamese regulars. You hear me, boy?"

"Anything you say, general. Anything you say. Hey, Murphy, turn on the tube — I want to see how lucky I really am," Jimmy said.

A brother offered him a swig of Rolling Rock, but he refused it. His throat was dry and he was spooked bad, but he was determined to act cool.

An announcer said the Selective Service was presenting a special program, and stone-faced functionaries soon assembled around a plexiglass drum.

"Looks like those stupid game shows you clowns are always watching," Jimmy said, now feeling unaccountably giddy.

Salerno smiled and said, "You're on a roll tonight, Clarke. Man I'd love to be your D.I. I'd turn your sorry ass inside out. Now just shut up and watch. All right?"

"Yes, sir."

Jimmy tilted his chair back against the wall and folded his hands behind his head. As always, he was doing a fine job of masking his inner turmoil. To those around him, he was a conceited rich jerk from the Philadelphia Main Line whose old man had bought his way into the chapter. He was a goody-two-shoes with no time for intramurals, except swimming. But that was sissy shit even though he always took first in everything.

Brother Clarke was good-looking all right. Weighing 178 and standing 5'11", he had the classic fraternity stature, but he wasn't a team player.

From Jimmy's perspective, his brothers were a bunch of beefy boors bound to become insurance salesmen and phys. ed. teachers. If they wanted to get their asses shot off like Salerno, then that was their business. Jimmy had better things to do with his life.

A functionary rolled the drum and withdrew a capsule containing a birthday.

The house hushed.

Salerno consulted the chapter book and grunted disappointedly, "Nope. Not yet."

There was a murmur of nervous banter and suddenly everyone was lighting cigarettes. Jimmy, the militant non-smoker, even bummed one.

"Man, I haven't had this much excitement since they told me to bend over and spread my cheeks at the draft physical," Jimmy said, coughing.

The government's doctors had found Jimmy to be in excellent physical condition, and his draft board had subsequently advised him to keep in touch.

The draft officials continued rotating the drum and withdrawing birthdays — no Alpha Chi winners yet.

Jimmy was born on May 7, 1948, three years to the day after the Third Reich called it verlassen. The officials pulled a May day, and Jimmy's heart dropped into his bowels. His scalp itched, and he got a nervous erection. Others did too, hunching forward to hide their distress.

"This is it, Clarke," Salerno said, popping out his leg rest. "'Halls of Montezuma' for you, pal. Hell, when old Charlie sees you, he's gonna think we're sendin' the women and children."

Jimmy felt his head swell as they continued drawing other young men's birthdays. Now he knew how Charles Darnell felt as he stood at the foot of the scaffold in TALE OF TWO CITIES. He was waiting for the kiss of cold steel.

"So far — so good," Jimmy whispered as they got past number 30 without drawing his birthday. He was sweating profusely now and wanted to stick his head out the window and scream. But he kept his unfocused eyes riveted on the television screen.

"Don't talk like that, Clarke. I got money ridin' on you, boy," Salerno said. "But I'm gonna have to turn those love handles of yours into solid muscle if you're gonna be squared away in your dress blues. Can't have no Alpha Chi's in the silly-ass army."

Jimmy rubbed his moist palms together and considered prayer. It offered no solace, because there was no one there to accept the call. There hadn't been for years.

"Number 35," the Selective Service official said, "May 7th, number 36 . . ."

Jimmy prayed.

"Hey!! That's you, Clarke!! That's you!!"

Salerno stabbed the chapter book with his forefinger and grinned enormously.

"Hey, brothers, let's hear it for Private James Clarke, U.S.M.C. God, I wish I could be there when you march your sorry ass into Parris Island. They're gonna turn you inside out! Hell, I might re-up just so I can be your D.I. Man, I'd be on your ass like flies on shit."

Jimmy was still in shock. "Parris Island? That's near Charleston, isn't it?"

Salerno laughed. "Yeah, but it might as well be on the moon, 'cause they ain't gonna give you liberty for a long, long time, sucker. The only dates you're gonna have are with mosquitos and water moccasins."

Jimmy was rebounding now and said, "None of which were virgins after you left, right, general?"

Salerno sprang from his seat and pinned Jimmy against the wall. He wasn't much bigger, but he had the weight training and surprise in his favor.

"God damn it, Clarke, you'd better get serious for once in your blueblood little life. Real serious. You understand me? You're draft bait now. You're goin' to Vietnam. You know, just like that hippie faggot song you're always singin' — 'don't give a damn, next stop is Vietnam.' Well, your next stop is Vietnam. You hear me?"

Jimmy looked into Salerno's eyes and saw something akin to concern.

Salerno looked into Jimmy's eyes and saw something akin to glass. He shook Jimmy, and the shock wore off.

"You're number 35. Number 35, and you've got less than two months on your 2-S, Jimmy Boy. Tricky Dick and Henry Kiss-off want your ass over there. Real soon."

"I could go to Canada," Jimmy said, dazed.

"Why not Sweden? Or Cuba, you pinko bastard."

"I'm not a communist. I was an Eagle Scout."

"Then be a man and join the marines. You hear me, boy. You better start gettin' your ass in shape for boot camp. Hey, I'll even help you. Startin' tomorrow, we'll roll out at 0500 and run a mile. The next day we'll build up to two, and then . . ."

Jimmy shook his head. "Al, you don't understand. I love my country, but I don't believe in this war. I . . ."

"You're a chicken shit, Clarke. But I'm gonna change that. Startin' tomorrow morning." Salerno shoved Jimmy away and returned to his throne to watch the rest of the show.

When none of the other brothers got numbers lower than 150, Salerno went back to Jimmy and said, "Well, Clarke, looks like you're the only one who's goin' for sure. So what do you say — tomorrow mornin' — 0500. I'm gonna whip you into shape like you've never been whipped before."

As his brothers burst into: "From the halls of Montezuma to the shores of Tripoli . . ." Jimmy Clarke surprised everyone but himself by punching Al Salerno solidly in the sternum.

Salerno collapsed with a wounded gasp. Several brothers sought to help him to his feet, but he brushed them aside with an angry growl. He had nearly straightened when he saw the murderous look in Jimmy Clarke's eyes. Salerno took a slow breath and opened his hands in supplication.

"Maybe you should take a little walk, Clarke. Cool off. Do you good," he said.

Jimmy was still smoking. He had enough adrenalin cooking in his veins to kick Canada's ass. He scanned the room for takers. The brothers of Alpha Chi wisely cleared a path, and he strode belligerently out of the chapter lounge and into the damp, dark night.

Chapter Two

After three miles of trying to pound his feet through the pavement, Jimmy found himself at Elaine's door.

He desperately needed to talk to someone, and Elaine Roberts was the only person on campus in whom he could confide.

They had met two years earlier at a Zero Population Growth rally and put their complimentary condoms to immediate use. Elaine was brash; pretty in a dark, Slavic way, and the purveyor of dynamite reefer. She was a year older than Jimmy and the progeny of a drunken Pittsburgh steelworker and his battered wife.

A professional student, Elaine Roberts was a semester or two away from a Masters of Social Work. She lived off grants and fellowships from leftist foundations and planned to be a feminist therapist. But she was content for the time being to practice on Jimmy Clarke.

Jimmy was about to rap on the door to her dingy, three-room apartment when he remembered Elaine's cardinal rule — call first. Always phone first.

Jimmy liked to think they had some sort of arrangement — maybe not a relationship exactly, but hell, they had been getting it on at least once a week for two years, and that had to count for something.

But Elaine wasn't about to sell her soul and body to any man. She liked Jimmy, but she liked a lot of other men and needed lots of them to satisfy her various needs. She chided Jimmy for not doing likewise.

Jimmy cupped his hands around his eyes and peered into the L-shaped apartment. Elaine had lighted her love candle and was playing her only Charley Parker album.

"It's that prick Pearson," Jimmy muttered.

Eugene Pearson was the graduate assistant who had nearly flunked Jimmy out of zoology his freshman year. He was African-American, bright, and, according to Elaine, bigger and better than Jimmy.

Reminding himself that he was really an open-minded liberal at heart, Jimmy backed away from the window. He turned and kicked a post, catching it wrong and bruising his big toe.

Jimmy bit his tongue hobbling down the steps and nearly tripped at the bottom. Tears welled in his eyes, and he wanted to collapse on the sidewalk and have a good cry.

Instead, he stomped back to campus. The union and library were closed, and having no immediate use for liquor, he passed the beer joints on College Avenue without a second glance. Presently he found himself at the stone "Nittany Lion" statue his father's class of 1940 had bestowed on Penn State. Jimmy climbed atop the lion and wondered what his father would do. Or, what he would have done if he had been in his father's place in 1941.

The Old Man didn't know he was going to sit out the war in New England when he enlisted in Officers' Candidate School, Jimmy thought. For all he knew, the navy was going to put him on a PT boat somewhere in the South Pacific.

Jimmy glanced at Alumni Hall and thought of his late grandfather, the original James G. Clarke. Grandfather Clarke had sacrificed a track scholarship in 1917 for the army. He had been one of the first Americans wounded in the great war — at Cantigny. He had come back to Penn State and Alpha Chi after the war and had lettered three times in track despite his war injuries. There was a plaque with his picture near the indoor track. Grandfather Clarke died when Jimmy was a baby, but he had always loomed large in his grandson's life.

"You'd enlist in a second, wouldn't you?" Jimmy said.

Despite his legendary achievements, Grandfather Clarke could not speak from the grave.

Jimmy took a deep breath.

His mother was forever telling him to confide in his father. Like it had been his fault all these years that he and the Old Man weren't Ward and Beaver Cleaver. Jimmy rubbed his face and wondered if it wasn't his fault.

He found a pay phone in the lobby of the Nittany Lion Inn. Having no money on him, he placed a collect call to the big, brick house at 322 Forest Drive, Wynnwood, Pa.

Jimmy glanced at his watch after the fourth ring and realized it was 11:30. His mother always went to bed at 11, and his father . . .

"Hello," a husky male voice said, "Clarke residence."

"Collect call from James Clarke; will you accept the charges?"

Jimmy could just see his father fumbling with the phone next to his leather chair in the study.

"James Clarke? I'm James Clarke."

"Dad, it's me — Jimmy," Jimmy said over the operator.

"Sir, will you accept the charges?" the operator said.

"Yes, goddamn it. I'll accept the charges. But this had better be the last damn time. For Christ's sake, Jimmy, do you know what time it is? You'll wake your mother."

Just then, Louise Maye Clarke picked up the bedroom phone and said in a sleepy voice: "Hello?"

"I've got it, Louise. Go back to sleep."

"Hi, Mom. It's me — Jimmy."

"Jimmy? Is that you, dear??" Louise awakened instantly.

"Yeah, it's me, Mom."

"Is something the matter, dear??" Calls from her only child were infrequent and never came at night.

"No, Mom. Actually, I wanted to talk to Dad. But as long as you're on the line, I wanted to remind you that I'm planning on being home this weekend for Jill's wedding."

"Oh good," Louise said. "I was counting on you being there. Can your lady friend, uh . . ."

"Elaine?"

"Yes. Will she be able to join us? She could sleep in the guest room."

"No, Mom. Elaine's got to give a lecture Saturday afternoon."

"That's too bad," Louise said, unable to mask her glee. She was sure Elaine Roberts was the wrong woman for her boy. So far, they all were.

"Well," she added, "I'll let you two have your little chat. See you Saturday morning, dear. Unless you'd like to come home Friday night."

"No, I'd rather drive over in the morning. I'll see you about 10. Good night, Mom."

"Good night, dear."

James Gordon Clarke II had meanwhile freshened his scotch and water and took a loud sip. "So, what is it this time — your checking account overdrawn again?"

"You happen to watch the news tonight, Dad?"

"Yes," he said. He had passed out before Walter Cronkite opened his mouth. "But I didn't see anything about Penn State. What tree did you wrap your car around this time?"

"I didn't do anything, Dad. It's the government that did something. They started a draft lottery tonight. I'm number 35. They're gonna draft me in two months, Dad. I'm gonna go to Vietnam. Dad, what should I do?"

James G. Clarke II swilled his drink and said: "There was a demonstration at the Naval Yard the other day. Some of those Italians from South Philly went down there and kicked the shit out of those goddamn hippies."

Jimmy stared at the phone. He should have known better.

"Dad, what has that got to do with . . ."

"Kicked the shit out of those goddamn long-haired bastards. If you ask me, they should have thrown the goddamn bunch of them in the Delaware River."

Jimmy tried to yell "Fuck you, Dad" into the phone but he managed only a meek, "I'll see you Saturday, Dad."

Chapter Three

"Bummer, man. I can't believe it. If I were you, I'd be on the next bus to Canada. No question about it." Elaine Roberts chugged the last of her Rolling Rock out of the green "pony" bottle and pulled the thick black hair out of her eyes. "Jimmy, are you nuts? You can't let them do this to you."

Jimmy shrugged and stared at the black-eyed beauty seated opposite him at the Rathskeller. Penn State's most popular beer joint was crowded with students raucously celebrating the end of another week. The smell of surreptitiously smoked marijuana, stale beer, and urine permeated the close quarters.

Jimmy had called Elaine, half expecting her to still be in bed with Eugene Pearson. But she was all his — until her next class at 2.

"You know," he said, licking the foam off his lips, "my old man used to drink in here. In fact, he had his last drink here before he joined the navy. Well, one of his last drinks. He graduated in 1940 and joined the navy in '41 — before Pearl Harbor, actually. He carved his initials in one of these tables, but I never could find them. Too many other initials. Well, what do you think?"

"Of your old man's initials?"

"No. Of me enlisting — like my father. In Officers' Candidate School. Hell, they're gonna draft me in a couple of months anyway. I'd look great in navy blue and gold. Elaine, my student deferment expires in June. Maybe if I enlisted, they'd send me to Europe or give me some cushy desk job in the Pentagon.

"Maybe I could do Shakespeare in some officers' club in Hawaii or something. They're not all a bunch of goons. Maybe there's some general or admiral out there who's been thinking of starting a theater company on his base. Maybe I could teach drama at the Naval Academy or something. Maybe . . ."

"Jesus, Jimmy, you should hear yourself. I've been trying to talk sense into your thick head for an hour, and you sit here telling me you're gonna teach drama at the fucking Naval Academy. Jesus H. Christ!"

Jimmy sighed and kneaded his fingers.

"Elaine, you know I'm not some crazy radical. I could give a shit about politics. I believed in the domino theory until it started looking like I was going over there."

Elaine lighted a Marlboro and glanced around the bar. "What is this — a speech for the fucking American Legion? Lighten up, boy. It's me, remember? Elaine. Earth control to Jimmy."

"Let's change the subject, all right?"

"Fine. What do you want to talk about — the weather? I bet it's awful nasty in Vietnam right now." Elaine took his hand and said, "What's going on in that head of yours anyway?"

Jimmy looked her in the eye. "I came by your place last night after they pulled my number. I wanted to talk to you then, but . . ."

". . . I had company."

"Right."

"So? You know what our arrangement is."

"Yeah, I know, but . . ."

"I'm not on call, Jimmy."

"Right. How stupid of me to forget," Jimmy said. He was tired of this modern crap. He was tired of being cuckolded by Eugene Pearson and God knows who else.

"Look, if you're gonna lay that jealousy bullshit on me, I've got other things to do, Jimmy. You told me you wanted to talk about this draft thing. Now: do you or don't you?"

"Yeah, I do."

"Well, then go to Canada. What's the big deal?"

"I don't know, Elaine. I just don't know. I really don't feel comfortable running off to Canada. I mean it's a nice country and all, but this is my country. It's just not me."

"Why not? Do you have to get killed in Vietnam to get your father's approval?"

Jimmy laughed.

"What's so funny? I know I'm a natural comedian, but I didn't think that was funny."

"I called my father last night after I . . ."

"After you peeked in my window and saw me getting it on with Gene."

"Yeah."

"Yeah, and . . ."

"Well, I tried to have a real heart-to-heart with him. And you know what?"

"Surprise me."

"All he could talk about was a bunch of goons from South Philly beating up demonstrators outside the Philadelphia Naval Yard. Like that was the answer to my problem. Maybe it was a cryptic message or something. You know how engineers are."

"No mystery to me, Jimmy—your dear father thinks more of whale shit on the bottom of the ocean than he thinks of you. Great, huh?"

Jimmy squeezed Elaine's hand.

"You look like you could use another beer," she said, smiling. "It's on me."

When she returned with four fresh ponies, Elaine continued her attack, saying: "You already tried to get his approval by joining that fascist fraternity. What did that get you?"

"Well, he does like to talk about how much better the chapter was in his day, but that's the way he is about everything. Everything was better in his day."

"Yeah, because you weren't even born. Jimmy, do you know what that says about you? He doesn't even care if you exist. You're just the drunk on the next barstool."

"At least my father doesn't use my mother as a punching bag," Jimmy said.

Elaine chewed her lip. "Let's change the subject, all right?"

"No. You were the one who wanted to discuss this. So let's discuss it, Elaine. You sit there and tell me how fucked up me and my family are—well, what about you and your family? I don't see you on the cover of THE SATURDAY EVENING POST."

Elaine's knuckles whitened around her pony. "Don't you have somewhere to go?"

Jimmy pushed his beer at Elaine and got up. "Yeah, as a matter of fact, I do. Thanks for nothing, Elaine."

Jimmy walked out before she could reply.

Chapter Four

Saint Matthew's Episcopal Church in Wynnwood was packed with prosperous Protestants.

Jimmy's maternal uncle, Phillip J. Maye, had spared no expense for his only daughter's wedding, and the stately old church was crammed with flowers.

Jimmy and his mother went to the second pew on the bride's side, and Louise Clarke habitually dropped the kneeler and knelt. Episcopal calisthenics.

She elbowed her son and he reluctantly knelt. While Louise Clarke asked Almighty God to guarantee her niece's everlasting happiness, Jimmy Clarke begged whomever was listening to keep his ass out of Vietnam.

He waited until his mother was finished and tried to get comfortable in the straight-backed pew. No way. There's no danger of this place ever being renamed the Church of the Holy Comforter, Jimmy thought.

Jimmy studied the old-money oak and stained glass and chuckled softly. "At least You've got taste," he thought aloud.

Louise Clarke glared at her son. To her, talking in church, genocide, and pederasty were sins of the same order.

"At least I'm here," Jimmy whispered. "More than I can say for Dad."

Louise adjusted her mink stole and stared at the ruby-encrusted gold crucifix on the marble altar. Hardly glancing at her only begotten son, she whispered, "You know your father! He hates to go to church. But he's here in spirit."

He's with spirits all right — scotch, bourbon, gin, vodka, and vermouth. Jimmy pictured the Old Man ensconced in his den with a scotch and water in one hand and the channel selector in the other. What a life.

Father and son had been painfully polite with one another that morning. Jim Clarke's only reference to his son's call for help had been: "I checked with the phone company — you owe me $1.78 for that phone call the other night."

Jimmy wrote the check and handed it to the Old Man without comment.

The organist finished an energetic "Ode to Joy" and nodded at the narthex. Jill's intended, a swarthy Armenian rug dealer from suburban New York, entered with his dark party and stood ready at the nave. Despite their gray morning coats and fresh haircuts, they looked like a plot to overthrow the Turkish government.

Jill had met him at a junior college in northeastern Pennsylvania, and the family was relieved to learn he wasn't Jewish.

"Do you suppose their babies will look like that?" Louise Clarke whispered.

"Probably be born wearing fezzes," Jimmy whispered back.

The organist pounded into Mendelssohn's "Wedding March" and all eyes gratefully shifted to Jimmy's adorable, five-year-old second cousin, Rebecca, as she led the procession of beaming matrons and maids of honor.

Uncle Phil, resplendent in his black tux and fresh crew-cut, marched his "little girl" down the aisle with the precision of an ex-marine. Except for a curt nod at the family, he gazed unbrokenly at his precious daughter all the way to the altar rail, and then he kissed her so long and hard that the groom and his men tensed for action.

Jimmy was glad Uncle Phil wasn't Turkish or they'd have to switch sacraments.

But he liked the dramatic tension and thought the lighting was terrific.

But the costumes needed help. The groom's party should all be wearing burnooses and jewel-handled scimitars. The bride would be better off with less lace. And cranberry did nothing for her portly party. Elizabethan finery would flatter them better and suit the subtle lighting. As for the extras — can the polyester and dress them in the natural fibers worn by 16th Century peasants. That would do.

Jimmy, of course, was nattily attired in a navy blazer, gray pleated slacks, oxford button-down, Florsheim loafers and a red, silk tie. Joe College.

As he watched the cast stumble into position, Jimmy wondered why he was here. Except for the time they played doctor behind their grandfather's cottage at the Jersey Shore, Jimmy and Jill had never been particularly close.

Still, it was an excuse to get away from Salerno and his bimbo brigade. They hadn't let up on him since the lottery. And Salerno had actually tried to roust him at 5 o'clock the next morning for his P.T. The crazy bastard actually thought Jimmy was going to Vietnam.

Jimmy glanced at his mother and wondered what she thought. She had been a Red Cross volunteer during World War II. She had seen the boys who didn't come back in one piece. She knows what a klutz I am — does she think it's going to be any different for me?

Enraptured by the nuptial nonsense unfolding in front of her, Louise Clarke was not thinking about Vietnam. Or her son. She was too busy being a blushing bride again to have another thought.

The presiding minister, a handsome young fellow with a dense mustache, daring sideburns, and horn-rimmed reading glasses, waited until the church was solemnly still. Then he smoothed a wrinkle in his starchy clean surplice and fiddled with his stole.

Opening his gold-leafed BOOK OF COMMON PRAYER, he read: "Dearly beloved, we are gathered together here in the sight of God, and in the face of this company, to join together this Man and this Woman in holy Matrimony; which is an honourable estate instituted of God, signifying unto us the mystical union that is betwixt Christ and his Church . . ."

Jimmy tapped his mother's wrist and whispered: "What happened to Dr. Gibson?"

Annoyed, Louise cupped her hand over his ear and said, "If you hadn't stopped coming to church, you'd know that Dr. Gibson retired two years ago and moved to Florida. He's a supply priest in Tampa. This is our new rector, Mr. Carlisle. He's quite popular."

She resumed her reverent pose.

Jimmy could see that the young priest was certainly a hit with the ladies — especially his mother's contemporaries. Jimmy had never thought of the clergy as sex objects, but this dude sure seemed to have the old girls in a state.

Hmmmm.

". . . Into this holy estate these two persons present come now to be joined. If any man can show just cause why they may not lawfully be joined together, let him now speak, or else hereafter forever hold his peace."

A few throats cleared, but no one spoke.

Cranmer's soothing ceremony continued, binding Jimmy Clarke in its spell.

And he couldn't fault this Carlisle character's delivery. The guy could probably be coached through an act or two of Shakespeare.

Plus, he lives rent-free in one of the finest houses on the Main Line. And the ladies are probably always fighting over who gets to have him over for dinner next, and there's no heavy lifting. No heavy lifting, and . . .

". . . Jill, wilt thou have this Man to be thy wedded husband, to live together after God's ordinance in the holy estate of Matrimony? Wilt thou love him, comfort him, honour and keep him in sickness and in health; and . . ."

And James G. Clarke III had his epiphany.

He felt it first in his scalp as a prickly sensation. Then the amazing manifestation made his whole body electric.

Louise Clarke sought to calm her quaking son with a quiet hand. "Ow," she said, examining her fingers for burns.

Jimmy shook and shimmied with the sure knowledge that the divinely-inspired U.S. Constitution absolutely guaranteed separation of church and state.

"4-D!" Jimmy exclaimed.

Horrified, Louise Clarke put her hand near her son's mouth. "Shhssshhh!"

Jimmy jumped up and shouted: "4-D, everybody! 4 fucking D! How could I be so stupid — they don't draft ministers, priests, and rabbis. God, it was right there on my draft card all along. Praise the Lord!"

Everyone was absolutely shocked and offended.

Except for the Mayes' black maid, Beulah.

She was so glad to see the spirit at work in the white folks' church, that she clapped her hands and shouted, "Amen, brother!"

Chapter Five

The Bishop's secretary, Gwynn Worden, peered over her spectacles.

"May I help you, young man?"

Jimmy reckoned the Red Army would have trouble getting past this lady. Even though he came complete with his best wool suit, fresh haircut, and shoeshine, he felt small and stupid in her presence.

"Uh yes, I have an appointment with the Select Committee at two o'clock."

"You mean to say the 'Standing Committee.'"

"That's it. I want to be a priest."

Gwynn Worden pursed her lips and found Jimmy's name in the Bishop's gold-leafed appointment book and slashed it with a sharpened pencil.

"Have a seat, Mr. Clarke. The committe will be with you presently."

She resumed her fast, letter-perfect typing as Jimmy settled into a chair and browsed a magazine. He found himself trying to read an article titled: "Planning Liturgy for the Spring and Summer."

Oh my God, he thought, breaking into a cold sweat. Elaine was right, I should go to Canada.

". . . this year Pentecost falls right in the middle of the Memorial Day weekend . . ."

Great, Jimmy thought, I'll make plans now. Jeez, I can't wait.

". . . Meditative hymns to the Holy Spirit, such as 'Breathe on me, Breath of God' will not work as processional hymns . . ."

Jimmy laughed; Gwynn Worden withered him with a look; Jimmy was quiet.

Jimmy put down the magazine and stared at Bishop Hamilton's solid oak door. They were grilling some other poor bastard in there. If you passed muster, they made you a postulant and sent you off to seminary school. After the first of three years there, you became a candidate for Holy Orders. Then, if you were graduated in good order, they awarded you a Master of Divinity degree and ordained you a deacon. Then a priest, and, if you prayed your cards right, you got to wear a bishop's mitre, pectoral cross, and ring with a smart dash of purple.

Jimmy wondered if they were holding the other applicant's feet over hot coals or tearing out his fingernails one-by-one. Like the good-old-days — the Crusades, the Spanish Inquisition, Oliver Cromwell in Ireland. Hernando Cortes in Mexico. Even the Marlboro man would have gone to church in those days.

He was contemplating the Salem witch trials when the door opened, and a middle-aged man emerged with a beatified look on his frail face.

The Right Reverend Charles Francis Hamilton, or "Plus Charles" for the cross he always included after his signature, patted the postulant-to-be on the back and said, "We'll inform you of our decision in a fortnight, Mr. Heckler."

Certain he had a calling from God, William L. Heckler turned and gratefully kissed the Bishop's ring. Jimmy was shocked. They never did anything like that at Saint Matthew's.

Heckler departed in peace, and Bishop Hamilton turned to Jimmy with pleasure. At last, he thought, a cradle Episcopalian who wants to be a priest, and a well-adjusted one to boot.

Heckler had come over from the Baptists because he adored the Episcopal liturgy, and he could go back as far as Bishop Hamilton was concerned, but the committee loved him. Having just finished a 20-year tour in the Army, Heckler was a first-class sniveler.

"So good to see you, Jim," Bishop Hamilton said, extending his hand.

Glancing nervously at the silver episcopal ring, Jimmy was surprised by the Bishop's grip. The man had the hands of a concert pianist but the grasp of a plumber.

"It's good to see you again, Bishop Hamilton. It's been such a long time; I'm surprised you remember me."

"Miss Worden tells me I never forget a face," the Bishop said, laughing. "But don't ask me where I left my umbrella."

Jimmy produced his red BOOK OF COMMON PRAYER. "Look, Bishop Hamilton, you autographed my prayer book after you confirmed me."

The Bishop chuckled. "Autographed? I never thought of it that way."

"Well, I sure did. I remember it like it was yesterday. And

remember, you took us all out to the Lion's Share for breakfast."

"I've never seen anyone enjoy blueberry pancakes more," the Bishop said. He fondly inspected the book. Moments like this made up for all the fights over funding.

"You were all so afraid I was going to give you a good hard clop on the head that you closed your eyes when you knelt in front of me. I felt like the executioner. Do you know, I almost broke out laughing."

"Dr. Gibson warned us that you liked to give everyone a good hard slap when you confirmed them," Jimmy said, laughing.

"Did he now? I'm sure you were pleasantly surprised when I turned out to be such a soft touch."

Jimmy shrugged. "Oh, I don't know, Bishop Hamilton, I think you might have loosened a few teeth. But don't worry, I'm not going to sue."

"I'm glad," the Bishop said, putting his arm around Jimmy's shoulders. "Well, shall I introduce you to the committee? They're most anxious to meet you."

Jimmy took a deep breath. He wanted to slip the Bishop a C-note and say, 'look, man, just fix it so I don't have to go to 'Nam, all right?'

Instead, he said, "Yes, Bishop Hamilton, I'm ready."

Jimmy entered the handsome office and looked down a polished walnut table at six men dressed just like his father. The seventh, Peter Martin, wore a silk ascot and a beige, linen suit. His was the only name and face Jimmy remembered after the Bishop's introductions.

Bishop Hamilton invited Jimmy to sit on his right, next to Peter Martin, and began by saying, "Gentlemen, Mr. Clarke comes to us this afternoon from Penn State where he is completing his studies in drama and history. Perhaps you could begin by telling us about yourself, Jim. Mr. Martin here has a great interest in history, and I'm sure he would like to know what period most intrigues you."

"The Elizabethan, of course," Jimmy said. "How can you not admire Elizabeth the First, Drake, Bacon, Raleigh, Donne, Marlowe — to say nothing of Shakespeare."

Delighted, Peter Martin turned to face Jimmy. "Don't forget the Archbishop," he said.

"Right. Of course Thomas Cranmer technically wasn't an

Elizabethan since Mary had him burned at the stake two years before Elizabeth took the throne, but you're absolutely right. I get goose bumps every time I read the Prayer Book. The Catholics can have their Latin or whatever they're using these days. I'll take Cranmer's English any day."

"To whom are you referring, Mr. Clarke?" said Glenn Couch, the grayest of the gray six.

Jimmy looked down the table. "I wasn't aware that there was more than one kind of Catholic," he said.

Glenn Couch nodded smugly. "Shall I enlighten this misinformed young man, Bishop?"

"Don't bully him, Glenn," Bishop Hamilton said. "What Mr. Couch meant to tell you, Jim, is that some Episcopalians, such as Mr. Couch, consider themselves Anglo-Catholics. But coming as you do from a good, solid Low Church background, I wouldn't expect you to know that. And I certainly don't see it as grounds to bar you from seminary."

Peter Martin patted Jimmy's hand. "Perhaps you could finish your discussion of Archbishop Cranmer. I believe you were going to add something when you were interrupted."

"Well, I was just going to say that Cranmer's actions certainly had a profound effect on Elizabeth. Not only did he move the church closer to the Reformation, but he basically was the one who helped Henry put her mother's head on the block."

"I wouldn't quite put it that way, Mr. Clarke," Glenn Couch said. "I wouldn't put it that way at all. And I certainly wouldn't want to hear any priest in this diocese refering to Archbishop Cranmer as a cold-blooded killer. If anything, the man should be regarded as a saint."

"I wasn't calling anyone a cold-blooded killer, Mr. Couch."

Bishop Hamilton nodded. "I'm sure you weren't. Now then, you were baptized into the faith as an infant — in 1948 at Saint Matthew's by the Reverend Doctor Gibson. I confirmed you there in 1959. Perhaps you can tell us the rest, Jim."

"Well," Jimmy said, directly addressing Bishop Hamilton and Peter Martin, "I was an acolyte from sixth grade through most of high school. I was never in the choir, because I can't hold a tune to save my life, but I was president of the youth group, and I led two retreats."

"That's all well and good," another gray man said, "but what have you done for the church lately? You filed your application at the last possible moment, and Father Kingsley at Penn State says he's only seen you in chapel the last few weeks. Forgive my cynical nature, Bishop, but I think it's pretty clear what we have here."

"Another Saul on the road to Damascus, Carl?" Bishop Hamilton said, smiling.

"Hardly. Mr. Clarke, would you mind telling us what number you got in the recent draft lottery?"

Shit, Jimmy thought, I blew it. "I'm not sure exactly."

"You're not sure?" Glenn Couch said. "You're a senior in college, on the verge of losing your student deferment, and you're not sure what your draft number is."

"I don't know—it was under 100. But what difference does it make if I was number 1 or 365? Anyway, I've been thinking about applying to become a navy chaplain. I know you're having a hard time finding positions for everyone, Bishop Hamilton, and I've heard it's pretty much the same in other dioceses, so I've been giving some thought to being a chaplain. My father was a naval officer, and . . . "

"And so was I," Bishop Hamilton said, beaming. "That's an excellent idea, and one I'd like to discuss in detail with you once you've settled in at the seminary. Speaking of which, have you given any thought to which one you'd like to attend?"

"Well," Jimmy said, recalling his stilted conversation with the psychiatrist he had seen as part of his application, "Dr. Fischbein thought it would be good for me to get away from Pennsylvania. So I've been thinking about Gatesbury in Chicago."

"My alma mater," the Bishop said.

"What better recommendation?" Jimmy said.

Bishop Hamilton stood and said, "Gentlemen, I think this young man will be a credit to the church. I'm sure you all join me in praying for his success. Jim, I think that will be all. We'll inform you of our decision within a fortnight."

Peter Martin took Jimmy's hand and gave him a reassuring wink.

Jimmy turned to the Bishop and spontaneously kissed the ring.

He was halfway through the lobby when he realized he had forgotten his prayer book. Gwynn Worden was away from her desk when he returned, so he eavesdropped at the Bishop's door. It was the six gray men against Peter Martin and the Bishop.

" . . . I won't have the Episcopal Church become a sanctuary for draft dodgers," Glenn Couch declared.

"Fine, Glenn. You can take your money and influence across the street to our fundamentalist brethren anytime you want. You've stood in my way every time I've tried to do something worthwhile for our young people. But not today, Glenn. I have the power to dismiss you from this committee — all of you. And you can take your checkbooks with you as far as I'm concerned, because I'm not going to let this fine young man get himself drafted and . . ."

"May I help you?" It was Gwynn Worden with a freshly powdered nose.

"Er, yeah," Jimmy said, yanking his ear away from the door, "I, ah, forgot my prayer book."

She nodded curtly and fetched it for him. Jimmy caught a glimpse of the Bishop and gave him a heart-felt smile.

* * *

Al Salerno saw the mailman coming up the flagstone walk and rushed to intercept him. He knew the notice was due and wanted to be the first to see it. As he expected, there WAS a letter from a suburban Philadelphia draft board among the junk mail, dunning notices, copies of PLAYBOY, SPORTS ILLUSTRATED, and official fraternity mail.

"Hey, Clarke," he yelled, "guess what YOU got?"

A dozen Alpha Chis tore themselves away from the tube and rushed to the living room where a remarkably serene James Gordon Clarke III appeared but made no attempt to claim his letter.

"Go ahead, Al, you've been looking forward to this more than I have," he said, suppressing a smile.

"Better start doing those push-ups, Clarke, or those D.I.s are gonna chew you a new asshole, you sorry son-of-a-bitch," Salerno said, tearing open the envelope. He stared at the contents with profound puzzlement. "What the hell . . ."

Jimmy's fraternity brothers crowded in for a closer look as he calmly took the letter from Salerno.

"Says I'm 4-D," he announced.

"What the hell's that?" a brother from Buffalo asked. "Pansies and transvestites? You gone queer on us, Clarke? I always figured you would."

"No," Jimmy replied, pointing to the fine print, "4-D: divinity students and clergy. Exempt, as in not going. Praise the Lord, brothers, I've been drafted into God's army!"

Chapter Six

The storm hovered overhead, thundering the leaded windows and rattling the oaken doors.

Jimmy cowered in his suite of ancient rooms watching the weather and wondering if God was trying to tell him something. And also wondering if Elaine wasn't right. Canada, even though he had never been there, certainly had to look better than Gatesbury Theological Seminary.

From the little Jimmy had seen so far, it was nothing more than a one-block square of gothic dormitories, classroom and administration buildings, a chapel, and some boxy married student housing built in 1962 when someone realized that even postulants liked to procreate.

Old dad had waited until the last minute to tell his son that they couldn't pay his full tuition, so he had sold his car to cover the first quarter. Saint Matthew's was rebuilding its organ, so it had no money to spare, and the Bishop said he'd try his best. Meanwhile, he advised, get a work scholarship.

Jimmy surveyed the compound and saw somebody drive by in a red Ford station wagon with Wisconsin tags. The guy actually had a crew-cut.

Oh, my God.

Then he saw a spindly figure hurry out of the classroom building with an armload of books.

Lord protect me.

Jimmy had taken the train from Philadelphia and had been fleeced by a Chicago cabbie who took him on a $35 ride to north suburban Evanston where the venerable seminary sat in a secluded corner of the Northwestern University campus.

He had been shown to his rooms by an anemic second-year student, or middler, and was just beginning to unpack when the storm broke. The middler, whose name he immediately forgot, told him Lake Michigan was but two blocks to the east.

"Great," Jimmy said, grabbing his Speedo, "let's go for a swim."

The middler blanched. Lifting bibles was all the exercise he ever got.

"Besides," he said, "I think the beach is closed."

"Closed? What, are they crazy? September is the best month of the year to swim. Well, when this storm breaks, I'm heading over there for a swim. Hey, do you guys ever go to Chicago? Looks like a terrific city. I've never been there before, and I thought maybe tonight we could . . ."

"Ah, no, I've some reading to do," the middler said, slinking out of Jimmy's rooms.

"Reading? Today? Classes don't start for a week."

"I'm doing an independent tutorial on the Oxford Movement for Father Wiltwright. I'll be in the library if you need anything."

The Oxford Movement?

"Right." Jimmy was surprised that the little wimp made it safely to the library.

You're wise to me, he thought, watching the angry black clouds surge over the seminary. If I'm not going to play the game and go to Vietnam like a good boy, you're going to make me suffer here. And then become a missionary and go to Africa.

Right?

I thought so.

It was the first time Jimmy had really considered the consequences of his action. Until now, it had seemed like a joke – a creatively funny solution to the draft.

But things were starting to look and feel a whole lot different. Sure, that Carlisle guy at Saint Matthew's was living the good life, but how many cups of tea could you sip with menopausal women?

Do I really care if the "Breath of God" is the right processional for Pentecost? Or the rising cost of candles?

Jimmy felt itchy and short of breath. As long as the draft and that wonderful little war continued, and there was certainly no end in sight, then he was going to have to hide out in the seminary. But the seminary was only a three-year gig. If the war was still on after graduation, then he'd actually have to become a priest.

Better learn to like tea, Jimmy thought, collapsing on a lumpy sofa.

God, all I want to do is take off for a year or two, you know, hitch out West. See America first, like old Lady Bird was always telling us.

By the time the train hit Chicago, Jimmy was just getting into it. He was all set to cross the platform at Union Station to the SAN

FRANCISCO ZEPHYR and plant himself in one of those inviting dome cars.

Rockies, here I come.

The poor kid was 22 and had never been west of the Monongahela. Plus, he had been in school continuously for 16 years and needed time off.

It was September 19, 1970, and the first-year, or junior, orientation week was to begin on the 21st. Jimmy had read the seminary's letter with severe misgivings particularly where it talked about "letting down barriers" and "getting real with one another."

Father Kingsley at Penn State had been into all that touchy-feely crap, and Jimmy had played along because he needed the man's recommendation. But he hated having fat strangers hug him until his ribs cracked.

Still, it was better than stepping on some punji stake in the middle of the jungle.

Jimmy went to his room and unpacked his toilet kit and a monogrammed towel. Mom was expecting a collect call to announce his safe arrival, but he wanted to wash the train grit out of his hair before he did anything else.

So Jimmy went to the white-tiled bathroom and turned on the shower. He groaned as ugly brown water sputtered out of the faucet. But clear water soon followed, and he peeled out of his stale clothes.

Jimmy carefully adjusted the levers and indulged himself in a leisurely steam cleaning.

He was bending for the soap when the curtain was drawn back and a firm but delicate voice said, "Oh, don't tempt me."

Straightening quickly, Jimmy peered through the mist and saw a fine-featured fellow in a navy blazer and tortoise-rimmed glasses. Jimmy covered himself with the curtain and turned off the water.

"Hi," Jimmy said, wrapping a towel around his waist and extending a dripping hand, "I'm Jimmy Clarke. You must be Terry Groves."

"No, I'm Bob Edwards. And I was just joking about the soap. I hope you don't think . . ."

"No problem," Jimmy said, keeping his distance just the same.

"Terry Groves isn't due until tomorrow. Well, don't let me interrupt your toilette. We've got all evening to get acquainted."

"Ah, actually, Bob, I've been invited to have dinner with some friends in the city, so ah . . ."

"Oh, what a pity. I thought I might interest you in a cozy little game of cribbage. Accompanied by some excellent French brandy, of course."

"Sounds terrific, Bob. Why don't you give me a raincheck?"

"Certainly. And I'll hold you to it," Bob Edwards said, leering.

"If you'll excuse me," Jimmy said, "I've got to get dressed and on my way."

Jimmy went straight to his room, put fresh clothes over his Speedo and, ignoring the rain, went to the beach and took a long, languid swim in Lake Michigan.

Chapter Seven

Gatesbury Theological Seminary's class of 1973 assembled in the refectory for their first meeting with the dean.

Jimmy sat in back by himself and tried not to gawk at his 22 classmates.

They all seemed 35 or older, and every last one of them had been "called" away from his second-rate bank or failing insurance agency to help God keep the Episcopal Church afloat.

Jimmy hadn't bothered to remember anyone's name yet, because he was still sure he could slip the dean a C-note and get him to snow his draft board while he hitch-hiked out West.

Speaking of whom, the Very Reverend George Manoogian entered the long, vaulted room. He wore a short-sleeved clerical shirt, tan chinos, and a relaxed smile.

Bob Edwards shot to his feet and stared at Jimmy.

"On your feet," he hissed.

Terry Groves gave Jimmy the same look.

When the rest of the junior class followed their example, Dean Manoogian was amused.

"That's very kind," he said, lighting a Lucky Strike, "but this isn't a military academy. Please sit down and make yourselves comfortable." His voice was rich and self-assured.

Jimmy settled uncomfortably in his hard-backed chair and studied the dean. There was a depth of feeling in that warm Armenian face that made him instantly want the man as his own father.

"I think I've met most of you in the last few days," Dean Manoogian said." But for those I haven't met, I'm George Manoogian, your dean and humble servant . . ."

Jimmy wished he had extended himself.

"And, I might add, a fellow newcomer to Gatesbury. So I'll be counting on you to help me adjust to my new position. This seminary is as much yours as it is mine, and my door will always be open. For the church to be a dynamic force in society, we all need to constantly consider what can be changed and improved."

He drew unfiltered smoke into his broad chest and smiled. Jimmy smiled back.

"And in keeping with this spirit of change, we have decided to give your junior orientation a slightly different twist than it had in years past."

So this touchy-feely crap is your idea. Hmmm.

"To enable you all to get better acquainted in a short period of time, I have asked the North Shore Human Resources Development Company to conduct a week-long series of encounter sessions. I think you'll find them both useful and fun."

A plump woman with short frizzy hair squirmed happily in her seat." Oh goodie," she announced. "Warm fuzzies. I love warm fuzzies."

The Dean restored Jimmy's confidence by giving her a dour look.

But she was not discouraged." I can't wait to get to know each and every one of you," she bleated. "Oh, Dean Manoogian, you're such a beautiful human being. I love you already."

Dean Manoogian blushed under his tan. "Thank you, Pam. Well, why don't we break for coffee and reassemble across the way in the Hornby Room, and you can get started."

Jimmy slipped out of the room and gulped the crisp air. Vietnam was looking better all the time.

Remembering that he still hadn't called his mother to report his safe arrival, Jimmy went to the pay phone on the landing above his suite and placed a collect call to 322 Forest Drive.

Louise Maye Clarke eagerly accepted the charges and was asking a thousand questions before the operator switched off.

"Mom," Jimmy hollered over the bad connection, "I'm fine. Just fine."

"Oh, Jimmy, your father and I were so worried. You were supposed to call Sunday night. When you didn't call, we thought the worst. I called the seminary, but there was no answer. I thought there might have been a fire or something. I didn't know what to think. I called the weather service, and they said the Midwest had a terrible storm Sunday. I thought . . ."

"Mom, I'm fine. Calm down, will ya? Jeez, I'm 22-years-old; I should be able to take care of myself by now. I'm a college graduate, for God's sake."

"Jimmy, please don't take the Lord's name in vain. Especially now that you're . . ."

"Now that I'm practically in the pulpit, right?"

"Well, it wouldn't do to have one of our fine young ministers taking the Lord's name in vain, would it?"

Jimmy wondered what his mother would make of Pam Millar in the pulpit of Saint Matthew's. One "warm fuzzy" and fat Pam would be down at the unemployment office.

"I'll try to watch my language, Mom."

"Good. Now why didn't you call us Sunday night like you promised?"

Because I was depressed as hell and wanted to swim to Canada.

"Because I had to unpack and meet my classmates. And get the grand tour. You know — that sort of stuff."

"What are your new friends like, Jimmy?" Louise said. My son the priest, she thought.

"Well, they're — uh — older."

"Older?"

"I'm the youngest member of the junior class — by far."

"Oh, well, they'll be a good influence on you, dear. Do you have enough money? Do you need more?"

"Plenty of money, Mom. I paid my tuition and room and board yesterday. There's plenty left over. I'm even opening accounts at the bank here. And I'm going to get a work scholarship filling the Coke machine. Believe me, I'll let you know when I need more."

"Good," Louise said, relieved. "Well, tell me all about the seminary. What does it look like? Have you met any of the faculty? What courses are you going to take? I'm sure they're all interesting. How's the food? I hope they're feeding you enough. What about your room? Do you have enough blankets? I understand Chicago winters are absolutely horrid. Is there enough heat?"

"Mom, everything is fine. Just fine. By the way, we just had a meeting with the dean. He's new too. And you know what — he's Armenian."

"Armenian?!? At an Episcopal seminary? Well, the church is very active in Africa, so I suppose . . ."

"Mom, Armenia's in central Asia, not Africa. I know — if I had gone to Philadelphia Theological like you wanted, I wouldn't be running into all these foreigners. Right?"

"Enough said about that, dear. It's so wonderful to hear your voice. Your father and I are so proud of you, Jimmy. You were the talk of the coffee hour after church Sunday. I'm the first mother at Saint Matthew's with a son in seminary in more than 20 years."

If you only knew why I'm really here, Mother dear.

"Look, Mom, I gotta be going. Give my love to Dad."

"I will, dear. And I'll remember you in my prayers. You'll call again next week I hope? Collect, of course."

"You sure Dad doesn't mind?"

"You let me worry about your father."

"All right. I'll call next week. Bye."

"Good-bye, dear."

Jimmy cradled the phone and wiped his palm on his pants. Turning, he collided with a bearded classmate wearing a red flannel shirt and faded jeans.

"Sorry."

"Talking to Mommy?"

"Yeah, you know . . ."

"Worried about her little baby, is she?"

Jimmy forced a smile. "Something like that. Hey, we'd better get over to that orientation thing—it should be starting any minute."

"You run along, momma's boy, I got some phone calls to make. I've gotta line up some gigs, or I'm not gonna eat this quarter."

"Gigs?"

"Yeah, gigs. My mommy and daddy aren't putting me through this joint. I play the trumpet for a living. If you're through with the phone, I'd like to use it."

"How do you know my parents are paying my expenses?"

"I was in line behind you at the bursar's office yesterday. I got good ears. Now run along and play fuzzies with your friend Pammie. I've got work to do."

Jimmy wanted to stay and get to know this gruff billy goat.

"I'm in no hurry. I'm Jimmy Clarke."

"Mmmm huh. I'm Bruce MacKenzie."

They shared a firm handshake and looked one another in the eye. Finally, Jimmy thought.

"Could I ask you a question, Bruce?"

"Shoot."

"What's your draft number?"

"Three-hundred-sixty-five. Right on the money. But it don't matter, because Uncle Sugar already got his pound of flesh out of me."

"Really, I thought you were younger, you know . . ."

"It's the beard. If I shaved it off, I'd look like I was 50. Actually, I'm 29."

"Twenty-nine, huh? Well, I guess I can trust you for another year at least."

"What a thrill. Hey, are you old enough to drink in this state?"

"Damn straight. You've gotta be a college graduate to get into this place."

"I thought maybe you just had a note from your mommy."

"I'll see you around sometime, Bruce," Jimmy said, turning away.

"Look, Clarke, I'm just in a pissy mood. Don't mind me, all right?"

Jimmy turned around, slowly. He wasn't exactly thrilled with the prospect of befriending this bearded bimbo, but what choice did he have?

"Sure."

"Good. Look, maybe we'll go out and have some drinks down in Chicago sometime. This damn town's dry as a bone thanks to those old broads at the Women's Christian Temperance Union. Their national headquarters is right down the street. Can you believe it?"

"So we'll throw our empties on their front lawn."

"Good idea. Look, I gotta make some calls. See you later, huh?"

"Aren't you going to the . . ."

"Fuck, no."

Chapter Eight

Pam Millar hugged Jimmy until his eyeballs bubbled.
"Let it all hang out," she said, her breath thick with natural peanut butter. "Loosen up, baby!"
Jimmy let his arms go lax along her folds of fat.
"Come on, Jimmy, let go!" Pam said, cracking his back.
"Oooff!! Pam, let up a little, would ya?"
"What?"
"I need to experience my own space for a while. Okay?"
Clearly not. A pouting Pam Millar said, "If you want to be repressed and uptight, that's your business. But believe me, Jimmy, it's going to inhibit your ministry. You can't be a helper if you don't know how to be helped yourself."
Although they were supposed to be concentrating on their partners, the other juniors paused to listen. The crew-cut from Wisconsin found Jimmy and Pam particularly amusing. Jimmy gave him a withering look.
The program facilitators, an androgynous North Shore couple in matching black turtlenecks, watched the "game" from the middle of the cheerless room with indifferent expressions.
Jimmy shrugged helplessly.
The facilitators, Irv and Edna Blackman, responded with hollow stares.
"Hey, could I take a break?" Jimmy said.
Irv and Edna nodded no. As they had carefully explained at the outset, their function was merely to "facilitate the free exchange of feelings. We're not referees."
Pam took the opportunity to lock Jimmy in another death grip. She knew she wouldn't get this close to such a good-looking hunk for a long, long time, and she was determined to hug her fill of warm fuzzies.
"Come on, Jimmy, let me give you a great, big warm fuzzy. If men got more warm fuzzies, they wouldn't get ulcers and heart attacks all the time."
Fat Pam's first husband, Fred, had suffered a fatal myocardial infarction at the dinner table after ten years of her cholesterol-laden

cooking. Her new husband, Warren, was a worried little man who took most of his meals away from their chaotic Evanston home.

Jimmy tried to escape Pam's embrace, but the woman held him firm. Her melon breasts splayed across his chest, and she nuzzled her thatchy hair against his cheek.

"Isn't this wonderful?" she said, dreamily. "I mean, Jimmy, if everybody touched everybody and hugged everybody and was really free with their feelings like this, there wouldn't be any hatred or killing. Or wars. Or violence. Can't you just feel all your tension draining away?"

"Actually, I just feel my breath draining away, Pam. Could you loosen your grip a little?"

"Oh, I'm sorry. A big, gorgeous man like you? I didn't think I was hurting you. There, how's that?"

"Dreamy."

"Really?"

Jimmy looked down into her baby seal eyes. Then he looked up at God and thought, this IS some kind of joke, right? It gets better next week, right?"

God wasn't talking.

"Really, Pam. It's just dreamy."

Pam cried.

Jimmy cringed.

"See," Pam said, her face glistening, "all you have to do is surrender to it. Just go with it. It's natural for women, because we're feeling creatures. But you can't help being uptight and repressed because you're a white male. That's why you subconsciously exploit women and other minorities.

"Society trains you to be an oppressor, practically from birth. You're taught to hold your emotions inside where they poison your mind and body. I'm so glad I talked George into having this."

Ah, the plot thickens. What else could the poor guy do but give in. She probably threatened to plant her warm fuzzy in his office until he relented.

"George?"

"The dean, silly. Now just relax and go with your emotions. Connect with me."

Pam rubbed her thigh against Jimmy's connector for emphasis.

Jimmy heard Terry Groves stifle a laugh. Bob Edwards was leering at him, and the others were watching out of the corners of their eyes. He and Pam were the featured attraction.

"Actually, Pam, I'm getting in touch with my bladder. I think it wants to express itself."

"Good," Pam said. "Get in touch with your body. Get in touch with mine."

The image of her naked flesh flashed through Jimmy's mind, and he feared he would never get another erection.

"I am in touch with my body, Pam. And it's telling me I'd better take a leak pretty damn soon."

"Do your thing, Jimmy. If that's the way you feel, then go with it."

"That's the way I feel all right. I'll be right back, all right?"

"Do what you've gotta do, sweetie."

Jimmy broke loose and raced for the hallway. Irv and Edna intercepted him at the door. He tried to skirt them, but they blocked him again. They acted in such unison, Jimmy wondered if they were siamese twins.

"Excuse me," Jimmy said, straining to be polite.

"The game isn't over," Edna stated.

"Yeah, right. But I have to go to the bathroom. Okay? Be right back."

Irv smoothed his silver hair and said in a loud voice, "Is it okay with the group if this person goes to the bathroom?"

Everyone stopped being real and stared at Jimmy.

"Heck," Terry Groves drawled, "If the man's gotta take a damn leak, the man's gotta take a leak."

Everyone but the crew-cut from Wisconsin, Lance Gordon, nodded in agreement.

Gordon, who had served two terms as mayor of Ash Lake, population 5,576, cleared his throat and proclaimed, "I think it's important that we get to know one another. I'm sure a lot of us have to go to the bathroom or want to check on our kids or any number of things, but we're here for a purpose and that's to get to know one another so the class of '73 will be the best Gatesbury has ever had."

Lance was an asshole, but he was a persuasive asshole, and he would soon be president of the junior class. A majority of the group voted that Jimmy Clarke should not be excused until Irv and Edna declared a break.

"Oh goodie," Pam Millar squealed, rushing to embrace Jimmy. He tried to back away, but it was too late.

"I told you I had to go," he said, watching his brown shoes turn black.

Chapter Nine

Bob Edwards was at the library where he had already claimed a study carrel and crammed it with commentaries and theological treatises. Jimmy had taken one look at that stuff and wanted to vomit.

Jimmy was sitting in their suite's common room watching Terry Groves pump out push-ups, marine style.

". . . 59, 60, 61, 62, 63, hey, come on, y'all. Get down here and join me, boy."

"No thanks, Terry. I already worked out today."

"You did? Where?"

"At the pool. Northwestern. You know, that university across the street."

"How far you swim?"

Jimmy watched Groves hit 100 and keep going. Here's a guy who's going to keep his Sunday school in line, he thought.

"A mile."

"Damn, boy, that's not bad. Come on an' do some push-ups. You haven't done a proper work-out until you've done your push-ups."

"Not tonight. I might go out for a little walk. Nice night. Maybe I'll hit the books later. You going to study tonight?"

"I ain't never been much fer books. Reckon I'll just put it off to the last minute like I always done when I was in college. 'Sides, this stuff ain't exactly the most stimulatin' readin' I ever come across."

"You can say that again," Jimmy said, glancing at the pile of books for his classes in Church History, Greek & Hebrew, Theology I, and Introduction to Pastoral Counselling.

He had cracked a few of the history books and had taken an immediate interest in the atrocities visited by the Crusaders upon their brother Christians in Constantinople. But he doubted he could get through three years of seminary on looting, sacking, and pillaging.

"All I can say is I'm sure glad they started a pass/fail system this year," Jimmy said. "I'm burned out from college. I'm not ready for another three years of this stuff."

Sweat now stained Groves' U. S. Marine Corps T-shirt and fatigue pants. He rolled on his back, propped his feet under the oak bookcase, and began a set of 200 serious sit-ups.

"So why don't you take some time off," he said, between breaths. "I'm sure the Lord wouldn't mind."

There he goes with that "Lord" bit again, Jimmy thought.

"I'd love to take off and bum around the country, Terry, but I've got this little problem with the draft."

"The draft? 28, 29, 30, 31 — hell, join the marines, son — 32, 33, 34, 35 — then come back to the seminary — 36, 37, 38 — you'll be a lot better preacher for it — 39, 40, 41 — believe me — 42, 43, 44 . . ."

"You go to Vietnam, Terry?"

"No. I was processin' out when it was heatin' up over there. I was in Okinawa mostly. Spent some time in Guantanamo Bay. Wasn't a day didn't go by that I didn't pray that Fidel Castro would accept the Lord in his heart."

"I think I'm gonna take that walk, Terry. See ya later."

"Hey, son, ain't you forgettin' somethin'?"

"What?"

"Your turn to clean the can. I don't aim ta get some social disease next time I take a crap because you shirked your duty. Now git in there and clean it up. It's dirtier than a damn swamp in there."

Jimmy sighed and went to the bathroom where he took a few half- hearted swipes at the sink with a sponge. He poured cleanser in the toilet and flushed it twice. Good enough for government work.

"Make sure you get under the sink and behind the can. Y'all missed 'em last time," Groves called.

"Yes, sir," Jimmy said, saluting himself in the mirror. He was dropping to his knees when he saw Bruce MacKenzie stroll by the window. Jimmy opened it and whistled.

"Hey, momma's boy, how's it goin'?" MacKenzie said."They got you on clean-up again tonight?"

"Yeah. Hey, where're you headed?"

"Off campus, kid. You keep an eye on things around here, okay?"

"Wait. I'm comin' with," Jimmy said, climbing out the window.

Bruce grunted. They got in his battered '62 Beetle and headed south for Chicago.

"Wanna smoke some reefer?" he said.

"Hell, yes! Where is it?"

"In the glove compartment. Dynamite Panamanian. Roll a coupla big fat ones."

Jimmy savored the pungent aroma as he opened the zip-lock bag.

"Don't play with it, man. Just roll some joints."

"All right. It's just that this is the first pot I've had since I've been here. I was starting to think I was going to have to get high on God. Did you know that Terry Groves talks to the Lord all the time?"

"So what's wrong with that? This IS a seminary."

Great, Jimmy thought. He finished rolling the joint and lighted it. He took a deep hit and passed it.

"No," Bruce said, "keep it. Roll one for me, and we'll each have our own. Like real grown-ups."

Jimmy nodded and rolled one for Bruce. They smoked in silence for a while, letting the THC work on their nervous systems.

"You talk to the Lord, Bruce?"

"So what if I do, Clarke? Like I said before, this is a seminary. Or are you just using it to hide from the draft?"

"Call me Jimmy, all right?"

"I'll tell you what: I'll call you Jim. Jimmy is a little kid's name."

Jimmy ground his teeth. They were slowing for a stoplight. Loyola University was on the left, and the student bars were on the right. Jimmy was tempted to jump out and transfer on the spot.

"Okay, you call me Jim, and I'll call you Mac. How's that?"

"I don't like to be called Mac."

"And I don't like to be called Jim. All right?"

Bruce made a gutteral sound.

"Good," Jimmy said.

"So answer my question — Jimmy."

"What question?"

"Are you high already?"

"Hell, yes. Aren't you?"

Bruce stopped smoothly at the light and rolled down his window.

"Hey," he called to some jocks crossing the street, "you guys are living proof that the Jesuits fucked monkeys."

The Catholic students did a double-take and went for the windshield.

"Hang on!" Bruce yelled, accelerating around them, running the red light, and roaring south on Sheridan Road.

When they stopped laughing, Bruce said, "Now answer my question, Jim."

"I thought you were going to call me Jimmy, Mac."

"Whatever. Look, what are you doing in a seminary if you don't believe in God?"

"Who says I don't believe in God? And who are you to ask? You sure as hell don't act like the typical seminarian. You could have killed those guys back there."

"Relax. Nobody got hurt. So you think we're two peas in a pod, huh?" Bruce said.

"Something like that."

Bruce laughed. "Right. But you're wrong, because I'm no fuckin' draft dodger. I didn't get a low draft number and run off to Canada or any of that crap. I didn't suddenly get right with God and hide out in a seminary like some people I know."

Jimmy watched the old ladies with blue hair walk their toy poodles in front of their lakefront highrises.

"So I'm not the first, and I sure as hell won't be the last."

"From what I've seen you're the only draft dodger at Gatesbury."

"Yeah, but Gatesbury's weird. Look at Wesley—hell, most of those guys make Abbie Hoffman look like a Young Republican."

Wesley was the Methodist seminary across the street from Gatesbury. The two shared faculty and facilities. Gatesbury was popularly known as "Jesus West," Wesley as "Jesus East."

"Shit, what do you expect from those creeps. So you figure you're the only draft dodger at Gatesbury?"

"I wouldn't put it that way, Bruce."

"How would you put it?"

"Look, I got 35 in the lottery, all right. I was going to lose my deferment in June, and I went to this wedding last spring, and it just hit me. I mean there was this minister or priest or whatever, living the good life. I figured that could be me. You say I don't believe in God, but how do you know God didn't put that idea in my head?

"Maybe God wants me to go the seminary. Maybe I really do have a calling. Maybe it's none of your damn business. Anyway, what about you? You sure as hell don't strike me as the church type."

"That's because I'm not."

"So what are you doing in a seminary? You going to be chaplain to the Hell's Angels? Absolve them of Altamont?"

"Dude fucked with their bikes. Got what he deserved if you ask me."

Jimmy glanced uneasily at Bruce."You're serious, aren't you?"

"Damn straight."

"So what are you going to do when you graduate?"

"Go to Alaska."

"Alaska? What, and be a chaplain to the polar bears?" Jimmy laughed so hard his nose ran.

Enraged, Bruce steered the car into a driveway, braked abruptly, and grabbed at Jimmy's neck.

Jimmy swiped his hand away and locked MacKenzie's cranium in the crook of his arm. He increased the pressure until Bruce's eyeballs bugged. "You want to fuck with me, pal, go right ahead."

Bruce thrashed around for a while, but Jimmy had him. He finally surrendered with a weak wave.

That broke the tension between them, and they were laughing heartily when Bruce took a hard left and sent them soaring south on Chicago's magnificent Lake Shore Drive.

"Hey, Bruce, how about I roll us some more joints?"

"All right, Jimmy, but roll 'em tight this time."

Jimmy set the pot on his lap and let his wandering attention fix on Lake Michigan off to the left. A northeast wind was blowing down from Canada, heaving the lake against the concrete breakwaters protecting the "Drive."

"Hey, Bruce," he said, "let's go body surfin'. Those waves are almost as big as the ones at the Jersey Shore."

MacKenzie eyed the lake and shook his head. "Those are pussy waves. You ever seen the Pacific?"

"This is the farthest west I've ever been."

"Figures. You come out to Oregon sometime, and I'll show you some real surf."

"I'd love to see Oregon."

"It's Or-e-GUN. The last syllable is 'gun' not 'gon.' Got it?"

"Right. So you're really going to Alaska after you graduate?"

"I'm going to be a bush priest. I've got my pilot's license. Hell, my parish could be the entire Brooks Range. Minister to trappers, Indians, and Eskimos. The church needs priests up there. It's the last frontier, man. They need priests up there who can hack it. Not like the pussies down here.

"It ain't like the Lower 48 where you chit-chat in the undercroft and get blisters on your ass from sitting around all the time trying to talk old ladies into leaving their estates to the church so you can get the damn organ fixed," Bruce said.

Jimmy just laughed.

"What's so funny?"

"Nothin', man. Nothin'." Jimmy watched the panorama unfold for a while and then asked, "You told me you were in the service, right?"

"Yeah. So?"

"Well . . ."

"I was in the navy. All right?"

"Just asking," Jimmy said. He wasn't ready for another battle-tested marine.

"I was up north with the marines in I Corps. I was a corpsman, but I killed more people than I saved. I weighed 170 pounds when I came back from Vietnam. Some dude looked at me wrong on the street, I wanted to kill him. That's the way you live over there. But you'd be surprised how fast you adjust to it. Hell, even a pussy like you'd be a cold-blooded killer after a few months in that country."

"Thanks, Bruce, I love you too. Seriously, I'm thinking about being a navy chaplain when I graduate."

"But you've never been in the service."

"So? My bishop was in the navy, and he says I'd make a terrific chaplain."

"That's because he doesn't have any place to put you when you graduate. I can just see you tryin' to relate to some jarhead with half his face blown away by a VC rocket.

"Man, you can't be a chaplain unless you've done your time. Nobody's gonna respect you otherwise. If you're really serious, quit and do some time in the navy. See what it's like to be a squid. Go through boot camp, bounce around in the bottom of some ship for a while. Hit the beach in Kaohsiung and fight it out with those Australian motherfuckers or get the clap from one of those chink whores. Then talk to me about being a navy chaplain. And only then," Bruce said.

"This thing work?" Jimmy said, pointing at the tape deck.

Bruce nodded.

"DOORS okay?"

"Shit yes. Morrison's my main man. I'd marry that son-of-a-bitch if the church would let me."

Jimmy didn't doubt Bruce.

"Hey, didn't I just read that Morrison beat some lewd and lascivious behavior rap?"

"It's oppression. Dude was just expressing himself."

"Beatin' off on stage? That's expressing yourself?"

"If God didn't want us to jerk off, he wouldn't have made our arms so long."

Jimmy let it go at that.

Bruce had to hit the tape player with the butt of his hand to get it to work. It picked up Morrison and the boys halfway through "L.A. Woman."

Neither Jimmy nor Bruce could carry a tune, but they crooned along as the Beetle hopped over the hill at LaSalle Drive. The stately Drake Hotel and the Playboy Building with its rotating "Bunny Beacon" were overshadowed by the frankly phallic Hancock Center, or "Big John."

Lake Shore Drive looped gracefully to the left at Oak Street creating a delightful dance of lights, buildings and water.

Traffic was light, and the October air crisp.

Jimmy was in love with this wonderful city. Nobody in the East ever talked about Chicago except to complain about layovers at O'Hare and Daley's fascist cops. Or to laugh at the '69 Cubs who had folded in the closing days of the season to the New York Mets.

"What a beautiful city," he said.

"It's all right. You want to see a city, go to San Francisco. Now that's a city."

"Right. Where're we headed?"

"Rush Street."

"Any women there?"

"Is the Pope Catholic?"

Chapter Ten

Jimmy got a hard-on just looking at all the beautiful women.

He and Elaine had only seen one another twice that summer, once in State College and once in Wynnwood, and she hadn't been in the mood either time.

"Will you look at that one, Bruce! And that one! God, I think I'm going to have a heart attack."

"Keep it in your pants, lover boy," Bruce said, calmly looking for a parking place in the bustling night-life neighborhood. "Don't you have a girlfriend?"

"She might come out for a visit, but it's hard to tell. Anyway, she's in the middle of Pennsylvania, so what good is she tonight?"

"Absolutely none to you. But I'm sure she's doin' a lot of good for some other dude."

"Very funny. What about you? You got some mountain woman stashed away somewhere? Or are you still mourning poor old Janis?"

"Janis Joplin was the only woman who could have tamed me," Bruce said. "Man, I'm still bummed out. A damn junky—shit, what a waste of beauty and talent."

"Yeah."

Bruce found that elusive parking place, and they strolled along Division Street oogling the beautiful women, many of whom were headed for a brightly lighted bar named "O'Lear's."

"How come you didn't card him?" Jimmy asked when the bouncer detained him after waving Bruce through.

"'Cause he looks old enough to be your old man."

Jimmy resisted the urge to say something cute and produced his Pennsylvania driver's license and a Wanamaker's credit card in his father's name.

"You're a long way from home, aren't you, Mr. Clarke? Sign says you gotta have three I.D.'s. You don't get in unless you got one more."

Patting his pockets, Jimmy found his Gatesbury picture I.D.

"Here," he said.

"Whoooaaah!" the South Side Irishman said, holding his heart in mock horror. "Okay, Padre, you're cool. Hey, maybe you can turn some water into beer for us. Manager'd love it."

Jimmy made the sign of the cross in front of the meathead's face. "Bless you, my son, for you know not what you do."

He disappeared into the dark, throbbing bar before the bouncer could figure that one out.

There was no hope of finding Bruce, so Jimmy muscled his way to the bar and ordered a Johnny Walker and water. His father would approve of his choice.

Jimmy took a long, appreciative sip and surveyed the action.

You'd never know there's a war on, he thought, realizing that the odds were three-to-one against him. He was dressed casually like those having the least luck with the ladies — it was the guys straight from work in their sincere suits who were scoring.

As for the women, most traveled in pairs or threesomes, with a beauty and a beast in every bunch.

Jimmy sipped his scotch and ruled out the groups. MacKenzie could find his own woman. Catching sight of himself in the mirror behind the bar, Jimmy lifted his glass and smiled confidently.

Then he turned and scouted the bar. There she was — Ms. Wonderful. Blonde, beautiful, and braless. Well, maybe not a real blonde, but good enough for bar lighting. Model maybe. A bit on the skinny side. Hell, borderline anorexic, but Jimmy didn't like fat women.

He took another sip and picked up his drink. An empty suit was closing in on Ms. Wonderful, so he rolled left, dodged right and got to her two seconds ahead of the lawyer with the red, silk tie.

Puffing out his chest, the legal type tried to insinuate his way into the woman's life, but Jimmy deftly upstaged him. The little lawyer sneered at Jimmy's wardrobe and backed off a short distance, like a hyena waiting for a lion to finish feeding.

Jimmy set his drink on the bar and glanced at his pick. She wasn't quite as beautiful up close as she had appeared from a distance. A little too much make-up, but who was he to judge? Besides, he hated this meat-market mentality and just wanted to get laid.

But it was hard with some legal beagle barking at your heels.

"Hey, pal, I think I hear your mommy calling. Past your bedtime."

The lawyer lunged forward, took another look at his adversary and decided to save his Saks suit for another encounter. He skulked off.

"Bravo," the woman in the white sweater said. She wore sensible gray slacks and had friendly brown eyes and a genuine smile. "Come here often?"

"Not really. I'm from Philadelphia."

She laughed. "First prize — one week in Philadelphia. Second prize — two weeks in Philadelphia."

"Touche. I'm Jimmy Clarke." Jimmy extended his hand.

"Debby White." She took his hand. "So what brings you to Chicago, Jimmy Clarke?"

Jimmy was too ashamed to admit he was a seminarian.

"Actually, I'm going to school in Evanston," he said.

"Evanston? Oh, Northwestern."

"Yeah. Close."

"Undergrad or grad?"

"Graduate, actually. I'm older than I look."

"You look quite mature to me. So what are you studying?"

"Comparative religions. I'm not sure what I'm going to do with it yet, but I might go up to Alaska and do an independent study of native religions."

"Alaska? Far out. I've always wanted to go to Alaska," Debby White said.

Jimmy smiled. "Can I buy you another drink, Debby?"

"Sure," she said, moving closer.

Jimmy ordered another round and asked Debby about herself.

She was 21, worked as a teller at a downtown bank, and was applying for stewardess school with three airlines. She thought she had her best chance with United.

"I love to travel," she said, "but I don't think I could live anywhere but Chicago. I love this city."

"It sure is beautiful. Coming down on Lake Shore Drive tonight — wow, it was something else."

"You have a car?"

"No. But I'm going to get one. I came in a cab."

"I've got a car. Maybe we could go for a drive. It's awfully hot in here, and I love to show off Chicago. What do you say?"

Jimmy looked Debby White full in the face and saw that she was ready for some good times. "I say, let's go."

They clinked glasses and downed their drinks.

They were almost out the door when Bruce MacKenzie intercepted them and said loudly, "Come on, momma's boy, time to go back to the seminary. You've got to get up early tomorrow for chapel."

Debby White stopped and stared. "Seminary? I thought you were studying comparative religions?"

"I am actually," Jimmy said through clenched teeth. He gave Bruce a hateful look, but MacKenzie wouldn't budge. "Look, Debby, I ah . . . "

"God, I can't believe this," Debby White said. "I almost picked up a priest."

"Look, I'm not in a Catholic seminary. We're allowed to date and . . . "

"Sure, Reverend," Debby said, turning back to the bar and the lawyer's attention.

Jimmy watched the little hyena move in for the kill and sadly shook his head. At least guys in Vietnam get laid, he thought.

Bruce tugged at his sleeve and motioned to go.

Jimmy yanked his arm free. "Don't touch me, man. Don't touch me."

"My, aren't we jumpy tonight?"

"Bruce, I was gonna score. Why didn't you just let me go? God, I can't believe you did that." Jimmy bolted out the door and was halfway to State Street when Bruce caught him.

"Did what? Tell the truth. What kind of lines were you feeding that little dolly, anyway?"

"I sure as hell didn't tell her I had to get up and go to chapel in the morning."

"I hate to rain on your parade, man, but you ARE in seminary school. And if you make it through, you're gonna have to wear a backwards dog collar the rest of your life. So you might as well face it now."

"Man, I was gonna get laid tonight."

"So take a cold shower. Better yet, I'll buy us a six pack for the ride back."

They drank it in silence and threw the empties on the front lawn of the Women's Christian Temperance Union.

Chapter Eleven

The Reverend Godfrey J. Wiltwright licked his thumb and dispensed the term papers.

Pam Millar pouted when she spotted a B- atop her rambling discussion of Gnosticism in the early church.

Bruce MacKenzie got a C+ for his paper, "The Arian Controversy after the Council of Nicaea," and an admonition "to spend a little more time in the library and a little less time playing your bugle."

"It's a trumpet, man," he grumbled, scowling at the red-marked paper.

"I don't care if it's a flugelhorn," Mr. MacKenzie. It would do well to retire it to its case while you retire to the library for the duration," Wiltwright said.

Jimmy wanted to gloat, but he was afraid Wiltwright had worse in store for him, so he looked away when Bruce muttered an obscenity.

Bob Edwards, of course, got an A+ for his "incisive exposition" on the conflict of Paganism and Christianity in the Fourth Century.

Terry Groves was given another syllabus and a firm reminder that the library was open every evening and on weekends. Lance Gordon received a C for attempting to equate the spread of early Christianity with the advent of the Episcopal Church in rural Wisconsin.

Finally, Father Wiltwright peered over his pince-nez at the class iconoclast. Clenching Jimmy Clarke's paper, he had to go to the leaded window before he could speak.

Jimmy gulped and watched the pigeons pirouette over the refectory. Father Wiltwright adjusted his Anglican collar, dusted his immaculate academic robe, and faced young Mr. Clarke.

Jimmy stared back and wondered which of the rumors about Wiltwright was true. He was forced to flee Harvard Divinity School because:

A. His drinking got worse.
B. He was caught sleeping with another faculty member's wife.
C. He was caught sleeping with another faculty member.
D. All of the above.

Definitely D, Jimmy decided.

"I've seen some interesting source material teaching Church History, Mr. Clarke, but never, I repeat, never THE HISTORY OF TORTURE."

Wiltwright waited for the snickering to subside before adding, "Pray enlighten us, Mr. Clarke. Where under God's good heaven did you find such a . . . such a graphic book?"

Jimmy cleared his throat and smiled at his classmates. "Well, I know it wasn't on the syllabus, but I had it from college, and, well, you have to admit, it added some pizzazz to my paper."

"Pizzazz?" Wiltwright said, his face reddening. "That is the understatement of the year. I think 'gratuitous violence and pornography' is a better description."

Holding the paper as far from his delicate nose as possible, Wiltwright dropped it on Jimmy's desk without further comment.

Jimmy forced himself to look at it. He breathed a deep sigh of relief. Wiltwright had penned in his perfect hand: "A+. You write extremely well, and your knowledge of history is impressive. However, the history of Christendom is not, as you suggest, an unending series of atrocities, torture, and carnage. How about accentuating the positive next time?"

Jimmy was disappointed. He had been planning to write about the atrocities the Crusaders had visited upon Christian Constantinople on their way to the Holy Land. But Church History was the only class he wasn't taking on pass/fail, so he figured he'd look elsewhere for inspiration. But he couldn't imagine where.

While Jimmy was ruminating, Bruce MacKenzie leaned over and snatched Jimmy's paper.

"Wow," he exclaimed, flipping through it.

Wiltwright halted his chalk in mid-letter and slowly turned his head. "You find it interesting, Mr. MacKenzie?" he said, his thin lips curling.

"Yeah, this is great," Bruce said. "Hey, Clarke, why didn't you tell me you were such a pervert?"

"Perhaps you could give us a dramatic reading, Mr. MacKenzie — now that you've completely disrupted the class. And perhaps then I can get on with the Middle Ages."

You love it, Jimmy thought, watching the twitches of anticipation flash across Wiltwright's porcelain face.

"Ah, here's a good one," Bruce said, running his finger down a page: "Another unique Roman torture was described by St. Gregory:

"The people of Heliopolis took young girls and after stripping them naked cut open their bellies and then, while the innards were yet quivering, they stuffed them with barley, sewed them up, and allowed wild hogs to tear them open. Some of the martyrs who died in this fashion were St. Prisca, St. Agnes, and St. Euphema of Aquileia. Since it was against Roman law to execute a virgin, the girls were first raped by gladiators.

"He goes on to say . . .

"That will be enough, Mr. MacKenzie. Quite enough," Wiltwright said, turning quickly back to the blackboard to hide his titillation.

You love it, Jimmy thought.

When class was over, everyone dutifully headed for the Guthbertson Memorial Chapel for Evensong. Daily chapel attendance was no longer required, but skipping more than a day was considered bad form, and Jimmy was deathly afraid that some faculty member would hold poor chapel attendance against him, so he attended at least once a day and often twice. The bell that summoned students to Morning Prayer every day at 7 a.m. was right across from his window, so he couldn't sleep in if he wanted. But he had arrived late more than a few mornings.

Jimmy took a seat in the last high-backed pew just as the minister, Lance Gordon, solemnly intoned: "Almighty God, who has given us grace at this time with one accord to make our common supplications unto thee . . ."

Jimmy glanced across the aisle and realized Pam Millar was staring at him like he was some demented sex murderer. Jimmy obliged her with a deranged look, and she buried her head in her fat hands. Well, he thought, that's the last warm fuzzy I'll ever get from her.

" . . . and dost promise that when two or three are gathered together in thy Name thou wilt grant their requests; Fulfill now, O Lord, the desires and petitions of thy servants, as may be most expedient for them; granting us in this world knowledge of thy truth, and in the world to come life everlasting. Amen."

Most expedient, Jimmy mused as everyone else asked for God's goodies. How about most expediently ending the draft so I can get

the hell out of this looney bin? How about most expediently putting
a little pussy in my path?

Lance Gordon held his black leather BOOK OF COMMON
PRAYER in his left hand and raised his right as a sign of blessing as
he said: "The grace of our Lord Jesus Christ, and the love of God,
and fellowship of the Holy Ghost, be with us all evermore. Amen."

Everyone prayed silently for a moment and then the more
Catholic-inclined crossed themselves. The low churchmen like
Jimmy just blinked.

Jimmy got up off his knees, adjusted his academic gown for
comfort, and settled back for the highlight of his day, choirmaster
Douglas Heck's evening organ recital.

As Heck arranged his music, the majority of the congregation
noisily exited for the refectory which opened in five minutes.

Swine, Jimmy thought, watching them go. He gave Pam Millar a
smarmy smile as she passed. She flew for the door.

Then the accoustically perfect chapel swelled with the first notes
of Bach's "Jesu, Heart of Man's Desire." Jimmy stretched his legs
and joined his hands behind his head. He drifted with the soaring
music and was far from the seminary when it was over.

When the last notes of a Bach cantata faded into the vaulted
ceiling, Jimmy sat up and applauded. Remembering where he was,
he stopped abruptly. But another pair of hands was clapping, so he
resumed.

Douglas Heck was moved. He had labored too long without
acclaim, and now someone was responding to his artistry.

Finally.

He stood at his organ and bowed to the welcome applause. Then
he dabbed at his eyes and exited quickly.

Jimmy stood up and realized that the other fan was none other
than Dean Manoogian.

"Marvelous, isn't it?" the dean said, smiling.

"Yes, sir. Really takes the edge off the day. Well, I'd better get to
the refectory before they close the line."

"I've got a better idea," Dean Manoogian said, placing a hand on
Jimmy's shoulder, "Why don't you come to the deanery for dinner? I
put a leg of lamb in the oven this afternoon, and I'm sure Claire and
I can't eat it all ourselves."

Jimmy loved lamb. "Well, if you've got some mint jelly, I suppose I could be persuaded."

"Just bought two jars and some bottles of a very lovely Greek wine that goes wonderfully with lamb. Now what do you say?"

"I say: let's go; I'm starved."

Chapter Twelve

The deanery was a multi-gabled, red-brick mansion with timber trim and a slate roof. It was set back from the seminary and hidden from view by a weeping willow that was clinging tenaciously to its yellowing leaves.

"It's a little big for just the two of us," Dean Manoogian confessed as they crossed the threshold. "But our youngest daughter, Jennifer, will be joining us after Christmas. Claire, I've brought a guest home for dinner."

Jimmy was struck by the similarities to his parents' house. Even the leathery, lived-in smell was the same.

There were footsteps at the top of the stairs followed by a firm, feminine voice. "Wonderful, George. Be right down."

"Jimmy, why don't you make yourself comfortable while I go up and change into my civvies. Bar's over there. Should be ice in the bucket. Glasses are in the cabinet. Make yourself at home. I'll be right with you."

Jimmy saw that the dean shared his father's good taste in liquor, and, feeling a bit homesick, he poured himself a Black Label on the rocks and added a dash of water. The old man had been totally useless when it came to little things like sex, life, women, and maturity, but he was a wonderful teacher of mixicology. Jimmy had long thought his father should open the Clarke Academy for the Preparation of Proper Drinks.

Jimmy took a few sips and let the scotch warm his throat. Then he wandered through the living room and looked at the oak-frame family portraits and paintings. Substitute the faces, and it could have been his mother's tastefully appointed living room.

Smiling, he settled on a sofa and set his drink on the end table after first finding a monogrammed coaster. Jimmy picked a family portrait off the table. There was the dean, his striking wife, clearly not Armenian, and three adult daughters. The eldest were, well, handsome. Nature had not endowed them with either parent's distinctive features, but they had friendly, confident faces. They both appeared to be in their 30s.

The youngest — hadn't the dean called her Jennifer — was the real beauty. In the portrait, she was wearing a light blue cardigan sweater and a gold heart locket. She had a shy smile and long, silky brown hair. She had her father's thick Armenian eyebrows and curls and her mother's fine Nordic nose and chin. There were individual portraits of the daughters on the bookcase, so Jimmy took Jennifer's and studied it, his heart racing.

"That's our Jennifer. Pretty, isn't she?"

Jimmy turned and blushed. "Yes, she certainly is. And she obviously takes after her mother."

"That's very kind of you to say," said Claire Manoogian, extending her hand. "It's a pleasure to meet you, Jimmy."

"Likewise," Jimmy said, taking her hand.

"George tells me you're from the Main Line."

"Yes. Wynnwood to be exact."

"I love the Main Line of Philadelphia. Have you ever attended the Devon Horse Show?"

"In a manner of speaking. I worked it a couple of summers while I was in high school. I didn't have much time to watch, what with setting up all those jumps and all."

"I can imagine. As George has probably told you, we're from Boston originally, but his last post was in Baltimore. Not a bad city, but I prefer Chicago."

"Me too. This area reminds me of the Main Line, and I love downtown Chicago. Have you been down there?"

"Oh yes. Marvelous. You must have lunch at the Walnut Room at Marshall Fields. It's simply wonderful."

Jimmy wondered if Jennifer was as agreeable as her mother. He certainly hoped so. Claire went to the bar and fixed herself a scotch and soda with a twist. "Can I freshen yours?"

"Oh no, I'm fine."

She invited Jimmy to take a seat, and they faced one another across a coffee table adorned with a vase of dried flowers that emitted a rich, fall aroma. Jimmy settled back, feeling really good for the first time since he had arrived at Gatesbury.

"What kind of work do you do, Mrs. Manoogian?"

Claire Manoogian was delighted with the question. Despite their liberal posturing, the Gatesbury faculty were a sexist lot.

"Please, call me Claire. Heavens, you make me feel like an old grandmother when you call me Mrs. Manoogian. Of course, I am a grandmother, but certainly not an old one. At least I don't feel old. But to answer your question, I've gone back to school at the University of Chicago."

"The University of Chicago — I'm impressed."

Claire Manoogian was liking this handsome young man more every minute. "Why, thank you."

"What are you studying?"

"I'm working toward a Masters in Social Work."

"That's terrific," Jimmy said, wishing his mother would do something like that. She had devoted her life to bridge and fad diets. "Are you going to be a therapist?"

"Yes, but I'm not quite sure if I want to go into private practice or do agency work. Right now, I just want to get through this quarter. How about you, Jimmy? What are your plans after seminary?"

Jimmy took a long look at Claire Manoogian and realized he couldn't bullshit her if he wanted to.

"Well, to tell you the truth, I don't have the slightest idea. I told my bishop I want to be a navy chaplain after I graduate, but that was just something that popped into my head when I went for my interview. I just want to get through this quarter."

"What classes are you taking?"

"Church History, which I love. In fact, I'm probably going to major in it. Theology with Dr. Marshfield, which is a real trip; Greek and Hebrew with Father Brownmiller and Pastoral Counselling across the street at Wesley."

"Jesus East, you mean?" Claire said with a wry smile.

Jimmy nearly choked on his drink. "You've heard that too?"

"I'm afraid I've never been very good at playing the prim and proper priest's wife. Life's too short. Don't you agree?"

"Absolutely."

"How do you like your counselling course? I would think you're a natural."

"It's all right. But if you ask me, I think they ought to add a modern language like Spanish to the curriculum. I mean it's nice to understand the languages of the Bible and all, but what if you end up in the inner city or something? How are you going to relate to all those Spanish-speaking people? Seems to me the Episcopal Church had better start getting more relevant, or all our beautiful churches are going to be empty."

Claire nodded enthusiastically. "Oh, I agree. Absolutely."

The dean appeared at the top of the stairs and descended. He had changed into a blue-and-white striped sports shirt and looked ready for an evening of good food and pleasant conversation.

"George, this young man has just suggested a wonderful idea for the curriculum."

"What's that?" the dean said, fixing himself a scotch and water.

"Why don't I let Jimmy explain since it's his idea. Jimmy?"

"Well, I was telling your wife, er, Claire, that it might be a good idea to add Spanish to the curriculum. I know a lot of people might have had it in high school or college, but, you know, a refresher wouldn't hurt. I hardly remember any of my college Spanish. I know not everybody's going to need it in their ministry, but those of us who are going to big cities or institutions certainly will." Jimmy shrugged. "I don't know, it was just a . . ."

"It's a marvelous idea." The dean said, sipping his scotch. "As a matter of fact, the Curriculum Committee is meeting next Thursday. How would you like to come and make a formal proposal? I've been trying to think of some ways to make the curriculum more relevant. You're just the ally I need."

"Well, sure. I'd be delighted, Dean Manoogian."

"Please, in my house, it's George."

George, no less.

"Okay. Well, George, how about if I put my thoughts in writing?"

"That'd be wonderful, Jimmy. Make about 10 copies. That should do. Well, if everyone has a fresh drink, why don't we retire to the kitchen and get dinner ready?"

The Manoogians enjoyed cooking together and found a spare apron for Jimmy and put him to work washing lettuce and chopping vegetables for the salad.

Having never had any proper instruction, Jimmy fumbled with the knife. The dean showed him how to hold it, and he was soon slicing and dicing with ease. This is the kind of father I should have, Jimmy thought.

"We love our time together in the kitchen," Claire said, smiling. "It's the happiest room in our house. I hope you don't mind being pressed into service, but we look at meals as a celebration, and the preparation is the most important part."

"Speak for yourself, Claire," the dean said, patting his ample middle. "The dining room has certainly brought us its share of pleasure over the years."

"Too much, George," she said, pinching his love handle.

"Ouch!"

Jimmy was amazed. They were acting like a couple of newlyweds or something. He couldn't imagine his parents carrying on like this, and yet these two were about the same age and judging by the ages of their daughters, had been married longer.

The dean opened the oven and inspected his leg of lamb. The aroma was wonderful. "A few more minutes," he reported.

Claire lifted the lid on the rice and nodded. "What teamwork. Do your parents cook together, Jimmy?"

"Usually my mother does most of the cooking. But I haven't been home much the last four years, so maybe things have changed. My father can make a mean melted cheese sandwich when he wants to. Is there anything else I can do? The salad's ready."

Claire admired his handiwork. "A work of art. Why don't you decant the wine and light the candles? By then everything will be ready."

When all was ready, the dean helped his wife into her chair and asked Jimmy to say grace.

Jimmy racked his brain for the one his mother always mumbled before his father erupted.

"Let us pray. Bless O Lord this food to our use and us to Thy service. And thank You for this wonderful weather, this bountiful harvest, this fine seminary, and bless everyone at this table. And bless the world with peace. Amen."

"Amen," Claire Manoogian said.

"And a special amen to peace in the world," Dean Manoogian said, sharpening his carving knife.

The lamb was delicious and the Greek wine was the perfect complement. They combined with candles and lively conversation to create the most magnificent evening in Jimmy's memory. He had never known such pleasure at the family dinner table.

"So you think we have no business in Southeast Asia?" the dean asked.

"Well, I don't know if I'd go that far," Jimmy said, "but unless the South Vietnamese really want to fight, what's the point of being over there?"

"Enough war talk," Claire said. "George's too modest to tell you, Jimmy, but he was awarded the Bronze Star for bravery during the Battle of the Bulge."

"Really?"

Dean Manoogian nodded. "I think it was Lee who said something to the effect that it is good that war is so terrible, otherwise we might grow too fond of it. Anyway, Claire's right, enough war talk. Certainly a good-looking young fellow like you must have a pack of ladies nipping at your heels. Do you have a girlfriend?"

Jimmy reached for the mint jelly and spread it on the last of his lamb. "Well, I guess you could say Elaine Roberts and I are still going together. She's at Penn State getting her masters in, well, the same thing you're studying, Claire."

"Wonderful. I'd love to meet the young woman. Is she planning to come for a visit?"

"To tell you the truth, we really haven't discussed it much. Maybe this quarter."

"Well, if she does come, you tell her she's welcome to stay at the deanery. We've got more room here than we know what to do with," Claire said. "It's a shame to let such a big house go to waste."

"I'll tell her," Jimmy said, wondering if he really wanted to see Elaine again. If there was a woman he wanted to be with, it was the Manoogians' daughter, Jennifer.

"Please do. It sounds like Elaine has a mind of her own," Claire said.

"That's for sure."

"What does she think of your being in seminary?" the dean asked.

"Let's just say Elaine's not real big on organized religion."

The Manoogians exchanged knowing looks. There is hope for Jennifer, they silently agreed.

"Is Elaine Episcopalian?" Claire asked.

"No, and I don't think there's much chance of her becoming one. To tell you the truth, she thinks I should have gone to Canada."

"Canada?" Claire asked.

"I think he's trying to tell us he got a low draft number," the dean said.

Jimmy reddened. There was no bullshitting these fine people. "I might as well 'fess up—I got the big call from God when I got number 35 in the draft lottery this spring."

They had all finished eating, so Dean Manoogian lighted a cigarette, savoring it.

"Did you know that Lincoln had to send combat troops to New York in 1863 to suppress the draft riots?" he said.

"Yes, I know. It was practically a second front. People went crazy after they heard about the losses at Gettysburg," Jimmy said.

The dean took another puff and patted Jimmy's hand. "I don't care if you had number one in the lottery—if you say you have a calling to Holy Orders, then no one here is going to question you. Is that clear?"

Jimmy nodded at his dearly beloved dean.

Chapter Thirteen

Episcopal seminarians are required to report their spiritual, mental, and physical condition to their bishops four times a year. Named for the church's four periods of fasting and abstinence, these "Ember Letters" are to be brief and written in the seminarian's own hand.

Jimmy clicked his blue Parker T-Ball Jotter and tried again. It wasn't that he was a poor writer — if anything he was an excellent writer — he just couldn't seem to combine the right blend of reverence and candor that the Rule of Faith called for. Finally he just decided to be himself and the words appeared as fast as the Parker could jot.

"Ember Letter Michaelmas Quarter
Dear Bishop Hamilton,"
So far, so good.

"I am comfortably settled in a pleasant suite with a fellow from Oregon who wants to be a missionary in Alaska. I had been rooming with two older guys, but I seemed to hit it off better with this guy, Bruce MacKenzie, so I moved.

"Don't worry, I don't plan to run off to Alaska after graduation, but I have been rethinking my ministry. I know I expressed interest in being a navy chaplain, but I'm not so sure at this point. I'm really just trying to get through this quarter.

"I think I'm doing pretty well with all my courses, and I know I'm doing real well with Church History because Father Wiltwright just gave me an A + on my first paper. Also, I made a presentation to the Curriculum Committee the other day and suggested they add Spanish. They said they'll consider it. I think a modern language is as necessary to our training as ancient Greek and Hebrew. Not that Greek and Hebrew aren't important, but they sure won't help you in the inner city.

"I particularly like Dean Manoogian and his wife and had a wonderful dinner at their house recently.

"I haven't chosen a faculty advisor yet, but I'm leaning toward Father Wiltwright.

"My chapel attendance has been good, but I have to admit that I often have my best talks with God while walking on the beach at Northwestern.

"Give my regards to Miss Worden. Maybe I'll see you when I'm home for Thanksgiving.

Respectfully,

Jimmy Clarke"

Bishop Hamilton's reply came by return mail. Jimmy could just picture Miss Worden typing it. It read:

"Dear Jimmy,

"I am delighted to learn that you are adjusting so readily to seminary life. I am disappointed that you are rethinking the navy chaplaincy, but there is ample time to consider vocations, and you are right to focus your attention on your present classes.

"You're right about Spanish—it is a useful language for a priest to know, especially those ministering in the inner city. However, one cannot be a proper priest without a sound understanding of the Bible. And one cannot truly understand the Bible until one masters the languages in which it was originally written. I too found Greek and Hebrew to be difficult, but my diligence was rewarded with a deeper understanding of the record of our faith. I encourage you to perservere.

"I would be delighted to see you when you're home for Thanksgiving. Please make arrangements with Miss Worden. Friday would be a good day for me.

"The Episcopal Church is indeed fortunate to have fine people like Dean Manoogian and his lovely wife, Claire. You couldn't find a better role model. Why not ask the dean to be your advisor?

"Finally, the Church provides the ideal forum for the worship and adoration of our Lord Jesus Christ. Even Saint Francis saw fit to follow the Rule of Faith. Please remember that, Jimmy.

"Again, I hope to see you during your Thanksgiving break.

Yours in Christ,

Charles Francis Hamilton + Bishop of Philadelphia"

Jimmy filed the letter, then took another look at Paul Tillich's formidable SYSTEMATIC THEOLOGY and shook his head. Jimmy returned the five-pound book to its shelf and went back to Joseph Heller's CATCH-22.

Chapter Fourteen

Jimmy forgot he had invited Elaine to come out for a visit until he received a letter from her saying she was coming the second weekend of November.

Although he wasn't a fanatic football fan, Jimmy thought the Notre Dame vs. Northwestern game would be worth their while and offered to get tickets. Elaine, after all, had been known to yell herself hoarse at Penn State games.

But she promptly replied:

"Jimmy:

"Don't clutter up the weekend with a bunch of college crap. We've got a lot to talk about.

— Peace and Freedom, Elaine"

Jimmy crumpled the letter and threw it against the wall.

"Bitch!" he said, clenching his teeth. He was heading for the phone to tell her not to come when his new roommate, Bruce MacKenzie, intercepted him.

"You talkin' to yourself again, man? That's a bad sign. Real bad sign. I saw a dude do that in Vietnam, man. Carried on complete conversations with himself, and old Charlie ended it real quick with a bullet in his brain. Anyway, maybe you ought to see a shrink," MacKenzie said.

"No — it's just my girlfriend, or whatever she is." Jimmy didn't really want to talk about it, but Bruce was blocking his path.

"So what's the problem?"

"She's coming for a visit a week from this weekend."

"What's wrong with that? You're finally gonna have sex with somebody besides your right hand."

Jimmy was still mad at Bruce for sabotaging his "date" with Debby White. The last thing he wanted to do was talk to him about Elaine.

"I don't know. I should have broken up with her last spring. Anyway, she's coming, but I'm not looking forward to it. Hell, she doesn't even want to go to the Northwestern game, and they're playing Notre Dame. I mean, how often do you get a chance to see the Fighting Irish?"

"Go to Belfast and you'll see 'em fight any day of the week. So go to the stupid game yourself, and I'll screw her brains out."

"You don't like football, Bruce? What, are you a communist or something?"

"A something."

Figures, Jimmy thought.

"Anyway, do you mind if she stays here? Obviously she's gonna sleep with me, but . . ."

"If she leaves her curlers in the sink, or if she backs up the toilet with her damn Kotexes, I'll wring both your necks."

Jimmy was going to laugh before he realized Bruce wasn't kidding.

"Thanks, Bruce. I knew you'd be a sport."

* * *

Jimmy cut classes on the day of Elaine's arrival and carefully feathered their "love nest" with an FM radio, black light and posters, incense, oversized pillows, and a dozen ribbed condoms. Non-lubricated, of course. Once in the mood, Elaine provided all the motion lotion they ever needed.

Bruce MacKenzie was impressed.

"I even cleaned up the bathroom," Jimmy told him. "I was gonna alert the Biology Department at Northwestern about that stuff that was growing in the toilet, but I didn't want to freak them out. I'd better head downtown. Her train gets in in a hour-and-a-half."

"How long do you think it takes to get down there?"

"I don't know. But I want to give myself plenty of time."

"Calm down, man. Here, sit down and let Brother Bruce roll you a nice little attitude-adjuster. Gange, man. Fresh imported from Jamaica."

"All right! But just one joint, and then I gotta go."

The room was clouded with cannibis 45 minutes later when Jimmy realized he had only 45 minutes to get downtown to meet Elaine.

"Oh shit!" he said, looking at his watch. "Bruce, you gotta let me use your car. Come on, I really need it."

"What, is she gonna cut your balls off if you're a couple of minutes late? Anyway, I already told you, man, I've got a gig in

Skokie tonight. If you catch an Evanston Express in the next ten minutes, you'll be there in plenty of time for your little dolly. Besides, the train'll probably be late anyway. They always are."

Jimmy missed an Evanston Express by two strides and had to wait 15 minutes for the next one. To make matters worse, the BROADWAY LIMITED was unaccountably early that day, and Elaine Roberts had been waiting 20 minutes in Chicago's unsavory Union Station when Jimmy finally appeared. She took one whiff of his breath and refused his kiss.

"Where the hell have you been — in some gin mill? Jesus, I go through hell on that god-awful train to get here, and you show up stoned. I told you we had things to talk about."

"Look, I'm really sorry. The time just got away from me — that's all. Anyway, it's good to see you."

He leaned forward to kiss her on the cheek, but she backed away. "Here, take this bag. It's got a ton of books in it. Where did you park?"

"I didn't. I took the el."

"The el? What the hell's that?" Elaine rubbed her forehead. She was wearing a navy CPO, jeans, and a red bandana — the uniform of protest and professional studenthood.

"It's what they call the subway here. Actually it's not a subway at all because it runs on elevated tracks. Which is why they call it the el." Jimmy was stoned enough to find that amusing.

"Nice to see you still have your childish sense of humor. How far is it to this el?"

A lot farther than the next eastbound train, Jimmy thought.

"A coupla blocks. No sweat. Come on, we used to tromp all over State College like it was nothing. What's a coupla blocks?"

"You call that a couple of blocks?" Elaine complained when they had walked three blocks to the nearest elevated station.

"Well, what do you expect, they're city blocks. This is Chicago, not State College."

Jimmy wanted to ditch her and her books and head for the nearest tavern for a long talk with the bartender, but he figured he still had a fair chance to get her in the sack. So he paid their fares and waited patiently while Elaine schlepped her bags through the turnstyle. I really must be horny to put up with this, he thought, watching her curse and complain.

The train was packed with week-weary commuters, so they had to stand all the way to the city line at Howard Street. Elaine didn't want to talk until they were alone, so Jimmy stared out the window at the backs of three-flats and tenements. Glimpsing Wrigley Field, he vowed to hit a game in the spring even if the Cubs continued their losing tradition.

When they finally arrived at the Noyes stop near Gatesbury, Jimmy asked Elaine if she'd like to have dinner. There was a little Greek joint by the station, and it wasn't crowded yet.

"Let's talk first, and eat later," she said, sighing.

She was not impressed with the seminary and less so with Jimmy's love nest. "Gimme a break," she said, throwing her bag on the bed. She went to Jimmy's dresser, found the condoms, and threw them in the trash basket. "You're not going to be needing these, lover boy. I didn't come all the way out here to be a sperm bank."

"Then why did you come all the way out here, Elaine?"

Elaine went into the common room and took a seat.

"I came out here to talk some sense into that thick head of yours, Jimmy."

"Like what kind of sense, Elaine? Canada? The Weather Underground? Pour blood on my draft files?"

Elaine took a deep breath and let her facial muscles relax. She removed her bandana and shook out her matted, greasy hair.

"Look at this place, Jimmy. It's not you. You know that. This is dishonest. Do you actually expect to put on that silly get-up and do all that voodoo when you get out of here?"

Jimmy laughed self-consciously. "I'm hoping the draft'll be over by then."

"But what if it's not, Jimmy? What if that war never ends? What if those fascist pigs keep on bombing Asian women and children until doomsday? What are you gonna do then? Are you really going to keep playing this ridiculous game? Reverend Clarke — give me a break! I just can't see you wearing a dress and preaching a bunch of voodoo nonsense to rich old ladies."

"So what do you want me to do, Elaine — come back to State College and hide under your mattress?"

"I want you to be honest, Jimmy. I want you to have some backbone. I want you to be the Jimmy Clarke who wasn't afraid to stand up for what he believes in. The Jimmy Clarke who . . ."

She circulated in that vein for a full 15 minutes, telling her "boy" in certain terms how he had made a mess of his life and what he could do to correct it.

Jimmy let her run off at the mouth because he was flattered at first that she cared so much. Then he realized that she regarded him as nothing more than a lab specimen from Sociology 301. That annoyed the hell out of him, but he let her run on a while longer, hoping it might lower her resistance to his amorous advances.

But once Elaine Roberts got on a soap box, there was no pulling her down.

" . . . so what I'm saying, Jimmy, is I'd really respect you if you split to Canada. You're an actor, for Christ's sake. Go to Toronto. There's plenty of good theater up there. Or learn French and go to Montreal. Their government supports the arts. There's no shame in going to a civilized country that puts its money into the arts, not into killing people like this police state we live in. Or at least resist the draft. Stand up for what you believe in. Tell those pigs war is immoral and refuse to go. Go to prison if you have to, but stand up, boy. Don't hide behind some damn frock or gown or whatever the hell they call those stupid things ministers wear. This is no solution. It's a cop-out, man. It's too fuckin' weird for words, man.

"A seminary! I still can't believe you actually went through with this. I mean, who the hell believes in God anymore? I mean . . ."

"Maybe I do, Elaine. Maybe I'll surprise you and everyone else and make a damn good priest. Maybe it's none of your fuckin' business what I do with my life, or how I deal with the draft. Let's face it, Elaine, it's a problem you and all those bitchy feminist friends of yours don't have to face. You can sit there and preach all the radical bullshit you want, because the simple fact is — they're not gonna draft your sweet little ass."

"It's not my fault we live in a John Wayne society. If women were running things, there wouldn't be . . ."

"I know, there wouldn't be a draft; there wouldn't be a dirty little war in Southeast Asia; there wouldn't be oppression, torture, and starvation; and there would be peace and love for everyone every day of the week and twice on Sunday."

"Very good," Elaine said, smiling grimly.

Jimmy took a deep breath and stared at her. She stared back. They went three minutes before they broke the tension with belly laughs.

There was a commotion across the way as Evensong ended, and the hungry mob hurried toward the refectory. Elaine went to the window and watched them.

"Look at those people, Jimmy. You've got to be kidding. Do you really think you fit in with such a bunch of weirdos?"

"No, I don't. I knew that the first day I got here. And you're right, weirdo is the perfect word for them. See that guy with the crew-cut?"

"Oh, my God!" Elaine said, slapping her thighs. "I don't believe it."

"He's the president of my class, no less. Lance Gordon — a real grade-A dork."

"Oh, Jimmy," Elaine said, sitting beside him.

When she put her arm around him, her braless breasts caressed his bicep. She was so warm and close, and it had been so very long.

"Where are you going?" Elaine asked.

"To get my condoms out of the garbage," Jimmy said.

"Good idea," Elaine said.

* * *

A strong northeast wind delivered a crystal blue fall morning complete with golden oak leaves and great white cumulus clusters. There had been a frost during the night, but the bright sun was burning it all away and beckoning everyone to frolick one more time before winter asserted itself.

Jimmy went to the window and grinned.

"Elaine, you should see it out there — it's beautiful. Let's go for a walk along the lake and have a nice leisurely breakfast in downtown Evanston. I know a great greasy spoon that has terrific pancakes and sausage. How's that sound?"

Elaine rolled on her side and played peek-a-boob with the sheets. "Sounds lovely, but don't you think we ought to work up an appetite?"

"Your wish is my desire, but I'd better take a leak first."

Urinating with an erection is a difficult enterprise at best, and Jimmy was still groggy, so he was making a royal mess of it when Bruce MacKenzie blustered into the bathroom.

"Hey, Clarke, why don't you stand on your head? It'd be a hell of a lot easier, and you wouldn't piss all over the floor."

Startled, Jimmy missed the toilet all together.

"Shit," Bruce said, "Watch what you're doin', man; You almost pissed on my new shoes."

"Sorry," Jimmy said. "Take care, Bruce, I gotta get back to . . ."

"Fuck her once for me, man," Bruce said, practically shouting.

Jimmy shushed him, but it didn't do any good.

"I heard you pumpin' away in there when I came in last night. Sounded like you were gonna drive her through the mattress," Bruce said, leering. "Too bad you got such small equipment. Why don't you let me go in there and show her how a real man makes love."

"Jimmy?"

"I'll be right there, Elaine."

Jimmy faced his roommate. "Hey, Bruce, would you mind takin' off for a little while? You know, while we . . ."

"While you fuck her brains out again? Didn't you get enough pussy last night? Jeez, what are you — some kind of sex maniac or something? Anyway, I ain't goin' anywhere. I live here too. But don't let me spoil your little orgy, Romeo. I'll just sit outside your door and beat off."

Jimmy wanted to put his fist through MacKenzie's smirking face, but he wanted to get back to Elaine.

"Thanks, Bruce. I'll remember this next time you need a favor."

Bruce MacKenzie laughed. "Break my heart, man. Next time your mommy sends you cookies, I guess I don't get any — right? My heart pumps peanut butter."

"Fuck you, Bruce," Jimmy said, stomping back to his room and slamming the door.

"Jimmy, what's wrong? Who were you talking to?" Elaine was sitting up in bed with her breasts fully exposed.

"Come on, let's get dressed," Jimmy said, grimacing. "My goofy roommate's pulling his usual shit. Let's go for that walk and have breakfast. Maybe he'll be gone by then and . . ."

"God, look at those tits," Bruce said, barging into the room.

Jimmy punched Bruce so hard in the stomach he thought he broke his wrist.

Get the fuck out of here, or I'll fuckin' kill you, you asshole!"

"Nice tits, baby, real nice," Bruce said, backing out of the room.

Jimmy slammed the door and locked it.

He tried to apologize, but Elaine was already packing.

Chapter Fifteen

"Elaine, would you please stop and listen to me."

Elaine was halfway up the steps to the Noyes elevated station.

"There's nothing to listen to," she said, not bothering to turn her head. "If you stay, you're as crazy as he is. I've had it with you, Jimmy. I really have. I thought I could reason with you, but this is ridiculous."

"Elaine, please. At least let me carry one of your bags." Jimmy heard himself whining and didn't like it, but he wanted Elaine to stay. At least long enough to make love one more time.

Elaine slowed and unslung a bag from her shoulder. "All right. Take this one with the books. It weighs a ton. But let's go, I don't want to miss that train, because I'm not . . ."

"I know, because you're not staying here one more second. Look, I'm really sorry about what happened. Bruce is really a strange dude."

"Strange?!? They call it psychotic where I come from. How can you room with a creep like that? He makes those goons at your stupid fraternity look almost civilized." Elaine shuddered.

"He was in Vietnam. He wants to be a chaplain in Alaska. I don't know. You're right: he's crazy, but you should meet the rest of them. The two guys I was rooming with before acted like it was boot camp and I was the private and they were the drill sergeants. It was real crazy."

"You don't have to convince me." Elaine settled on a bench and looked fixedly down the track as if willing a train to appear.

"Look, give it one more chance, all right? The dean and his wife said you could stay at their house. They're really nice people, and you'd love her. She's your kind of woman. In fact, she's getting her Masters in Social Work. Come on . . ."

"Jimmy, I'll never set foot in that insane asylum as long as I live. If you want to have any kind of relationship with me at all, you're going to have to leave — the sooner the better, boy."

"Sure, girl."

"Don't call me girl."

"Then don't call me boy."

"I was just teasing. You don't have to take everything so seriously."

"I was just teasing too."

The train was crowded enough that they couldn't sit together, and that was fine with both of them. When they got to Belmont, Jimmy grabbed Elaine's hand and led her off the train.

"What are you doing?!?" she said. "This isn't downtown."

"Come on, it's more scenic on the Ravenswood, and it'll drop us off closer to Union Station."

"Jimmy, I'm not interested in sightseeing. I just want to catch that train and get as far away from this hellhole as possible. Are you sure this is going to work?"

"Elaine, I've been here for almost three months now. Of course, I'm sure. Trust me."

She did, and Jimmy mistakenly got them on a northbound train. "Hey," he said to the conductor, "Where the hell's this train going?"

"Lawrence and Kimball — where it always goes, man," the young black man said. "Where the hell do you think it's goin' — Mars?"

"It's supposed to be going downtown."

"That's cause you got on the wrong platform, dude. You'da read the signs, you'd be on the right train. Get off at the next stop and go down the stairs and up on the other platform and get a southbound train."

"Shit!" Elaine said, looking at her watch. "You fool! Goddamn it, I'm not going to miss that train. Do you hear me? Come on, let's go."

She went to the door and stared impatiently at the conductor, willing him to make the train go faster.

He shrugged and stuck his head out the window as the train approached Southport.

"Southport — watch your step."

Elaine pounded on the doors and screamed, "Open them, goddamn it!"

"Be cool," the conductor said, flicking the lever and watching the weird honky bitch take off down the steps like her pants were on fire.

A southbound train was approaching, and she just might catch it if she hauled ass. The conductor hoped she tripped and broke her face.

Elaine was halfway up the opposite steps before she realized Jimmy was not following her.

"Jimmy," she screamed, "I need my goddamn books!"

There was no reply, and the southbound train was gliding to a stop above her head. Elaine decided she could live without her books and bolted for the train.

"Hold the door!" she shrieked, and the conductor obliged.

She was settling in a window seat when she saw Jimmy Clarke on the opposite platform. She expected some pathetic gesture, so she was surprised to see him calmly dump her books, including the one autographed by Gloria Steinem herself, in the trash.

Elaine caught her train with minutes to spare and fumed all the way back to State College, Pennsylvania.

Chapter Sixteen

Jimmy watched the southbound Ravenswood disappear and shrugged. He didn't know whether to cry or shout for joy, so he looked down along Southport Street and settled for the nearest saloon.

He went in for a few beers and ended up spending most of the day watching college football, shooting pool, and bad-mouthing women in general with some salty city workers.

He had a pleasant beer buzz on when he returned to Evanston that evening. The sun was setting somewhere over Skokie, and the trees were full of its fading fire. Jimmy's windbreaker was poor defense against the chill, so he trotted along Orrington Avenue to stay warm. He nearly collided with Claire and George Manoogian as he turned on Seminary Avenue for the seminary.

"Oh, hi," Jimmy said, embarrassed. "I'd better get headlights if I'm going to run at night."

"Jimmy, what a pleasant surprise," Claire said, stepping aside so he could join them.

"Lovely evening, isn't it?" the dean said, smiling. "We're just coming back from our evening constitutional. And you?" He was wearing civvies — chinos and a blue cardigan sweater.

"I was down in the city."

"You have friends in Chicago?" Claire said.

"No, I was just doing some sightseeing, and I found this nice little neighborhood tavern and ended up watching football there. It was nice."

The dean smiled, thinking he would have rather been there than sitting in committee meetings all day. "So did Penn State win?"

"Did they win? They annihilated Syracuse. Never looked better. I made 15 bucks on them. Of course, I lost 20 bucks betting against Notre Dame. That should teach me not to gamble. Boy, Northwestern really stinks! I'm surprised they let them stay in the Big Ten."

"Maybe Gatesbury could take their place," the dean mused. "You look like you could throw a mean football if you wanted to. You could be our starting quarterback."

"Well, I'm not bad, but swimming's my main sport."

"I bet you're quite a swimmer," the dean said.

Jimmy automatically wanted to disagree, but he realized the dean was absolutely right. He was so accustomed to his father's condescending comments that he didn't quite know what to do with fatherly love.

"I'm not bad. I made the team at Penn State my freshman year, but I just kind of lost interest."

Actually, he just kind of developed a stronger interest in booze and pot.

"I'm impressed," Claire said. "You look like a swimmer. I'll bet you're really at home in the water."

"Yeah, I guess I am. My father had me in the Atlantic before I was knee-high to a grasshopper. I've always liked the water. Maybe I'm part fish."

They laughed and walked a while in silence, savoring one another's company. Jimmy took a deep breath and cleared his throat.

"Remember me saying my friend, Elaine Roberts, was coming out for a visit?"

"Yes," Claire said, eyeing her husband. Their daughter, Jennifer, had just announced that she was transferring to Lake Forest College and would be living with them starting in December.

"Wasn't this the weekend Elaine was coming?" Claire said. "Did she change her plans? I hope nothing's wrong."

"Well, ah, to tell you the truth, she was here, and we, well, we broke up. In fact, she's on her way back to Pennsylvania right now. That's the real reason I was in the city. I took her back to the train station. Well, I was taking her back to the train station — anyway, it's a long story." Jimmy exhaled and bit his lip.

The dean put a warm hand on his shoulder. "I'm really sorry to hear that."

Claire took his hand and squeezed his fingers. Just wait until you meet Jennifer, she thought.

They walked him to their house and fed him the finest meal he had had since he last dined with them.

* * *

"I'll clean up tonight," Claire said, when they had eaten the last slice of pumpkin pie. "You two relax and talk man talk."

She stacked the dishes and disappeared into the kitchen.

"Cigarette?" the dean said, opening a fresh pack of Lucky Strikes.

"Well, all right, let me try just one."

The dean tapped the pack, and a Lucky leaped out. He lighted it for Jimmy with his Zippo.

Jimmy took a big pull and felt like Bobby Hull had just slapped a puck into his lungs from the blue line.

"Wow," he said, coughing. "That's some cigarette! How do you smoke these things?" Jimmy dabbed his eyes with the napkin.

The dean chuckled. "It's an acquired taste. I've been smoking these things since I was in the army, and I've never stopped. Even when they came out with the filter cigarettes. You don't have to finish it."

"Oh no, I'm kind of getting used to it," Jimmy said, inhaling carefully. Some tobacco stuck to his lip. He reached for his wine and took a big gulp. That didn't do it, so he swallowed some water. That was better. He took another drag, and although it went down a little easier, he could practically feel the cancer cells forming.

"I take it you don't smoke," the dean said, settling back in his chair.

How do you tell the dean you only smoke pot, Jimmy thought. You don't.

"No, I never really liked it. And nothing will ruin your swimming faster than cigarettes."

"My doctor has been after me for years to take up swimming or bicycling, or something that will get me to stop smoking these nasty little things. I guess it's the Armenian in me, but I just don't want to quit. Maybe this New Year I'll make the big resolution. Claire would love it. Oh well."

They enjoyed their cigarettes for a moment, and then Jimmy cleared his throat. The dean smiled, signalling he was ready to listen.

"I'll put it to you straight, Mr. Dean . . ."

"Please — George."

"Right. Well, it's like this, George, that roommate of mine, Bruce MacKenzie, he's, well, he's drivin' me crazy. Without going into any detail, he was part of the reason Elaine and I had that big fight. Not that we wouldn't have had a big fight anyway and split up — I think it was inevitable, and to tell you the truth, I'm kind of relieved it's finally over, because it was just dragging along anyway. But this thing with Bruce, I don't know. I mean I try to get along with him, but he's just . . ."

"Crazy?"

"Yeah," Jimmy said, surprised. "How did you know?"

The dean blew smoke through his nose and grinned. "His bishop is on the board of directors and is a major contributor to the alumni fund. Bruce saved his nephew in Vietnam. Apparently the young man was shot up pretty bad and would have bled to death if Bruce hadn't braved open fire to treat him. Yes, Bruce MacKenzie is a disturbed young man, but he's also a war hero, and his bishop is deeply indebted to him. And as much as I'd like to live in a world without politics, I am not in a position to ignore Bishop Mitchell."

Jimmy looked at the dean and sighed. "So what you're saying is: I should just live and let live."

"That's about it. Unless you want to move back with Terry Groves and Bob Edwards. But I don't think you'd be any happier with them, and there's just no other space available in the dorm."

"What about moving off campus?"

The dean shook his head. "I know how you feel, but I have to draw the line there. If I let you go, I'd have to let everyone else go. I'll be honest with you, it's not just a matter of preserving our sense of community. It's a matter of money. We'd be in a financial pickle if we didn't have income from the dormitory. So that's the long and short of it. Give Bruce another chance. I know he's trying, and to be perfectly honest with you, I'm not exactly wild about him myself, but in our business you have to accept all conditions of men and women. Otherwise you just won't succeed. Believe me, I've learned the hard way."

"That's the best sermon I've ever heard," Jimmy said, without trying to be funny.

Just the same, the dean laughed until his eyes watered.

Chapter Seventeen

Jimmy was about to turn the key in the lock when he heard Bruce clearing his trumpet's spit valve.

It was only 9:30, and having had three cups of killer coffee, Jimmy was too wired to face Bruce, especially since he still wanted to strangle him.

So he crossed Sheridan Road and wandered around the Northwestern campus looking for some kind of excitement. He found himself next to the lake where the wind was gusting out of the northeast. Jimmy looked east across the waves and tried to mourn Elaine but he couldn't.

Face it, he thought, it's been over for a long, long time. He was more mad than anything, so he kicked a rock and howled into the wind. When the pain subsided, he wondered what the hell he was doing out by the lake on a cold, dark November night.

Jimmy wanted to be with people, but the Manoogians had retired, and there was no one else at the seminary he wanted to see. So he headed back toward campus thinking he might find a party or something.

When he chanced upon fraternity row, he realized he had never visited the local Alpha Chi chapter, much less considered visiting it. Now it almost seemed like a good idea.

The NU Alpha Chi's occupied a handsome three-story tudor affair with a weeping willow. Frisbies and half-deflated footballs littered what had once been a lawn. Jimmy walked through the unlocked door and introduced himself to a pledge who directed him to the chapter room. Ours is bigger, Jimmy thought, but their rug is cleaner and they have more trophies.

The Northwestern brothers were drinking beer and hazing a pledge when the brother from Penn State appeared.

"Help you?" a brother said, freezing his paddle in mid-swat.

"I come in service, that brotherhood may never flounder," Jimmy said, trying to keep a straight face.

"The crescent is our guide," the brother replied.

"And the sword our strength."

"I'm Chip Sumner. High Alpha." He extended a moist hand.

They interlocked their little fingers and depressed their thumbs three times — two short and one long — in fraternal greeting.

"These are the brothers of Zeta Rho chapter," Sumner said. "Pledge, get Brother Clarke a drink. Old Style okay?"

"I'd rather have a Rolling Rock, but it'll do."

"Hop to, Bickley!"

Sweating profusely and clad only in jockey shorts, the red-faced pledge got Jimmy a beer.

"Thanks," Jimmy said, embarrassed for the pledge.

"Bickley," Sumner said, "aren't you forgetting something?"

"What, sir?" Bickley had been having a hard night and wasn't thinking too clearly.

"A glass, you imbecile. Alpha Chi's don't drink out of the bottle. Get Brother Clarke a glass, or your ass is mine for the rest of the night." Sumner's delicate face hardened as he spoke.

He'll go far in corporate America, Jimmy thought.

Bickley had a glass etched with the Alpha Chi crest in Jimmy's hand before he could blink. "Sorry, sir. I beg your forgiveness, SIR!"

Jimmy shrugged. "Hey, don't mention it. We drank off the floor at our chapter."

Sumner gave Jimmy a disparaging look and said, "Assume the position, Bickley."

Bickley spread his legs and bent at the waist, grabbing his left ankle and testicles.

"You holdin' your family jewels?"

"Yes, sir!"

Smiling sadistically, Sumner handed the paddle to Jimmy. It was five-layer plywood and laminated for extra strength. Jimmy remembered that the three-ply paddles that had been broken on his butt had been enough to leave major welts.

Jimmy handed the paddle back to Sumner. "No thanks, I'm not into S and M anymore."

Sumner grabbed the paddle, cocked it, and followed through with a sharp forehand that would have had Jimmy Connors running for cover. The blow lifted Binkley three inches off the floor and forced the air from his lungs, but he did not peep.

"What'dya say, maggot brain?" Sumner hollered in the pledge's ear. "Thank you, sir, may I have another?" Binkley's husky voice was cracking at the edges.

"You sure can, fuck face."

This time Sumner took a running start and cracked the paddle on Bickley's ass. Blood stained Bickley's shorts, but he asked for another which Sumner graciously gave him.

Jimmy put his beer on the piano and walked out. Now he knew why he hadn't bothered to stop by sooner for a visit. He also wondered why he had ever joined a fraternity in the first place. You'll go to any length to get the old man's approval, won't you, he thought.

Not anymore.

Jimmy was looking for his jacket when a wild man with a beard and overalls burst into the room, screaming: "The Alpha Chi Liberation Army hereby frees all pledges from the fascist, pigdog oppressors. Up the revolution! Off the pigs!"

The pledges waiting to be paddled looked uncertainly at the crazy active. He was a tall, lanky guy who moved like a weasel in the bush. His beady gray eyes were bloodshot, his beard was long past needing a trim, and his greasy brown hair fell over his eyes. He completely contradicted his well-dressed brothers.

Jimmy was intrigued.

"Rise humble slaves. Throw off your shackles and join the fight for freedom and justice. Peace, love . . ."

". . . tits, ass," Jimmy added.

"Yeah," the wild man said, grinning. "Yeah, and lots of dope." Sumner and his retainers could not quiet the restive pledges.

"O'Neal," Sumner said, turning to the intruder, "I told you you're not welcome in this house until you pay your dues. And I don't want you near the pledges. We're trying to turn these wimps into Alpha Chi men, not drug addicts."

The wild O'Neal produced a red bandana, carefully swabbed each nostril with it, and offered it to the perturbed president. "Want some, brother? Fresh out of the oven. Mm mm."

"Leave, or we'll throw you out, O'Neal."

O'Neal reddened. "Anybody lays a hand on me, I'll break his face." Everyone backed away, knowing O'Neal could back up his threats.

"Hey," he said to Jimmy, "wanna go to a decent party? You look like you got more sense than to hang around this dump watchin' sick pricks like Generalissimo Sumner here do his fascist military routine on these poor dickheads."

"I'm with you," Jimmy said, ready for whatever came his way.

"I don't want either one of them in this house again, you hear me?" Sumner said.

"Yes, sir," they chorused.

"Fools, dupes, lackies," O'Neil said, opening the door. "Toodles, brothers. May you all suck on the mighty sword of fellowship."

When they were a block south kicking through the leaves of the oak-shrouded campus, O'Neal displayed his loot — sticks of butter, packets of sugar, two jars of jelly, one of peanut butter, and two apples. He had been quietly stuffing them in his jacket while Bickley was taking his swats.

"Think I hang around that fuckin' freak show for my health? Assholes tried to throw me out of the fraternity two years ago for smokin' dope. Shit, can you believe it? What a throw-back to the Stone Age. A bunch of fuckin' troglodytes. Hey, by the way, I'm K.C. O'Neal. My name's really Kevin Charles Ignatius O'Neal, but I've been called K.C. since I was a little kid."

"Jimmy Clarke. Glad to meet you, K.C."

The two white boys gave one another the hooked handshake of black brotherhood.

K.C. said he was a senior, majoring in journalism and "looking for a steady gig after I blow this joint. Man, I'd really like to write for the ROLLING STONE, but those fuckers won't even talk to me, man. Anyway, what's your major?"

"Actually, ah, God."

K.C. laughed. "What — comparative religion? You gotta be kiddin' me."

"Actually, it's worse than that. I'm a student at Gatesbury. I'm a seminarian."

K.C. dropped his jaw. "What?!? Come on, you're pullin' my leg."

"No," Jimmy said, proceeding to tell his new friend the whole story. And," he concluded, "that's how I ended up at Jesus West."

"Better than goin' to 'Nam, man. You did the right thing." That was easy for O'Neal to say, because he was 315 in the draft lottery. "Hell, I was gonna go to a seminary. Or I thought I was when those nuns had me brainwashed. I was gonna be a Jesuit. Goddamn

Jezzies are the Marine Corps of the Catholic Church. I was plannin'
on torturing publics."

"Publics?"

"Yeah, you know, publics. That's what we called 'em on the South
Side, anyway. I went to a Catholic church and a Catholic school
which made me a Catholic. So the kids who went to public schools
and public churches were publics. Couldn't be simpler."

"I never thought of it that way, but then there weren't many
Catholics around when I was growing up."

"Figures — you probably burned them all at the stake."

Jimmy was surprised to see that K.C. was serious.

"No, there just weren't many Catholics in my neighborhood,
that's all."

"Catholics need not apply, right?"

"Hey, look. I can't help it that I'm Protestant and you're Catholic.
What's the big deal, anyway?"

K.C. chewed his cheek for a while and said, "Well, the nuns
always told us that publics were goin' straight to hell, but I figured
the only ones who were goin' straight to hell were those sick old
penguins. Which reminds me of this joke I just heard."

"Do I have a choice?"

"No."

"OK. Shoot."

"Well, there was this leprechaun, see, and he goes up to his
convent, and he says to the Mother Superior: 'Sister, has there ever
been a leprechaun nun?' And she says: 'No, there's never been a
leprechaun nun.' So he goes back to his leprechaun buddies and says
there's never been a leprechaun nun, and they say: 'Then that was a
penguin you fucked last week.'"

They shared a good laugh, and K.C. asked Jimmy if he'd like to
smoke some dope.

"I thought you'd never ask," Jimmy said.

They did a number as they walked past the Millar Chapel and
were soon babbling about the meaning of life and other cosmic
questions. K.C. led Jimmy to a two-story, gray frame house near the
WCTU headquarters and said, "It's party time."

Was it ever.

Jimmy was quickly introduced to a motley coed crew and given a lukewarm Schlitz, two hits of dynamite hash, and an earful of the late, lamented Jimi Hendrix.

God, what a contrast, Jimmy thought, drifting into an alcohol/drug fog. What's a good little seminarian like me doing in a place like this, he wondered. Partying hearty, he decided. Elaine crossed his mind for a moment. She could be here with me right now, he thought. She'd sure like this scene a lot better than the seminary. Of course she wouldn't like the posters or the music and she'd probably want to go home right away. Good thing we broke up, he decided.

K.C. tapped him on the shoulder. "Hey, man, this is my old lady—Jill Gaines. This is, ah, hey man, what's yer name again?"

"Jimmy. Jimmy Clarke," Jimmy said, turning to face a raven-haired beauty who reminded him of Elaine. But this one was much better looking, he decided, taking Jill Gaines' warm hand.

K.C. went off to find some more pot, and Jill and Jimmy settled on the floor to talk. Jill was an army brat and had most recently lived near the Fort Ord Military Reservation south of San Francisco.

Shades of Elaine, Jimmy thought, listening to Jill explain, "I would have graduated by now, but I changed my major from philosophy to art history. God, it's almost like starting over again. Anyway, when I do graduate, I'm thinking maybe I'll open a gallery in Florida or something. So, what about you?"

Jimmy took another toke and told her the truth. She was a good listener, and he liked looking into her dancing, dark eyes as he talked. It was dim, so he couldn't tell if her eyes were brown or hazel, but they were beautiful.

". . . so that's how I joined the God squad," he concluded.

"But you don't really believe in God, do you?" Jill asked, leaning forward to pass yet another passing joint.

A Creedence Clearwater Revival album dropped onto the turntable, and John Fogerty started wailing through his nose about the view from his back door. Jimmy bopped to the cajun beat.

"You like this hillbilly stuff?" Jill asked.

"It's not hillbilly stuff," Jimmy said, offended. "Man, CCR is down-home swamp music. Yeah, I like it. Why not?"

"Because it reminds me of all those rednecks I knew when Daddy was stationed at Fort Benning. Anyway, you didn't answer my question."

"What question?" Jimmy was too stoned to remember.

"Do you believe in God? Do you really believe all that stuff they're teaching you at the seminary?"

Jimmy shrugged. "I don't know what I believe at this point. I think God is this big cosmic cucumber that sort of floats around the Milky Way and every now and then bumps into the earth and causes earthquakes and tidal waves and all that horrible shit. I don't know."

"Well, I know I don't believe in God. I mean how could God let six million Jews die in the gas chambers?"

"Well, they call them the chosen people — maybe God chose them to suffer. I know some so-called Christians would probably say they got what they deserved for killing Christ. You know, let His blood be on us, and all that."

Jill's nostrils flared, and Jimmy wondered for the first time if she was Jewish. Jimmy had horrified his parents by having a Jewish girlfriend in high school.

"Do you believe that?" Jill said.

"Of course not. Look, why don't we talk about something nice, like . . . "

"Like quit hittin' on my old lady, or I'll break your thumbs," K.C. said, settling between them.

Moving to make room for him, Jimmy realized he had a full erection. He had been subconsciously lusting after Jill's body, and K.C. was right to be jealous.

"Hey, I was just talkin' theology with her — that's all," Jimmy said defensively.

K.C. playfully rubbed his knuckles on Jimmy's head. "Just stick with theology, Padre, and everything'll be fine. Now who wants some hash?"

The party wound down at 2 a.m. when most of the house's hirsute inhabitants retired to their black-lighted rooms to screw one another into submission. Jimmy had ended up in K.C.'s and Jill's room where he was staring dreamily at a Janis Joplin poster.

"Hate to kick you out, Padre," K.C. said, stripping matter-of-factly to his Jockey shorts, "but me and the old lady are headin' to the South Side first thing tomorrow mornin'. My nephew's baptism. You know, Catholic shit."

"Yeah, sure," Jimmy said, not wanting to leave. "Hey, thanks, K.C, Jill. Thanks for a terrific time. Well, probably see you after Thanksgiving break, huh?"

Yawning, Jill removed her shoes and socks and sat on the unmade bed ready to remove the rest as soon as Jimmy left. Jimmy stared at her, wishing she would forget herself.

"Yeah, we'll see you after Thanksgiving, man," K.C. said. "Now, if you don't mind, me and Jill'd like to cop some Zs."

Jimmy edged toward the door, thinking how he'd like to take K.C. out with a quick karate chop and have Jill all for himself. "Sorry. Yeah, I'm pretty tired too. And I'm supposed to go to church on Sunday mornings, but to tell you the truth, I think I might sleep in."

K.C. went to his dresser, saying, "Hey, I didn't mean to give you the bum's rush. We just got a lotta family shit tomorrow, that's all." He found what he was looking for. "So here's a little holiday treat for you, brother. It ain't a turkey or a pumpkin pie, but it sure is something to be thankful for."

He handed Jimmy a carefully folded piece of aluminum foil. "Take it in good health, man."

Jimmy unfolded it and found what looked to be a shard of tinted glass. "What the . . ."

"Window pane, man. Acid. You've tripped before, haven't you?"

"Oh, yeah. Yeah, lotsa times," Jimmy lied. "Sure, sure. Hey, thanks."

"Sure man. Be careful with that stuff, man. It's powerful shit," K.C. said.

"Oh, I will," Jimmy said, taking a long, last look at Jill.

Chapter Eighteen

"Sir, you'll have to leave the airplane. This flight terminates in Philadelphia. Sir?"

Jimmy Clarke was still in the clouds. He peeled his face off the window and blinked. "Huh?"

"You'll have to leave the aircraft, sir," the stewardess said.

"Leave the plane? What plane?" Jimmy looked out the window, and his disordered mind threw the two-hour flight back at him, complete with gremlins and angels on ten-speed bicycles. "We're on the ground?" He tried to grasp "ground" but could not.

"We've been on the ground fifteen minutes, sir, and you're ..."

"Trouble here, stewardess?" the captain said, tall and Texan.

"This gentleman doesn't seem to want to leave the plane, sir," the stewardess said, rubbing her hands.

One look, and the pilot pegged Jimmy as a rich draft-dodger high on some expensive drug. "You don't get off my aircraft in one minute, mister, your ass is in one hell of a sling. You hear me, boy?"

Standing and saluting, Jimmy replied, "Yes, sir, general." He saw his distorted image in the aviator's sunglasses and laughed. "God, I need a shave." He touched his chin and the tendrils felt like tentacles. "Wow."

"Off my aircraft. Now!"

"My luggage, man. What about my luggage?"

Jimmy dropped to his knees and searched under the seats. When he tried to look up the stewardess' skirt, the muscular captain grabbed his shirt collar and shoved him off the plane. Jimmy was too loose to resist.

"That was terrific," Jimmy said as the captain pushed him down the ramp. "Do it again."

"Next time take the bus, you goddamn worthless, draft-dodgin' hippie, scumbag son-of-a-bitch," the pilot said, wiping his hands on his pants.

The wind had a sweet chemical taste, and the sky was unremittingly gray. Trying to remember why he had taken such an amazing journey, Jimmy gaped at the terminal and saw a middle-aged woman waving at him. He wondered why people waved at one another and was nearly run over by a speeding fuel truck. The rush of airport activity was too intense, so he decided to go inside and see about this waving woman.

She turned out to be his mother, and she thought he was sick.

"Let me have a look at your eyes," Louise Clarke said, after she had given her only child a heartfelt hug. "My goodness, you ARE sick, dear. Your pupils are bigger than quarters. Have you been getting enough sleep lately?

"What are they feeding you at the seminary? Oh, Jimmy, it's been so lonely without you."

She hugged him again, and he realized that he had come home for Thanksgiving and had better smell the turkey.

"Oh, Jimmy," Louise continued, "I've been so worried about you. You've hardly written, and you almost never call. Then I thought you had missed the flight. You didn't call before you left, so I could only assume you would be on this flight like you said in your letter. And then the pilot brought you off the plane, I . . ."

"He was helping me, Mom. I'm sick. I think I've got the flu or something. I just had mid-terms, and I've really been cracking the books, you know, staying up half the night and studying. Plus the food really stinks. You should see what they call meatloaf. Looks like something they picked off the highway."

"Oh, Jimmy," Louise said, delighting in her son's presence.

She had put on a few pounds and wrinkles and was keeping something from him, but he wasn't ready to ask.

"Mom, I, ah, didn't get a chance to go to the bathroom on the plane. Can you wait a second?"

"Certainly, dear."

* * *

Jimmy splashed cold water on his face and looked in the mirror. He shuddered. For a moment the water looked like blood. Then he could see the layers of tissue under his skin. When he saw maggots crawling out of his eye sockets, he had to turn away. Jimmy rubbed his face with a paper towel.

A hippie came out of the crapper with a buzz on. "You got any more of that shit, man?" he asked.

Jimmy blinked. "Huh?"

"The acid you're on, man. You got any more?"

Jimmy nodded. "I'm not on acid. I've just got a headache — that's all."

"Sure, man."

The hippie left, and Jimmy took some deep breaths. He could still see Donald Duck and the other Disney characters floating under his eyelids.

"You can take a nap in your own bed when we get home," his mother said when he emerged from the restroom. "I made it this morning with those Davy Crockett sheets you had when you were little. The guests won't arrive until three so there's plenty of time for you to get some rest. Your father and Uncle Phil are trying to get in one last round of golf before winter, so the house will be nice and quiet."

"Speaking of the devil, how is he?" The thought of his father brought Jimmy down several notches.

"Jimmy, I wish you wouldn't . . ."

"Sorry. Well, how is he?"

"Your father has been, well, he's under a lot of pressure at work, and . . ."

She collided with a sailor and apologized profusely.

Listening to her, Jimmy wondered if she had apologized to his grandmother for being born. But he was glad for the interruption because he didn't need to hear that the old man was going to cut him off.

They went to the baggage claim area, and Jimmy screamed at a bewildered attendant before he realized that he had forgotten to bring any luggage. He had packed all the necessities before he dropped the little tab of window pane, but once that was in his system, it was all he could do to get to the airport.

"Sorry, man," he said, sheepishly. He was coming down hard now and so pushed his mother's hand away when she offered him the keys. She always told him what a good driver he was, which was generally true.

"You mind drivin', Mom? I don't think I could handle it."

Jimmy dimly remembered warning the cabbie in Chicago to watch out for falling planes.

When they were in the familiar blue Fairlane cruising across the Penrose Avenue Bridge enroute to the Schuykill, or "Sure Kill," Expressway, Louise asked if Elaine was coming to dinner.

Jimmy was preoccupied with the Philadelphia Naval Yard which spread beneath them. An enormous aircraft carrier caught his eye, and he wanted to catapult off its deck on a big Harley.

"Oh, Jimmy, how could I forget such an important thing — the bishop's secretary, Miss Worksmith . . ."

"Ah, it's Worden, Mom. Miss Worden."

"Right. Well, she called yesterday to say the bishop will see you tomorrow at 11 in his office. Is anything . . ."

"No, I just mentioned in my Ember Letter — that's this letter you have to write to the bishop four times a year — I think I might have mentioned it to you in one of my letters — anyway, I said I'd be home for Thanksgiving and suggested I stop by for a visit. That's all."

Louise beamed. Her boy hobnobbing with Bishop Hamilton. Well, that would be one for the coffee hour.

"How lovely," she said. "Would you like to take the car? I won't need it tomorrow, and I'm sure your father . . ."

"No, that's all right. I'll take the train. If it's still running."

"It's one thing the Penn Central hasn't ruined. Maybe I could come down with you, and we could meet your father at Bookbinder's for lunch."

"I don't know how long I might be with the bishop, Mom, maybe we'd better wait on that."

"Whatever you say, dear."

Jimmy settled back and closed his eyes. But the cartoon characters were waiting under his eyelids, so he blinked and stared at the John F. Kennedy Stadium where crowds were forming for the army/navy game.

"Jimmy, didn't you hear me before? I said: Is Lorraine coming for dinner this afternoon? I'll have to make more food if she is."

Lorraine? Oh, that's right, Jimmy thought, good old Mom's never quite gotten their names' right. Except for Susie Blake, the bimbo down the block.

"Do you mean Elaine, Mom?"

"That's right. Why do I always call her Lorraine?"

Because she tried to steal your baby.

"Well, whatever you want to call her, she's not coming. She's staying in State College for the holiday."

"That's nice," Louise said, smiling inwardly. "Susie Blake's living at home now. She's got a job with an insurance company out at King of Prussia. I don't suppose . . ."

"I'll take a pass, Mom."

"Well, maybe you'll see her at church on Sunday."

"Actually, I booked myself on an early flight, so I don't think I'm going to be able to make it to church Sunday."

Louise's jaw dropped about three miles. She had been looking forward to her son's triumphant return all fall. "Couldn't you take a later flight?"

Jimmy saw his mother's disappointment. He really didn't want to deal with all those stuffed shirts at Saint Matthew's, but he didn't want to hurt his mother's feelings.

"All right, I'll take a later flight if I can get one. I just thought it'd be better for you if I left early—you know, you wouldn't get caught in all that traffic at the airport. Half of humanity is going to be flying Sunday."

"Jimmy, it's never too much trouble. You know that. I'm so glad you'll be able to go to church Sunday because Mr. Carlisle has a little surprise for you."

"Money?"

"Uh, no, dear. The new organ's . . ."

"I know, it's costing a small fortune. So what's the big surprise?"

"Mr. Carlisle wants you to give the sermon at the 11 o'clock service."

"The sermon at the 11 o'clock service? Wow, the big time. But I haven't taken homiletics yet. They don't let us get near a pulpit at Gatesbury until our second year."

"That's all right, dear. Mr. Carlisle just wants you to talk about your experiences at the seminary. That sort of thing. Isn't that nice of him?"

Jimmy looked down at the Schuykill River and wondered if it was warm enough for a swim. Donald Duck assured him it was.

"That's real nice of him, Mom, real nice."

* * *

James G. Clarke II grimaced as he took his place at the head of the table. "Would you help your mother?" he said to his son, who had settled next to his cousin, Jill Maye Hakobian.

Jimmy's nap had been a farce; the cartoon creatures had distracted him, and he had had diarrhea all afternoon. Now, the burgeoning table made him want to barf, but he was determined to please his mother and keep his old man quiet.

"You need help, Mom?"

"Would you pour the wine, dear? It's in the other refrigerator. And please light the candles." She was smooshing gobs of real butter on the real mashed potatoes.

He wobbled around the table and served Uncle Phil, Aunt Edna, Jill, and her mustachioed groom, Mikael. "Glass of wine, Dad?"

His father, a heavy-set man with thick waves of black and gray hair, angrily dropped his carving tools. "Goddamn it, Jimmy, how many times do I have to tell you I don't drink wine? We go through this every holiday. Get me another scotch. And don't drown it like you usually do."

Jimmy made the drink the way his father liked it, two ice cubes, a drop of water, and the rest scotch, but the old man complained that it was too weak. He stomped off to his kitchen corner bar and overflowed a fresh cocktail glass with Black Label. He poured Jimmy's drink down the sink, prompting his harried wife to say, "Jim, that's expensive scotch."

"To hell with it. Damn kid still doesn't know how to make a decent drink." Jimmy and the others overheard, and he smiled thinly as he lit the candles and took his seat. He was uncomfortably accustomed to this. His mother rushed in with a bowl of her wonderful cole slaw, perking Jimmy's appetite.

He held her chair and said, "Mmmmm, I love your cole slaw, Mom. Best in the world."

"Jimmy, you've been saying that since you were a little boy."

"What'dya mean, since? He still is a little boy." Big Jim Clarke grinned and went after the turkey with the knife he had been sharpening for fifteen minutes.

"Remember the time you tried to carve the bird, Jimmy?"

Jimmy blushed and shook his head.

"He made a real mess of it," Big Jim said. "Looked like somebody ran the damn thing over with a power mower." His voice was loud and slurred.

Louise took a deep breath and said, "Would you stop that for a minute, Jim, while we say grace?"

"Don't let me stop you." He continued carving, and Jimmy was happy to see he was not doing such a hot job of it.

"How about if our seminarian leads us? Jimmy?"

Jimmy wanted to call God's wrath down upon his father, but instead he said, "Let us pray. Bless, O Father, these thy gifts to our use and us to thy services, for Christ's sake. Amen. And Happy Thanksgiving everybody."

"Boy, that was fast," Uncle Phil said, eagerly unfolding his napkin. "You'd make a great Marine Corps chaplain. Ever thought of that?"

"I thought the marines didn't actually have their own chaplains. The navy provides them—like corpsmen and that sort of thing."

"Then you have thought about it. Of course, being a chaplain, you won't command troops. But at least you'd be serving your country as well as your God."

Jimmy's ears burned. His uncle, the insurance adjustor from Paoli, still looked like a model for a Marine Corps recruiting poster—from the chest up, anyway.

Glancing to his left, he could see that his father was nearly finished carving and would soon join the conversation. He had that faraway look on his face which signalled a long, maudlin story about any or all of the following: his war in the Atlantic, Winston Churchill's wartime speeches, the latest barroom wisdom, the good old days at Penn State and Alpha Chi, and/or the dirty little Japs and why they deserved a good nuking.

Eager to thwart his father, Jimmy turned to his cousin-in-law and said, "Did you know that the dean of my seminary is Armenian?"

Mikael, who had been politely uncomfortable, smiled in relief. "Is that right? What's his name?"

"Father George Manoogian. He wasn't born in Armenia. I think he's from Boston originally. Real nice."

"I know the name. He's quite a theologian, isn't he?"

"Yeah, I guess he is. I'm afraid I haven't read any of his books yet, but I plan to next quarter."

Big Jim had his wife fetch him another drink while he brooded over his white meat. "I thought you were going to an Episcopalian seminary?" he asked, looking up suddenly. "What's all this 'Father' stuff? When I was growing up, we called Doctor Gibson 'Doctor' Gibson, and that was it. What's this 'Father' stuff? Since when have we become a bunch of goddamn mackerel snappers?"

Louise returned with his drink and tried to placate him, saying, "Jim, you haven't been to church in years. You don't even go on Christmas and Easter anymore. How do you know . . ."

"That's because they've got some young hippie over there at Saint Matthew's. Next thing you know he'll be serving pancakes to little bush bunnies from North Philly. I know that when Doctor Gibson was around the Episcopal Church was the Episcopal Church. Sounds to me like the damn Catholics are taking over. I suppose the next thing you're going to tell me is that you're going to confession." He took a long drink and pursed his lips.

"As a matter of fact, a Franciscan brother is coming next quarter to hear confessions. I thought I might give it a try. That's what I like about Gatesbury, they're open to high and low church customs." Turning, he added, "You're Catholic, aren't you, Mikael? Armenian Catholic, I mean."

"Well, I was raised in the Armenian Catholic Church, but the masses are too long and full of old DP's so I go to regular Catholic churches when I go."

"That's interesting. The Armenian Catholic Church is affiliated with Rome, and the Apostolic Church is Orthodox, right, which means . . ."

"Doctor Gibson always said you could call him 'Doctor' Gibson or 'Mister' Gibson. Never 'Father' Gibson. I never heard him ask somebody to kiss his ring, and if he had lit some incense or tried to have confession or any of that other Catholic crap, we would have run him out of town on a rail."

"Jim, you hardly ever went to Saint Matthew's when Doctor Gibson was rector. You . . ."

"Bullshit."

Phil stirred. Louise patted her brother's hand and smiled bravely. Big Jim drained his glass in two gulps and plunked it in front of his wife who went to make him another drink.

Jimmy was too physically and emotionally wrecked to eat and dropped his silverware. "Dad, Doctor Gibson was a low churchman. He was called 'Doctor' because he had earned a Doctorate of Divinity degree. Some people call Father Manoogian 'Doctor' because he has the same degree. And some people call him 'Dean' or 'Mr. Dean' because he's dean of the seminary. In fact, he even asked me to call him 'George' when I'm at his home."

Louise perked up. "Oh, you've been invited over to the deanery. How lovely."

Yeah, Jimmy thought, and I'd rather be there right now. "Yes, it was lovely," he said. "Anyway, it's stupid to argue about semantics, especially when Mom has cooked such a terrific meal."

Jimmy rubbed his forehead and glanced at his father. "Plus, you're sitting here insulting the Catholic Church when you know damn well Mikael's Catholic. How would you like it if I asked who won the big golf game today? Huh? Especially since you've carefully avoided saying one word about it. That's gotta mean Uncle Phil won, right, Dad? The Marine Corps beat navy again, didn't they, Dad?"

Enraged, Jim Clarke grabbed the turkey in both hands and hurled it at his son. Jimmy ducked as the stuffed carcass sailed over his head and landed on his mother's clean carpet with a wet thud.

"Goddamn son-of-a-bitch!" Big Jim cursed, charging his son.

Uncle Phil got between the jousting Jims and said, "For Christ's sake, Jim, sit down and take it easy. It's Thanksgiving, remember? Come on, let's all relax and have a good time. What do you say?"

Jim Clarke worked his jaws, producing a garble of oaths and epithets.

Finally, he pushed past his brother-in-law, stomped through the living room, and slammed the front door with such force everyone's ears popped.

Jimmy exhaled and unclenched his fists. He was so tense he was dizzy.

Louise came from the kitchen with tears of shame streaming down her face. As he had done so many times before, Jimmy went to his mother and put a protective arm around her shaking shoulders.

Chapter Nineteen

Gwynn Worden tapped Jimmy's knee and said, "The bishop will see you now."

Jimmy rubbed his eyes. He had fallen fast asleep reading a lively article about selecting the right lessons and carols for Advent. He wiped his mouth with the back of his hand and realized he had been drooling.

"Thank you," he said, struggling to his feet. He had taken an early train so he wouldn't have to face his father, and it had cost him that extra hour of badly needed sleep.

Bishop Hamilton had a healthy tan and a hearty handshake.

Jimmy glanced at his ring and decided to take a pass. A handshake's going to have to do, he thought, matching the bishop's firm grip.

"It's great to see you, Jimmy. I'm so glad you were able to stop by for a visit. Well, please have a seat and tell me all about your first quarter at Gatesbury."

They settled on sofas opposite the bishop's clutter-free desk. Gwynn Worden brought them coffee and rolls, and Jimmy gave the bishop a carefully worded account of his life and studies at Gatesbury, concluding with, "And so Father Wiltwright thinks I should major in church history."

"I hope you take this in the spirit in which I offer it, Jimmy, but I just don't see you with your head buried in a history book. Not when the need for active young priests is so great. What happened to your interest in being a navy chaplain? Frankly, I was distressed by your Ember Letter. I hope you're not having second thoughts about your calling."

The bishop added a bit of cream to his coffee and stirred it clockwise, then counterclockwise. He took a slow sip and looked thoughtfully at the young seminarian. He had such hopes for this young man, but he was beginning to wonder. The reports from Gatesbury had not been good.

Jimmy wrung his hands and fiddled with his coffee before taking too big a gulp. Damn, I burned my tongue.

"Well, I don't know, Bishop Hamilton. I know I sounded real gung-ho before about being a chaplain, but the more I think about it, the more I realize that you really have to do some time in the navy or Marine Corps or whatever before you can minister to those guys. I mean, they're not going to relate to some guy who's never had to swab a deck or whatever. Don't you think?"

The bishop had to agree. "So what kind of ministry are you thinking about now? I'll be quite frank with you: this diocese isn't the only one with declining membership. The Reverend Mr. Carlisle is a young man, and openings at churches like Saint Matthew's just don't come along very often anymore. What I'm really looking for are young priests who are willing to find another source of support."

"You mean like find another job?" Jimmy was crestfallen. He had always seen himself living in an ivy-covered rectory on the Main Line. If you had to go all the way with this weirdness, it might as well be cushy.

"That's exactly what I mean—working priests. It's hardly a new idea. You're taking church history—look at the deacons of the early church. It looks like we're coming full circle. With your interest in acting, maybe you could support yourself on the stage and serve as a supply priest on Sundays," the bishop said, sipping his coffee.

"That's why you were so encouraging about my being a chaplain."

"That's right."

"Well, I'll have to give it some more thought."

"Do that. Please do that. Now then, you haven't said a word about your private life. How is that young lady of yours—Elaine Roberts, I believe?" As always, Gwynn Worden had briefed the bishop well.

"Well, to tell you the truth, ah, we broke up about a week or so ago."

"I'm sorry to hear that." The bishop leaned forward and patted Jimmy's knee. "How are you taking it?"

Jimmy shrugged. "All right. Things were pretty much over a while ago anyway. It's just as well because she didn't really, well, she didn't think too much of me being in a seminary. Elaine's not really the church type."

"Well then, it's just as well, because it's a rare woman who can be a good rector's wife. Believe me, I know."

Bishop Hamilton was rumored to have broken off a love affair prior to his ordination as a bishop. His fiancee had allegedly asked him to choose – her or the church. She didn't want to be stood up for the rest of her life for committee meetings and confirmations in remote suburban churches. Bishop Hamilton chose the church without hesitation.

"I'd say the dean's wife is one of those rare women," Jimmy said.

"Claire Manoogian is a fine church woman. Say, I don't suppose you've had a chance to meet their lovely daughter, Jennifer, have you?"

"No, but I've seen her picture. I'd sure like to meet her."

"Well, I'm sure you'll have your chance before long – Dean Manoogian tells me she's moving in with them next month. She's transferring to Lake Forest College. A good choice, I must say."

Maybe I will go back to the seminary, Jimmy thought. As if I had a choice. At least now I have something to look forward to.

Gwynn Worden appeared at tht door right on cue.

"Well," Bishop Hamilton said, rising, "I see our time is up." He casually presented his ring.

Jimmy stared at it for a long moment before remembering that he had gratefully kissed it at the conclusion of his last visit. Of course, he thought, I was so damn glad that he was going to keep me out of 'Nam, I would have kissed his ass. Still, he did tell me Jennifer's going to be around, so . . .

Jimmy bent and kissed the episcopal ring as Bishop Hamilton and Gwynn Worden smiled approvingly.

*　*　*

Big Jim Clarke stood looking out the front window with a scotch-and-water in his hand. He watched his son come up the walk and grimaced. Whatever possessed me to have kids, he thought, taking a good gulp. I mean kid. How the hell was I to know Louise would lose the first one. God, what she went through to bring this one into the world. Oh well, she wanted him, so she can have him. Anyway, he's given her something to do all these years.

Jimmy didn't see his father until he came around the big blue spruce, and then it was too late to duck around to the side door like he had done so many times before. He had just finished a joint and definitely didn't want to ruin his high by hassling with the old man. But there was no avoiding him now, so he strode boldly through the front door and said, "Hi, Dad, how's it goin'?"

Big Jim took another drink and shifted his weight from his heels to his toes. "'Bout yesterday," he said, clearing his throat.

"Yeah," Jimmy said, facing him fully.

"It was the booze talking." He grabbed his boy's shoulder and gave it a hard squeeze. "'Nough said. All right?"

"Sure, Dad," Jimmy said, wanting to kill him.

"How about a drink before dinner?"

"Sure, Dad."

Chapter Twenty

"... and I believe in the Holy Ghost, The Lord, and Giver of Life,
Who proceedeth from the Father and the Son; Who with the Father
and Son together is worshipped and glorified; Who spake by the
Prophets; and I believe in one Catholic and Apostolic Church; I
acknowledge one Baptism for the remission of sins; and I look for
the Resurrection of the dead: And the Life of the world to come.
Amen."

The Reverend Mr. David Malcolm Carlisle turned to his
well-heeled congregation and bid them be seated. Louise Clarke
settled in her customary spot, the aisle seat in the second-to last pew
on the Gospel, or left, side of the church. She was so proud she
wanted to shout. Instead, she just sat up straighter and bobbed her
head.

The handsome young rector adjusted his purple stole and
cleared his throat. The women of the church were all eyes.

"We're in for a real treat this morning," Carlisle said, "because
I've asked our young seminarian, Jim Clarke, to take my place in the
pulpit. But I hope he doesn't get any ideas, because I'm much too
young to retire."

There was a ripple of polite laughter.

"As most of you know," Carlisle continued, "Jim grew up in this
church and was baptized here by Doctor Gibson and confirmed here
by Bishop Hamilton. He was graduated from Penn State in June and
was active in the campus ministry there. He's completing his first
quarter at Gatesbury Theological Seminary in Chicago, and he tells
me he's giving some thought to majoring in church history.

"Well, if our organ wasn't in such a state of disrepair, I'm sure
that we would offer him generous financial support. He is, after all,
the first young man Saint Matthew's has sent to seminary in quite
some time. But I'm sure we can all give him the spiritual support he
needs by remembering him in our daily prayers."

Carlisle turned to Jimmy, who was sitting behind the choir.

"Remember," he said, smiling condescendingly, "no souls are
saved after the first ten minutes."

At Carlisle's insistence, Jimmy wore a red acolyte's cassock. He had taken the biggest one he could find, but it was still too small, and he felt like a damn fool as he ascended the pulpit steps.

But then he surveyed the congregation from this new perspective and was surprised to see that every single woman, young and old, had glued her eyes to him. Especially Susie Blake who was sitting with her mother three pews in front of Louise Clarke.

Jimmy gave Susie the once-over. She was wearing a heavy gray dress that hid her large breasts but could not disguise the fact that she had been eating a little too much of momma's cooking. Her already round face had gotten more so, and she had cut her hair too short. She still had her freckles, and her blue eyes were as lively as ever. She had been Jimmy's heart throb in the eighth grade, but he had never gotten up the courage to harken to her siren call.

Susie Blake had collided with puberty back in the fifth grade, and by eighth grade was operating with heavier equipment than any two other girls combined. She was a lusty little kid and would have welcomed Jimmy Clarke's advances, but the poor boy was so riddled with guilt and misinformation, he was sure he'd get hand cancer if he touched her. They had gone their separate ways in high school and had gone to different colleges, but Susie still burned a candle for Jimmy Clarke. Especially now that he was up THERE.

Embarassed by the intensity of Susie's gaze, Jimmy looked away, wondering what it would be like to buy the whole scene with her. She'd sure make the perfect rector's wife — no doubt about it. Makes her own dresses, probably dress the kids too in her own creations. Kids. Who said anything about kids? Susie'd sure as hell want them. But do you?

Jimmy looked at the other women and remembered all the attention Carlisle had gotten at his cousin's wedding and realized there was something to this.

Jimmy cleared his throat and fished the 3" x 5" index cards out of his pocket.

Nodding at Mr. Carlisle, Jimmy said, "Thank you, sir, for that fine introduction. And thank you all for being here for my first sermon."

Jimmy removed the paper clip from the cards and realized he was perspiring so heavily he had run the ink beyond recognition. He couldn't make out a single word. So big deal, he thought, you're an actor — improvise.

"As our dear rector said, no souls are saved after the first ten minutes, and I will self-destruct if I go a second over. Anyway, I seemed to have used disappearing ink on my notes, so I'm going to have to ad-lib."

Jimmy paused to tear up his index cards and got a good laugh. Carlisle shifted irritably in his seat. He didn't like having his thunder stolen, especially by a wise-cracking junior seminarian. When he was a junior, he hadn't been allowed to open his mouth unless spoken to, and he wouldn't have dreamed of giving a sermon. But Bishop Hamilton was keen on this kid, his mother was more than generous every Sunday, and it was rumored the kid's old man was about to drink himself out of a job. But the pompous priest also sensed that this kid had more personality in his little finger than he would ever have, and he hated him for it.

Jimmy continued: "The good rector forgot to mention an important item – the Gatesbury Saints, for the tenth year in a row, trounced his alma mater, the Cranmer Crosses, on the sacred gridiron. This year's score was only 30-to-6 because we took pity on the poor souls, and I'm happy to report there were no injuries and plenty of good Christian fun."

Carlisle nodded tightly at Jimmy, and Jimmy judiciously described the seminary and his life there.

". . . and so," he concluded after 590 seconds of lively monologue, "I'm taking church history, theology, Greek and Hebrew, and pastoral counseling. No P.E., but then as good Episcopalians we do plenty of calisthenics in the chapel every day. I take the counselling course across the street at Wesley Methodist. We call them Jesus East, and they call us Jesus West. We're thinking of having an East-West football game and calling it the Lavabo Bowl."

The Reverend Mr. Carlisle preempted the laughter by standing and clearing his throat. "Thank you, Jim. Most illuminating." He nodded at the organist and said, "Remember the words of the Lord Jesus how he said, 'It is more blessed to give than to receive.'"

Passing Jimmy on his way back to the altar where he would receive the alms and oblations of his flock, Carlisle added under his breath, "You wouldn't get a dime from this church if we had it to give."

Jimmy sat and fumed for the rest of the service. When he went to receive communion, he kept his eyes closed so he wouldn't have to look up Carlisle's pointy nose. What an asshole, he kept thinking.

Still, I could be in 'Nam with an officer like him sending me into an ambush, so I suppose I should be grateful.

Louise Clarke was waiting in the church basement, or undercroft, with Susie Blake and her prim and plump mother, Eloise. Jimmy took one look at them and clutched his stomach.

His mother rushed to his side, saying, "Are you all right, dear?"

"I think I still have a little flu bug floating around, Mom. Mind if we go home?"

He really did feel ill, but not from the flu. He just couldn't face Susie and the rest of them. And Carlisle was over there giving him a haughty sneer.

Louise was crestfallen, but she would never hesitate to nurse her son. "Maybe some tea would help, dear."

"No, Mom, I really think I need to go home and lie down a little while. All right?"

His mother looked at all those jealous ladies and tried to hide her profound disapointment. "All right, dear," she said.

* * *

Jimmy had been back at Gatesbury a week when his mother called. She was still in shock, so her message was short and simple: "Dear, your father has been forced to take an early retirement. If you want to stay in seminary, you'll have to find some way to pay for it. I know this is quite a jolt, but we're even thinking of selling the house. Jimmy? Are you all right?"

Jimmy stared at the receiver. He was breathless and didn't know if he should laugh, cry, or do both. Chopper blades whirred in his head and little Vietnamese kids tried to hand him exploding Coke bottles. He saw himself bleeding to death on a jungle trail or prodded into a Viet Cong tiger cage.

I'm going to Vietnam.

"Jimmy, are you all right?"

He exploded. "Why don't you divorce that drunken bastard and marry somebody who really appreciates you? Why don't . . ."

"James Clarke, I don't ever want to hear that kind of talk from you again. Do you hear me?" Louise was all ice. Her devotion to her husband was absolute; her denial that he was a drunken bum complete.

There was no use: she would never leave him. "Sorry. I'm really sorry, Mom. I didn't mean it. Look, I'd better be going. I've got to get to church history class."

"Jimmy, dear, I'm sorry I spoke that way. We're all upset. It's been hard on all of us, dear. But we'll make it. And there's always the Maye Trust if . . ."

"But that's for your old age, Mom. I couldn't . . ."

"It's there if you need it."

"No, Mom, I'll manage somehow. You'll see. I'm a big boy now. I'll manage. Look, I've really gotta go. I'll call you this weekend — on Sunday afternoon after you get home from church. Bye."

"Goodbye, dear. God bless and keep you." Louise Clarke cradled the phone and cried.

Her son cradled the pay phone and ran to church history class where he presented a paper discussing in detail the atrocities visited upon the Huguenots by the French Catholics.

Chapter Twenty-One

"Almighty God," Jimmy prayed, "who hast given us grace at this time with one accord to make our common supplications unto thee; and dost promise that when two or three are gathered together in thy Name wilt grant their requests. Fulfill us now, O Lord, the desires and petitions of thy servants, as may be most expedient for them; granting us in this world knowledge of thy truth, and in the world to come life everlasting. Amen."

As the minister of that December morning's prayer, he could keep them waiting as long as he wanted. He had plenty of supplications for Almighty God, and if everyone was in such a hurry to get to breakfast, then they could just go. Their lives were happy; most of them had wives who worked, kids with clean teeth, and cars to take them places. Most of them had money.

Jimmy was mad at God and doubted his higher power's lines were open anyway, considering the competition. He fidgeted for a while wondering if hard kneelers caused cancer of the knee cap and finally whispered, "You know the whole story. If you've got any ideas, I'd sure appreciate a little help, or cash. Amen."

He got to his feet, extended his right hand, cleared his throat, and said, "The Grace of our Lord Jesus Christ, and the love of God, and the fellowship of the Holy Ghost, be with us all evermore. Amen."

Jimmy quickly extinguished the candles and tidied the sacristy and thus got to Dean Manoogian before anyone else.

"Good morning, Jimmy. What can I do for you this fine morning? Why don't you join us for breakfast?"

"Us?"

"Yes, I'm having breakfast with Lance Gordon and some of your classmates to discuss Clinical Pastoral Education. If you're thinking of doing your CPE this summer, I suggest you join us."

"Ah, actually, Mr. Dean, I'd like a word with you in private, if you don't mind."

"Let's go to my office."

The Dean's office occupied a full corner of the Gatesbury building, had tall leaded windows with leaded sills, noisy radiators, and friendly clutter. Jimmy took a seat in a comfortable chair opposite the great oak desk and wondered how best to begin. Dean Manoogian fussed with some phone messages, offered Jimmy a Lucky, took one for himself, and said, "Well, my friend, what's on your mind?"

Watching the man enjoy his cigarette, Jimmy said, "On second thought, maybe I will have one of those." The smoke seared his throat and nearly closed his carotid artery.

"I still don't know how you smoke these things," he said, his head spinning.

"You should see what passes for cigarettes in Armenia," George Mannogian said. His laughter led to coughing, and he quietly added, "Claire wants me to quit these nasty things, but I . . ."

He took a long drag and exhaled with obvious pleasure. "What can I say? We all have our little vices. Well, I'm sure you didn't come here to hear about my addiction to nicotine."

Jimmy snuffed his half-smoked cigarette and said, "Well, things have taken what you might call a downturn in my life lately. My father, ah, took an early retirement, see, and, well, I'm broke. I talked to my mother yesterday, and she said they might even have to sell their house. I'm paid up through the end of this quarter, but I don't know what I'm going to do about next quarter, and that's less than a month away."

Jimmy fought the tears but a few slipped down. He took a deep breath and asked for another cigarette. This time he kept the smoke down.

Dean Manoogian leaned back and regarded the junior with compassion. "What about your parish? Saint Matthew's — isn't it?"

"Yeah, that's it all right. I called Mr. Carlisle last night, and he was sympathetic and all, but he said they don't have a dime to spare because they're rebuilding their organ."

Besides, that tight-assed SOB wouldn't give me a dime if he had it.

Dean Manoogian contemplated his cigarette and said, "I'm sorry to hear that. But if you ask me, seminarians are more important than organs any day. What about a leave of absence? A quarter or two off so you could work and earn enough to pay the rest of your way. How does that strike you?"

"Great, except for that little matter of the draft. Remember, I'm number 35 in the lottery, and I'm afraid ..."

"... you'd end up in Vietnam before you blinked twice."

"... right."

Dean Manoogian was considering a solution when Lance Gordon appeared at the door and cleared his throat. "Be right with you, Lance."

"Doctor Marshfield's theology class starts in 40 minutes, Mr. Dean, and ..."

"I'm well aware of that. I'll be right with you." Dean Manoogian wanted to take Jimmy for a long walk.

Lance Gordon cocked his eye at Jimmy and left to tell his classmates that Clarke was having a pow wow with the dean, meaning, of course, that the misfit from Philadelphia was finally being expelled.

"Well, George, what do you think? I guess I could join the navy. Probably wouldn't go to Vietnam, or, if I did at least I'd be safe and sound on some ship a hundred miles off the coast."

"Nonsense. You're not going in the navy, the army, or even the coast guard. You're staying right here at Gatesbury if that's where you want to stay. You leave it to me, Jimmy, I'll work something out. Now how about some breakfast?" the dean said, standing.

Jimmy went to him and hugged this amazing man.

* * *

After Father Leslie Swann had read the Collect, the minister appointed, Jimmy Clarke, stood before the good and gay people of St. Augustine's Episcopal Church and read the Epistle for the Fourth Sunday after Epiphany: "... for they are God's ministers, attending continually upon this very thing. Render therefore to all their dues; tribute to whom tribute is due; custom to whom custom, fear to whom fear, honour to whom honour. Here endeth the Epistle."

Normally, seminarians did not begin parish work until their middler years, but Dean Manoogian had pulled some strings and assigned Jimmy to St. Augustine's on the north side of Chicago. It paid $60 a month, which together with Jimmy's work scholarship stocking the pop machine outside Father Wiltwright's classroom, made it possible for the young man to continue avoiding the draft.

And all he had to do was show up every Sunday morning and help Father Swann with his priestly chores. The easiest sixty bucks I ever made, Jimmy thought.

As he backed away from the leather-bound Bible, he noticed she was sitting in the front pew again. Last Sunday she had invited him to her apartment for brunch, but he had declined, saying he had urgent business back at Gatesbury. And what was that, he thought.

Mooning after Jennifer Manoogian?

He had fallen in love with her as soon as he saw her drive by his window in the dean's black Mercury.

Jennifer was wispier than Jimmy had imagined. She had an ethereal quality about her that, at least from where he stood peeking through the curtains, reminded him of his mother's fine crystal. She was beautiful, all right, more so than her photograph suggested, but she seemed so fragile. Not that Jimmy wasn't dying to meet her, but the bad business with Elaine had left him feeling unsure of himself.

So Jimmy was waiting for the correct occasion in which to meet Jennifer. The best thing would be dinner at the deanery. But it was a busy time, what with the holidays and finals coming up, and he figured he might just have to wait. Plus, he was punishing himself for the business with Elaine.

Jimmy glanced again at the woman in the front pew, Sharyn something-or-other. She was wearing a clingy, low-cut, black silk dress that accentuated her massive cleavage and earthy hips. She wasn't a raving beauty, and she could spare 20 pounds, but she sure looked like she knew how to bump and grind with the best of them. Her hair was red and curly, her eyes blue and cool, and her lips red and hungry.

She moved like a cat in heat when she came to the altar rail for communion. Jimmy remembered reading about how the Crusaders had raped Greek nuns on the altars of churches in Constantinople and wished he was alone with this lusty creature. God will surely strike me dead, he thought, wiping his chalice and watching her kneel at the end of the rail.

As a seminarian, he was only allowed to administer the Blood of Christ; the Blessed Body was Father Swann's department.

Father Swann began dispensing the wafer-thin wisps of white unleavened bread to the faithful, and Jimmy followed with the port wine.

"The Blood of our Lord Jesus Christ, which was shed for thee, preserve thy body and soul until everlasting life. Drink this in rememberance that Christ's Blood was shed for thee, and be thankful. The Blood of our Lord Jesus Christ, which was shed for thee . . ."

His tongue tangled completely when he stepped in front of Sharyn.

Jimmy's hands were so sweaty he had to grip the chalice for dear life.

The woman in black seized the cup and leered at Jimmy.

He took a deep breath and said, "Drink this in remembrance that the Blood, of, ah, was shed for thee which, ah, shall, ah, the Blood of Our Lord Jesus Christ for thee."

Releasing the chalice, she brushed his hand and quickly crossed herself. Jimmy noticed she had left lipstick on the rim and wiped it with his cloth. He watched her return to her pew.

"Would you watch where you're going?" Father Swann hissed. "This is a church, not a singles bar."

"Sorry, Father," Jimmy said.

When Mass was ended, and Father Swann had blessed his flock and bid them go in peace, Jimmy joined him in the vestibule to greet parishoners. The old guard consisted mainly of little old ladies in furs and blue hair who lived in lakefront high-rises. A few still had doddering old husbands, but most had happily graduated to widowhood, like crazy old Violet Worthington. She told Father Swann that she had seen three ghosts that week.

Father Swann gently admonished her to think more on the Holy Ghost.

She told Jimmy she had see her late husband last night, and he nodded indulgently. Having entrusted his fate to Father Swann, he didn't want to say or do anything that would prejudice his position.

Located in Chicago's nefarious New Town neighborhood, the old graystone church attracted a large number of gay men who enjoyed Father Swann's fastidious rituals. Though he had not stepped all the way out of the closet, the righteously Reverend Leslie Algenon Swann was widely said to be one of the boys. Jimmy had heard and figured as much, but he didn't care as long as the good Father left him alone.

"Well, what do you think, ah, Father ah . . ."

"He's not a priest, Mrs. Worthington," Father Swann said. "He's only a seminarian. That's why he wears that black stripe on his collar — so you can tell he's not been ordained to Holy Orders. I told you last week, just call him James or Mr. Clarke, but please don't call him 'Father.' Only priests are called 'Father.'"

"Very well, James, what do you think?"

Father Swann was listening, so Jimmy forced a smile and said, "I think Father Swann's right, Mrs. Worthington, the only ghost you should think about is the Holy Ghost." Father Swann smiled approvingly.

To discourage the persistent woman, Jimmy gladly took the next hand and wished Robert somebody or other a good morning.

Robert Boswell wished Jimmy the same and gently squeezed his hand. "I'm having a few people over for brunch," he gushed, "and we'd love to have you join us."

That Sharyn creature was within earshot, so Jimmy gave her just the nod she had been waiting for.

Chapter Twenty-Two

"You did all this yourself?" Jimmy said, impressed.

"Yeah," Sharyn Craig said, "and the fireplace too. No big deal. Want another bloody Mary?"

"Yeah. That'd be great." Sharyn went to fix the drinks, and Jimmy looked enviously at the yards of oak floors, and the trim she had hand-stripped. He couldn't hammer a nail straight in.

"Can I use the john?" he said.

"No, go out in the yard."

"Huh?"

"That was supposed to be funny," Sharyn yelled. "Don't they teach you to laugh at Gatesbury?"

"No, as a matter of fact, they don't."

Peeking in Sharyn's medicine cabinet while the toilet was flushing, he spotted a birth control pill dispenser and noticed that today's tablet had been taken. There was also a Lady Gillette razor and a valium prescription signed by a Doctor Gerald Gronsky.

"You get a lot of calls while you're in here?" he asked when he saw the phone mounted next to the toilet.

"I like to give decrees from the throne. My shrink says I'm a phone maniac. What can I say? In case you haven't noticed, there're phones all over the apartment. Eight last time I counted."

"You go to a shrink?"

"Yeah. What about you?"

Jimmy had gone once — as a requirement for seminary admission. The old fart had spent the hour trying to keep an enormous black cigar lit while pontificating about the need for more psychology courses in seminaries.

"Nah. Hey, how long have you lived here? This is a terrific place."

"Yeah, if you can fight your way through the Puerto Ricans. I've been here two years. When I first moved in, I was the first anglo on the block. Now there's three more. Pretty soon we're gonna start our own street gang."

They went to the spacious living room, sipped their drinks, and listened to some Moody Blues. Sharyn asked about Jimmy's family and he said he had a happy one.

"I wish I could say the same," she said, lighting another Kool. She blew the smoke at him and added, "God, I've been going to shrinks for four years to figure out my parents, and I feel like I'm just beginning."

"Four years? How old are you? If you don't mind my asking?"

"Twenty-four. What about you? No, let me guess. You're 21, and this is your first time away from home."

"I'll be 22 in May, and I was away four years for college. Hey, you got some pot?"

"Sorry. I've been in treatment so long, I must sound like a shrink myself. I'll get my stash."

She rolled the most perfect joints he had ever seen.

"To your health, Father Clarke," she said, firing the first one. It was wonderful. The second and third were even better. "You get body rushes?"

He was leaning back on the couch watching the black tree limbs rattling in the wind. "Huh?"

"Hey, why don't you take that collar off. You'll get more oxygen to your brain." Before he could do it, she leaned forward and removed the white plastic tab. "Leslie's is different," she said.

"Leslie?"

"Of course. Think I'm going to call him 'Father Swann'? When I get stoned I can feel the blood in my veins. I can feel it going into my eyes and ears." She moved closer on the couch and gave him the joint. "I've never smoked pot with a man of the cloth before. God, this is so kinky, I can't believe it."

Jimmy fiddled with his plastic collar and tapped a foot a beat behind the music.

"Are you a virgin?" She was looking deep into his eyes.

"What?"

"You a cherry? You sure as hell act like one."

"Whatd'ye mean? Just because I'm a seminarian, you think I'm some kind of sissy, right? Like . . ."

"Like Leslie? He's a fag, so what? He's also a beautiful man. But that's not the question. The question is you, and you act like you've never been alone with a horny woman before. You're not gay too, are you? Is that why Leslie picked you? It's okay if you're gay, I've been the first woman for a lot of fags. I look at it as one of my missions in life."

"He picked me because Dean Manoogian recommended me. Normally, you don't do field work like this until your middler year, but I've got some real problems with money, and Dean Manoogian worked out this special arrangement, see, and I'm going to . . ."

"Jimmy?"

"Yes?"

"You wanna fuck or what?"

"Well, yeah, but . . ."

"Then come on, lover boy. It'll more comfortable in my bedroom. Unless they teach you to do it on the floor at Gatesbury."

"No, we do it on the pews. It's good for the spine."

Chapter Twenty-Three

Jimmy's stomach soured as he watched the man emerge from the green and white van.

"You really think we need a phone?" he said, grimacing.

"Maybe you like being a hermit," Bruce MacKenzie said, opening the door for the installer, "but the phone is my bread and butter. I've missed four good gigs because some jerk had that stupid payphone tied up. Probably talking to his mommy or something."

"Yeah, I guess you're right."

"What's the matter, you afraid that crazy chick's gonna call you up? I don't understand why you let some broad get you all worked up. Geez, Clarke, how old are you anyway?"

Bruce MacKenzie admitted the installer and showed him to the empty third bedroom — the site they had selected for the phone. Jimmy watched for a while, worrying that Sharyn or his mother would call as soon as the thing was connected.

"I think we can handle this," MacKenzie said, annoyed by his roommate's radiant anxiety. "Why don't you take a cruise up Sheridan Road or something?"

"Good idea," Jimmy said, pulling Bruce into the hall. "Hey, man, can you spare me a coupla joints?"

"Cheap bastard. Why don't you buy some from those Northwestern friends of yours?"

"I will, but I need some for right now. Okay?"

"All right. Two joints, but that's all you get until you buy some of your own."

Jimmy gratefully accepted the hand-rolled happiness and turned to leave. "Oh, I almost forgot. You gonna be able to come to church with me Sunday? I kinda . . ."

"You don't want that crazy broad raping you again, and you want me to protect you, right?"

"That's not exactly what I . . ."

"Sure. Well, I suppose I could fit you into my busy schedule. As long as I'm not playing too late Saturday night. And speaking of forgetting, when are you going to refill that pop machine?"

"Oh shit — thanks for reminding me."

Jimmy pocketed the joints and went to the bin in the musty basement where he stored the pop. He opened the ill-fitting door and hoped the smell was gone, but it was even stronger. Through his carelessness and haste he had smashed some cans last time the truck came and he had been too lazy to clean up the mess. Now the smell of sweet decay was overpowering, and cockroaches were feasting on the hardened soft drink. Holding his breath, Jimmy grabbed two cases off the top of the stack, kicked the door shut and muscled them up three flights of stairs, opened the machine, and began rolling the cans down the chutes.

He was starting on the second case when an ashen Father Wiltwright tapped him on the shoulder. "I appreciate your enthusiasm, Mr. Clarke, but I am trying to conduct a class next door. Perhaps you could come back in half an hour and finish that?"

Jimmy shrugged. "Sure thing, Father Wiltwright. Sorry. By the way, did you happen to get to that paper I did on the Crusades?"

Wiltwright gave him his most withering look. "Oh yes," he said. "And I would like to discuss it with you in my office. At your earliest convenience. I don't know what kind of game you think you're playing here, Mr. Clarke, but you're not going to pull it on me. Now, if you don't mind, I've got some serious students to teach. But I am glad you finally found the time to fill the machine. It's been an age or two since you last filled it."

"Yeah, Clarke," Lance Gordon called from the classroom, "we thought you defected to Montgomery."

"Not a bad idea," someone else muttered.

"Maybe we could trade you for a pew," Groves said. All but Pam Millar burst into laughter. She gave Jimmy one of her soulfully sympathetic looks, and he wanted to throw up. His black robes billowing behind him, Father Wiltwright returned to his classroom, quickly and quietly closing the door behind him. Jimmy thought of giving them the finger, but got a better idea. Before securing the soda machine, he stuffed his pockets with booty from the coin bin.

Mike Harper, a mild-mannered middler who handled student accounts, never hassled him about his bookkeeping, so why not?

If they're gonna treat me like a piece of whale shit on the bottom of the ocean, Jimmy thought, then I'll take their charity. Jimmy wandered out into the wet, gray February Friday and hoped the sun would make an appearance. Looking at the formless clouds, he doubted it would, but the grayness suited his mood. It was in the mid-30s and last week's snow was melting into a fine mist that made Northwestern's gothic and modern buildings seem soft and far away.

Jimmy crossed Sheridan Road and lit the first joint as he skirted the massive Tech building. He finished the second as he rounded the Hyanek Observatory. It was bad weed and only gave him a headache. He looked at the gray expanse of Lake Michigan and wanted to be out there on the bottom somewhere.

He walked on the concrete blocks used to create the university's new landfill and saw that like-minded students had painted their depressed thoughts on the rocks. Reading the self-involved doggerel, he realized he was acting a might foolish and walked back to the center of campus where he hoped he would be part of something.

But the busy Northwestern students acted as though he was invisible. They had their own friends and concerns. Jimmy went to the Norris Student Center, sat in a chair facing the lake, and tried to read the newspaper, but the marijuana made the words dance. He went to the university library and got more depressed looking at all the books he was too stoned to read.

Then he remembered Mr. Larson, the bursar, had said the library wanted to hire seminarians as part-time attendants. Maybe some other day, Jimmy thought, heading for the nearest exit.

He went to K.C. O'Neal's house only to learn that he was at class. Rich Feuerstein, a skinny dude from Long Island who was putting himself through engineering school by dealing drugs and repairing stereos, was the only one home.

"I don't suppose you'd like to go to Chicago or something?" Jimmy said, standing on the front porch with his hands in his pockets. He didn't really know Feuerstein and didn't really want to know him, but he was lonely.

"No, man, I gotta lab in an hour."

"You know when K.C.'s gonna be back?"

"I don't know, man. Look, I gotta study."

"You don't have any pot by chance? I just smoked some rotten shit that gave me a headache. I really need to cop a good buzz. God, it's Friday."

"Yeah, and the Pope's Catholic. Come on up to my room. I think I might have just the cure — some nice blotter."

"Yeah?"

"Sure. Thirty bucks a hit."

"Thirty bucks?!?" With the coins, Jimmy had maybe $45, but it had to last. "How about twenty-five?"

"Thirty bucks, man. Take it or leave it. Like I said, I gotta study."

"I'll take it."

Feuerstein took Jimmy up to his tidy room and produced a cedar pencil box. He carefully removed a piece of paper towel that was systematically splattered with blue dots and detached one for his customer, saying, "I'd only do half at a time if I were you, man. This is potent stuff."

Jimmy counted out five five's, three singles, seven quarters, two dimes and a nickel, and said, "Not much for thirty bucks. Oh well, you only go around once, right?"

He plopped the whole affair in his mouth and smiled. And then added, "Tell K.C. I stopped by, will you?"

Feuerstein stared at the stupid goy and shook his head.

The sun was making a brief appearance, so Jimmy removed his blue-and-white Penn State stocking cap and unzipped his green Air Force parka as he strolled toward the elevated station. He fingered his matted, greasy hair and wished he had washed it this morning, but so what — the sun was shining and he just might get high if Feuerstein wasn't ripping him off.

The large, lived-in homes along the way reminded Jimmy of the Main Line, but he took no comfort in the comparison because he realized how hollow these houses were. They were painted real nice and had slate roofs and big yards with towering oak trees but their insides were rotten with fathers who seduced their secretaries and drank martinis out of Styrofoam cups on the 5:08, frustrated women who were realizing too late that having children was not all there was to life, and alienated kids who took to pot for comfort and joy.

Jimmy encountered an occasional housewife heading with furrowed brow to her consciousness-raising class. They regarded him with fear and suspicion. The only men they knew wore white shirts and worked in Loop skyscrapers as high-powered attorneys, architects, and accountants.

Eager to evade Evanston, Jimmy quickened his pace and reached the platform just as a two-car Evanston Express arrived. There were plenty of empty seats, so he took the last one and settled back for what he hoped would be an interesting ride, provided Feuerstein hadn't ripped him off.

Five minutes later the train cleared the Howard Street station and began its 12-mile express run to Chicago's Loop.

As was his custom, the conductor started at the rear. He was two years shy of retirement and liked the dull routine of the mid-day trains. "Evanston Express 'round the Loop — have your fares or surcharges ready, please," he chanted, "fares and surcharges ready, please."

The wide-eyed white kid in the last seat appeared deaf, so he raised his voice and repeated, "Fares and surcharges ready, please. This is an extra-fare train. Cost you ten cents to ride to the Loop."

He waved a hand in front of the honky golfer's face, and the kid sprang a foot off the seat.

The conductor backed off, saying, "You can ride for free today. I ain't hasslin' no zombie."

Chapter Twenty-Four

The rails rushed together and trailed off in a long silver thread. Jimmy leaned with the train as it curved past Loyola University and accelerated with it into the two-mile straight-away to Wilson Avenue. His heart racing and his pupils dilating, the acid-soaked seminarian clenched his fists and bit his bottom lip.

"This is great!" he shouted. "This is fuckin' great!"

Jimmy's flashing thoughts fixed briefly on Feuerstein and for that moment he loved Feuerstein. Then his head was a movie camera, and he was filming the mist and the tracks and the blur of factories and Uptown tenements. They overtook a Jackson Park B train, and he cranked his right arm. "Lights, camera, action. God, this is great shit. Fuckin' great!"

The other passengers, an elderly couple headed downtown to pay their utility bills, an Iranian student, and a young mother who worked part-time at the Art Institute, watched helplessly as the young man in the last seat bounced up and down, exclaiming, "God, this is great! God, this is great!"

Together, they quietly moved to the head car leaving jumping Jimmy alone in his hallucinogenic happiness.

Now he was a tailgunner in a B-29 Flying Fortress high over the Ruhr Valley and that B train there was a ME-109 at twelve o'clock, and he had the stupid kraut in his sights.

"Bam bam bam bam bam bam bam, you're dead, Spaetzle breath!"

Checking six for other enemy planes, he realized that the other passengers had gone. He thought there had been other passengers, but now he wasn't so sure. He wasn't certain there were other people on the planet. He pondered this and other meaningless matters all the way downtown and realized at the last Loop stop that this was where he meant to get off.

"Loop the Loop. Loop the Loop," he said, stumbling off the train that had just circumnavigated Chicago's central business district. "They call it the 'Loop' because it makes a loop," he told the black woman in the ticket booth. "Wow!"

She rolled her eyes and wondered when all these crazy white children would grow up and take all the good jobs.

Jimmy walked east, then down LaSalle Street, reckoning from all the establishment types that he had just returned from a space capsule after an absence of many light years. He was convinced he was invisible until he collided with a portly banker.

"Watch where you're goin'," the man in the London Fog fumed.

"I was invisible," Jimmy muttered. But what does it matter, I'm higher than a kite and got money in my pocket, and I'm ready to do some walkin'.

As he moved north along Chicago's avenue of avarice, he could see, feel and hear his leg muscles and bones working in unison to propel him forward. He was amazed and delighted. Suddenly, he could feel the life force in his guts. The sensation of his circulating blood was so vivid, he stopped to watch.

"God does it," he told a man who looked and dressed like his father. "God makes your blood circulate."

The businessman mumbled something about "dirty hippies" and pushed Jimmy out of his path.

The rush of blood in his body suddenly felt ridiculous and he realized it would stop one day and he would be dead and worms and insect larvae would devour his eyes and brain, and he would just have to lie there and take it no matter how much embalming fluid they pumped into him. What kind of life was that just lying there for centuries rotting away until you were nothing more than a skeleton for some archeology student to fondle?

Eventually, he realized he was being jostled by an endless stream of men in dark suits. Four-legged giant ants, he thought, wanting to be somewhere quiet with his random thoughts and sensations.

Crossing LaSalle Street, he saw a traffic cop and wondered if he should ask. His heart raced and his chest tightened as he approached the pot-bellied, silver-haired man under the white hat with the blue-and-white checkered band. Chicago cops killed hippies and blacks for fun, Jimmy remembered, touching the hair that hung halfway down his neck. He remembered the televised reports of the Democratic Convention in Chicago.

Wondering whose head this "McNamara" had bashed in in 1968, Jimmy took a deep breath and said, "Excuse me, Officer, could you tell me where I could find the Art Institute?"

"Two blocks east on Adams. Can't miss it. Got two big lions in front." McNamara turned away to blow his whistle at a cabbie. When he turned back, the kid in the green jacket was still there. "You wanna direct traffic, talk to your precinct captain. Scram, or you're gonna get run over."

Certain McNamara was going to club him, Jimmy braced himself and asked, "Uh, where's Adams?"

"You're on Adams, fuckhead. They teach you punks to read anymore, or what?"

Jimmy was certain McNamara knew he was tripping because all cops could tell when you were tripping, and McNamara would arrest him, and they would torture him in the basement of some police station and starve him to death and pull his fingernails out and make him shit in a bucket and . . .

"Jesus, watch where the hell you're goin'!" he screamed at a Checker cab that nearly hit him as he careened away from the cop and trotted east on Adams to get away from the faceless flannel androids who infested LaSalle Street.

Enroute to what he was sure would be the ultimate experience with art, he asked ten people if he was still on Adams, and if Adams was on earth, and if earth was still in the solar system, and if would soon see stone lions.

He soon saw stone lions and they winked at him and wagged their tails. He knew the acid was permitting him to see this and was grateful. The straight people around him were missing a lot. With acid you could see that other world that moved at 120 seconds a minute.

An old man in a red blazer stopped the wondering boy at the entrance and directed him to a counter where he had to pay something, however little. Jimmy liked the silence and sunlit stairway that lay beyond the guard, so he unloaded a handful of coins on the ticket taker.

"Here," he said, grinning like an idiot, "this is to feed the lions. They're starving, can you dig?"

Another hippie comedian, the woman thought, giving the jerk his ticket and diving back into the latest Harold Robbins novel.

Jimmy gave his ticket to the man with the amazing red blazer and clambered up a steep staircase. The place was patronized only by a few ragamuffin art students and the occasional group of blue-haired old ladies. Jimmy wandered into a gallery of medieval art and was alone with the suffering saints and crucified Christs. He stopped to consider the beheading of John the Baptist and got blood on his shoes. The crowd at the foot of the cross turned on him and chased him to another room where Christ begged to change places.

"No way," Jimmy said, rubbing his palms together. "Sorry, but you're on your own."

He nearly collided with a cowering St. Peter. "Man, I can dig it. I can dig it."

Peter kept on cowering, so he ran/walked into a bigger gallery and watched the Blessed Virgin Mary ascend through the skylight without breaking the glass.

He was on his knees praying and sobbing when a guard strolled by. Jimmy got up, wiped his eyes and said, "I'm a Catholic."

The guard, a Missionary Baptist, nodded nervously and decided to keep an eye on this guy.

Trying to stay cool, Jimmy advanced through the centuries, seeing scenes of torture and depravity. Though they evoked extremely strong reactions, he bit his lip and dismissed the acid because he could hear the guard's footsteps behind him. He took a series of deep breaths and tried to dispel the paranoid fantasy in which every guard and cop in the world was stalking him. They would finally corner him and roast him alive like they were going to do to that poor soul in the bronze relief he had just seen and . . .

"Sorry, excuse me, I'm sorry. Whoops," he stumbled through the group of little old ladies, trying not to crush their feet or bother their blue hair. The young woman who had seen him on the train was leading the lecture tour.

"Why don't we move into this next gallery, ladies?" she said, motioning the group away from the obviously deranged young man.

Jimmy remembered seeing her somewhere but couldn't make the connection. Certain she was part of the plot to roast him, he clattered off to a gallery containing work of the French Impressionists. The young woman summoned the guard who summoned assistance.

Glancing back, Jimmy saw them talking and wanted to scream. He turned his head and Vincent Van Gogh climbed out of his self-portrait and offered him a knife. "Cut your ear off, Jimmy. It's fun. I did," Vince implored.

The serene characters in Seurat's "Sunday Afternoon on the Island of La Grande Jatte" hissed at him as he walked by, and Monet's haystacks burst into flames.

Jimmy was about to hyperventilate. He didn't care what anyone said now; he had to get out of this horror show before these painted people caught him and dragged him behind the walls. He was sure Rod Serling was going to appear momentarily and announce: "Jimmy Clarke is traveling through another dimension, a dimension not only of sight and sound, but of mind; a journey into a wondrous land whose boundaries are that of imagination. Next stop the Twilight Zone."

So he sprinted to the exit where the guards awaited him.

He wrestled with the old men, screaming, "Let me out of here! Let me out of here! God damn it, let me go! They're after me!"

Someone went to call the police and the ruckus aroused an administrator. "Let him go," he said. "But don't ever let him back in here."

Two spindly old men in red blazers pushed Jimmy into the revolving door. Jimmy was immediately mesmerized by the contraption and delighted in the "pocketa, pocketa, pocketa" sound the rubber flaps made as he spun the amazing door faster and faster. He howled until the administrator jammed a chair in the door, sending the troublemaker tumbling toward the steep steps.

Jimmy caught himself in time and looked up at the buildings lining Michigan Avenue.

"Wow," he said, watching the sky spin around the buildings and then the buildings spin around the sky.

He had to sit for a moment to catch his spinning head. When he looked up, he saw a police car and ran around the side of the building and over the Jackson Street bridge that crossed the Illinois Central tracks. A gunmetal green electric commuter train passed below, and he stopped to play with his train set. Remembering that every pig in the world was after him, Jimmy jaywalked the busy street, nearly catching it in the middle, and finally found the solitude he had been seeking in Grant Park.

He was starting to come down and didn't like it. His body seized and quivered, and there was a faint rumbling in his bowels that would lead, he knew, to acute diarrhea.

He found a bench near a statue of Abraham Lincoln and had just sat down to collect his riotous thoughts when a beaming black man in a broad-brimmed hat approached him and said, "Say, man, you wanna buy some reefer?"

Chapter Twenty-Five

Jimmy took another toke and looked over Raymond Kennedy's shoulder.

"That still Lake Michigan?" he said.

The 32-year-old man of independent means removed his mirrored sunglasses and considered the wild-eyed white boy. "Man, you is some kinda hick. That damn lake is big, man. You see the other side?"

Jimmy peered at the flat gray expanse. "No, man. I don't see the other side. Weird, huh? I mean it's like the Atlantic Ocean almost. But no sharks, right? You ever see the Atlantic Ocean, Raymond? Now there's a big body of water."

"When I was a little kid, the lifeguards used to keep us outta the water by sayin' there's a shark alert. I thought there were sharks in that lake for the longest time after that. But you know, I don't see no reason why some shark couldn't just swim on down from the Atlantic Ocean, adapt hisself to fresh water an' all, and just start eatin' at the beach everyday. Man, he could take his pick — white meat or dark meat."

Taking the joint from Jimmy, Raymond maneuvered his black Electra around a slow-moving CTA bus.

"I seen lots of sharks when Uncle sent me to fight them damn gooks in Korea. Sailors used to dump garbage off of the ship, and them sharks be everywhere just like that.

"Sometimes we'd shoot one or two of 'em, and the rest of them sharks would eat 'em. Pretty soon all them sharks'd be eatin' each other. I think a shark would eat itself if it could bend around far enough. Damn, that's one bad animal. I still don't go into the lake just in case one of them bad old sharks decides to take hisself a little trip down the Saint Lawrence Seaway." He took a succession of heavy hits and carefully placed the smoldering roach in the ash tray. "Say, Eddie, why don't you roll another one of them killer weeds?"

"Eddie Smith" happily complied because the potent pot and straight-talking black dude were just what he needed.

"Korea, huh? What was that like? Man, I was just a little kid when that was goin' on."

Raymond's eyes slowly went out of focus. He took a long toke and held the smoke deep in his lungs.

"Yeah, I wish I was a damn kid then, too. Maybe someday I'll tell you about it. But not now. Right now I feel like gettin' wasted, if that's all the same to you."

"Yeah, sure." Jimmy accepted the joint and took a hit.

Raymond's expression darkened suddenly. "Can you dig, honky, you like a pig, but you ain't got no gun."

"Ah, no, I, ah . . ."

"Man, I was just jivin'," Raymond said, grinning. "You think I'd take you to my 'hood if I didn't like you?"

"No, I guess not." Still, Jimmy wondered if he'd live to see tomorrow.

"Well, lighten up and live a little, man. Come on, I'll show you where all us gentle colored folk live, and then we'll do that drinkin' thang."

The temperature had climbed to 42, bringing people out of hibernation.

They knew it was old Mother Nature playing one of her dirty tricks, but it was nice to get out of the crib for an afternoon. The sun had just dipped below a cloud bank in the western sky, silhouetting the skyline. The warmth was rising from the streets and sidewalks and the melting snow softened everything with a fine mist.

Without signalling, Raymond cut across two lanes of traffic, exited the Drive at 47th, swung north on Drexel, and headed west on 43rd Street.

"You live around here?" Jimmy hoped he didn't sound too shocked. This was every bit as bad as North Philadelphia where his mother's maid, Beulah McBride, lived. Maybe worse.

"Yeah," Raymond said. "You said you wanted to see my 'hood, man. What'd you expect, the damn Gold Coast?"

"No, it's just, well, you know."

"Yeah, I can dig it. Your momma kept your lily-white ass in the suburbs so you ain't never seen where us poor colored folk live."

"I've got lots of black friends, and . . ."

"Shut up and roll that joint. Man, I'm gonna show you some soul tonight. You sure you still want to see it?"

"Yeah, I said so, didn't I?" Jimmy finished rolling the joint, lighted it, took two tokes, and passed it to Raymond. He worried about getting sickle cell anemia from sharing the joint.

"What you study up there at that country club, Eddie? Your daddy payin' to put you through that joint or what?"

"I study drama, and my old man ain't puttin' me through school. I'm doing it all myself." Jimmy wondered if this guy wasn't just leading him along.

"Oh, yeah," Raymond said, fingering the joint, "How? By hosin' them rich bitches up there along Sheridan Road whilst their fat cat husbands are downtown fuckin' they secretaries? You some rich old lady's hired dick, ain't you?"

"Yeah, Raymond, I'm the biggest stud on the North Shore. But I usually don't charge for it, because I like pussy more than anything."

"You eat pussy, man?"

"Hell yes."

"You crazy, man. I wouldn't eat that if some bitch paid me ten thousand dollars and gave me a hundred blow jobs. Man, pussy'll give you cancer. You crazy, man." Raymond puckered his face and spit out the window.

Seeing no point in arguing, Jimmy settled back and wondered why he let the acid and pot talk him into taking off on some hair-brained scheme like this.

At 35th and Prairie, "players" — junkies and pushers lined the darkened street.

"Used to be a lot more of them dudes," Raymond explained, "But the pigs been down on their case real bad. An' they like to kill each other, too."

Heading north on Giles, they saw two white patrolmen frisking a black man in a baggy, gray overcoat in the familiar manner still begrudgingly accepted on the South Side.

"Damn stool pigeon," Raymond muttered. "Yes sir, mister white POLICEman, please don't throw me in jail. Damn wino, stool pigeon."

Raymond swung back on 35th Street and they stopped to watch two elderly men fighting in the middle of the street. One waved a silver pocket knife at his opponent as spectators gathered to egg the men on. Guns drawn, two husky detectives, one white and one black, quickly stopped the disturbance and dispersed the crowd. The white officer stopped Raymond and peered into the window.

"Get a load of this," he said to his partner. "Another salt-and-pepper team. And I thought we were the only one in the District. You fellas must be from downtown, right?"

He was teasing of course, but Jimmy took him seriously, saying, "Yeah, how'd you guess?"

The black cop pulled Jimmy out of the car and spread-eagled him against the roof. "That's enough, funny boy," he said, patting him down, then examining his wallet. "Hey, Dan, look what we got here. A child of God. Now ain't that nice. What you doin' down here, Mr. James G. Clarke the Third, bringin' the word of de Lord to us poor colored folk?"

Jimmy sheepishly shrugged at his startled acquaintance who was facing him over the vinyl car top. Raymond gave him a bitter, betrayed look and glanced away. When he looked back, he laughed and shook his great head. "I shoulda figured. You didn't look like no Eddie. James G. Clarke. The Third, no less. Damn. I shoulda let you sit in the back seat. Damn, a real high-king white man."

"Shut up," the white dick said, kicking Raymond's feet apart.

When they finished searching the suspects, the dicks cuffed them and herded them to the streetside of Raymond's car. The black dick trained his revolver on them and radioed for a backup car while his partner searched the car. "Not a good idea to bring your customers down here, Raymond. Wimps like this could get hurt," he said. "Downtown, my ass. They wouldn't let scum like you shovel the sidewalk at the police academy."

Turning to Jimmy, he said, "Hope you don't write an angry letter to your daddy about this. We do our best to serve and protect down here."

Jimmy felt urine trickle down his leg. "No, no, I'm not gonna say a word to anybody about this."

Meanwhile, Raymond was saying to the other cop: "I ain't no dealer, man. I don't know where you . . ."

"Oh, yeah," the white dick said, backing out of the car with Jimmy's lid dangling from his hand. "What's this, Raymond, oregano? You gonna open an Italian restaurant on Indiana Avenue and sell soul pizza to the brothers? Say, bro', give me a large pizza with cheese and chitlins."

While the cops had their cheap laugh, Jimmy whispered, "These guys know you?"

Craning their necks, Jimmy and Raymond watched as the cop emptied the baggie on the wet, filthy street and ground the contents with his heel. "How much you pay for this shit, kid?"

"I didn't pay for it. It's mine. I was gonna sell it to Raymond. It's not his."

The white cop hammer-fisted Jimmy in the rib cage. Jimmy slumped against the car, gasping for breath.

"Well, whoever owns this shit, it's gonna taste real good now. Real good. Now it's real street dope."

The cops cracked up.

Then the black partner found Raymond's Kools and slowly ripped the pack in half and sniffed loudly at the torn cigarettes. "Hmmm, smells clean to me. Sorry, bro'." He stuffed the two halves back in Raymond's shirt pocket, watching him all the while. Raymond swallowed and looked passively at the crowd forming across the street.

A blue-and-white patrol car arrived, and the uniforms quickly scattered the Friday night fun seekers. "Nothing to watch, nothing to see here," they repeated, using their leaded night-sticks to prod the pedestrians.

Jimmy shook with paranoia. He was too high to handle all this.

This sucks, Jimmy thought loud enough that his lips moved.

The black investigator continued taunting Raymond while his partner returned to their car to run a background check.

"You think I'm a 'Tom' don't you, boy?"

"I think you just doin' your job, man," Raymond said, avoiding the detective's mocking eyes. "That's all. Just like I do my job."

"And what's your job this week, Raymond — pimp? Dealer? Fence? Or you got your old lady on the street again?"

Raymond took a deep breath. The muscular cop clenched his powerful fists and waited on the balls of his feet. Raymond exhaled and withdrew his last reserve of calm. "I told you — I'm an honest businessman just tryin' to get by."

"My ass. You wanna be an honest businessman? Then start lettin' me know what's goin' on with them gangbangers you hang with. I wanna know every time Fort and the rest of them P. Stone Nation dudes take a shit, you understand?"

"I ain't no snitch, man, and I don't know no Jeff Fort and none of them dudes. I'm an honest businessman, and that's it. Just caught me with a little pot, that's all, and you know the State's Attorney is gonna throw that right out. Right out, Officer Oreo." The two men glared at one another.

"Come on, Bob, let's leave these clowns to their little games. They'll get theirs," the white cop said, patting his partner's shoulder. "Besides, they're clean."

The black dick slapped his partner's hand away, saying, "One of these days, Raymond, you and me is gonna have a little private talk. You dig?"

His eyes burning and his lips tight, Raymond barely nodded.

Before releasing their suspects, the spiteful dicks "tossed" Raymond's car, tearing out the back seat and dumping the contents of the trunk on the street. "Do yourself a favor, white boy," the black dick said. "Stay up there in Evanston and learn about this shit in your pretty books. Scum like him ain't gonna teach you nuthin' but trouble."

Jimmy started to give the departing cops the finger, but Raymond checked him, saying, "No, man, it don't mean nuthin'. It don't mean nuthin'."

Chapter Twenty-Six

Jimmy awakened to the sound of rattling metal and squinted uncomprehendingly at the world rushing past his window.

He rubbed his throbbing temples and moved his swollen tongue. There were dried particles of something or other lodged against his gums. He looked down at his jacket and realized he had been sick.

He gasped, and his head throbbed until he was sure it would burst. The world was still flying by the window, and he could not look at it without feeling sick again.

A disembodied voice suddenly announced:"IIT – 34th Street's next."

The motorman abruptly braked his two-car Jackson Park B train, and Jimmy lurched into the forward seat. The momentum reversed sharply, shoving him back into his own seat like a dummy in a test car. He looked dumbly about the car and fixed on a plump black woman seated across the aisle.

"Did he say, Evanston?"

The woman rolled her eyes disapprovingly. "Child, we is goin' south. This is 34th Street. If you want to go to Evanston, you best get off and get a train goin' the other way."

"Thanks."

His head reeling, Jimmy stumbled to the door and got off as soon as it opened. He was greeted by a blast of cold Canadian air that had slipped down the lake during the night. He zipped up his parka and faced the wind, shivering and blinking. Anything to wake me up, he thought, uneasily realizing that he had no idea where he had been for – God, the last thing he remembered was being in that all-black bar on 43rd Street he and Raymond had gone to after their run-in with the cops. Thinking about that gave him an orange headache, and then he remembered that he had consumed vast quantities of screwdrivers there.

He remembered that the bartender wore a beret and sunglasses and said he was a jazz musician looking for gigs – a drummer, Jimmy thought. He wondered if he had given the guy Bruce's name, and thought he hadn't. But he did remember talking a mile a minute about how race relations would improve overnight if the government required blacks and whites to drink together for an hour every day.

Someone had proclaimed him the "Mayor of Woodlawn," and he thought he had done an Irish jig on a table, but he wasn't sure. Somehow, he realized, I kept drinking for a long time after I ran out of money.

Tottering in the refreshing wind, he realized he had to urinate and seeing that he was alone on the platform, he pissed on the tracks, careful not to hit the third rail for fear of electrocuting himself. He realized with satisfaction that he was becoming a real city dog and scanned the soulless Illinois Institute of Technology campus with disapproval.

Looking around, Jimmy guessed that it was a few minutes after sunrise, although it was difficult to tell for sure because the sun was hidden by a thick paste of gray clouds. Someone had forgotten to turn off the mercury vapor street lights.

Two students crossing State Street glanced up at the gesticulating figure on the elevated platform and decided to split a cab to the Loop.

The fragrance of frying bacon wafted across Jimmy's flared nostrils, reminding him that he had not eaten for at least 24 hours.

Unless — no, he was sure he and Raymond hadn't eaten anything except. Except — that's right, he remembered, nearly retching, pickled pigs' feet at that joint on 43rd Street. Or was it 47th Street?

When his stomach steeled, he thought he might have breakfast at IIT. He was pretty sure there was an Alpha Chi chapter on campus, and maybe the old brotherhood routine would get him a free meal. It was the only way he was going to eat because he had spent everything but three cents. The fresh air was doing him some good, but he realized what he really needed was some sleep in his own bed, certainly not another hassle with the frat rats. Besides, he could see, hear, and feel an approaching northbound Howard train.

He claimed the front seat and watched with growing fascination as the tracks descended suddenly south of Roosevelt, dipping the train into darkness. Then there was a dazzling display of red and green signal lights and a rapid succession of stations schemed in red, blue, brown, green, red, blue again, and then bright sunlight as the train suddenly returned to elevated status.

"God," Jimmy gasped, "what happened to the clouds?" Chicago's indecisive weather was what had cleared the sky, but Jimmy attached deeper significance to it.

He tapped on the motorman's door. The man shook his head and pointed to a sign warning passengers not to talk to the motorman while the train was moving. Fearful of further contact with the police, Jimmy folded his hands and sat upright in his seat until the train had come to a complete halt at Fullerton Avenue.

Then he politely knocked on the door, and the exasperated motorman, a middle-aged black man in coveralls and a Casey Jones hat, poked out his head and said, "What is it, man? I got a train to operate."

For a moment Jimmy thought the man was Raymond Kennedy, and he had a vivid recollection in which Raymond was shouting and telling him to run.

"Huh?" he said, wondering what this guy wanted with him. He was just riding the train and minding his own business.

"I said, what do you want? I got a train to operate." The motorman stared at the disheveled honky and shook his head. "Man, you is a mess. And you got one hell of a lump on your head." He slammed the door, waited for the conductor to close the doors and started the train with a jerk of the throttle that threw Jimmy into his seat.

He sat dumbly exploring the knot on his forehead with his fingers and wondered where in God's name that had come from and why he hadn't noticed it sooner and if he was ever going to get back to his room. Beads of sweat appeared on his forehead and dripped into his eyes as his heart raced and his lungs labored for air. Jimmy was afraid he would die. Maybe the blow had left a blood clot that was about to seep into his brain and kill him, or worse, kill part of him. He would be a vegetable for the rest of his life.

Willing his heart and lungs to cool it, he closed his eyes and tried to think comforting thoughts, but his overworked brain only served up a profusion of paranoia. Blinking, he watched the train's rapid transit, marvelling at how it seemingly zipped the rails together. His heart and lungs were still working too hard, but he could control his brain as long as he kept his eyes open. He began to reconstruct last night's activities, easily recalling the run-in with the cops and the beret-wearing bartender. He knew the soreness in his throat stemmed from his exclamations at the bar — the "Unique Dude's Club" came to mind.

And the cigarettes. He had bummed them from a buxom lady in a tight burgundy dress. Pearl. Pearl Davis maybe. She had called him "white sugar," and he remembered that she laughingly approved of his proposal for ending racial tension.

"Except," she had said, "you have to bring your own cigarettes next time, white sugar."

He had recited parts of OTHELLO to her, but it got fuzzy after that. For some reason, he recalled, rubbing the bump on his head, people at the bar had turned on him.

He remembered Raymond grabbing him by the collar and hustling him outside, saying, "Man, you crazy? You see that big dude at the end of the bar? Pearl lives with that dude. You hittin' on his old lady. Man, you wanna die young, you on you own, but as long as you drinkin' with me, you gots to be cool."

From there, Jimmy remembered, they had gone by car to Raymond's "crib" which was on the top floor of a crumbling 12-flat on a desolate side street with shot-out streetlights and a pistol-brandishing Blackstone Ranger "guard" who had admitted them only after Raymond vouched for Jimmy's inherent blue-eyed soulness.

Raymond's old lady, a woman who doubtless had been attractive before the worry wrinkles and anxiety eating, had been friendly enough to Jimmy, but she had taken Raymond aside and screamed at him.

"You no good," was what Jimmy remembered. Jimmy thought he may have heard flesh striking flesh, but he wasn't sure what was hearing and what was hallucination. He did remember that when they left, Raymond said a Ranger with a rifle had been watching him from an adjacent rooftop. Jimmy's palms got greasy just thinking about it.

From there it was almost impossible to recollect even though those events were most immediate. Jimmy monitored the train's progress for a moment and felt chilled and disoriented. He touched the bump and wished he could recall the night's final act. It was important, but so was staying awake until he got to his room. That seemed so distant now he wondered if he would ever get there. He willed the train to go faster, but it did not.

He was nodding off when the train reached Howard, but he responded this time to the angry buzzer and the conductor's repeated, "Howard Street end of the line. Everybody off the train. Far as we go. Howard Street."

Stumbling across the platform to an awaiting Evanston shuttle, Jimmy vaguely recalled having been here before. Then he realized he had blacked out and stayed on the train as it was brought around the yards.

No wonder I ended up on the South Side again.

Jimmy was frightened. His drinking had been manageable most of the way through college. At least he thought it was. He hadn't even started drinking until the very end of his junior year in high school. Until then he had vowed never to follow in the old man's alcoholic footsteps.

But he was panting at the old man's liquor cabinet by the end of his junior year. Jimmy got drunk the first time he tangled with the old man's liquor — in that case green creme de menthe on the rocks.

In college, he learned to mix booze with drugs, marijuana mostly, but so was everyone else. No big deal; it was part of the college scene. Sure, he passed out once in a while, but that was usually on Friday nights after a hard week in the classrooms, and he wasn't alone. He was never alone.

And nothing like this ever happened before, Jimmy realized, as the Evanston train slowed for the Noyes stop. Shit. I gotta do something about this.

Oh well, I've been through a lot. What the hell?

Jimmy pinched his leg and walked the three blocks to the seminary in a somnolent stupor. But he made it.

He was glad to find that Bruce MacKenzie was asleep because he had no desire to explain himself. Collapsing on his unmade bed, he kicked off his shoes and unzipped his jacket.

As sleep swiftly enfolded him, his mind fixed momentarily on 63rd Street. They had gone to that hellish place to get some whiskey so they could continue their scintilating conversation by the lake.

That was it.

Jimmy remembered the elevated tracks overhead and the flashing neon "Schlitz" sign and the first of many gun shots.

Gun shots, he thought, sitting up in bed.

But sleep claimed him before he could roll the next reel.

Chapter Twenty-Seven

"Wake up, man. Come on, sweetheart. Rise and shine. Reveille, reveille. Drop your cocks and grab your socks and hit the deck. Come on, sleeping beauty, you've got a phone call."

"Huh?" Jimmy tried to hide in his damp pillow, but Bruce MacKenzie snatched it away. He opened the curtains and tugged his roommate's foot. "Hey, what the hell you doin'? Close those goddamn curtains. Jesus!" Jimmy started to pull the soiled bedding over his head, but MacKenzie threw it on the floor.

"Nice pajamas. At least you took your shoes off. Must have been one hell of a night. Come on, get up, you've got a phone call."

MacKenzie opened the windows and a blast of cold air hit Jimmy in the face.

Groaning, he coiled into a fetal position. "Who is it?"

"That's for me to know and you to find out," Bruce said, enjoying his roommate's discomfort.

Jimmy rolled on his back and rubbed his eyes. "Bruce, seriously, who is it? A black guy, by any chance?"

Bruce laughed. "Hey, what time we goin' to that stupid church tomorrow? I want to know so I don't play too long tonight."

Jimmy tried to sit up but could not, so Bruce helped him. Jimmy took a few shallow breaths, and the room spun madly. It had done that when he first collapsed, accounting for the vomit that caked his sheets and hair.

"Church?" he said, wondering. "Oh, yeah it's Saturday, isn't it? Church. How about we leave about 9:30? I like to be there around 10, or Father Swann gets nervous. Now who the hell's on the phone? Male or female? Black or white?" Jimmy could think of no one he wanted to talk to.

"Hey, buddy boy, I'm doing you a favor tomorrow, remember? Keepin' that crazy chick off your back, remember? I wouldn't take that tone of voice if I were you."

"Sorry." Jimmy rubbed his face and rediscovered the lump on his forehead. It frightened him.

"Black guy, huh? Looks like he did a number on you. What the hell happened to you, anyway?"

"I don't know. It's a long story. Bruce, can't you tell 'em I'll call back? I'm sick, man. Would you tell 'em I'll call back?"

MacKenzie caught Jimmy before he fell back on his back. "Uh uh. You've got a phone call, and I gotta be downtown in less than an hour."

Bruce left, slamming the door.

Moody asshole, Jimmy thought, shuffling for the phone."Hello," he said, his voice slurred and surly.

"Jimmy, this is Dean Manoogian."

"Dean Manoogian, what a surprise!"

"Claire and I thought you might like to join us for dinner tonight. You haven't had a chance to meet our Jennifer yet, and we thought this would be the perfect opportunity. That is if you don't have other plans. I tried earlier, but you must have been out."

"I was out all right."

"I hope you like roast beef and Yorkshire pudding."

Jimmy muffled the phone and slapped his face. He couldn't believe he was having this conversation. The dean should be telling him the police were on their way to evict him.

"You bet, and I'd love to come. Sorry to have kept you waiting. I ah . . ."

"How's 6:30?"

"That'd be fine." Jimmy looked at his watch. It was already 4 o'clock. "That'd be fine. Can I bring anything?"

"Just your appetite. See you at 6:30." The dean was delighted. "Bye."

Jimmy cradled the phone and shuffled into the shower, mumbling to himself. Halfway through his long, hot shower, he remembered he was still wearing his clothes and peeled them off so the water could soak the sin out of his system.

* * *

Resplendent in another of her stunning Jaeger outfits, Claire Stewart Mangoogian greeted Jimmy at the deanery door, saying, "Jimmy, what a pleasure to see you." She extended her hand.

"Nice to see you again, Mrs. Manoogian," he said, taking her hand.

"Claire, please call me Claire."

"Right. It's nice to see you, Claire, and it's nice to be here. I was going to get a bottle of wine, but you know Evanston." He fumbled in his pocket. "Here, they're not real fancy, but they're . . ."

Claire accepted the box of Marshall Field's "Frango Mints" and cooed. "Ohhh, you shouldn't have. I just adore Frango Mints, and so does George. That's very sweet of you. I've been trying to get George off sweets, but I don't suppose a few Frango Mints will hurt him. Or me." She pecked him on the cheek and led him into her home. "Let me take your coat, and you can make yourself comfortable while I finish setting the table." She noticed his bump and asked how he had gotten it.

"I slipped on the ice walking to Field's. Some people just can't be bothered to shovel their walks I guess." Jimmy didn't like lying to people he liked.

"Oh, dear. Would you like an ice pack or some aspirin?"

"It's fine, Claire. Really."

"You're sure?"

"I'm sure."

"Well, you know where the bar is. Why don't you make yourself a drink, and I'll get George and Jennifer."

Jimmy went to the bar, took one look at the booze, and nearly retched. He took another peek and decided maybe he needed a little hair of the dog that bit him.

He was halfway though his second soothing vodka tonic when the dean and his daughter presented themselves.

Jennifer was more hauntingly beautiful in person than in her picture, even in faded blue jeans and worn, navy turtleneck sweater. She wore her auburn hair long and straight. It had a just-washed sheen to it, and her thin, but perfect lips had an impish quality.

She boldly took Jimmy's hand and said, "How do you do? I'm Jennifer Manoogian." Her voice was deeper than Jimmy had expected but pleasing to his ear.

Charmed, he lightly grasped her hand. "Nice to meet you, Jennifer. I'm Jimmy Clarke." Turning to the dean he added, "Hi, Dean Manoogian."

The dean clapped his back, "Glad you could come, Jimmy. That looks pretty good. What is it?"

"Vodka tonic."

"Hmmmm, still a little cold for those. I think I'll stick with scotch until we get some real spring weather. Jennifer, dear, can I fix you something?"

"Just a ginger ale, Daddy."

Jimmy watched her take her drink and decided she was a bit underweight, but the effect was more enchanting than pathetic.

"Well, here's to our health," the dean said.

They clinked glasses and smiled at one another. Claire called for help from the kitchen, and the dean responded.

"So," Jennifer said, settling cat-like on the couch, "you're a student here? You into God or what?"

Propping an elbow on the mantlepiece, Jimmy wasn't sure if he liked her directness.

He took a long sip and replied, "Do I detect a little sarcasm?"

"No, you just don't look like the seminary type. Daddy said you're from Philadelphia. How come you came here when there are so many seminaries back east?"

"I wanted to get away from home. What's wrong with that?"

"But it's so depressing here. No mountains, no ocean, nothing. Where we used to live, you could hop on a train and be in New York in an hour." Jennifer shrugged. "Oh, well."

"I don't know if I'd want to be in New York in an hour or two days for that matter," Jimmy said. "The place is falling apart at the seams. Take Chicago. It's a lot cleaner and New York sure doesn't have anything to compare to Lake Michigan. I mean, how many beaches have you seen on the Hudson River, and Coney Island looks like the Bay of Pigs. Anyway . . ."

"You didn't answer my question," Jennifer said. "You sure don't look happy to me. If I were you, I would have stayed in Philadelphia. Actually, if I were you, I wouldn't be in a seminary at all. I think this is all quite silly, especially since there's no God in the first place."

Jimmy glanced at the kitchen to be sure the dean was out of earshot. "Wait a minute, your father's dean of this seminary, and you're telling me you don't believe in God."

"So? What Daddy does is Daddy's business. You're going to tell me you believe all this crap." She held him with a penetrating look.

Jimmy stared back.

Jennifer pursed her lips.

Jimmy pursed his.

Jennifer wrinkled her brow, and Jimmy did likewise.

They were sticking their tongues out at one another when the dean came to summon them for dinner.

"Well," he said, smiling, "I see you two are hitting it off. I hate to interrupt, but dinner's ready."

Dinner consisted of: a standing rib roast, baked potatoes with sour cream and chives, string beans with butter, sourdough bread with strawberry preserves, good French wine, and a salad with Jennifer's homemade herbal dressing.

Jennifer picked at her food and drank water with her meal, lamenting her failure to go to the health-food store and get some mineral water. She didn't touch her meat, but at her father's insistance, she had a sip or two of the wine, conceding that some experts thought a glass a day wouldn't hurt.

"More juice?" Claire asked Jimmy.

"You bet. This is delicious. I haven't had roast beef like this since — I can't remember."

"Surely your mother must make an excellent roast," Claire said.

"She does. It's just that she hasn't made it for a while." Jimmy smiled at Jennifer. "I understand you spent some time in Italy."

She was feeding carrots and bean sprouts into her face with her fingers. She paused and said, "It was wonderful. Italians know how to eat. Fresh vegetables every day. I never felt better. You can't go into a restaurant around here and find fresh food. New York, but not here. And the grocery stores — God, they have a lot of nerve calling that stuff fresh produce. Do you know what kind of insecticides they put on crops? Ever scrape an apple with a knife? Know what that stuff is? I think it's a plot by Dow Chemical to kill us all. It's . . ."

Jennifer went on like that through the rest of dinner and into dessert, which consisted of fresh-ground French roast coffee and Claire's homemade German chocolate cake. Jennifer produced a jar of natural peanut butter, stirred the top oil into the thick mass, and ate spoonful after spoonful.

"Want some?" she asked.

"No thanks," Jimmy said, glancing at the dean and his wife.

Claire was wearing a "my children — they are so wonderful" smile, while the dean regarded his youngest child with affectionate amusement.

With Jennifer's mouth temporarily out of action, Jimmy decided to make his graceful exit. "This has been a wonderful meal, Claire."

"Care for some more cake, Jimmy?" she said.

"Thanks, but I couldn't eat another bite. Well, it's been a long day, so I'd better be . . ."

Jennifer swallowed a lump of her hard peanut butter and said, "You can't go. I've got some new Joni Mitchell albums I want you to hear. You like Joni Mitchell, don't you?"

"Sure, I like Joni Mitchell."

Jennifer's room was on the uppermost floor under a gable and contained: a bed with a bright quilt and wrought iron frame, a window that faced the alley, a neat little desk with a tidy stack of college catalogues on it, a ficus plant, a guitar, a Zenith portable stereo and small stack of albums, and a poster. Set against the poster's blue background was a green turtle and these words: "Behold the turtle — he only gets ahead when he sticks his head out."

Jennifer had used a red felt-tip pen to change the pronouns from masculine to feminine.

Jimmy beheld the turtle and wondered how he was going to get ahead with this crazy woman. Jennifer put Joni and her old blue jeans on the turntable, and as her heroine sang wispily of "cloud fantasies" and "mysterious devotions" plopped herself on the bed and said, "You smoke pot?"

Jimmy looked at her, wondering where he was supposed to sit. He opted for the hard desk chair. "I don't know. What about you?"

"It was impossible to get in Italy — at least in Celano where I was staying. God, they lock people up forever there for just having a little pot. I only tried it a couple of times before I left, but it always gave me a headache."

"Yeah, that's what I've heard."

"You have any pot?" Jennifer asked, matter-of-factly.

"No, I don't have any. I only tried it a couple of times, too."

Disappointed, she slumped back on the bed.

Jennifer invited him to sit with her on the bed and turned the talk to a lurid description of dogs she had seen copulating in Italy.

Listening to her prattle on about, Jimmy wondered what would happen if he kissed her.

Her lips were like cold aluminum, but she did not push him away. Rather, she placed her hand on his pants. He hovered a hand over

Jennifer's breasts, but she pushed it away. He put his arm around her and kept kissing her metal lips while she rubbed him in a rough motion.

"Oww," he said.

She stopped and looked quizically at him. "It hurts?" she asked.

"Yes, it hurts. What do you think it's made of — cast iron?"

She giggled. "Do you have a name for it? I've heard a lot of men have names for theirs."

Now Jimmy knew he was still tripping. "No, I don't have a name for it."

"When I was in Celano, I lived with this family, and they had a 13-year-old boy. One time I came into the bathroom without knocking, and he was playing with his thing. Do you play with your thing?"

"Jennifer, your parents are right downstairs."

"So?"

"They'll hear us."

"So?"

Chapter Twenty-Eight

Sharyn Craig, who had sat in the front pew staring through Jimmy's cassock, was outmanuevered in the receiving line by Bruce MacKenzie.

This allowed a blushing Robert Boswell to get to Jimmy first. "No excuses this week," he scolded, taking Jimmy's hand. "I'm making a spinach quiche this morning and it's going to have your name on it."

"I'd be honored," Jimmy said, pretending to ignore Sharyn. "Mind if my roommate tags along?"

"Your roommate? I didn't know you had a roommate." Jimmy pointed to Bruce, and Robert nodded approvingly. "By all means. I've got plenty of eggs and spinach. We may have to get some more vodka for the bloody Marys. Good God, he's big."

"No problem, Robert. I've got money." Jimmy smiled. This was turning out just the way he wanted — a day without women.

"Bobby, call me Bobby," Boswell said, winking.

"Okay, Bobby. I'll be with you in a minute."

When it came time to greet Sharyn Craig, Jimmy's knees buckled. He knew there was no good reason to be afraid of this woman, yet he was.

She gave him a measured look, saying, "I guess you've got other plans this morning."

"I guess I do." He didn't know what else to say, so he looked away.

Bobby's Victorian flat had naked oak floors and trim and was neater than a Japanese garden except for the omnipresent bird shit. Ruby, the guano maker, made a surprise appearance, frightening Jimmy and Bruce. Bobby extended his finger and made puckering noises. The green parakeet alighted on his finger and pecked at his lips. Bobby opened his mouth, and the bird clattered about, cleaning his teeth.

"God," Jimmy said, "won't you get a disease or something?"

"Not from Ruby. Best little toothpick I ever had. Want to hold her? She's quite friendly, and I assure you, you won't get VD from Ruby."

"No thanks."

"How about you, Bruce? Would you like to hold my baby?"

"Sure."

Sensing a friend, the bird hopped to MacKenzie's finger.

"Well, you two get acquainted, and I'll get brunch started. Anybody for a bloody Mary?"

Jimmy only had to think for a few seconds. The first thought of a drink made his head spin and his stomach churn. The second thought made his mouth water. "You bet. And when you run out of vodka, I'll make a run."

They repaired to the well-stocked kitchen, and Bobby furnished them with drinks and started brunch. Bruce volunteered to help and was soon whisking eggs, washing spinach, and grating cheese.

Jimmy perched himself on a stool and made short work of his drink. He was about to get another when Ruby alighted on his head. He automatically swatted at the bird, hitting it squarely. Feathers flew, Ruby squawked, and Bobby was apoplectic.

"Oh, my poor baby," he said, anxiously coaxing the frightened creature to perch on his finger. "Are you all right, baby? Oh baby, talk to Daddy."

Ruby chirped, indicating she was just fine.

"I'm sorry, Bobby, I . . ."

"Why don't I put Ruby in her cage, and we can all relax," Bobby said, grinding his teeth.

While Bobby went to put his bird away, MacKenzie said, "Off to a real good start, aren't you, Padre? What are you gonna do next, light the kitchen on fire?"

"Maybe I'll blow up the whole block, Bruce."

Bobby returned with a caged Ruby and a little brown bottle. "Now that the bird crisis is over, how about some 'locker room?'"

Bruce regarded the bottle and assented.

"What the hell is it?" Jimmy asked.

"What kind of language is that for a boy of God?" Bobby scolded.

"Boy of God! You know what you can do . . ."

"Jimmy, he was just kidding. Would you lighten up? For Christ's sake! Try some of this stuff, and you'll feel a hell of a lot better," Bruce said.

"What is it?" Not that he wasn't up for a new high; he just didn't want to lose control in the presence of these two characters.

Bobby opened the bottle and held it under Jimmy's nose. "Take a big sniff. Go on, it won't hurt you."

Jimmy did as he was told and was overwhelmed with the medicinal odor. He was recalling childhood visits to the doctor's office when his arteries suddenly dialated, rushing a double order of blood to his brain. Exhilarated beyond expectation, Jimmy ran around the kitchen screaming, "God damn! God damn!"

A superstitious old Puerto Rican lady living across the gangway heard him and came to her window. Seeing a man in a Roman collar convulsing in her crazy neighbor's kitchen, she crossed herself and rushed to consult her blue plastic Blessed Virgin Mary.

His face flushed and his heart racing, Jimmy wanted to simultaneously fly, run, and swim. Although it was mostly a head rush, his whole body was energized and ready for adventure.

When it wore off a few moments later, Jimmy said, "I don't know what that shit is, but it's great. Fuckin' great!"

"It's amyl nitrate. Poppers. It's what they break under your nose when you've had a heart attack. Like those guys do on TV all the time. Gets you going, doesn't it?" Bobby said.

"Damn! I thought I was gonna blast off there for a minute. Man, that shit really gets you goin'."

"Ready for some more?" Bobby asked.

"Yeah," Jimmy said, taking a deep breath.

"Bruce?"

"Why not?"

"First, a little music. Any preferences?"

"Yeah," Jimmy said, "THE DOORS."

"Good choice. God, I love Jim Morrison. What a yummy man. Those tight leather pants he wears — mmmmm," Bobby said, going to spin the platter.

Jim Morrison — yummy?

As Jim Morrison woke up this morning and had himself a "beee-- aaah. . . yeeer," Bobby reappeared with a fully loaded hash pipe. "Let's do this right," he said, igniting it.

When they had each taken two enormous hits, Bobby uncorked the amyl nitrate, and they each inhaled as much as their lungs would hold. Jimmy closed his eyes and mimicked Morrison. When the song was over, he opened his eyes and nearly fainted from shock.

Bruce and Bobby were on the floor felatiating one another.

"Come on, Jimmy, we can make it three-way," Bruce said. Jimmy rocked on his feet, rolling his dialating pupils in time to the music.

"Are you just gonna stand there, or am I gonna have to pull your pants down?" Bruce said.

THE DOORS were doing some "L.A. Woman," and Jimmy decided they had the right idea. He was looking for his coat, when Bruce and Bobby attacked.

"Come on, Clarke, let me suck your delicious little cock," Bruce pleaded. Jimmy grabbed his coat and backed to the door.

"Bruce, I thought . . ."

"You thought I was a big tough lumberjack, that's what you thought. Well, you'd be surprised what we big tough lumberjacks do for entertainment on dark and stormy nights. Why do you think I chased that sleazy little bitch away from you that night we went to that bar? Why do you think I agreed to come today? Now, come on, and let us suck that pretty, little pink cock of yours." MacKenzie lunged for his roommate, but Jimmy was all speed and dodge.

He got out of the door before the two queers could grab him and ran the entire five blocks to Sharyn Craig's apartment. She was expecting him, but she was not expecting the ferocity with which he made love to her all afternoon.

Chapter Twenty-Nine

"Do you masturbate?"

"I beg your pardon?"

"I said, do you masturbate? You know, abuse yourself?" The Reverend Paul H. Jordan flexed his fingers and peered into the applicant's eyes.

Wondering what the hell he was doing inside on such a gorgeous spring day, Jimmy Clarke shrugged and said, "Sometimes. What about you?"

The sandy-haired Unitarian minister straightened in his chair. He wore a clerical collar, khaki wash pants, tennis shoes, and an inscrutable expression. "Why?"

"Why what?" Jimmy said, annoyed with this constipated twit and his irritating questions.

Why do you masturbate?"

"What does this have to do with me being accepted into Clinical Psychological Evaluation or whatever you call it?" Jimmy said. He looked longingly out the window and wondered how the weather was in Canada.

"Clinical Pastoral Education," Jordan corrected. "A lot. If you're going to spend the summer helping patients at St. Mark's get in touch with their feelings, you had better learn to be in touch with your feelings. Now, why do you abuse yourself? Self loathing? Fear of failure? Fear of intimacy?" He produced a Parker pen and opened a file folder.

Jimmy looked out the window and saw Jennifer Manoogian drive by in her daddy's big black car. He had been meaning to call her, but he was afraid she'd laugh at him for being such an inept lover. But, my God, the dean and his wife WERE right downstairs.

"Because it feels good, that's why."

Jordan nodded and scribbled. "Do you have a girlfriend? Fiancee?"

Jimmy had to chew that one for a while. Just last Sunday, Sharyn Craig had brought her dowdy suburban parents to St. Augustine's and introduced him as her fiance. Sharyn dismissed his complaints, saying she thought they had an unspoken understanding.

"For Christ's sake," she said, "you don't think twice about screwing me every chance you get. What do you think I am, some goddamn government-funded hooker for horny seminarians?"

Jimmy had stormed out and had not seen her since.

Glancing at his bloodless inquisitor, he shrugged and said, "No, not at the moment."

"Do you date anyone regularly, or do you engage in casual sex with pick-ups?"

"What?!?"

"Ahh. I knew there was some feeling under that jovial exterior. Tell me about it. What are you feeling right now?"

"Anger."

"That's better. You can discuss it with the group this summer. Ever had any homosexual experiences?"

Kids were playing in the parking lot and a cardinal was calling to its mate from the big cottonwood behind the deanery.

"No."

Jordan studied Jimmy. After a long silence, he said, "No?" Another long silence. Then more earnest scribbling, a knowing nod, and, "We can take that up with the group, too. Well, that about wraps it up. Is there anything you want to ask me?"

"No, I can't think of anything. Well, it's been nice meeting you, Reverend Jordan."

"Paul, please call me Paul." He gave Jimmy a dry, clean hand. "You're sure you'll be able to support yourself this summer?"

"Yeah, I think the job at the library is a sure thing, and what with St. Augustine's and the coke machine job, I should about make it. Besides, my advisor says the summer between the junior and middler years is the best time to do CPE."

"Very well. See you on the seventh."

"Yeah, see you then."

* * *

Father Brent Babcock turned to the congregation and spread his long arms. "Let us greet one another in the name of the Lord."

He nodded at his acolytes: Jimmy, Bruce MacKenzie, and Pam Millar, and they released the multi-colored balloons tethered to the altar rail. Rising, they collided with the felt peace and love banners

"Father Friendly" had erected throughout Guthbertson Memorial Chapel.

Jimmy was wondering what the old dead bishop would think of all this when Babcock suddenly bear-hugged him. "The peace of the Lord be with you," he said.

"And with you," Jimmy gasped.

"Pass it on," Babcock whispered, wandering off to share warm fuzzies with the Gatesbury community. Jimmy turned reluctantly to Pam Millar and let her crack his back. His bladder was empty this time, so he smiled and said, "A pox on your biscuits too."

"What?" she said, giggling.

"It's Latin."

"Oh." She kissed him on both cheeks before releasing him. Then she waded with Babcock into the congregation for a host of hugs.

Jimmy folded his hands and faced the altar. Maybe Bruce will go away if I ignore him, he thought. But MacKenzie wanted words with his estranged roommate.

"What about me, Jimmy? Don't I get a hug, too? Or aren't I pretty enough for you?"

Embarrassed, Jimmy gave Bruce a half-hearted hug and said, "Hey, I'm, sorry I haven't . . ."

"Yeah, I was beginning to wonder what you looked like. If you're that repelled by me, you could move off campus. I mean just because there aren't any other rooms in the dorm doesn't mean you have to stay with some commie faggot like me," Bruce said.

Jimmy looked away. "Bruce, I don't think of you like that. It's just that . . ."

"It's just that you don't even use our toilet anymore. What do you think's gonna happen—giant crabs are gonna bite your dick off?"

"Sscchuuussch. We're in church. They're gonna hear us," Jimmy said.

"Don't sscchuussch me. They're too busy groping to hear us. So where the hell do you sleep half the time? At least you could tell me if you're not coming home. I do worry, you know," Bruce said.

Pooped from passing too much peace, Father Babcock and Pam Millar returned to the altar.

"Look," Jimmy whispered, "why don't we talk about this some other time, okay?"

"Sure, man, sure."

When the mass was ended, and the congregation had gone to feast, Jimmy slipped upstairs to the pop machine and emptied the coin receptacle into his pockets.

K.C. O'Neal and Jill Gaines were waiting when he returned to his room.

"I thought this was gonna be a stag party." Jimmy was annoyed. He and K.C. had agreed — absolutely no women.

"Feuerstein had to go to some bar mitzvah or something," K.C. said. "Besides, I get horny in the woods. Ain't that right, honey?"

Jill, who was braless under her tie-dyed T-shirt, bounced and giggled.

"All right, we'll all go to the North Woods. You ever fish before, Jill?"

"What, you think a woman can't fish as good as a man?" she said.

"That's not what I meant. I just, hey, I'll go get Mike, and we'll get underway. Might as well do as much driving as we can while it's still light."

Jimmy jangled over to the second block of married student apartments and rapped on Mike Harper's door.

No answer.

He rapped again, and someone peeked through the curtain. He heard some shuffling and almost fell over when the door opened. With his wife, Shirley Anne, and two little girls, Anna and Elizabeth, gathered around him, Mike Harper looked Jimmy in the eye and said, "I'm not goin'."

Jimmy regarded the lanky Oklahoman with astonishment. "What? Man, we've been plannin' this trip for weeks. You were gonna teach me to shoot your gun. We were going to . . ."

"Jimmy," Mike said, "I'm not goin' 'cause I quit drinkin'."

"What?!?"

Shirley Anne and the little girls glared at Jimmy and clung closer to Mike.

"Jimmy, I've joined AA. I'm an alcoholic, Jimmy. I can't drink no more, 'cause it'll kill me." Mike hugged his women close.

"AA? You mean like Alcoholics Anonymous? Those old winos on skid row? Mike, are you serious? Man, you can hold your liquor the best of anybody I know."

Mike Harper regarded his younger classmate with newfound patience and detachment. "You call what I did last month at that bar on Howard Street holdin' my liquor?"

"Mike, that guy had it comin'. He was lookin' for trouble."

"Uh-uh, Jimmy, I was the one. I was lookin' for trouble. I was lookin' for trouble every time I took a drink. I'm a sick man. I wanna get better. Goin' fishin' up in Wisconsin would be nothin' but trouble."

Shirley Anne bit her lip but the tears came anyway. Anna and Elizabeth hugged their daddy's legs and stared at Jimmy. They wanted daddy back, and they weren't about to let this boogey-man take him away again.

Jimmy exhaled and slapped his thighs, jingling the coins. "Wow. Heavy. Well, I guess some guys can't hold their liquor. But AA, that's — big time."

"It's the only way, Jimmy. It's not as bad as you think, and it's not just the bullshit winos from West Madison."

"Yeah, well, I don't suppose we could like borrow your car for the weekend? We'd fill up the tank when we got back. Man, we've been plannin' this trip for weeks — you know that."

"No, Jimmy. The answer's no. And you can't keep the money from the pop machine, either. I went over the books last night, and the pop fund is short $456. That's a lot of money to steal from anybody — especially a seminary school," Mike Harper said.

Jimmy bit his tongue. "But, Mike, I need this money for the trip. I thought we had an understanding. I thought . . ."

"The understanding's off. I'm getting someone else to take care of the pop machine. I know $456 is a lot of money, but I'm gonna expect you to make an effort to pay at least part of that back."

"But, Mike, you . . ."

"No. I let you get away with it, and I let you buy me drinks with that money. That's why I'm gonna pay back the other half. You could start by giving me what you got in your pockets there."

Jimmy glanced sheepishly at his bulging pockets. "I need this for the trip, man. It's the only money I've got."

"All right — I'll add it on to what you owe. Motor easy, Jimmy."

"Well," K.C. said, when Jimmy returned, "where's Harper? Where's his car?"

"You're not gonna believe this."

"Believe what, man?" K.C. said, pacing.

"The dude up and joined AA. I went to get him, and he says he quit drinkin'. Cold turkey. I can't believe it."

"I can." K.C. said. "The guy can't hold his liquor. Look at the way he snapped after he got loaded. I mean that wasn't normal behavior. Plus, his old lady's got him pussy-whipped. Face it, Jimmy, the guy's a wimp."

"Yeah, I guess you're right. Well, what do we do now?"

Surprised, K.C. and Jill stared at Jimmy. "Hey, man, this trip was your idea. You were the one who said you'd line up a car. What about that homo roommate of yours? He's got a VW, doesn't he?"

"Yeah, but . . ."

"But nothin', man. We gotta go on this trip, man. I copped some dynamite windowpane from Feuerstein, man, and I sure wouldn't want to waste it sittin' around this fuckin' place all weekend. Go ask him. Tell him we'll give him blow jobs, butt fucks, whatever he wants. Go on, lover boy, put the moves on him."

This was definitely not the way Jimmy wanted it. But he could see there was no other way. They didn't have enough to rent a car, and there was no one else at the seminary he could ask.

"All right. It might be kinda awkward, but I'll give it a try. Wait here, okay?"

"Sure, man."

"Good luck, Jimmy," Jill said, flashing her long eyelashes.

Jimmy walked into the refectory just as the dean began the Doxology: "Praise God from whom all blessings flow . . ."

Moved by George Manoogian's sonorous voice, Jimmy stood against the wall and listened appreciatively. Bruce's big voice boomed above the rest, and Jimmy sidled next to him as he sang, "Praise Him all creatures here below. Praise Him above ye heavenly host. Praise Father, Son, and Holy Ghost. Amen."

"Hey, Bruce, can I talk to you for a second?"

MacKenzie was amazed to see his roommate at a community dinner. "What's the matter, your gin mill burn down?"

Faculty and students, some who barely recognized Jimmy, were eavesdropping, so Jimmy grabbed Bruce and led him out of the great hall.

"Look," he said, "I know I haven't been such a great roommate lately, and I'm really sorry. Really, I am. And to make it up to you, I wanted to invite you on a little fishing trip we were planning . . ."

"What's the catch?"

* * *

They were at the Wisconsin line when Jill found it. "I see," she said, "you've got to put it this way and then hit it. Wanna hear some jams?"

"Shit, yes. God, you've been fuckin' around with that thing long enough," K.C. said, annoyed. He and Jimmy were in the backseat. "And gimme another beer, will ya?"

Jill pushed the button and gave her boyfriend a beer. "It's so dark, I could hardly see what I was doing."

"Turn it up."

"Speaker's cracked," Bruce said, holding the road with his steady gaze.

"So we'll listen to cracked music," K.C. said. "Turn it up, baby."

Backed by Big Brother and the Holding Company, Janis Joplin wailed at Bill Graham's Fillmore Auditorium as the four fools from Chicago screamed along.

Between them, they had: K.C.'s childhood Zebco rod and reel, Bruce's trumpet, Jill's birth control pills, four hits of acid in Reynolds Wrap, $62 in small bills and coins, the remnants of two warm six-packs of Schlitz, a "nickel" of killer Columbian, two packs of Job rolling papers, and a Texaco credit card in Jimmy's father's name. And no maps.

K.C. claimed an intimate knowledge of the Badger State's highways and byways.

". . . no, no it just can't be . . . there's just got to be an answer, and everywhere I look there's none around," Janis whined.

Jill joined her, and K.C. reached around the seat and grabbed her left breast. She squirmed and giggled.

"God," K.C. said, "why'd she have to go and OD? Man, I woulda loved to do about three hits of acid and fuck her brains out. I woulda done it doggie-style, 'cause Janis was the kinda woman who appreciated animal love. What do you think, Brucey? You think she liked to do it doggie-style? Or you think she liked it

Greek-style — right up the old brown canal?" K.C. had been baiting Bruce like this from the start.

And Bruce had been responding in kind, saying, "How would a queer boy like me know what women like?"

Annoyed, Jill brushed K.C.'s paw off her breast.

"Anybody want to smoke some pot? This stuff is dynamite," she said.

"I thought you'd never ask," Jimmy said.

Chapter Thirty

"Clarke, wake up!"

"Huh? Wha?"

K.C. shook Jimmy until his eyes rolled open. "We're here. Wake up and go to sleep."

Jill and Bruce were already unloading their goods into a pine cabin with a green shingle roof. The sky was a gun-metal blue, and the cold, damp air hung low and heavy. Jimmy's head ached and his tongue had dried to the roof of his mouth. He had slept fitfully. He forced his eyes open as a chirping bird pounded his eardrums.

There looked to be a lake out there through the trees, but Jimmy didn't care. He just wanted to crash.

The smell of damp pine needles filled the Beetle, prompting Jimmy to arise. His left leg had fallen asleep and his bladder was bursting, so he wobbled into the woods and relieved himself against a pine tree. He watched his steam rise for a moment, rubbed his face, shook his leg, and headed for the cabin.

K.C. intercepted him, saying, "Hey, man, let's go to town and get some brews. We need a fresh supply for the weekend."

"Naw, I wanna sleep," Jimmy said, pushing past him.

"Sleep? You were crashed out all the way up here. You don't need sleep. Come on, man, get the keys from your loverboy, and let's go. I'm ready for adventure." K.C. grabbed his shoulders and spun Jimmy around.

Jimmy stretched and considered the morning sky. "What time is it?"

"Six ten. Who gives a fuck? This is party time, man. Get the keys. I didn't come up here to sleep."

"Aren't you tired?" Jimmy couldn't imagine where K.C. got his energy.

"Fuck no. Feuerstein gave me a black beauty before we left. I've been flyin' all the way up here."

"Thanks for givin' me one. You got any more?"

"No, man, but I'll give you a hit of acid if you get the keys. I guarantee that'll keep you wide awake, man."

"You got a deal," Jimmy said, smiling.

Bruce and Jill were busily organizing the musty, dusty cabin, which consisted of two bedrooms, a common room with a kitchen in the corner, and a washroom with a rust-stained sink and toilet. They had a kettle going on the stove and had opened the windows to freshen the place.

"Jimmy, you're alive. I thought we'd lost you," Jill said.

"I was pretty tired. Hey, Bruce, could we borrow your car for a second? We wanted to go to town and get some beer."

Haggard from having driven the entire 300 miles, Bruce looked askance at his roommate. "You know I don't like other people driving my car."

"No kiddin', Bruce. Look, all we want to do is drive into town and get some beer. Won't take long. Honest."

Bruce contemplated his keys. "You'll come right back?"

"Yeah. Of course."

"All right, but be careful. And get some food for breakfast while you're there. And some coffee . . ."

"And toilet paper," Jill added.

Jimmy ran to the car, hopped in the driver's seat, and fired up the Beetle. K.C. climbed in. They roared down the dirt road past the shuttered caretaker's cabin to Wisconsin Highway 77.

"Which way, K.C.? You're the guide."

"Take a left, man."

The rising sun was hemorrhaging across the sky, and unbroken ranks of tall pines and birches stood green-and-white guard along the roadway. Jimmy chewed his cheek and contemplated the surrounding beauty. It reminded him of parts of Pennsylvania except there were no mountains.

"Hey, don't fall asleep, man. I'll drive if you can't handle it."

"No, I'm all right. I was just thinkin' about Mike Harper joinin' AA. Man, I just can't believe it."

"Hey, the guy's a wimp. Every time we went drinkin' with that dude, he'd end up cryin' or yellin' or some crazy shit. Or pickin' fights with the biggest asshole at the bar. The guy couldn't handle his liquor. I mean, some guys are born wimps. Let him stay home and get pussy-whipped all weekend. Serves him right," K.C. said.

"Yeah, I guess you're right. Hey, what about that acid?"

"Now you're talkin'. Cost you ten bucks."

"Ten bucks?!? I thought you were gonna GIVE me a free hit."

"You think Feuerstein gave me this shit for free?"

"No, man, but . . ."

"So why should I give it to you for nothin'?"

"For one thing, I got the car. I got MacKenzie to drive us up here. And I'm the only one with a gas card. I'll tell you what — I'll pay for the gas if you give me a hit." Jimmy couldn't take his eyes off the crumpled aluminum foil K.C. had pulled from his pocket.

"All the gas?"

"Well, maybe . . ."

"All the gas, man, or no acid." K.C. dangled it in front of Jimmy's face.

"All right — all the gas."

K.C. carefully unfolded the foil, saying, "Open your mouth and close your eyes and get ready for a big surprise."

Jimmy took his foot off the accelerator and did as he was told. "I hope this is as good as that last shit I bought from Feuerstein," he said. "I was flyin' for two days on that shit." K.C. swallowed his acid whole, saying, "Don't worry, man, this is grade-A, prime, government-inspected acid."

They motored easy to Clam Lake, an unincorporated collection of taverns, bait shops, and filling stations, and chose "Stu's Place" because an inviting Leinenkugel beer sign glowed in the window.

Still waiting for the acid to activate, Jimmy climbed out of the car, saying, "What kind of beer is that? I can't even pronounce it."

"LIE-nin-coo-gill. What's so hard about that, man? It's the greatest beer in the world," K.C. proclaimed, bursting out of the car. "They also call it squaw piss, in case you were wonderin'."

"Bet it's not half as good as Rolling Rock. That's the best beer in the world. Hey, don't you think we ought to get the food and stuff first?"

"Naw, man. We'll get that shit later. Come on, let's go get some brews."

Jimmy took K.C.'s arm and whispered, "Hey, you gettin' off on this shit?"

"Give it some time, man. Give it some time." K.C. jerked away from Jimmy and bounded into the bar.

Jimmy trotted after him.

Although it was only 7:30 a.m., the bar was lined with men in flannel shirts and chino pants. Most were drinking bottled

Leinenkugels from stubby glasses, but a few were chasing sips of bourbon with coffee. They all stared at the city slickers, particularly the one in the purple high-tops, green corduroys, and a loud lavender shirt.

"Kinda early for fishin', ain't it, boys?" one of them said, eyeing K.C.'s clashing clothes.

"We're goin' for muskie," K.C. announced, cocksure of himself.

"Muskie?!?" another man said. "And where, might I ask, are you gonna catch muskie around here this time of year? In a deep freezer?"

Assuming they were laughing with him not at him, K.C. bellied up to the pine bar and grinned winningly at the bartender, a weathered old man wearing a wet, white apron over a white shirt.

"Two bottles of squaw piss, barkeep," he said.

Wondering when they were going to be killed, Jimmy squeezed in next to his foolhardy friend. The bartender set them up, and K.C. elbowed Jimmy.

"Oh yeah," Jimmy said, reaching in his jeans pocket. "Here you go," he said, plunking a pile of stolen change on the bar.

As Jimmy was trying to fill his glass in a manly manner, the acid blew his brain. He managed to put a perfect head on his beer. Hoisting it, he was entranced by its endless effervescence.

K.C.'s acid was kicking in too, but he took an outward tack. "Man, we're gonna get us some big muskie this weekend. I got it on good authority that they're just waitin' for the right lure."

"And what might that be," the bartender said, "a hand grenade?"

K.C. chortled and clapped Jimmy's back. "You hear that, bro'? This guy thinks I'm gonna catch muskie with a hand grenade. A fuckin' hand grenade. That's terrific." When he could control himself, K.C. turned back to the bartender and said, "I've got a secret lure, man. You just wait."

Jimmy wiped the splattered beer from his face and contemplated the muskellunge mounted over the bar. Its mouth was agape, exposing a set of savage little teeth. "Man, I'd use a grenade if I saw one of those things coming at me."

"Hey," K.C. said to the flannel shirts, "don't mind him. We just drove all the way up from Chicago, and he's still a little tired."

"You say Chicago?" the bartender said.

"Yeah," K.C. said.

The bartender squinted and lighted a Pall Mall. "You know South Shore?"

"Man, I was a lifeguard at Rainbow Beach for four summers. Best goddamned beach in the world."

"It WAS the best beach in the world until those damn Mau-Maus started taking over. I had a bar on 71st Street. Damned good one too. God, you should have seen that street in the 40's and 50's. Greatest place in the city until the shines showed up. I bet that neighborhood looks like hell by now."

K.C. squared his shoulders. "When was the last time you were there, man?"

"I got out in '68 when the gettin' was still good. But any fool could see where things were going. They would have stolen us blind during the blizzard of '67 if we didn't have the citizens' patrols."

"If you haven't been there since 1968, you don't know what you're talkin' about, man. And why shouldn't blacks live in South Shore or anywhere else? Why shouldn't they live here, for that matter?"

There was a stirring along the bar. Jimmy put his beer down and looked for the door. For an anxious moment, he thought it had disappeared.

"How you know so much about South Shore, friend?" the bartender asked. "You live there?"

Not now, man. I live in Evanston. Most integrated community in America. I used to live in South Shore when I was a kid, but my parents moved to Beverly because . . ."

"Because they knew what was coming and they wanted to move to a nice, safe, all-white neighborhood while they could still get a good price."

K.C. tapped the bartender's arm and said, "Gimme a smoke, will ya, man?"

"There's a machine by the wall."

"Get us a pack of Marlboros, will ya, Jimmy?"

Jimmy finally got the machine to work and had himself a smoke after giving K.C. one. It tasted so damn good, he lit another with the remains of the first.

But you don't smoke, he told himself.

I do now, he replied.

Cigarette dangling from his puss, K.C. continued: "My parents moved to Beverly because they needed more room, man. But we go back to South Shore all the time, man."

"What? To go to the country club and be waited on by your black brothers," the bartender said.

"Yeah, but . . ."

"But nothing. If they let a nigger or Jew in, your old man'd quit in a minute. I know your kind."

"It's gonna change, man. Listen, the point I'm tryin' to make is that you can't run and hide from the blacks. We've got to treat them as equals, or they're gonna come after us. There's gonna be a race war, and I think we've got it comin' if you ask me."

"If there's a race war, I pity any nigger that comes up here lookin' for trouble," the bartender declared.

"Damn right."

"Yeah."

"You said it, Stu."

K.C. considered them and laughed. "Man, I'd fight with the blacks."

"Even if they were attacking your home? What if they killed your parents?" Jimmy said.

"Even if they were gonna rape Jill. Don't you see, we started it. We brought them over from Africa. We starved them to death on those slave ships and threw them overboard in the middle of the ocean when they got sick.

"We put them in high-rise slums and created the welfare state to keep them in slavery. We continue to . . ."

"Hey, K.C., you're gonna burn your lip."

"Oh, yeah. Thanks, man." K.C. plucked the smoldering filter from his mouth. "Like I was sayin' — the blacks got every reason in the world to rise up against us, and I hope they win."

K.C. lighted another cigarette and spilled the last of his beer. When he waved the empty glass in the bartender's face, the man froze. "Hey, what's the matter, pops? Come on, get me another beer. We got a whole fuckin' pile of money on the bar. What's your problem, gramps? Can't take a little honest discussion?"

K.C. leaned over the bar and tried to grab a beer out of the cooler.

"Come on, K.C," Jimmy said, taking his arm. "Let's get out of here."

"That's real good advice, kid," the bartender said.

But K.C. brushed Jimmy aside and reached for the beer. "Fellas, how about a hand with these dirty hippies?"

There was a bum's rush of shoves, punches, and kicks until they were somehow speeding away in MacKenzie's straining car. K.C, who was bleeding profusely from the ears, nose, and mouth, rolled down his window and shouted, "Death to all fascist pigs!"

Jimmy, who was more bruised than bleeding, gripped the wheel and peered nervously in the rearview mirror. No one was following, but he hammered down just to be safe.

"Jesus, K.C, you coulda got us killed in there. Are you nuts, or what?"

"You know what your problem is, man?"

"What?"

"You don't know how to relax and have a good time. Slow down and pull in there," K.C. said, pointing in no specific direction.

"Where?"

"There."

There was a gravel drive curving back behind a stand of pines. There was a white sign with a shamrock and "Emerald Isle Tavern" hand-painted in green.

The little car spewed gravel as it labored through the abrupt turn.

"Hey," Jimmy said, "why don't you let me go in there and get a couple of six packs, and we'll head back to the cabin. Jill and Bruce must be wonderin' what the hell happened to us."

"Fuck them. Come on, man. Lighten up. You act like you were back at that fuckin' seminary. This is the North Woods — time to party hearty. Let's go get us some Guiness. 'Guiness Stout is good no doubt,'" K.C. said.

"K.C, you're bleeding like a stuck pig. You can't go in there like that."

"Sure I can. Let's go."

Jimmy followed his crazy friend and listened as he explained to the incredulous bartender that they had been in a slight accident but were just fine. They just hadn't seen the stop sign, and the other guy and his car weren't even scratched. "So what's to worry?" K.C. said, the voice of reason.

The Emerald Isle Tavern was a plain white room with no Guiness Stout, no Harp Lager, and no Irish music on the box save for what K.C. called "a bunch of worthless Bing Crosby shit."

"Maybe we ought to go," Jimmy suggested. He just wanted to go somewhere quiet and enjoy his high.

"Shit no," K.C. said, swaggering to the bar. "Put some of that loot of yours in the juke box, and we'll have us a party."

The bartender was a burly young man named McManus from Milwaukee. His mother was German, and his interest in Ireland was purely commercial. Enough Chicago Irish frequented these woods during the summer season to keep his coffers filled, so why not hang out a shamrock even if it looked more like a sagging sow's ear. He explained that his father's people had probably been Ulster Protestants, adding, "I just wish they could end their troubles over there and live in peace."

"Not me, man," K.C. said, gulping his Leinenkugels. "There ain't gonna be any peace in Ireland until the last dirty Prot is moldin' in his grave."

McManus leaned over the bar, contemplating this one. His slow fuse was sizzling. "What kinda attitude is that?" he said.

"Yeah, K.C." Jimmy said. "In case you forgot, I'm Protestant too."

"Yeah, and I'd kill you too if we were over there. I'd blow up every Prot church I saw, especially if they were full of little Prot kids. Did you know that the English used to hang Irish priests just for wearing clerical collars? So don't give me your Main Line Protestant peace and love bullshit, man. And who the hell do you think you are, puttin' a shamrock on your stupid sign? Up the IRA!" K.C. guzzled his beer and demanded another.

The phone rang, and McManus tromped off to take the call in an adjacent room.

"Hey, K.C," Jimmy whispered, "Drink up and let's go. Jill and Bruce are gonna be wonderin' what . . ."

"Give me a break, man. What the hell'd you come on this trip for anyway? All you been doin' is bitchin' and moanin'." He leaned over the bar and drew himself a Leinenkugel. "Wait outside if you don't like it in here. I'm not leavin' until I convince this guy that he's a stupid Prot."

McManus returned to the bar with a scowl on his face and a revolver in his hand. "I just got a phone call from Stu Smith down the road. Said he just escorted you two bums outta his place and suggested I do the same if you showed up here. There's the door!"

Terrified, Jimmy headed for it.

K.C, however, held his ground, coolly sipping his purloined beer. McManus cleared his throat and shifted his weight. "Out! Now!"

"Ahhh," K.C. said, appreciating his suds. "Good old squaw piss. Hey, Clarke, where're you goin'? Get back here and have a beer. It's on the house."

Jimmy stood at the door, staining the knob with his sweaty palm.

"Suit yourself," K.C. said, taking another sip. He smacked his lips and studied McManus' piece. "Smith and Wesson, model 19. Lot of Chicago cops carry 'em. Fires both .38 and 357 ammo. Bet you got that baby loaded for bear." He leaned forward for a better look. "Yeah, just what I thought — hollow points. Those little suckers pancake out when they hit something like a nice, soft abdominal cavity. Come on man," K.C. said, patting his stomach, "Give me a good gut shot."

McManus blinked and rocked on his feet.

Jimmy held his breath, ready for a stack of lead flapjacks. He exhaled. "I'm leavin', K.C."

"Suit yourself, sissy," K.C. said, not even looking at his friend. Jimmy went to the car, started it, and shifted into reverse. He couldn't leave, but he couldn't go back inside. He just wanted to lie down somewhere near a nice clean toilet.

A gunshot scattered the birds. K.C. burst out of the bar and jumped into the car. "Come on, man, let's get the fuck outta here! That dude's crazy! Come on!"

"You hit?"

"No, I'm not hit, and get your hands off me. Let's get the fuck outta here. Now!"

Jimmy gunned the car, nearly killing it.

"Jesus Christ, you stupid asshole. Let me drive."

It was too late. McManus was in the doorway drawing a bead on them. Jimmy could feel red pancakes all over his body. He willed the car to move and it spun madly backwards down the drive.

McManus squeezed off two rounds. They crashed harmlessly into the pines, splintering wood and cones.

K.C. was laughing his ass off when they hit the road.

Jimmy lightened up when he got the car moving forward. He howled too when K.C. told him how he had thrown beer in the bartender's face.

"The stupid fuck fired over my head and knocked out that Hamms sign with the sky blue waters. Funniest fuckin' thing I ever saw," K.C. said, tears running down his cheeks.

"Yeah," Jimmy said, "stupid fuckin' Prot."

Thrilled by their brush with death, Jimmy gunned the little car through the gears and got it up to 80.

They were aboard the Starship Enterprise headed for a distant galaxy when K.C. spotted the cutoff for their cabin and screamed, "Turn here!"

* * *

Bruce put down his trumpet and wiped his mouth with the back of his hand. "Please don't stop," Jill said. "I was enjoying that."

MacKenzie peered out the cabin door. "Where do you suppose those two are? They've been gone for more than an hour. I'm going to look for them."

"They'll be back. Maybe the store wasn't open yet, and they went to the next town."

"Maybe they fell in some bar and got loaded. Look, I don't know you, and you don't know me, but I do know my roommate's outta control when it comes to liquor. And if you want to know the truth, the only reason he asked me along on this trip was so he could take off with my car like he's doing now."

"Why don't we walk down to the road and see if they're coming," Jill suggested. "They should be along any minute."

They were halfway to the highway when they saw the car start its skid. Shocked, they stood and watched as it sheared off a "Soft Shoulders" sign at its base. The toppling sign shattered the unbreakable windshield, and Bruce's Beetle skidded another 90 feet before imbedding itself in the muck and gravel that lined the road.

Jill and Bruce raced for the car, fearful of what they would find. "Listen," Jill said between strides, "they must be alive. I hear them."

K.C. and Jimmy were alive all right, alive and laughing uncontrollably.

Chapter Thirty-One

"Collect call from James G. Clarke the Third. Will you accept the charges?"

"Hell, no."

"Yes, operator," a woman said, picking up another extension. "We'll accept the charges. Jimmy, is that you, dear? I've got the phone in the kitchen."

"Yeah, Mom, it's me. How are you?"

Jim Clarke snatched the phone out of his wife's hand. "What the hell have you done now—set that damn seminary on fire?"

"Jim, let me talk to him. I'm fine, dear. How are you? It's been so long since we're heard from you, Jimmy. I was about to send out a posse."

Good old Mom and her posses, Jimmy thought, watching the lumber trucks roll through Hayward. "It's been a busy quarter, but I'm okay. I'm sorry I haven't written or anything. It's just that . . ."

"How much money do you need, and what's her name?" Jim Clarke said, splashing some more scotch on his rocks.

"Well," Jimmy said, examining his father's Texaco card. "I don't need anything right now. I just wanted to let you know that I just ran up kind of a big charge on that gas card you gave me last summer."

"What gas card?!? What the hell's he talkin' about?" Jim Clarke said to his wife.

"Jim, you gave him a Texaco card last summer—in case he ever needed it. I remember quite well. I thought it was a good idea then, and I think it's a good idea now."

"Bullshit. We can't afford to have that jerk running around the country charging everything in sight. God, we can hardly afford to eat around here anymore."

"Don't listen to your father, dear. How could you run up a big bill if you don't have a car?"

"Car?!? He didn't buy a damn car with it, did he?" Jim Clarke pounded his fist on the counter.

"No, Dad, I didn't buy a car with it. It's kind of a long story." Jimmy turned in the phone booth and smiled wanly at the others who watched as a repairman fitted a new windshield in the Beetle.

"Remember me mentioning my rommmate Bruce MacKenzie from Oregon?"

"Oregon?" Louise Clarke said, puzzled.

"It's a state, Mom. It's on the West Coast. Anyway, we're up in Wisconsin with Bruce's car on a fishing trip, and we had a little accident, and . . ."

"Oh, dear—are you all right, Jimmy? Are you calling from a hospital? Have you seen a doctor? Do you need blood? Is there an airport near where you are?"

"What's it gonna cost?" his father demanded.

"Uh, it looks like about $250. Something like that."

"And you put it on my credit card? Are you nuts? What about your pal; it's his damn car. How come he's not paying?"

"Because I was driving, Dad, and because I'm the only one with a credit card. The others'll chip in when we get back to Evanston. I'll send you a check to cover it as soon as I get back. I just wanted you to know in case they called to verify or something. Don't worry, I'll take care of it. I'm not a little kid anymore."

"Coulda fooled me. Now, you listen to me, buster. When you get back from this little trip of yours, you cut up that credit card because I'm telling the gas company not to accept anymore charges from you. You hear me?"

"Yes, sir." Jimmy's wanted to tell that bastard what he really thought of him, but he needed to get back to Evanston.

"Now say something nice to your mother, for Christ's sake. You didn't even send her a Mother's Day card, you selfish punk." He slammed the phone and poured himself some more scotch.

"Mom? Are you still there?"

"I'm still here, dear." She was trying not to cry. "You didn't tell me if you're all right."

"I'm okay."

"Good. Hey, I'm sorry about Mother's Day. Happy Mother's Day, Mom. Sorry I forgot. I . . ."

"Oh, don't pay attention to your father. He's had a little too much to drink, that's all. It's the scotch talking."

"I know. Anyway, nobody was hurt. Bruce's car just got banged up—that's all. You're not gonna believe this, but we were behind a logging truck and a log fell off and hit the windshield."

"Oh my Lord, that must have been awful. Are you sure you're all right?"

"Yeah, and it looks as though the car's gonna be okay too. Uh, since I was, uh, drivin', and it was an accident, I was wonderin' if Dad could call Mr. Myers at the insurance company and . . ."

"Dear, you just heard your father. He hasn't had any luck finding a new job, and we've had to sell some of our stock. I think you'd better get your friend to pay his share and send the check like you said."

"Mom?"

"Yes?"

"Could you help me out a little?"

"I don't know, dear. We've even been thinking of selling the house and renting an apartment in Villanova. How much is a little?"

"Well, I'm kinda tight at the moment, but things'll be better in a coupla weeks when I start workin' at Northwestern's library. I don't know, maybe $75 or so."

"All right, but this is the last time I can help you until your father gets a job. And that could be — well, I'll see what I can do."

"Thanks, Mom. Thanks a lot." Jimmy was about to hang up when he realized she might want to talk about her own problems. "Are you sure you're okay, Mom? Is everything all right at home?"

"Things will be better when your father gets a job. Well, I've got to go. He'll be wanting his lunch. Please be careful driving back to the seminary."

"I will, Mom. Talk to you soon."

"Goodbye, dear."

Jimmy left the phone booth and stretched. The acid had gone sour, and he wanted to sleep. But first he had to face the group.

"Well," K.C. said, folding his arms, "you get your old man's insurance to cover it?"

"Not exactly. I still think the fair thing would be for us to split it."

Bruce grimaced and turned away.

Jill looked imploringly at K.C. who shook his head and said, "No way, man. You were drivin'. Your responsibility, man."

"But, K.C, you were the one who screamed at me to make that turn. I never woulda done it if you hadn't screamed at me like that," Jimmy said, totally exasperated.

"It's your problem, man. I can't afford something like this. If you weren't such a pussy, you woulda got your old man to pay for it through his insurance. You said you were gonna." K.C. folded his arms across his chest and stared stubbornly at Jimmy.

"Yeah, well, there're some problems at home." Jimmy took a deep breath, counting to five.

He wished he had listened to Mike Harper. Mike Harper had the right idea — booze and drugs were nothing but trouble. He took another deep breath, but he still wanted to kill K.C.

He let his anger dissipate a little and said, "Well, we can talk about it later back at the cabin. Man, I'm so tired I'm gonna fall asleep on my feet."

* * *

Jimmy was awakened by the sad laugh of a loon on the lake. He was bathed in sweat and had been dreaming of headless people and hopelessness. He propped himself on his elbow and rubbed his eyes with the back of his other hand. A faint twilight haunted the cabin. Jimmy sat up too quickly and nearly vomited. His body and brain were in turmoil. He decided a bath or shower would soon put them right, but he seemed to remember that the cabin contained no such accommodations.

"K.C.? Jill? Bruce? Anybody here?"

Jimmy fumbled around, barking his shins on various objects before he found a light. He was frightened by his reflection in a mirror.

Jimmy poked around, quickly realizing he was alone. He was sure he was the only person left in the world. But that didn't make sense, because nobody sleeps through World War III.

Maybe they just got fed up and went back to Evanston without me, Jimmy thought.

He went outside to confirm his sorrowful suspicion and was glad to find Bruce's car under the pine tree where they had left it.

Jimmy rubbed his face, trying to reconstruct the recent past. There was the acid and that slow-motion sign shattering the windshield. Jimmy wondered why he and K.C. had found it so funny. They could have been killed. And there was a bar, or were there two?

Two.

And that guy with the gun and those crazy lumberjacks or whatever they were at that other place.

God, it was nuts.

And I talked to Mom, and the Old Man. Did I just see them? Are they dead?

Am I dead?

No, I just talked with them on the phone. But why? Two-hundred-fifty dollars, that's why. You just ran up a $250 charge on the old man's Texaco card, dummy, and he wants you to pay it all.

Jimmy picked out a trail and followed it to the lake. He walked to the end of a fishing pier, stripped, and dove into the dark water. The cold grabbed his chest, but he spread his arms and glided gracefully down through the copper-colored lake, hoping to find truth and beauty at the bottom. His lungs seemed to have limitless capacity, so he continued his effortless descent. The water got colder; his toes ached, but still he continued. Then he remembered the mounted muskie at the bar and realized its next of kin were out there eyeballing his toes and testicles.

When he was a kid, his folks took him to the Jersey Shore where they warned him against swimming at night because that was when sharks fed close to shore. Didn't it follow that those mean-looking muskies had the same nasty habit? They even looked like small sharks or barracudas.

His lungs ached for air, and the water was colder than he could stand, even with the residual acid effect. He paddled frantically but seemed unable to ascend. Terrified, he clawed desperately and gulped just as he got to the choppy surface. Coughing, he could barely see the pier. He had gone too far, and if the cold didn't claim him, the maddening muskies certainly would.

Forgetting everything his father had told him, he rolled his torso and lifted his head in a clumsy crawl stroke that finally got him to safety.

The dark woods encircled him as he stood shivering on the pier. He dried himself with his shirt and dressed quickly, wanting only the warmth of the cabin and the fellowship of his friends. Walking barefoot through the cooling forest, he wiggled his toes to be certain he had them all. He did.

Jimmy's so-called friends were gathered around a small perch K.C. had caught. They regarded him with horror when he came to the door.

"God Almighty, Clarke," Bruce said. "You're covered with leeches!"

"Huh?"

"Leeches, man! You didn't go swimmin' in that lake, did you? A guy just told us it was leech-infested," Bruce said.

Jill screamed. K.C, who had continued all day, tried to tear off Jimmy's shirt, popping the buttons. Jimmy looked and saw several brown annelids gorging on his chest. He was horrified that he had not felt them before and wondered if they had sucked him senseless. Obviously not because he wanted to punch K.C. for tearing his favorite shirt.

He shoved K.C.

K.C. shoved back, saying, "Hey, asshole, I'm just tryin' to help."

"You don't have to go tearin' my shirt off," Jimmy screamed.

Bruce was more or less sober and stepped between them. "You wanna get those leeches off?"

"Hell, yes!"

"Then calm down, and we'll get 'em."

"Jesus," Jimmy said, "all I did was go for a little swim in the lake. I didn't feel a thing."

"Gimme a coupla cigarettes, K.C." Bruce said, striking a match.

"Cigarettes?!?"

"Didn't you ever see The Bridge Over the River Kwai?" K.C. asked. "William Holden and that English guy, uh . . ."

"Jack Hawkins," Jill said.

"Yeah, Jack Hawkins. They were commandos, remember, and they got leeches all over, and they burned 'em off with cigarettes. Worked like a charm. Well, you ready?"

Jimmy held his breath. "Yeah, go ahead."

He heard and smelled the sizzle but didn't feel a thing.

A leech lay dying on the floor. Soon there were several.

K.C. and Bruce worked methodically until Jimmy's upper body was free of them.

"To hell with the dance and down with your pants," K.C. said, lighting a fresh leech killer.

Do you mind, Jill?" Jimmy said, blushing. In spite of it all, he was modest.

"No, I don't mind. I'll get sick if I watch any more of this. God, doesn't it hurt?"

"No, not really." Jimmy looked at the rivulets of blood running down his chest and at the spineless corpes on the floor. "But I sure wouldn't want to be one of those poor little bastards. If you listen real carefully, you can hear their little leech screams."

Jill laughed. "Come on."

"Really. They're in leech agony."

K.C. looked up at Jill.

She went to their room without further comment.

"We'll save 'em and use 'em for bait," Bruce said. "The fish love 'em."

"Speakin' of fish, I saw the biggest fuckin' muskie in the world when I was under water. I tried to catch it, but it got away," Jimmy said.

"Sure," K.C. said, "Now take your pants off before they chew your balls off." Jimmy dropped trou, and they found a fat leech feeding within three inches of his left nut. "Just in time," K.C. said, going for it." Another coupla seconds and that little bugger woulda had your family jewels."

"Careful," Jimmy said, afraid to watch.

"Hey, Brucey, you take his ass, okay, honeybuns? You'll be in familiar territory," K.C. said, lisping.

"Leave him alone, K.C." Jimmy said.

"It's all right," Bruce said. "Being around a big macho stud like K.C. has made me see the error of my ways. Starting tomorrow, I'm only gonna screw broads, like K.C."

They laughed their animosities away, and Bruce and K.C. finished the job with no discomfort to the patient.

Jimmy made the sign of the cross over the dead and dying, saying, "Bless them, Father, for they know not what they sucked." He was about to pull up his pants when he saw Jill peeping at him through a crack in the door. They winked at one another and she quietly shut the door. Later, Jimmy thought.

"Hey look, Brucey, you got the fucker so excited, he's got a hard-on," K.C. said.

Jimmy quickly pulled up his pants and nearly recircumcised himself with his zipper.

* * *

"Hey," Bruce whispered, "That turn you on?"

Wide awake, Jimmy stared into the darkness. What kind of stupid question is that, he thought. Who wouldn't be turned on listening to those two go at it in the next room. Hearing her through the wafer-thin wall, Jimmy could picture Jill with her legs spread and her mouth open. Only he was on top, not K.C.

Actually, it would be fine if she wanted to be on top. Just fine. You got a hard-on?" Bruce asked.

Shit, Jimmy thought, what kind of dumb-ass question is that.

"Come, baby," K.C. cried, "Come, baby —"

Jill moaned, but it sounded to Jimmy like fake-orgasm city. In fact, he KNEW she was faking.

Bruce reached through the darkness and got a hungry hand on Jimmy's hip. "Come on, I can make you happy. You don't have to lie there getting yourself all worked up. I can . . ."

"Fuck off, Bruce," Jimmy said, pushing his roommate's hand away. "I'm tryin' to sleep." Jimmy rolled on his side so his back was to Bruce.

"Hey, baby," K.C. said, "they're gettin' it on in the next room. Who's on top, fellas? You goin' Greek or French tonight? Don't play hard to get, Jimmy."

Jill laughed nervously.

Bruce said, "Oh, shut up!"

When K.C. and Jill had spent themselves, and K.C. was snoring loudly, Bruce made no secret of beating off and then fell into a deep, snoring sleep. Listening to the frogs and insects, Jimmy wondered what the hell he was doing in Wisconsin with these weirdos.

He wondered why he was in a seminary in the first place, and then he remembered the alternative and was thankful.

Unable to sleep, Jimmy padded to the bathroom to see about the swelling in his loins. He was about to lock the door when there was a soft knock.

It was Jill, and she was clad only in a diaphanous pink nightie.

Chapter Thirty-Two

When they returned to the seminary, Jimmy found a letter thumb-tacked to his door.

Written by Father Wiltwright, it read:

"Dear Mr. Clarke:

"I know you have a busy social schedule, so I shall not detain you long with this epistle. But I do want to call to your attention the appointment we had this past Saturday to discuss your rather relaxed attitude toward church history.

"I let you get away with one excess, but I cannot forgive two. Your final paper was the work of a cheap and lazy mind. I filed it in the trash basket where it belongs and am giving you a C- for the course. Please consider another major, for I do not have the patience to endure another term of your unpleasant presence.

"Others at this seminary might accept your sincerity, but I surely do not.

"Sincerely,

"The Reverend Godfrey J. Wiltwright."

"Shit," Jimmy said, crumpling the paper in his fist.

"Let me see," Bruce said, looking over his roommate's shoulder.

"Get the fuck away from me," Jimmy said, shoving Bruce.

"My, my, aren't we in a touchy little mood," Bruce said, pursing his lips and blowing a kiss at Jimmy. "Well, you just go off and cry in your corner. I've had enough of your moody bullshit. If you can't cut it here, why don't you just quit and join the military like a real man?"

"Maybe I will," Jimmy said. "Maybe I won't even waste the time going through boot camp. Maybe I'll just steal a helicopter from some army base and go over there and kill gooks on my own. How's that, Bruce? Would that fuckin' impress you? Huh?"

Bruce backed up a step.

"Yeah," Bruce said, "That'd be just great. But why don't you get a good night's sleep and leave first thing in the morning. Killin' gooks is hard work. You'll want to be well rested. See ya in the mornin', killer. It's been real."

Jimmy watched Bruce retreat into his room. Then he went to the window and looked for God. All he could see were the flood-lighted gargoyles atop the steeple.

Figures, he thought, I'm finally ready to pray, and the only thing to pray to are a bunch of weird little stone guys. Well, it's all part of your little joke, isn't it?

Jimmy was so tired he climbed into bed with his clothes on. But just before he fell asleep he kicked his shoes off and added, "Hey, God, if you're listening, how about givin' me a break? Okay?"

Chapter Thirty-Three

The old man would love this guy, Jimmy thought, listening to the Reverend Doctor J. David Marshfield tell for the ten-thousandth time how he and Winston Churchill had won the Battle of Britain.

Old Marshfield bore a strong physical and verbal resemblance to Churchill and enhanced the effect by keeping unlighted Cuban cigars perched in his puss. He got them, he said, from a cousin in Canada, but Jimmy wondered if the old guy wasn't a personal pal of Fidel Castro. He seemed to know everyone else.

They were in Marshfield's late-model Volvo station wagon and were heading west on Willow Road through a lovely, tree-lined section of Winnetka.

"Do you want to start with Kierkegaard, Tillich, or Teilhard de Chardin?" old Marshfield said.

Jimmy had never had an easier course than Marshfield's Theology of Modern Man. At least until now when the ancient Englishman actually expected him to have read all that crap. Jimmy smiled gamely and wondered if the old guy would like to hear about the Richard Brautigan book he had just read.

"Uh, what struck me about the reading was the role of evil in the twentieth century," Jimmy said, stalling for time.

Marshfield turned north on Illinois Highway 43 and looked expectantly at his student. "Evil? Yes? Do go on."

"Well, it seems to me that Adolph Hitler personified evil in the twentieth century," Jimmy said, eyeing his professor hopefully.

Marshfield's eyes widened. "Hitler? Yes, pray continue."

"Well, he started out tame enough. He was just an Austrian painter who couldn't sell his stuff. Then he was exposed to the horrors of war as an enlisted man on the Western Front and had to come home to a defeated country. The next thing you know, he's got the Luftwaffe bombing the stuffing out of London." Jimmy paused, knowing he need go no further.

Off to the left an A-4E Skyhawk cleared the runway at Naval Air Station Glenview. Marshfield watched it disappear into the sun and shook his head. "Yes, but good old Stuffy knocked the stuffing out of

Kesselring and Goering in the skies over London." His eyes misted over. "It was our finest hour!"

"Who's Stuffy, Doctor Marshfield?"

"Air Chief Marshal Sir Hugh Dowding, known to King and country as 'Stuffy.' I was a young assistant vicar at St. Benet's in Blackfriars trying to teach those infernal Welshmen the King's English and religion. Did you know St. Benet's was designed by Christopher Wren?"

"No."

"Yes, it's a beautiful church. Marvelous. On Upper Thames Street — if you know London."

"Unfortunately, I've never been there."

"Pity. Well, you must get there one day. Our Catholic brethren can blither on all they want about the splendors of Rome, but any Anglican worth his salt has spent some time in London discovering where true Christendom was forged between the anvil of Catholicism and the hammer of Reformation."

"And the result was the best of both worlds — the Church of England which spread throughout the world as the Anglican Communion, of which the Protestant Episcopal Church of the U.S. of A. is a part. Catholicism without popery and Reformation with comfort and joy." Jimmy had stayed awake in enough classes to remember his lines.

"Good lad. The Church of England, of course. Christianity the way Christ meant it to be. Well, do go on," Marshfield said, remembering why he had invited young Mr. Clarke along for the ride.

"Yes, of course. But before I do, weren't you going to tell me about Stuffy Dowding? I think you were going to make a point relevant to my point about Hitler and evil. The London Blitz. September, ummmm . . ."

"September 15th, 1940. 'Never have so many owed so much to so few.'" His eyes misted over again, making him miss a red light. Realizing his mistake, he stopped halfway through the intersection. A housewife turned up behind them in a Fairlane and hit her horn. "Good heavens," Marshfield exclaimed, "I do believe the woman's quite mad."

"Maybe you should keep going, Doctor Marshfield," Jimmy said.

"Really? Do you think so?" He seemed quite content to stay were he was, horn or no horn.

"Yes, I think it would be a good idea," Jimmy said as calmly as he could.

He nodded and continued driving. The housewife stopped honking. "Lovely, lovely. Now, then, where were we? Your term examination, I do believe."

"Ah, we were discussing evil in the twentieth century, and I brought up the bit about Adolph Hitler and the Battle of Britain, and you were telling me about Stuffy Dowding."

"Of course. Good old Stuffy. Should make that man a saint, they should. Of course, the old pope wouldn't think of making a Protestant a saint. Much less a proper Englishman. Anyway, it was September 15, 1940. A fine, clear autumn day. Jerry had been pasting us every night for months, but the lads in the fire brigades were always there to quell the fires. It had gotten so that sleeping in the underground was second nature to us. We could hear the bombing, of course, we could feel it, but we were safe, and we had steeled ourselves to meet the Hun when he landed.

"But September 15 was different because that was the day fat old Goering ordered an enormous daylight raid against London. He wanted to show his boss, Hitler, that the Luftwaffe was doing a proper job of it before the Jerries launched their invasion." Marshfield was in stride now. "Well, I tell you, young sir, it was our finest hour! Our finest hour! We could see the dogfights from Blackfriars and every time a Jerry got it there was a great cheer."

Marshfield's foot palpitated on the gas pedal, and the mist in his eyes became a downpour of tears. "Did I ever tell you about the poor Jerries who had to bail out over Soho?" he said, his voice now a hoarse whisper.

Of course he had, hundreds of times, but it would fill out the remaining miles.

"No, Doctor Marshfield, I don't think you've ever told me that one."

"Yes, well, Jerry was giving the East End a real pounding. We could see the bombs hitting from where we stood just outside the Blackfriars underground. But our lads were up there in their Spitfires and Hurricanes giving it right back, and they got a Flying Pencil that was a type of Jerry bomber — just over the river.

"We could see it burst into flames and then two Jerries bailed out. But the wind carried them right into the middle of Soho. If it had brought them our way, I expect we would have delivered them to the authorities."

"What happened to them?"

"Well, like I said, the East End had been getting a thorough pasting. The people were bloody furious. So when they saw these two Jerries drifting their way, they got their kitchen knives and cut them to pieces before their feet touched British soil."

"I hate to interrupt, Doctor Marshfield, but I think that this is it," Jimmy said, pointing to an enormous factory sprawled along a railroad siding.

"So it is." Marshfield's eyes were all aglow as he motored along the long service drive. "Modern industry—what a delightful horror. The mass production of our every need. Food, toilet paper, hot dogs—how much longer before they mass produce our thoughts, I wonder?"

"They already do—it's called NBC, ABC, and CBS."

"Touche. Well, shall we make our presence known to these merchants of mass production?"

"Why not?"

Marshfield found a parking space near the front office, and they were soon confronted by a perky young woman from the customer relations office.

"Welcome to the Leslie Sarah Corporation," she said, extending her hand. "I'm Bonnie Morgan, and I'll be your guide this morning. I think some of the others are already here, Reverend."

"That's 'Father,' not 'Reverend,'" Bob Edwards said, getting up from a green couch. "He's an Episcopal priest. Episcopal priests are properly addressed as 'Father.'"

"Not where I come from," Terry Groves said. "Call him 'Reverend Doctor' or 'Reverend Mister.' But not Father. Says right in Matthew, or is it Mark, anyway it says in the bible that you should call no man father but God."

"Terry, that's not what that really means. If you had paid more attention in Father Kemmerley's biblical languages class, you would know that . . ."

"Where I'm from, we call our priests by their first names. Why put them on pedestals?" Lance Gordon said.

Jimmy didn't care if his parishioners called him Brother Jimmy,
or Jive-Ass Jimmy, or Pope James the Fart.

Bruce MacKenzie insisted that Marshfield be addressed as
"'Mister Marshfield.' After all, we're Protestants. So let's talk like
Protestants."

"Speak for yourself, Brother MacKenzie. We Anglo-Catholics
refer to our priests as 'Father,'" Bob Edwards said.

A lapsed Baptist, Bonnie Morgan was baffled. "Well, anyway, uh,
ah . . ."

"Call me 'Vicar' my dear. Always liked being called 'Vicar.'
Rather suits me, don't you think?" Marshfield said, swelling his
chest.

"Yes," she said, smiling. "Yes, it does, Vicar. Well, if everyone is
here, perhaps we can begin our tour."

"Everyone's here, Father Marshfield," said Bob Edwards.

"That's right, Reverend Doctor Marshfield, everyone's here,"
Terry Groves added.

"Yeah, Vicar Marshfield," Jimmy added, "we're all ashore that's
goin' ashore."

"Very well." Bonnie Morgan said, suddenly a little less pert.
"Before we begin, you'll all have to put these on. We wouldn't want
to find hair in our Leslie Sarah products now, would we?" She
motioned, and a flunky fetched two handfuls of green hairnets. As
everyone was gamely donning their covers, she noticed Bruce
MacKenzie's beard and said, "You'll have to wear a cover on that."

The flunky got one and handed it to Bruce, who eyed the dorky
thing with utter contempt. Jimmy tried like hell not to laugh but
ended up blowing air through his eyes and nose.

"Oh shut up," Bruce said, donning the mask. Bruce had trouble
tying the strings behind his head and had to ask Jimmy for help. It
was the first time he had asked his roommate for anything since the
trip, three weeks ago.

"Sorry I laughed, Bruce. There, how's that?"

Bruce touched the damn thing uncertainly. "I look ridiculous,
don't I?"

"Well . . ."

"Fuck you," Bruce whispered, loud enough for the blushing
Bonnie Morgan to hear.

"Perhaps we should begin our tour. If you'll all follow me through this door, we'll start with our mixing room. This is where . . ."

You pass your test?" Bruce said as they followed the blithering blonde.

"Yeah," Jimmy said, glad to be speaking with Bruce again. "I got the old guy off on one of his 'finest hour' raps, and he babbled all the way here. Hey, man, I don't suppose I could get a lift back?"

Bruce eyed his erstwhile roommate suspiciously. "What's wrong, Jill not putting out for you?"

"What the hell's that supposed to mean? All I asked for was a ride back."

"I'm a light sleeper, Clarke. That a big enough clue?"

Bonnie Morgan was boring them with a monotonous monologue about "secret formulas, special ingredients, and highly trained and motivated personnel." The latter looked like they'd eviscerate you for a shot of tequila and a hot tortilla.

"That's all well and good, Miss Morgan," Marshfield said, butting in, "but let us consider the meaning of this carefully constructed chaos. Giant cookie mixes. Rivers of milk and mountains of chocolate chips. It weakens the mind to consider how much we've bartered away in the name of instant gratification.

"We've surrendered our dignity and freedom just so we can pop off to the convenience shop and get a tin of your miserable little biscuits. Where is the spirit of enterprise and human dignity in that?"

He paced to and fro with his arms behind his back. "I tell you, we're becoming a race of automatons. Lives without meaning, serving the endlessly clanking and clattering machinery of modern industry. Man in the modern age. Carried from the cradle to the grave on a continuous assembly line and fattened and fiddled with along the way by great greedy corporations like Leslie Sarah. No salvation — no hope — no joy. Nothing left to live for."

He shook his head, saddened by his private vision of gloom. "Ah, to be back in 1940. That was a year when men were men, and men called on a living God for deliverance."

Bonnie Morgan giggled girlishly and stopped talking. Cub Scouts she could handle, but this guy was too much. A pair of Mexican ladies in pink stretch pants looked up from the gops of goo rolling by their station on the way to a giant oven.

One of them pointed at Marshfield, and said, "El gringo gordo es loco en cabeza."

They laughed until Bonnie Morgan looked their way and threatened with her suddenly sinister eyes to have them deported.

"So you're a light sleeper," Jimmy whispered to Bruce. "What's that supposed to mean?"

"You gonna put the moves on her when K.C. splits?" Bruce said.

"K.C. split? What are you talkin' about? I never heard anything about K.C. splittin'. You're crazy."

"Yeah, well, I ran into him the other day on campus, and he said he got a job with some paper in Jackson, Mississippi. Can you believe it? He's leavin' after finals."

This was a complete surprise. Jimmy had figured K.C. for a job with a Chicago paper. Or he'd stick around Northwestern and get a masters in journalism. The asshole had number 315 in the draft lottery, so what did he have to worry about? Besides, he loved Jill too much to split like this.

Unless . . .

"He say anything about Jill goin' with him?"

"No. From what I heard, she's gonna stay here and get her masters in philosophy. Now's your big chance, lover boy. Maybe this time you can use a bed instead of a toilet," Bruce said, his voice quick and vicious.

"Maybe next time you and Bobby Boswell can use a bed instead of the floor. Anyway, I don't know what you're talking about. Come on, they're moving," Jimmy said, anxious to end this conversation.

"Bullshit, you don't know what I'm talking about. Sounded like you two were havin' some good lovin' that night. How'd you do it, anyway? You must be a contortionist, you savage."

"Hey, you gonna do CPE this summer?"

"What's the matter, lover boy? You don't want to tell your queer old roommate about how you screwed your buddy's girlfriend on a toilet while he was asleep in the next room?"

"Look, I don't want to talk about it. Okay?"

"Sure, Jimmy. Sure. And no, I'm not gonna do CPE this summer. Some of us have to work our way through school. Besides, how can you afford to do CPE? You've got to pay your old man for the accident."

"My mother took care of it. She sold some of her stock. She said her grandfather had left it to her for emergencies," Jimmy said.

What he wasn't willing to say was that Mike Harper, the prick, still expected him to pay back the $456 he had "borrowed" from the pop machine.

"And I start working at the library tonight, so I should be okay. Plus, I'll still be at St. Augustine's, so . . ."

"Jimmy, I hate to be the prick in your pink balloon, but they won't let you work while you're doing CPE because you have to be on call all the time. Just like doctors. Didn't they tell you that?"

"I don't remember. But I'm sure I can work something out."

"I wouldn't count on it. They take it pretty seriously. They like to pretend you're in medical school. Run you ragged, and all that shit. And second, the refectory's gonna be closed for the summer which means you're gonna have to eat off campus."

"You're kidding!"

"I'll spot you a coupla bucks until payday."

"Hey, thanks."

Bonnie Morgan ended her tour and welcomed them all to visit the outlet store where Leslie Sarah unloaded her scratched and dented merchandise.

Marshfield became a man possessed. He battled plump suburban matrons for king-sized containers of Heat 'n' Serve lasagna, German chocolate cake, and anything else Leslie Sarah had misprinted, mislabelled, or dented. They were practically giving the stuff away, and the old greedy glutton was not about to pass up a bargain. He had filled up three shopping carts when he was through, and the class formed a human chain to help him load it all into his car.

"A's for everyone if you help me unload this into the deep freezer when we get back," he said cheerfully. "I guess you'll have to get a lift from someone else, Mr. Clarke. Seems like I've gone and filled up the front seat with coffee cakes."

"No problem, Vicar. See you back at the seminary."

Bruce offered Jimmy a joint as they pulled out of the parking lot. It was dynamite reefer, and they were blasted when they got back. They gladly helped Marshfield unload his treasures, and Jimmy put his lasagna and German chocolate cake in the refectory refrigerator.

"God," he said to Bruce, as they walked back to their suite, "I could've saved myself a lotta bullshittin' if I knew that's all it took to pass this course."

"Spend a little time around here, and you find out all kinds of wondrous things. Wanna smoke some more reefer?"

"Yeah, definitely." Jimmy was still antsy about money and figured the dope would put his mind at rest.

They eagerly entered their dimly lighted alcove and were about to open their outer door when a figure stepped out of the shadows and said, "Can you dig, you like a pig, but you ain't got no gun."

It was Raymond.

And he was moving in for a while.

Chapter Thirty-Four

Jimmy started his library job the next day.

He spent the beginning of the four-hour shift worrying about Raymond. Raymond had appeared out of nowhere last night with some cock-and-bull story about being run out of his "crib" by his old lady and half the East Side Disciples. Now he was sleeping on Jimmy's couch.

But I can't worry about that now, Jimmy thought. I've got to worry about library books.

He wondered what it would be like to spend his whole life working in a library. Almost as bad as a lifetime career at the Leslie Sarah factory, he decided.

He was assigned to the core collection where his duties were to shelve borrowed books and to guard the non-circulating collection. He was too stoned to read and too tired to stay awake for long periods.

Thus, he was slumped over the desk by the electronic sentinel when a shattering buzzer sounded.

Jimmy awakened with a start, dribbling spittle on his shirt and the desk. A curly haired Northwestern undergrad stood trapped by the flimsy metal gate.

"You can't take that book out of here. This is a closed section," Jimmy said, rubbing his eyes and mouth.

The student sneered and turned to a friend who had already passed through the turnstile. "Here, catch," he said, tossing the hefty history text to his mate. He leapfrogged the turnstile, and the two of them were gone before Jimmy could focus his eyes. Miss Whatever-Her-Name-Was had carefully explained what to do in such an emergency, but he was damned if he could remember.

So he ran after the two thieves, shouting, "Stop! Come back here!"

They knew the labyrinthine university library better than he and escaped easily. Jimmy gave up at the main check-out desk and panted for breath.

"Did you see two guys with a red history book?" he asked the bored but beautiful coed stationed there.

"No," she said, returning to Bernard Malamud's latest, THE TENANTS. "Well, they stole a book from the core collection. We've got to stop them."

"Do you work there?" She shifted her gum to the left. It clicked annoyingly as she spoke.

"Yeah."

"Then what are you doing here? You're not supposed to leave your post. They could be stealing everything in sight while you're gone. Didn't you call security? That's what you're supposed to do."

She stared disdainfully at the drool on his shirt.

"Well, what am I supposed to do? This is my first night. Jesus, they're gonna fire me for sure."

"Don't have a heart attack, man," she said. "Go back to the core collection, and I'll call security. What'd they look like?"

"Well, one guy had dark curly hair, and the other guy had dark curly hair, and they were both wearing army jackets and blue jeans. Faded blue jeans."

"Terrific. That narrows it down to about half the student body. Look, man, just take it easy, okay? Whatever you're on is sure fucking you up."

"On? I'm not on anything. What makes you think I'm on something?"

"Must be my imagination. Look, just go back to your station, and I'll call security. All right?"

Jimmy took a deep breath. "Okay. Hey, I just read that book. Isn't it about two writers — one black and one Jewish — and they live together in . . ."

". . . a tenement in New York. Thanks for telling me. I never woulda known." She opened it and started reading.

"Say, what's your name?"

"Just leave, okay?"

"Okay."

When Jimmy got back to the core collection, the books that had been on the return cart were gone. He remembered a few titles and searched the circular stacks for them. Not there. Nor were lots of other books. The few remaining students snickered when he asked what had happened.

Jimmy admitted this further loss of books to the security man who said he'd have to call the core curator, Miss Dorothy Fielding.

She demanded to speak with Jimmy. He haltingly explained what happened. "When I asked the seminary if they could recommend some reliable students, I believed them. They always have in the past. Obviously they've lowered their standards. Well, Mr. Clarke, do you have anything to say for yourself?"

"I'm really sorry. I didn't get enough sleep last night, and . . ."

"And you left 44,000 irreplaceable books unattended. The library closes in half an hour. Do you think you can stay awake that long?"

"Sure, but . . ."

"I want to see you in my office tomorrow morning at 9 o'clock sharp. Do you understand?"

"Yes, Miss Feeling."

"Fielding."

"Yes, Miss Fielding. I'll be there."

"Very well. I'll see you in the morning. And don't fall asleep again."

Jimmy was too upset to fall asleep again. He promptly put away each book as it was left on the return cart and eyed each student with eager suspicion. He prowled the stacks on the balls of his feet, ready to karate-chop anyone caught tampering with the metal plates affixed to the bottom of each book. The last hour passed without incident and he was certain as he left that he could sweet-talk Miss Fielding the following morning.

Jimmy just didn't know what he'd do without the income. They were bombing the hell out of North Vietnam, but Ho's minions just didn't know when to quit.

Jimmy was entertaining all sorts of morose thoughts when he started across the Gatesbury campus. Passing by the married student apartments, he saw Mike Harper getting out of his car and tried to duck out of the light but it was too late.

"Hey, pardner," Mike said.

"Hey, Mike, how's it goin'?"

"Terrific. How's by you?"

Jimmy sniffed, wondering what Harper had had to drink. But there wasn't the faintest trace of alcohol, and Mike's face and eyes were radiant in the sodium-vapor light. The last thing Jimmy wanted to talk about was the $456 he owed the seminary, so he smiled and said, "You still goin' to those AA meetings?"

"Yeah, still goin'. In fact, I just came from one."

Jimmy stared at his feet. "Yeah, well, I guess it takes a while to recover, huh?"

"Jimmy, I'll be recovering until the day I die. And, God willing, I'll be going to THOSE meetings until the day I die."

"You're not gonna have another drink for the rest of your life? Not one? I thought the purpose of AA was to dry you out and then teach you how to control your drinking."

Mike Harper laughed until he nearly cried. "How would you like to go to a meeting with me? I go to an open meeting on Sunday afternoon. You wouldn't have to say a word. Just come and see what goes on."

"Hey, no offense, but not everybody's got a drinking problem. Okay?"

"Sure. But just let me know if you ever change your mind." Harper turned for his apartment. A thought struck him, and he turned back to Jimmy. "By the way, you only owe the seminary $228."

"What?!?"

"I figured I was as much a party to it as you were since I knew it was goin' on and let you get away with it. Hell, I drank up a lot of that money, too. You think you can handle that over the summer?"

"Sure, Mike. I just started workin' at the Northwestern Library tonight, so I should be able to pay it off by the end of summer, if not sooner. Hey, this calls for a — sorry, Mike."

"It's okay, Jimmy. Have a drink for me. Talk to you later."

Jimmy was practically floating when he walked into his suite. "Bruce? Raymond? You're not gonna believe what happened to me tonight. You're not gonna fuckin' believe it. Man, this calls for a party." Jimmy put Jim Morrison on Bruce's turntable and looked for a joint. He found a fat roach in the ashtray and lighted it. "Hey, where are you guys? Come on, let's party."

He went to Bruce's room and rapped on the door. "Hey, Bruce, wake up. It's party time." He turned the knob, but the door was locked. "Bruce, you asleep? Come on, wake up. I gotta tell you about how they ripped off half the library while I was passed out."

There was a shuffling noise, then Bruce whispered through the door, "I'm not coming out until you get rid of that fucking Mau Mau."

"What?"

"You heard what I said. Either he leaves, or I leave."

"Bruce, he just needs a place for a coupla nights. Until he gets his act together. What happened?" Jimmy turned the knob again.

"Either he goes, or I go," Bruce said.

"But you ARE goin'. . . you start house-sitting next week."

"I'll leave tonight if you don't get rid of that slimy African bastard."

"Bruce, would you come out here? What the hell happened?"

"Get rid of him, Jimmy, or I leave. Tonight."

Jimmy slapped his forehead. "Aye, aye." He went to his room and found that door was also locked. "Great. Raymond? You in there, Raymond?"

"That you, my man?"

"No, it's the fuckin' tooth fairy. Yeah, it's me. Open the door, would you, Raymond?"

"That sissy wid you, man?" Raymond asked.

"No, he locked himself in his room. The coast is clear."

Jimmy took a final toke from the roach and ground it out in the ashtray. Jimmy was ready for a party, not a diplomatic incident. "Would you please come out of there?"

Raymond Kennedy opened the door a crack. Seeing that Jimmy was alone, he pulled him into the bedroom. Then he locked the door and launched into it. "That damn sissy tried to fuck me, man. After you went to your job, we smoked some reefer and had us a nice friendly talk about jazz and lots of good shit. I figured he's a straight dude the way he's rappin'. I mean, he's my man's roommate, so he got to be cool, can you dig?"

"Yeah."

"So, I started gettin' sleepy. Man, after all the shit I been through the last coupla days, I needed to nod out. That's cool with your man, Bruce. He says he got things to do, so he leaves me alone while I crash out on the couch out there. Pretty soon I'm sleepin' like there ain't no tommorrow, and I feel some hands all over me. Like big ugly spiders. At first I think it's some kind of crazy-ass dream, but then I realize it ain't no dream. Bruce is all hot for some black meat and he's grabbin' for my tool. I open my eyes and he's standin' there buck naked. Can you dig?"

Jimmy shook his head. "Yeah, I can dig."

"No offense, man, but you got you' self one fruitcake-ass roommate."

"Funny how they can fool you, huh?"

"Damn!"

"Well, you still wanna crash here for a couple nights?"

"Man, I ain't got no other place to go. My old lady'll shoot my black ass if I go back to the crib, and them mother-fuckin' Disciples got a hard-on for me. No way Raymond Kennedy goin' back to the 'hood. Not for a long time. Besides, I like it up here."

"It is kinda nice, isn't it?"

"Yeah," Raymond said, raising his voice, "except for them damn sissies that try to butt-fuck a man while he's sleepin'."

"That's because brown sugar tastes so good," Bruce taunted from behind his locked door.

Raymond bristled and went for the door. Jimmy caught his arm. "Hey, let's blow this pop stand. How about hittin' some bars on Howard Street with a buddy of mine? I bet he's got some good reefer, too. Man, I feel like partyin'. I had a crazy night at that fuckin' library. I gotta tell you about it, but first I need some drinks."

"Sure, man. I can dig. Let's party."

"I'm just gonna make a quick phone call. Wait here, okay?"

"Man, I ain't goin' out there with that damn faggot waitin' for me."

Jimmy took a deep breath and headed for the empty third bedroom where they kept the phone.

Bruce heard him and said, "Is he leaving?"

"No. We're going out for some drinks. He's stayin' here tonight because I promised him he could. I don't suppose you'd be willing to change your mind and . . ."

"Jesus, Jimmy. Always gotta be everybody's pal, don't you? Don't bring him back, Jimmy, or we're through."

"What do you mean, WE?"

"You know what I mean."

"No, I don't know what you mean. We're roommates, and that's it."

"Is it?"

"Fuck you."

"Anytime."

Jimmy gave up in frustration and phoned K.C.

Jill answered. She had been cramming for a philosophy final.

"Hi," she said, embarrassed.

"Hi, Jill. How you doin'?"

"I'll be a lot better when these finals are over. I've got two tomorrow. God, what a bummer. How about you?"

"Okay. I aced a theology final." Jimmy didn't want to think about the rest.

"Well, listen, you probably want to talk to K.C. I've got to get back to the books."

"Sure. Good talkin' to you, Jill. Maybe I'll see you later. Think K.C. wants to go out and have a few beers? I've got a buddy up from the South Side and I figured K.C.'d get a kick out of meeting him. Course, you're welcome to come along too."

"Jimmy, I've got to study. I haven't opened a book all quarter. I'll get K.C. Talk to you later."

Jimmy heard her call K.C. and then plead with him not to go out. She said something about it being their anniversary and K.C. promising to be with her.

K.C. raised his voice, and the phone hit the floor. There were some harsh words and then K.C. was on the phone, all sweetness and life. "Jimmy! How the hell are ya?"

"Great, K.C. Hey, I was just tellin' Jill: I got this buddy up from the South Side and . . ."

"Yeah, so she said. What part of the South Side, man? It's a big place."

"Sixty-third and Cottage. Around there. You know where that is?"

"Sixty-third and Cottage?!? How the hell you know somebody from around there?"

"It's a long story, K.C. We'll pick you up in five minutes, and Raymond can tell you all about it."

"The dude's name is Raymond?"

"Yeah, Raymond Kennedy. He had to split because the Disciples were on his case."

Jill said something, and K.C. muffled the phone and replied sharply. Jimmy was sure he heard him say "bitch" several times.

"No problem, man. I'll be waiting out in front. Hey, I'm busted, so bring some money."

"I can't do that anymore. That goody-two-shoes Harper is on my case about payin' back what I ripped off. Can you believe it?"

"Bummer, man. Isn't that the dude who pimped out on our trip because his old lady made him go to AA or somethin'?"

"Yeah, that's the dude."

"He still goin' to that bullshit?"

"Yeah, as a matter of fact I ran into him tonight. Asshole tried to get me to go to one of those fuckin' meetings."

"Fuck him."

"That's what I say. So anyway, I can't rip off the Coke machine anymore. And I only got enough money for me."

"You want me to go drinkin' with you, you better get some cash, man. I'm leavin' for Jackson, Mississippi in a week, and I got to save what I got for movin' all that shit."

"Yeah, I heard you got a job down there. That's terrific."

"Yeah, I'll tell you about it when you get here. Got any reefer you can bring?"

"I'll see what I can scrounge up."

"See you in five minutes."

It was no use asking Raymond since he was nearly broke, so Jimmy rapped on Bruce's door and asked to borrow $10.

Bruce didn't open the door. "What's it worth to you?" he yelled through the wood.

"I just want to borrow $10, that's all. I'll pay you back as soon as I get paid."

"No way, Jose. I'll GIVE you all you want if you give me what I want."

"Bruce, just lend me ten bucks, all right?"

"You know the terms, sweetheart."

Jimmy threw up his arms, and then he remembered that Bruce had left his jacket in the sitting room. He rifled it and found his roommate's wallet. "Come on, Raymond, let's go party," he said, stuffing two twenty-dollar bills in his pocket.

K.C, of course, wasn't waiting out front, so Jimmy left Raymond in his big black Electra and knocked on the door.

Jill answered with a shy smile.

Jimmy looked at Jill and she looked away. Then she looked at him, and he looked away.

K.C. was in the next room cajoling some free joints from Feuerstein.

"You guys aren't gonna be real late, are you?" Jill said. Her eyes were red.

Jimmy's heart went out to her. He wished they were alone together somewhere far away and safe. No K.C, no Raymond, no Bruce, no draft, no finals — no Miss Fielding. Just the two of them, lots of dynamite dope, a decent stereo, and a warm waterbed.

"Nah, we're just goin' out for a coupla beers. Celebrate the end of the quarter and all. Sure you don't want to come?"

Jill bit her lip. "Actually, I was hoping Kevin and I would be together tonight. We've been living together two years today. It's kinda special. You know?"

"I understand. Hey, K.C, why don't we make it another night? Raymond'll be around for a while. We can catch up with you tomorrow or something."

"Fuck no," K.C. said, coming to the door with two freshly rolled joints in his hand. "We're partying tonight. Ain't that right, honey?" He squeezed her left breast.

Jimmy looked away.

Jill tried to wriggle out of K.C.'s love lock. "Kevin, I wish you'd stay home tonight."

"Fuck you," K.C. said, grabbing her ass. "I'm not gonna sit around and watch you study all night. That sucks. We'll have our anniversary fuck when I get home." He grabbed her breast again and gave her a big slurpy kiss. "Mmmm, me Tarzan, you Jane," he said.

Jill backed into the apartment. She choked back her tears and pleaded softly for K.C. to come back at a decent hour.

"I'll come home when I feel like comin' home. Come on, Jimmy, let's get the fuck out of here. This fuckin' women's lib bullshit's drivin' me nuts."

Jimmy swallowed hard, glanced quickly at Jill, and said, "Okay, let's go."

Chapter Thirty-Five

K.C. was in love with Raymond Kennedy before Jimmy finished the introductions.

Jimmy slumped in the big backseat as K.C. fired up a joint, speed-rapped with Raymond, and directed him to the "El Tap," so named for its proximity to the Howard elevated line.

It was dark, damp, smelled of urine and stale beer, and was fully integrated with black Chicago Transit Authority motormen and conductors, Mexican factory workers, and hillbilly truck drivers. It had a worn pool table with a broken Old Style beer lamp over it. It was all the bar they wanted and more.

Taking one of Jimmy's purloined twenties, K.C. procured a bottle of tequila, a sliced lemon, and a shaker of salt. "We're gonna drink Mexican-style," he announced. "You ever drink Mexican-style, my man?"

"Yeah, you ever drink Korean-style?" Raymond said, savoring his tequila.

"Shit, no. Hey, you're supposed to put some salt on your hand, like this, lick it off, like this, take a bite out of the lemon, like this, and then do a shot of tequila," K.C. said.

"Why waste all that time, man? Besides, I ain't hungry."

Jimmy laughed and chugged his shot minus the salt and lemon. "Yeah, K.C, why waste time?"

K.C. stuck to his ritual until they were halfway through the bottle. By then he was so blasted he threw the lemon over his shoulder, shook the salt in his mouth, and spilled most of the shot on his shirt.

Raymond had made the mistake of admitting that he didn't particularly like North Koreans, having nearly been incinerated by their phosphorus artillery shells at Taejon.

Jimmy knew nothing of the Korean War and remained silent as K.C. questioned MacArthur's every move.

"MacArthur didn't ask for my advice, man. And if I had to give it, I woulda said, 'General, let's get our black and white asses outta this damn icebox and let these gooks fight for it all by theyself.' It's theirs. Just like Vietnam. Same damn thing. We ain't got no business tellin' them peoples how to run they country. Unless we want to take it over and turn it into the 51st State or somethin', we should get our ass outta there."

"That's just the problem with Korea and Vietnam. The object is victory over those commie scumbags," K.C. said, pouring himself another shot. "Truman shoulda let MacArthur keep right on goin' when he got to the Yalu. Same thing in Vietnam, man. I heard the Nationalists on Taiwan wanna go over there and head north until they hit Peking. Let 'em hang that fat old Mao by his little yellow balls. They'd chew up them fuckin' commies. Just like Truman shoulda let Patton go all the way to Moscow. Fuckin' LBJ didn't have no balls. Just that stupid scar. And Nixon and Kissinger are a coupla pussies."

Raymond's face dropped. "Don't be bad-mouthin' my man LBJ. Dude done all right for black people, man."

Seeing his chance to get back in the conversation, Jimmy said, "Hey, Raymond, just what the hell did happen that night we were together on the South Side? Man, I just barely remember rappin' with some chick named Pearl after those cops hassled us."

Raymond rolled his eyes and took another shot of tequila. "Man, you is damn lucky you is alive. We was in the Unique Dude's Club on 43rd Street. You don't remember that, man?"

"Just barely."

"Man, you musta been in a black-out, 'cause you was the life of the party. Hell, they was callin' you the 'Mayor of Woodlawn.' You don't remember gettin' on that table and yellin' 'I'm an Irish jig', and then dancin' your fool head off?"

Jimmy broke into a cold sweat as K.C. gave him a look of profound admiration. "I said that?"

"Yeah. You said a lot of crazy shit that night. And then you put this heavy rap on Pearl D. while her old man's standin' right there."

"Damn," K.C. said, clapping Jimmy on the back. "You're crazier than I thought you were, brother. That calls for another bottle of tequila." K.C. took Jimmy's change and went to get it.

Raymond patiently reconstructed the events of that February night, frequently shaking his head, saying, "Man, I can't believe you don't remember. You really musta been wasted." The upshot of it all was that Jimmy had shot his mouth off at every turn, and every time Raymond used his cunning and tact to save his white ass.

"Why'd you stand up for me, Raymond?" Jimmy was pretty drunk now and wanted to know before he lost too many more brain cells.

Raymond shrugged. K.C. was coming back with the bottle, but with no lemon or salt. "I don't know, man. I like you — ain't that good enough?"

Jimmy had never had such a friend. "Well, how'd you save me from Pearl's old man?"

"Well, I just told the dude that you just got outta Manteno State on a weekend pass, and that you be in there for mass murderin' big black niggers, and that you really part Viet Cong, you know 'cause you eyes get all squinty when you drunk — like they is now, and everybody start thinkin' maybe old Raymond ain't just bullshittin', an' I got your white ass outta there before anybody could pull a splive."

K.C. took a swig from the bottle and passed it to Jimmy who did likewise.

Raymond followed suit, and they were halfway through it in no time.

"What happened at the end?" Jimmy slurred, his mind going fast.

Raymond was getting a might foggy himself and had to recollect a moment. "Yeah, now it's comin' back. We had gone to my crib, and me and my old lady had one of our usual fights — 'Raymond, why don't you get a job? Raymond, what you bringin' some white boy here for? You wanna get us all killed? You crazy nigger.' Well, I had enough of that old shit, so we split. We went over to the Point for a while and listened to them fog horns out on the lake and rapped about life and shit. You remember any of that?"

Jimmy shook his head. From Raymond's look of disappointment, he wished he could.

"Well, we drank up all our wine, so . . ."

"Wine? We were drinkin' wine?"

"Man, there wasn't nuthin' we wasn't drinkin' that night. At that point, we was workin' on a pint of MD 20/20. You wuz guzzlin' that nasty shit like it was soda pop."

"It stands for Mogen David, Jimmy," K.C. explained.

"Thanks, K.C. I never woulda known. So what happened next? All I remember is a Schlitz sign and some el tracks. And somebody shootin' and then I woke up on an el train. And you were gone. Man, I thought it was all a dream or something."

"It wasn't no dream, man. That Schlitz sign was the J & L Lounge on East 63rd Street. You wanted to go in there and rap your peace and love shit to the brothers. I didn't want to stop, so you put your damn foot on the brake and went flyin' against the windshield. Don't you remember that, man?"

Jimmy touched his forehead. It felt fine now. He shrugged.

"Man, I sure remember, on account of I had to get a new windshield. Anyway, I didn't want to stop because I seen a car full of them mother-fuckin' Disciples across the street. And as much as I tried to tell them dudes and the Rangers that I didn't want none of their bullshit, they started hasslin' me. I had told you to stay in the car and keep down, but you got your white ass out and started your fool rap about the brotherhood of the bottle.

"There was about 15 of them crazy muthafuckers, and they all carryin'. All I gots is my .32 and all you gots is your big mouth and bleedin' forehead. I seen one of them dudes pull his gun on you, so I fires over his head, and you take off runnin' like there ain't no tomorrow. Nobody ever seen a white boy run like that, and when you get under the street light, they can see the blood all over your face, and they musta thought you is super honky. The white boy what won't die even after he been hit in the face with a bullet.

"While they is all standin' there with they big black mouths hangin' open, I jumps in my car and head after you, but you already up the damn el steps by then. So I got my black ass outta there and figured you was okay. That's what happened, man. Hey, this bottle's about empty. Let's drink American-style. Get some beers, man."

"Yeah," K.C. added, his eyes glazing over, "let's have some brewskies!"

Jimmy set them up with six bottles of ice-cold Old Style, and the talk turned to pool. Jimmy hadn't played the game since he was ten, and for good reason: that was when he tore the felt on Uncle Phil's new table.

"Come on," Raymond said, "we'll play three-way."

"Yeah," K.C. said, "I'll show you chumps how this game is played."

Jimmy reluctantly took a cue stick and waited his turn. He had balls one through five and drilled the ten ball on his first shot. But the cue ball bounced off the table and crashed against the bar.

The bartender, a mean old hillbilly woman with thin greasy hair, bad teeth, and a half-concealed shotgun, shook her fist and yelled, "That's enough!! Get your ass outta here. Now! All of y'all!"

K.C. smiled winningly and went to sweet-talk her.

Red-faced, Jimmy looked for the cue ball and nearly upended a stool. Its occupant, a burly truck driver, cussed him and threatened to kick his ass. Raymond took one look at the hillbilly and the man was silent. Completely.

"Hey, don't worry about it, man," Raymond said, putting his arm around Jimmy. "I tell you what, why don't you go out and crash in the car for a while. Maybe you need a little sleep, huh, man?"

Jimmy grabbed the pool table to keep the room from spinning, but it didn't work. He was a lot drunker than he wanted to be and wondered what Mike Harper would think of him now.

Fuck Mike Harper.

Jimmy took a deep breath to clear his head, but it just made him dizzier and more nauseous. He had trouble focusing his eyes, which was why Raymond looked like a big ball of fuzzy brown wool. Jimmy took another deep breath and felt the bile rise in his throat. "Maybe a little fresh air. Yeah, that's all I need. Then I'll be ready for round two."

Raymond offered his keys. "Crash in the car, man."

"Nah, I'll just take a little walk, and I'll be fine. I just took too much salt with my tequila, that's all."

"You sure, man?"

"Yeah, I'm sure," he said, lurching out of the bar. He stumbled along Howard Street seeking sobriety. He didn't find it, but he did find Raymond's car and wished he had the keys. Oh well, he thought, leaning against it. He leaned farther back and was soon sprawled across the hood, snoring loudly.

Passers-by decided it was time to move to another neighborhood.

Jimmy was drifting into the deepest levels of sleep when the spinning started anew. He dreamed that he was in a boat caught in a whirlpool. The captain said they could save themselves by jettisoning ballast. Jimmy abandoned his—all over himself and Raymond's fresh wax job. Then he fell back into a dreamless sleep.

He was quite comfortable until someone began sprinkling his face. Water ran relentlessly up his nose, into his eyes, and down his neck. He rolled over but the water persisted. His few functioning brain cells told him that he was getting wet all over.

When Jimmy finally opened his eyes, he realized he was sprawled on the hood of a big black car that was parked on a mean and dirty city street in a pouring rainstorm. He realized too, that he had been sick on himself but was relieved to see that the rain had washed most of it away. Certain only that he was about to drown, Jimmy bolted off the car and took off down the middle of Howard Street. He was looking desperately for dry land when he was blind-sided by an unseen assailant. He flailed furiously, but his attacker had him in a vise-grip.

"Hey, Jimmy, it's me, K.C. Your Alpha Chi brother, man. Where the fuck you goin', man? You look like an Apache runner or somethin'. Take it easy. It's me, K.C."

Jimmy blinked. It WAS K.C. And then there was Raymond Kennedy and some of it started to come back.

"Chicago," Jimmy muttered.

"Hey, brother Jimmy, you doin' real good, man. That's right, this be Chicago," Raymond said, smiling. "Come on, man, we goin' home."

Motorists gawked as they detoured around the threesome, but offered no assistance.

"Come on." K.C. said. "Let's split before the cops come."

"All right," Jimmy said, putting about an eighth of it together. "But get the fuck off me, man, or I'll kick your balls in."

K.C. ground his elbow into Jimmy's shoulder and then sprang to his feet. "I was just tryin' to help, Apache Runner. Calm down, man."

"You call almost breakin' my neck tryin' to help?" Jimmy tried to straighten his rumpled clothes and glared at K.C.

K.C. glared back.

Raymond stepped between them, saying, "Come on, fellas. It's been a long night. We all tired. Let's split."

Jimmy blacked-out as soon as he hit the backseat. He was awakened sometime later by a tumultuous argument in the front seat. They were northbound on Sheridan Road and were just abreast of the Northwestern campus.

K.C. shouted, "Fuck you, man. I said corner pocket. You know I said corner pocket. I got witnesses, man. Let's go back there, and I'll prove it."

Raymond responded in a hard voice, "Don't be givin' me your bullshit, man. You said side pocket, man. I know you said side pocket. Now give me that ten bucks, or I'll kick your white ass across Lake Michigan."

Jimmy rubbed his throbbing forehead. The lights were killing him. Especially the blinding lights blinking in through the rear window. He craned his neck.

"Holy shit!" he said, coming to his senses. "Raymond! K.C.—there's two cop cars back there!"

They didn't hear him and they didn't see the cop cars.

"Fuck your ten bucks," K.C. said. "Let me outta here, man. I told you to let me out back there. But you kept goin'."

"You ain't gettin' outta this car until you gimme that ten spot, man. I'll drive to the fuckin' North Pole, if I have to. You didn't win on account of you said side pocket, and you put that ball in the corner pocket. Now gimme that ten spot, man," Raymond said, matching K.C.'s stubborn anger.

"Get your fuckin' ears checked, bro'. I said corner pocket, and you know it! Now let me outta this fuckin' crate."

No way, man. Not until you pay up."

"Hey, fellas," Jimmy said, "I, ah . . ."

"If you won't stop," K.C. said, grabbing the wheel, "then I'll stop this piece of shit."

The car jerked to the right, jumped the high curb, spun its wheels in the wet parkway grass, and then shot into Northwestern's forested campus, crushing a squirrel and ramming an oak tree. Half of the 90-man Evanston Police Department converged on the car and bathed it in harsh searchlighting.

The sergeant-in-charge deployed his forces, checked his own 357, put the loudspeaker to his lips, and said, "You are completely surrounded. Leave the car one at a time with your hands above your head. I repeat, you are completely surrounded. Leave the car . . ."

Chapter Thirty-Six

"Yeah, baby," K.C. said into the phone, "fifty bucks in cash. The bond is $500, but you only have to pay ten percent to get out.

"Yeah.

"Tell Feuerstein I'll pay him back as soon as I can.

"Yeah. I love you too.

"Nmmm huh.

"Yeah, as soon as I get back. No, I didn't forget. As soon as I get home."

K.C. cradled the phone and smiled at Jimmy. "Nothin' like a good woman, huh, Apache Runner. Bet you wish you had one right now."

"Bruce'll bail me out. You'll see."

"Like I said, nothin' like a good woman."

Jimmy took a deep breath and held it until K.C. returned to the holding cell. Then he called Bruce and exhaled as the phone rang repeatedly. He was about to give up when a sleepy voice answered: "Who the hell is it?!?"

"It's me—Jimmy. Bruce, I've got a little problem, and I . . ."

"And you called me in the middle of the night to save your ass. What time is it, anyway?"

"About three." It was closer to four.

Bruce rubbed the sleep out of his face. "Shit. I've got to be the minister for morning prayer at 7. Of course, you wouldn't know about that since you seem to be allergic to the chapel. Well, what the hell do you want from me? What have you done this time? Are you in a hospital or a whorehouse? Or a funeral home? That's it, you just chopped up half of Evanston, and the cops shot you, and you're about to be embalmed, but you can't pay the undertaker." Bruce laughed in spite of himself.

"Nothing like that, Bruce. We just had a little run-in with the police on our way back from the bars. Nothing serious. In fact, they'll let us go if I just pay a little money for a bond or bail or something. I don't understand all this legal shit, but it's no big deal, Bruce. I just need . . ."

"You just need your faithful old roommate to come down to the police station in the wee hours of the morning and bail you out. How much do I have to pay to get the pleasure of your company?"

"Ah, fifty bucks."

"Just a minute. Let me go see if I have that much."

"Bruce, wait. I took $40 out of your wallet before I left, and . . ."

"You what?!?"

"Well, you know. I wanted to go drinkin', and you wouldn't give me any money, so I just helped myself."

"You ripped me off, and now you want me to come down there and bail you out?"

"Yeah, that's about the size of it."

"What do I get for all this? What do I get for $90 — assuming, of course, I have another $50 to my name after you and your soul brother got through with my wallet?"

"He didn't touch it."

"Likely story," Bruce said.

"Honest. He didn't."

"All right, he didn't. So what kind of return do I get on my investment?"

Jimmy leaned against the wall to keep the room from spinning. "I'll pay you back, man. You know I'm good for it. You worry too much about money. There's more to life than money, you know."

"Sure there is — too bad you have to pay for it. You're gonna pay me back — hah! They're gonna drive you to the poorhouse in a Cadillac. You know damn well you're not gonna pay me back. You're a walking disaster when it comes to money. And just about everything else for that matter."

"You gonna just let me sit here and rot in jail? They're gonna hold me 24 hours. These guys are animals — they already called me a dirty hippie."

Jimmy was most worried about Raymond who was in an abusive, sinister mood. He didn't want to be anywhere near him, much less locked in a cage with him for a day.

"You gotta help me," he pleaded.

"What's it really worth to you?"

"What do you mean?"

"You know what I mean. Well?"

Jimmy looked down the harshly lighted corridor. He could see Raymond's powerful hands clenched around the bars of the holding cell. He could well imagine those hands closing around his neck.

"Let me think about it."

"You think about it and call me back. I'm going to bed."

"No, wait — they only let me make one phone call. Now run this by me again. I'm still kind of groggy . . ."

* * *

Although he was more than 10 minutes late for his 9 o'clock meeting with Miss Dorothy Fielding, Jimmy detoured to the university center to buy a pack of breath mints. He stuffed half in his mouth and chewed furiously as he sprinted up the library steps.

"Come in," Dorothy Fielding said in a pinched little voice.

She despised tardiness and regarded it as the foremost flaw of the male sex. She herself had never missed a day of school or work and had never, repeat never, been late for an appointment. She expected the same of the rest of the world, but was coming to the sad realization that tardiness was epidemic even among young women.

When she saw what walked through her door at 9:20 that bright June morning, she went into a full body twitch. It's not enough that he's 20 minutes late, she thought, eyeing him coldly, but he reeks of alcohol, his clothes are wrinkled and dirty, his hair is greasy and unkempt, and there is some ungodly white foam coming out of his mouth. She wondered if he was rabid. The campus squirrels had been known to bite students. For good reason, she was sure.

She took a measured breath and adjusted her bifocals. "Our appointment was for 9 o'clock," she said crisply.

Jimmy assumed a penitential position before her ordered desk and tried to organize his thoughts. The hangover hadn't hit him yet; he was still drunk. So there were no thoughts to organize.

"I'm sorry I'm late." He repeated the sentence and coughed.

"I don't know where to start. I have never had any trouble with Gatesbury students. Never. And now you come along, and in one night, five valuable reference books are stolen."

"Five? He only took . . ."

"The others were spirited away while you were having your little nap. Or should I be more precise and say, while you were comatose."

"Mind if I sit down?" he said, slurring.

"If you must."

"I must." It was cool and dry in the room but Jimmy was sweating profusely.

"Are you drunk?" she said.

"Nah. I just had a few drinks with some friends last night, that's all. Look, I'm sorry about last night. I promise: it won't happen again. I've been under a lot of pressure lately, and I haven't been getting all the sleep I need, and, you know."

"No, I don't know. I know you were hired to ensure that core books are not removed from the section. I know that you were not hired to sleep on the library's furniture, on the library's time, while half the collection disappears from under your nose. And I do know that I'm docking your pay to cover the cost of the stolen books."

"Does that mean I can have my job back?"

"Yes. I called your dean and he spoke well of you. Why, I'll never know, unless he sees something in you I certainly don't. It's against my better judgment, but I am retaining you because summer is starting and good help, any help, is hard to find."

Feeling the urgent need for another bout with the bowl, Jimmy got up to go. As he did so, he felt something rumble in his rectum.

"Well, again, I'm real sorry about what happened last night, Miss Feeling."

"'Fielding.' It's on the door, it's on my desk, and I've told you ten thousand times how to say it." She pursed her lips and folded her hands. "The seminaries really must be desperate these days. They had to scrape the bottom of the barrel to come up with a reprobate like you. Of course, you seem typical of your hopelessly narcissistic generation."

"I beg your pardon?"

"Oh, quit smirking like some naughty little boy with his hand in the cookie jar." She arched her back, cocked her head, and lay into him. "Let me guess: the only reason you're in seminary is to avoid the draft. Right?"

The truth hurt, but so did Jimmy's rectum. And now something cold and gelatinous was issuing from it.

"Look, I've got to get going, okay?"

"I guessed right, didn't I? And I'd be correct in saying you were spoiled rotten as a child and have never had to grow up and fend for yourself. I'd also be correct in guessing that you are a lazy degenerate who abuses drugs, alcohol, young women, and God knows what else for your self-gratification."

Something was definitely dripping out his backside. Jimmy wanted to get to the john quick and see if he was dying of rectal cancer. Then he remembered his "deal" with Bruce.

"Who the fuck are you to criticize anybody, Miss Touchy-Feely?"

She stopped in mid-harangue, leaving the last syllable of "hedonist" isting in her teeth. "I beg your pardon?"

"I said, take your crummy little job and shove it up your ass, if you have one."

Jimmy turned on his toe and strode manfully to the men's room to tend to his plumbing.

Miss Fielding twitched for a while and suddenly realized that she, too, had to tend to her plumbing.

Chapter Thirty-Seven

The Reverend Paul H. Jordan gave great attention to his pipe. When he finally lighted the damn thing, he leaned back in his overstuffed chair and smiled thinly. "I now pronounce you a group."

Two weeks of this and Jimmy was a basket case. He looked at his reflection in the one-way observation window and wondered what Gabi Wolter, Ph.D., was writing in her notebook this time. He stared at the middle of the gold-tinted glass, willing the Teutonic twat to squirm.

Sister Cecilia, a diminutive Dominican nun from India, folded her hands and smiled sweetly. Seated on Jimmy's right, she had come to America to learn how to better minister to her endlessly suffering people. Jimmy wondered why she had bothered to come all the way to St. Mark's Medical Center when it was obvious that she was the only one in Jordan's so-called group who knew the meaning of ministry. The others were hostile incompetents.

Like Mark McGann, the know-it-all Jesuit, who was nodding his head in thoughtful agreement. Or Byron Patton, the rich twerp from Kenilworth who arrived everyday in the white 1971 Electra his parents had given him for his 23rd birthday. A Presbyterian, Byron preferred penny loafers and chino pants from L.L. Bean.

And last and least, Fred Freeman the fat Franciscan—everybody's pal and nobody's friend. Jimmy watched Fred nod in unison with McGann and Patton and wanted to throw up.

Jimmy winked at the window and yawned. He wondered if he could survive 16 more weeks of this psycho-shit. He figured he would be a lot better off looking for a job, but his advisor had urged him to stick with Clinical Pastoral Education, or CPE.

"Well," Paul Jordan said, filling the stale air with his pipe exhaust. "Any comments? Reactions?"

Mark McGann helped himself to a Marlboro from Byron's pack. "I'd feel more comfortable if Jim was more forthcoming with his feelings."

Byron was there with the assist. "It's been two weeks, Jim, and I don't feel I know you at all. You just sit there and smile and present your happy-go-lucky facade to the world. If we're a group, I don't feel you're a part of it because I have no idea who you really are."

"I agree," Fred Freeman said, nodding. "I agree."

Jimmy fidgeted and reached for Byron's Marlboros, but Patton cut him off at the pack. He had told these assholes a hundred times that he preferred to be called "Jimmy."

Jimmy settled back on the lumpy sofa and stared out the window at the endless procession of gorgeous nurses.

"How do you feel, Cecilia?" Paul Jordan asked, striking yet another match.

Sister Cecilia took a deep breath. "Please call me 'Sister Cecilia.' If the rest of you want to be on a first-name basis, that's your business." Her English was crisp and mild. "I don't know about a group. This is nothing like any group I've been in. I think our time would be better spent on our wards with our patients."

Paul Jordan showed a trace of annoyance. "You knew the structure when you accepted. Would you please focus on the present? The group. Jim's role in the group. Or lack of it." He struck another match.

Sister Cecilia squeezed Jimmy's hand. "I don't know why you all pick on Jimmy. No wonder he doesn't reveal himself. You are like hungry tigers waiting for him to come out in the open so you can pounce on him."

Mark McGann leaned forward, ready for the kill. "You going to hide behind her habit again, Jim, or are you going to defend yourself?"

Jimmy snatched one of Byron's cigarettes and lighted it with Patton's Zippo. "You're right, Mark, I'm going to let Sister Cecilia fight all my battles. Obviously, I don't have a backbone of my own, so I have to let her stand up for me."

Sister Cecilia fixed her warm brown eyes on Jimmy and smiled. "You don't need anyone to fight your battles, Jimmy."

"I know," he said. "I know." Turning to McGann, he added, "But you don't seem to think so, do you, Mark?"

"No, I don't know, Jim. It's been two weeks, and I don't know anything about you, except that you seem to enjoy the role of the silent observer, and that you are perfectly willing to have Cecilia fight your battles."

"Yeah," Byron added, "whenever we try to draw you out, you let her stand up for you."

"Yeah, yeah," Fred Freeman said.

Jimmy looked to Paul Jordan for comfort, support and/or direction and got nothing more than a vacuous look. He exhaled. They had him this time. "Well, what do you want to know?"

"Now we're getting somewhere," McGann said, rubbing his hands. "For starters, how about telling us where you're at? Or where you're coming from? What's on your mind right now?"

"Yeah," Byron and Fred chorused.

"What's on my mind right now?" Jimmy said.

"Yeah."

"Well," he said, hoping for a laugh, "I've been watching that cute little blonde number out there, and . . ."

No one bothered to look out the window; no one laughed.

"Well, in all honesty, I'd have to say that the foremost thing on my mind right now, other than nurses, is money. Or lack of it."

"Ah," McGann said, "now we're getting somewhere. You've never said a word about money. From the way you dress and act, I thought you were well off. That your parents were supporting you."

Jimmy had been sitting on so much for so long, he didn't know where to start. But he did want to unburden himself, and as much as he distrusted them, these people were inviting his intimacy. Sister Cecilia gave him an apprehensive look, but he ignored it.

"Well, I don't know where to begin, but you're right, Mark, I do act like I've got a silver spoon in my mouth because that's the way I was raised. I never had to pay for anything. Other kids had summer jobs while they were in high school and college; I spent the summer at the family cottage at the Jersey Shore or touring Europe and Canada. Hell, I've been to Bermuda by boat."

Jimmy paused and looked at Byron Patton, hoping to establish some rapport. Byron looked away.

"The Main Line of Philadelphia, where I grew up, is a lot like the North Shore of Chicago—from what I've seen anyway. I've never had to worry about money until a few months back when my father lost his job. Then all of a sudden I've got this new responsibility, and I'm not equipped to deal with it."

"How are you dealing with it?" Paul Jordan asked, his voice cool and clinical.

"Not so hot. Well, I had a part-time job at the library at Northwestern, but I kinda screwed that up, and now I don't have any source of income for the rest of the summer. So actually, I've been kinda thinking about dropping out of CPE and getting a full-time job. I've got to get my act together financially, or I'm gonna . . ."

"Ah, now we're getting down to your hidden agenda," Paul Jordan said, dropping his pipe in the ashtray and leaning forward. "You're obviously using this business about money to mask your real feelings about CPE, the group, and intimacy. What I hear you saying is that you are afraid of intimacy, and instead of dealing with it, you're looking for some excuse to quit. If you didn't think you could afford CPE, why did you agree to take it this summer? You could have waited a year."

Now there was blood in the water, and the sharks were flashing their teeth.

They were only 15 minutes into the hour-long session, and he didn't know how long he could hold out. Kneading his brow, he looked longingly out the window. There were no nurses now, just a fat black woman looking for a cab.

"Because my advisor said I should take CPE this summer," Jimmy said. "I figured I could make it with this job I had at the library, but, like I said — that fell through."

"Why?" Paul Jordan wanted to know.

"Yeah, how come?" McGann seconded.

"Long story," Jimmy said, meeting their inquisitive stares with an obstinate look.

Paul Jordan cleared his throat. "When we spoke in May, you assured me you would have no trouble with money this summer. Now you spring this guilt trip on the group. I don't buy it."

"Neither do I," said McGann.

Patton and Freeman nodded.

Sister Cecilia gave Jimmy the look of assurance he needed.

"Well, believe whatever you want, but I'm having a rough time financially. I make a little money through my field work at St. Augustine's, but it's barely enough to cover my housing. And I've written to my rector and bishop for money, and they both turned me down. I guess new organ pipes or whatever are more important than putting one of their members through seminary, and the bishop is broke, or he says he is. Anyway, I'm having some hard times with money, and since you wanted to know where I'm at right now, I thought I'd tell you. But since you think I'm using it to cover up other feelings, you can all go fuck yourselves."

"Ooooooh," McGann said, clutching his heart with mock shock. "There ARE some feelings under that cool exterior after all. It's not all a performance. Come on, Jim, go with your anger. Tap into it. Let it all hang out."

Jimmy exhaled. They weren't worth the effort. He looked at Sister Cecilia and was ashamed of himself. "Forgive me for talking like that, Sister."

"Of course," she said.

Despite the best efforts of the gang of four, Jimmy sat in silence for the rest of the hour thinking of cool pine forests.

When it was finally over, and they were alone in the corridor, Sister Cecilia quietly slipped a wad of bills into Jimmy's hand. "Sister, you can't . . ."

Sister Cecilia put her fingers to his lips and smiled lovingly.

* * *

"You'll have to get off the train."

"Huh?"

"This is Linden Street. Far as the train goes."

Jimmy rubbed his eyes and blinked. He looked around, trying to figure out who he was and where he was. Putting his hand to his neck, he felt the Roman collar and the black strip of electrician's tape he had clumsily affixed to it. It signified he was a seminarian. His left hand was clamped around the neck of a wine bottle. He held it close to his eyes. There was a procession of ancient Greeks on the label and a full measure of red fluid inside. He recalled vaguely that he had consumed two bottles of the stuff with dinner and had bought this one "for the road."

"Roditys for the road," he remembered telling the equally inebriated owner. They had laughed and slapped one another's backs, and Jimmy remembered hollering something in Greek.

But I don't know Greek.

He also remembered having eaten squid or octopus or some cephalopod that sounded exotic when he ordered it. Now it sat writhing greasily in his stomach.

"Got to get off the train, Reverend." The black conductor was weary from a day of riding back and forth over the same rails.

Jimmy nodded too much, giving himself a savage headache. "Okay, man. Thanks for waking me up. I guess I kinda dozed off."

"You was passed out, Reverend." A Missionary Baptist, the conductor didn't take kindly to clergy who clung to the bottle.

"Yeah, well, thanks." Clutching his bottle, Jimmy lurched off the train and barfed in some nearby bushes. Then he headed through the heat toward the seminary, some three miles south.

He was reasonably clear-headed after the first mile. Remembering that Sister Cecilia had given him $50, he checked his wallet to see how much he had left. Only $20 remained.

He had just turned south on Orrington Avenue when he saw a middle-aged man trying to manage a ten-speed bike that was clearly too small for him.

"Shift gears," Jimmy called. "It'll be a lot easier. You gotta shift gears. You're in the wrong gear, pal, that's why it's so hard."

But the dumb guy wouldn't listen and continued struggling with the bike. Jimmy gave up and kept walking.

But he stopped short when he heard a familiar voice call: "Hey, Jimmy, wait for me."

Oh shit, Jimmy thought, it's the dean, and he's gonna see what a drunken jerk I really am. Jimmy wanted to run and hide, but instead he waited.

Red-faced and out of breath, the dean dismounted and joined Jimmy. He clapped him on the back and gestured at the girl's bicycle.

"My doctor's idea," he said, coughing. "And Claire's. It's Jennifer's bike, in case you were wondering. Well, what do you think, am I ready for the Tour de France?"

Jimmy looked at Dean Manoogian and couldn't help smiling. "Just about. All you have to do is quit the smokes and you're all set."

George Manoogian was wearing a sports shirt, bermuda shorts, and knee socks. He took a Lucky out of his pocket and lighted it.

He coughed, took a puff, coughed, and took another puff.

"Doctor says these'll kill me, but I think I'd kill dogs if I ever quit," he said, surpressing another cough.

He laughed heartily. Jimmy laughed too, but not so heartily because he felt the doctor had a good point. "I know what you mean, Mr. Dean."

He choked on his cigarette and coughed fitfully. He coughed for a full minute before he was able to draw a decent breath. Then he crushed the cigarette under his heel.

"Mind if I walk back to the seminary with you? I think I've had enough bicycling for one night."

"I'd be delighted," Jimmy said. "You know, it would help if you put the seat up. Your leg is supposed to be almost fully extended when the pedal is on the down cycle."

"Really? I think I'm going to stick to walking. This turned out to be a bit more complicated than I thought. Jennifer doesn't seem to have any trouble with this thing, but then she's young."

The dean lighted another cigarette and inhaled with only minor coughing. "So tell me, Jimmy, how is your clinical work going?"

Jimmy was sure the dean was going to ask about the bottle of wine, but the man seemed to accept it as the most natural thing in the world. Jimmy knew the Evanston police wouldn't look at it that way.

"Well, it's been pretty heavy. I think the worst thing I've seen so far was an autopsy. Open-heart surgery was a close second. Tomorrow, I'm supposed to see a delivery. That shouldn't be too bad. But I almost lost it on the autopsy. It was an old lady, and the way they cut open her rib cage with those clipper things — God, it was too much. I had to leave the room. I don't know how people can do that kind of work."

"Neither do I," the dean said. "But how about your group? How are you getting along in that department?"

"Well, as the French say, it's a pain in ze ass."

The dean howled, heedless of the surrounding suburban quietude. "Don't tell me — you've got a facilitator who's made a royal mess of things and a couple of hostile jerks who are taking advantage of it by jumping all over anyone brave enough to bare his chest."

"Yeah," Jimmy said, smiling broadly. "That's it exactly. How'd you know?"

"I took the course a couple of years ago — when they first came up with the idea."

"So what's the point? Why do students have to go through all that garbage?"

"I wonder sometimes. But in the long run, it pays off. I know its hard to imagine now," he said, eyeing the wine bottle, "but stick in there and you'll be a better priest for it."

"I don't know," Jimmy said. "I was ready to quit today. In case you haven't noticed, I had a few glasses of wine with my dinner."

"Rodytis," the dean said. "I know it well. Armenia isn't that far from Greece, you know. Did you have some saganaki?"

"Saga what?"

"The flaming cheese."

"Oh yeah. Yeah, I did. I thought the guy was going to burn the place down. It was terrific. Especially with the wine."

"I'd go easy on that if I were you. Take it from one who knows, it might go down like soda pop, but it can come back up like . . ."

"I know."

The sky was turning teal blue as the sun slipped behind the elevated tracks. Sleek nighthawks swooped above, searching wide-mouthed for insects. Their nasal "peeents" echoed pleasantly off the big houses. Evanston's enormous elms turned a bewitching green in the fading light, and the ancient streetlights twinkled on, enchanting the summer night. Jimmy and the dean walked silently, relishing the moment and one another's company.

Realizing that this was the kind of experience he longed to have with his own father, Jimmy wished the seminary was five miles away. He had so much he wanted to discuss with this marvelous man, but the familiar steeple was only two blocks away now.

"How's the job at the library?" the dean asked, wishing too that they had farther to walk.

"I'm afraid that didn't work out so well. What can I say — I quit. I'm just not cut out to be a librarian."

"So what are you doing for money? I thought that was why you took the job."

"Well, that's the $50,000 question, and money was why I took that job. God, that's the last time I work in a library. Anyway, St. Augustine's pays me $60 for field work, but that's about it. I tried my rector and bishop, but they both have other priorities right now. Try us later, and all that good stuff. So things are a little tight right now. In fact, I told the group today I wanted to drop out of CPE and get a full-time job until I got my act together. But that went over like a lead balloon."

Dean Manoogian furrowed his brow. "Sounds like you're between the proverbial rock and hard place."

"You could definitely say that."

The dean stopped suddenly and reached for his wallet. "Tell you what," he said, peeling off five fresh tens, "consider this a vote of confidence. Not a loan or a gift — a vote of confidence."

Before Jimmy could reply, the dean stuffed the bills in his shirt pocket.

"Thank you," Jimmy said.

They finished the walk in silence, and Jimmy was trying to give voice to his affection when Lance Gordon appeared and insisted on speaking in private with Dean Manoogian about an urgent matter.

"Maybe we can continue our talk tomorrow," the dean said as Lance Gordon led him away.

"Sure," Jimmy said, watching him go. He went to his dusty, dishevelled suite, found a corkscrew Bruce had forgotten, and downed the third bottle all by his lonesome.

* * *

"We have four for you tonight, chaplain. In fact we have one in acute labor; she should be ready any time now," the obstetrics nurse said.

Jimmy and Paul Jordan could hear the moans and occasional screams of the expectant mother emanating from the labor room.

"She should be ready by the time you've gowned and scrubbed," the nurse said, directing them to the appropriate room.

"What are you feeling right now, Jim?" Paul Jordan asked, unfolding a fresh scrub shirt. He was playing it cool and clinical.

"I don't know. After that autopsy, I don't think anything's gonna bother me."

"We'll see."

"What's the point of this anyway?"

"If you are going to minister to people, you've got to experience their lives with them. How can you deal with an expectant mother's fear or pain, if you haven't seen it first hand?"

"You've got a point. But then how can you counsel guys who were in Vietnam if you haven't been over there?"

"You'll need some shoe covers," Paul Jordan said, ignoring the question. "There's going to be oxygen in the delivery room. The covers guard against static electricity."

The nurse poked her head in the door. "Ready, chaplain."

"Okay," Paul Jordan said. "Let's go."

They scrubbed their hands, donned surgical masks and gloves and watched as a wailing black woman was wheeled from the labor room to the delivery room. She was just a kid—thirteen or fourteen at the most—and she howled: "I wants my momma—I wants my momma—"

Even Paul Jordan fidgeted. This wasn't going to be the kind of touchy-feely experiences he had "shared" with his wife.

The delivery room nurse, a no-nonsense black woman, shooed them out of the way as the obstetrician made his grand entrance. He was an imperious Indian gentleman whose formal manner commanded efficiency and instant obedience. He watched impatiently as the nurse and transporter coaxed the patient from the transport to the delivery table.

She was in deep labor and had difficulty moving, but the nurse assured her that it would be better to move herself.

"It hurts," she said, tears staining her dark chocolate face.

"You got to do it, girl. You got to do it," the nurse said.

Once on the table, the patient's legs were placed in stirrups, and the doctor prepared her for surgery while the nurse comforted the young woman and instructed her how she should contract her muscles.

"Didn't your momma tell you what to do?" the nurse said.

"My momma done turn me out for gettin' pregnant. She tell me I be a dumb bitch for gettin' myself knocked up. She say I gonna turn out jus' like her."

The nurse wiped the tears from the girl/woman's face. "What's your name?"

"Latrice."

"How old are you, Latrice?"

"Thirteen."

"What about the father? How come he's not here?"

"Tyrone be a gangster. He laughs when I tell him I'm pregnant, and says it's my own damn fault 'cause I ain't on no pill or nothin'. He say I ain't nuthin' but an old 'hore."

Jimmy looked at Paul Jordan and raised his eyebrows to indicate he was definitely feeling something. Paul Jordan's eyes remained impassive.

The Indian doctor had had enough of this ghetto chatter. "Please, girl, lie still and be quiet. Nurse, would you bring that instrument tray closer, so I can reach it? Gentlemen, are you comfortable?"

"Fine, doctor," Paul Jordan said.

Jimmy nodded. He had a clear view as the doctor shaved the patient's pubic hair.

Frightened by her intensifying contractions and the rising level of activity around her crotch, the patient rolled her hips, asking, "My baby been born yet? My baby been born yet?"

"Nurse," the doctor said sharply. "Please control her, or I shall have to adminster a sedative."

"Yes, doctor. Honey, you hear that? You lie still, or we'll have to put you to sleep." She patted the patient's hand. "Take a deep breath and let it out real slow. There, that's it."

The nurse calmed Latrice enough to allow the doctor to proceed with his work. Using a long needle, he anesthestized the cervical muscles so Latrice wouldn't feel any pain when she pushed her baby through the birth canal. She saw it when he was finished and tried to squirm off the table.

"Calm yourself, child," the nurse said. "You're not going to do either you or your baby any good by fighting like this. Relax, Latrice. That's better. That's much better. The doctor's not going to hurt you. You have to cooperate, so he can help you. Now take another deep breath — that's it. Okay, push down on those muscles — come on, Latrice, push — "

The doctor nodded his head.

"Come on, honey. You're not trying hard enough. Now push."

Latrice squirmed again and cried, "It hurts. Oooooooowww, it hurts so bad. It hurts, it hurts. Momma, I want my momma." Her voice trailed off and she closed her eyes momentarily.

"Nurse, we'll need forceps," the doctor remarked casually as he performed an episiotomy with a pair of surgical scissors.

Clutching the nurse's hand, Latrice bit her lip and asked if her baby had been born yet.

"Not yet, Latrice. You're almost there — just keep trying, keep trying. You're a woman now, Latrice, you've got to do this on your own. Are you ready now — push — that's it. Push again. Come on, get a deep breath — now push down like your life depended on it. That's it — come on — you've got it — that's it, Latrice."

The three men at the foot of the table watched as the baby's head appeared, or crowned, at the mouth of the birth canal.

The doctor carefully inserted the forceps into the birth canal. He fastened the two arms and positioned the instrument around the baby's head.

"Come on, girl, push. Push with all your might," he said. As she pushed instinctively, he carefully turned the baby around so the child faced upward. Another, more violent, contraction pushed the baby's head out. Immediately, the doctor inserted an oxygen tube into each of the infant's nostrils and mouth. There was a moment of watchful silence, then the joyful sound of the child's crying filled the room.

Jimmy was jubilant.

Even Paul Jordan did a happy little dance.

"You hear that, Latrice?" the nurse said, "that's your baby crying."

The young mother was soaked with sweat. She laughed girlishly between breaths, saying, "My baby, my baby . . . is it a boy or a girl?" She tried to sit up and see, but the nurses restrained her.

"You're not finished yet, girl," the doctor told her. "The baby is not born yet. Come now, you must finish."

Pushing hard and screaming, the young woman gave birth to her child. The doctor intercepted the pale, puckered baby as it emerged into the world.

Jimmy was astounded.

Cradling the wailing child in his hands, the doctor carefully cleansed her eyes.

Her pain passed, Latrice lay breathing great gulps of air. Holding the child aloft for its mother to see, the doctor said, "Say hello to your daughter."

Barely able to catch her breath, Latrice gazed lovingly at her child and smiled.

"My baby," she gasped.

The doctor deftly sutured the umbilical cord and cut it. After letting Latrice hold her baby, the nurse wiped the newborn clean and placed it in a lamp-heated incubator. She dusted the baby with talcum powder and rubbed its feet to stimulate breathing and circulation. Finally, she wrapped the baby in diapers and moved the incubator close to the delivery table so Latrice could adore her child while the doctor tended to the afterbirth and such matters.

Captivated by the scene, Jimmy jumped when Paul Jordan tapped him on the shoulder and said, "Come on, let's go have our debriefing."

"Sure," Jimmy said, reluctant to leave.

When they were alone in the gown room, Paul Jordan asked, "Well, what were you feeling in there?"

"I don't know—just that it's a shame that kid has to go live in the ghetto. Look, I gotta get back to Evanston before it gets too late."

"Wait a minute. Those are observations, not feelings. You've got to . . ."

"You didn't hear me—I've really got to go. The el gets real scary after dark. See you tomorrow."

Jimmy found a pay phone in a remote corner of the lobby. He had just enough change for a three minute call and was prepared to tell his mother how much he loved her for laboring him into the world when his father answered and slurred, "What the hell do you want?"

"Nothing," he said, hanging up and heading for the nearest bar.

Chapter Thirty-Eight

"How come we're slowing down? We're out in the middle of a cornfield. I knew we should have flown."

Taking the train to see K.C. in Jackson was Jimmy's idea.

Jimmy looked out the window. "There's a bunch of guys working on the track. Looks like they're putting in new ties and ballast."

Jill flagged the conductor and asked, "What's the matter? How come we're stopping out in the middle of nowhere?"

"Amtrak," the conductor said, through his teeth. "Worst wreck in ten years right here a month ago. All on account of them lame-brains from Amtrak. What do they know about a railroad? I was off that day, thank God. Amtrak!" He shook his head and walked away.

"What's Amtrak?" Jill asked.

"Don't you read the newspapers?"

"Yeah, but not about choo-choo trains. The New York Times is barred from publishing the 'Pentagon Papers' and I'm supposed to care about who's running the train. I bet you had a train set when you were a little boy."

"Yeah, I did as a matter of fact, but . . ."

"How Freudian," Jill said, half teasing.

Jimmy blushed. "Don't you want to hear about Amtrak?"

"Not really. But if you've just got to tell me, then go ahead."

"Well, I don't want you to think I'm some kind of train nut, but I am interested because I grew up along the Main Line of the Pennsylvania Railroad. What was the Pennsylvania Railroad. Anyway, Amtrak started as Railpax, but they changed the name this year. It's an attempt by the government to save intercity passenger trains like this one."

But everything on this train says 'Illinois Central.' Except for our tickets."

"Well, that's all going to change. You see . . ."

"Like hell it will," said the conductor, who was still within ear shot. "One of them Amtrak punks tries to tell me to take off my IC badge, and I'll tell him where he can stick it. It's nothing but goddamn socialism, if you ask me."

"It saved your job, didn't it?" Jimmy said.

"But I know a lotta guys who ain't as lucky as me. The way these jet jockeys from Amtrak is runnin' things, I'd just as soon get the sack or work the freights again."

Quiet was hard to find that afternoon on the southbound City of New Orleans. The old coaches were climatic catastrophies causing the passengers to cluck, complain, and fan themselves with newspapers.

Jill and Jimmy retreated to the vestibule where they opened the top of the dutch door and let the corn-cooled air rustle through their hair.

The fare was fine if you could stand the added heat in the diner, and Jimmy and Jill could long enough to gobble down their baked chicken and vegetables with plenty of salt from their perspiring faces. Most of the passengers, however, had brought along their own chicken, hence the train's moniker, the "Chickenbone Limited."

"It's interesting," Jill said, enjoying an after-dinner breeze.

"What?" Jimmy said, squinting into the wind at the speeding brown and orange locomotives.

"All these black people on this train. I bet a lot of them took this railroad to Chicago when they left the South to get away from Jim Crow. Now they're taking it back to visit their relatives in Mississippi. I wonder what they'll tell them."

"That life in a northern ghetto is no better than life in some crummy little Mississippi town."

"I disagree. Blacks have done a lot better in the North than they have in the South."

"Spoken like a true northern liberal."

"I still think it's interesting. You could write a thesis on the social relevance of this train."

"Probably."

The sensation of motion became soothing and sensual as the train hit full speed on a smooth track.

Jill leaned out for another look, and Jimmy grasped her waist.

"Careful, don't lean too far."

"I'm all right. I'm not going to fall out." She was alternately annoyed and delighted by the huskiness in his voice and the heat in his hands.

Jimmy was a true gentleman and part of her really wanted a sensitive man who was not afraid to express his feelings. But another, darker, side of her desperately needed K.C. and his aura of reckless adventure.

Jimmy dropped his hands. "Hey, I could ask the conductor if they've got any compartments free in the sleeper. I'm sure ten bucks would . . ."

"Jimmy," Jill said, backing into the vestubule, "no."

The conductor clumbered through the passageway and said he thought he had told them not to stand there with the door open.

So they returned to their seats where Jill read a John Updike novel, and Jimmy stared out the window until dark. Then the conductor dimmed the lights, and the babies started howling. Old men snored and fat ladies farted. It got hotter and stickier as they sliced through corners of Kentucky and Tennessee. Jimmy dozed off without saying good night.

He soon dreamed that he was alone and naked on a lovely beach. He settled belly-down on the warm sand and soon had an enormous erection.

Suddenly he was not alone.

The beach was now crowded with fully clad people and they were all pointing and staring at him. Embarrassed, he tried to cover himself, but somehow his arms were too short. The people kept pointing and commenting, but now it didn't matter because there was another naked person on the beach, and she was Jill, and she beckoned him to frolic with her in the waves. He chased her through the surf, feeling himself grow by at least another inch. She slipped sleekly into the sea, and he thought he had lost her.

Then she emerged with a burst of bubbles and was clinging warmly and wetly to him. He was bringing the matter to a logical conclusion when he was rudely awakened by a sharp slap to the side of the head.

"Stop it!!"

"Huh?" Jimmy felt another open hand strike his cheek and blinked, wondering what had gone wrong. He had rolled on top of Jill, and had worked his hand way up under her T-shirt.

Get your hand out of there, now," she hissed.

A flatulent fat lady awakened to the commotion and told them to "shush up."

Jimmy realized he had rolled on top of Jill and had been dry-humping her in his sleep. The sweat on his imprisoned hand turned cold as he tried to extricate it from Jill's tight little T-shirt. She mistook this for more fondling and slapped him again.

"Goddamn it, I'm trying to get my hand free," he whispered.

Another farting old black lady shushed them.

"Well, get it out of there. Now!"

"Hold still," Jimmy said, struggling to free his hand.

"All right. But get it out of there," Jill demanded.

When she settled, he freed his hand and slumped back in his sweat-soaked seat. Jill rearranged herself and wished she had worn a bra. She also wished she had a fresh set of panties handy, because she was awfully wet down there.

It wasn't like he snuck up on me while I was asleep, she admitted to herself. I guess I could have said something sooner. If he had only insisted a little longer that we get a sleeping compartment, then, oh well.

When she was sufficiently calm, Jill went to find another seat. There were none, so she came back and said, "You keep your hands to yourself the rest of the night, or I'll call the conductor and have you thrown off the train. God, you're just like some horny teenager at a drive-in movie. You're disgusting." She curled with her back to him and tried to go to sleep.

* * *

K.C. O'Neal was waiting impatiently on the platform when The City of New Orleans lumbered 30 minutes late into Jackson, Mississippi. There was a mound of half-smoked Marlboros at his feet and a half-pint on his breath. He wore a pair of mirrored aviator's sunglasses, a Hawaiian shirt, wash pants, and penny loafers with mismatched socks. His neck and forehead were as red as any native's.

Jill rushed into his arms.

K.C. took a final drag from his butt before kissing her.

"Hey, baby," he said, with a phony drawl, "y'all look terrific."

Carrying all the luggage, Jimmy awkwardly approached the lovers. K.C. put a possessive arm around Jill and cupped her left breast for Jimmy to see. "Well, hey, Yankee, y'all have a good little train ride?"

Jimmy swallowed and extended his hand. K.C. took it and, for a few seconds, they contested one another's grip strength. Jimmy didn't like looking at himself in K.C.'s glasses so he quit first.

"Yeah, it was fine, K.C," he said, stepping stiffly away. "Just fine. Hey, it's good to see you again. How's it goin' at the paper?"

"Real fine."

"Good. Well, let's go to your place and start partyin'."

"Or at least eat some breakfast," Jill said. "I'm half starved."

"You won't be after you have one of my rib-stickin' down-home breakfasts. Grits, biscuits 'n gravy, and ham and eggs. The best ol' ham you ever laid your sweet little eyes on."

"Let's go," Jimmy said, salivating and wondering when K.C. was going to cut the good old boy routine.

He wasn't, because, as he said, he had totally assimilated into Southern culture during his two month residence in Mississippi's capital. For proof, he pointed proudly to his car, a battered green '62 Ford Falcon.

"See," he said, kicking a clay-caked tire, "it's even got Mississippi tags. I am a genuine redneck, and don't you old Yankee dogs forget it."

Jill laughed nervously.

Jimmy searched the ashtray, saying, "You got any pot, K.C.?"

"Mississippi's finest, son. Home-grown in the Delta. K.C. proferred a fat joint. "Fire up that little hush puppy, and you'll never smoke that inferior ol' Mexican shit again."

Jimmy did as he was told, and the threesome were soon suitably high. Jimmy gazed through the rotting floorboard to avoid watching K.C. fondle Jill.

K.C. lived in a 12-flat in the poor white part of town. The first thing Jimmy and Jill noticed was the insect multitude. They scaled the walls and cavorted over K.C.'s piles of greasy pots and pans.

"Howdy boys," K.C. said, amused by his guests' amazement. "Don't worry; they're tame. These are good ol' Southern palmetto bugs. Look like giant cockroaches, but they ain't nuthin' but mild-mannered palmetto bugs. Keep me company. Even do tricks. Jimmy, throw your stuff on the couch in the living room. That's your room. Me and Mistress Jill will be retirin' to the master bedroom for our pleasures. There's some beat-off books in the bathroom for yours. Try not to hit the light bulb, okay?"

With a lascivious grin, he grabbed Jill's ass and hustled her into the bedroom. He put an Allman Brothers album on his scratchy stereo, and the rebel rockers soon stifled their low moans.

But Jimmy could still hear the high ones and wanted to go in there and strangle K.C. and take Jill for his own. He thought of taking K.C. up on his offer, but one look at the bathroom and he didn't even want to breathe in there. He thought of cooking himself some breakfast, but he couldn't stand the sight of the kitchen either.

So he found K.C.'s stash and rolled himself a fat joint. He was halfway through it when the phone rang.

"I'll get it," he said. Who the hell else was going to get it? "Hello, O'Neal residence."

"Hello, this is Tracy Lynne Montgomery. Is Kevin Charles there?"

"Kevin Charles? Ah, he stepped out to get some cigarettes. This is Jimmy Clarke. I'm a friend from Chicago. Can I have him call you when he gets back?"

"He didn't say anything about havin' a guest. Well, I just happened to be in the neighborhood. Doin' errands and such. Maybe I'll just stop on by and introduce myself. Unless y'all have other plans."

"Actually, I think K.C, er Kevin Charles, was planning to show me around."

Jimmy could hear them rutting in the next room. He remembered Jill insisting many times that K.C. was keeping the faith in Mississippi and wondered why he was covering for K.C.'s bare ass now.

"You couldn't get a better tour guide than Tracy Lynne Montgomery. I'm from the Delta originally, but I've lived in Jackson for more than ten years. And any friend of Kevin Charles's is a friend of mine. Just talkin' to you on the telephone, I can tell y'all is someone I most definitely would like to meet," she said.

Jimmy listened to the raw sex in the next room and grinned devilishly. "You know, Tracy Lynne, that sounds like a terrific idea. And I'd certainly like to meet some of Kevin Charles' new friends."

"Oh," she giggled, "we're more than just friends."

"All the more reason for me to meet you. See you soon, I hope."

"Why, certainly."

"Hey, dog breath." K.C. called from the love chamber. "Who the hell was that?"

"Oh," Jimmy said, relighting the joint with care. "Some friend of yours. T.L. Montgomery or something like that. Comin' right over. Wants to show us around town."

Jimmy inhaled deeply and smiled as he heard the sounds of hurried dressing.

"Come on," K.C. said, buttoning his shirt, "we're goin' to Red's Roadhouse for breakfast. He makes better grits than even me. Then we're gonna go see Mississippi."

Jill was as not quick to recover from the coitus interruptus and had to be goaded into action by her manic lover. Jimmy calmly smoked the marvelous Mississippi marijuana and smiled.

* * *

Red did make better grits than K.C, and there was all the iced tea you could drink, clean counter tops, no palmetto bugs, and a terrific air conditioner. Jimmy and Jill wanted to spend the weekend there, but K.C. had bigger plans.

"Come on," he said. "We're goin' to Vicksburg, scene of the greatest military stand of all time."

So they went west 45 miles to the Vicksburg National Military Park and saw what remained of the Confederacy's "Gibraltar."

"Weather was like this during the siege," K.C. said when they arrived. He wiped his brow and sighted down the barrel of a Union artillery piece. It was aimed at the scene of the bloodiest fighting of the 57-day siege, the Third Louisiana Redan.

"Yeah, hotter than a toad's ass on a Mississippi blacktop, and them damn Yankees was wearin' wool uniforms. Them boys was sure stupid," K.C. said.

"In case you forgot, K.C, you're a damn Yankee too," Jimmy said, tiring of his friend's act.

Jill looked wistfully at the pitched terrain and enjoyed her own company. She felt their tension, but decided not to do or say anything. She wasn't ready to take sides.

"I woulda fought with General Pemberton if I were around in those days," K.C. declared.

"K.C, I thought you were the big northern liberal who was going to reform all these redneck racists down here. Now you tell me you would have fought to defend slavery."

"You think there wasn't economic slavery in the North? You think there still isn't?" K.C. said, finally reverting to his normal nasal twang. "These people down here get along with blacks a hell of a lot better than you do in the North. We're not hypocrites down here."

"You call Jackson State getting along with blacks?"

"Hey, man, that was more than a year ago. Anyway, we don't say one thing to blacks down here and then do another, like you do in the North."

"What's this 'we' and 'you' crap? You've only been down here a month and a half."

"You know," K.C. said, "this really wasn't a Union victory. As a matter of fact, the North didn't really win the War Between the States."

"What are you talkin' about? That film we just saw said Pemberton surrendered to Grant on the same day Meade chased Lee's ass out of Gettysburg. And every history book I've ever read always shows Lee surrendering to Grant at Appomatox, not the other way around," Jimmy said.

"No, man. You got it all wrong. Shows you don't know shit from shinola about the Civil War."

Jimmy bristled. If there was one thing he did know a lot about, it was the Civil War. "All right, professor, perhaps you could enlighten me."

"Do you deny that the North had the South out-gunned, out-manned, and out-supplied from day one?"

"Nope."

"Do you deny that the Union had far more ships and trains at its disposal, more foundries, more capital, and vast hordes of immigrants to use as cannon fodder?"

"Ah, Irish immigrants. I knew you'd work the Irish into this somehow. I suppose the evil Limeys figure into this somehow too."

"Damn right they do," K.C. said, flushed with passion. "Bastards were real prick-teasers, man. Kept telling the Confederacy they were gonna support them, but they kept putting it off because they wanted to see who was going to win. After Lee's first attempt to invade the

North failed at Antietam, they backed the North. Fuckin' Limey pricks."

"The British didn't back either side. But they did refuse to recognize the Confederacy after Lincoln made it clear that the real issue was slavery. They had no choice," Jimmy said.

"Oh bullshit. Lincoln was the biggest bullshit artist in history. You ever read some of his early campaign speeches, man? The dude approved of slavery. He was just using the thing as an issue to get his ass elected."

"Fuck you, K.C. Why don't you grow up?"

"You wanna make me?"

They squared off in front of the cannon and were ready to trade blows when a motor-driven camera whirred nearby.

"Ausgezeichnet!" a thin man in socks and sandals declared after snapping half a roll of the pugilistic pair.

"What?" K.C. said, eyeing the dude's funny-looking glasses.

"Outstanding," the German tourist said. "Americans. Still fighting your Civil War. I can't wait to see how zey come out. If you vould be so kind as to give to me your names and addresses, I vill send you copies."

"Vat?" K.C. said, mockingly. "So you can send ze Gestapo to arrest us for crimes against der Reich?"

"I beg your pardon." The German hoped the American was joking. He had spent the war hiding in Berlin basements from the Nazis.

"Ah, tut mir leid," Jimmy said, drawing on his scant high school German. "Mein Freund ist verruckt." Jimmy grabbed K.C.'s arm and hustled him away.

K.C. jerked his arm out of Jimmy's grasp and said, "What the hell did you tell that fuckin' Hun?"

"I said that you were overheated. That's all," Jimmy said, smiling to himself.

Jill joined them and gave K.C. one of her pleading, "please don't" looks. K.C. exhaled and looked sharply at the German and then at Jimmy. He wasn't sure which one he wanted to hit first.

"What'd you tell him? What's the last word mean? 'Verfuck' or something. Sounds like German for 'fucked up,' if you ask me."

"What difference does it make? I didn't see any reason in getting into a fight with some guy just because he wanted to take our pictures and send them to us."

"You told that Nazi scumbag that I'm a mental defective, didn't you?"

Jimmy threw up his hands. "I'm goin' to the car. If you want to fight World War II again with that guy, that's your business. I've had enough."

K.C. grabbed his shoulder and was ready to punch Jimmy in the mouth when Jill got between them. He checked his swing but cuffed her sharply on the ear. It drew blood and she screamed. The German got his motor-drive moving, saying, "Ausgezeichnet! Prima! Amerikaner, sie sind alle Verruckt. Ausgezeichnet!"

* * *

Three six-packs and eight joints later, they were headed south on U.S. 49 and Jill had to visit the ladies room.

"Hey," K.C. said, pointing, "I'll stop by those trees up ahead and you can go squat in the woods."

"No, I'd prefer if we stopped at a gas station," Jill said, embarrassed that her biology had become the center of attention.

"Jesus H. Christ. Goddamn broads and your delicate plumbing. All right, we'll make a tinkle stop at the next gas station. That suit you, m'lady?"

"That's fine," she said, sitting on her hands and staring straight ahead until K.C. spotted a filling station just this side of Perkinston.

"Watch this," K.C. said, winking at Jill when Jill had gone to the rest room, and a good ol' boy in greasy coveralls shuffled leisurely over to the car.

Spotting the Mississippi tags, the gas jockey decided that at least these dirty long-hairs were home-grown.

"Howdy," he said, shifting his chaw of Redman.

"Howdy," K.C. said, slinking back into his affected Southern accent.

"Where you boys headed?"

"Biloxi," K.C. said, drawling out the second syllable. "How about you, Sonny, you wanna come along?"

Sonny wore his name over his heart.

Sonny gave a leering look at the rest room. "Yeah, I reckon I'd like ta come along with you boys. I reckon I most definitely would. 'Ceptin' some folks got to work for a livin'." He fiddled with the pump for a while and then ambled back to the windshield to make a few half-hearted passes with a half-dry sponge on a stick. "Where 'bouts in Mississippi y'all from? I ain't never seen any y'all 'round Perkinston before."

"That's on account of I'm from up Jackson ways. I'm a reporter for the Clarion-Ledger. That there gal o' mine and this here friend o' mine is visitin' from Chicago. But the governah give 'em all a special weekend passport."

"What's y'all name, son?" Sonny said, squinting skeptically.

"O'Neal. Kevin Charles O'Neal."

You any relation to the O'Neals in Pascagoula County?"

"Yeah. Yeah, I believe I may be distantly related. Least ways, that's what my daddy tells me."

Sonny stopped wiping the windshield and grinned toothlessly. "Well, boy, you must be related to thin air because there ain't no O'Neals in Pascagoula County. None that I ever heard of, least ways. An' maybe y'all livin' in Jackson now, but you sure ain't no native son. If you ask me, you ain't nuthin' but another no-good Yankee carpetbagger."

"No, man," K.C. said, persisting in his folly but reverting to Chicagoese. "I was born and raised in Jackson. Lived in Mississippi all my life, except I went to college in Chicago which is why I probably lost a little of my accent. Or maybe you just got some shit in your ears."

Sonny was contemplating his next move when Jill sashayed out of the rest room. He couldn't resist a wolf whistle.

"Hey, Gomer, that's my girlfriend you're whistlin' at."

"Why, was that me, Mr. Reporter? Heaven forbid." He pretended to recoil in embarassment, and then he was suddenly crouched and coiled with a huge wrench in his hand. Jimmy gulped and told Jill to get into the car fast.

K.C. regarded the wrench coolly. "What if I got a gun, Gomer?"

"What if you do, boy? You ain't man enough to use it, Yankee scumbag. Now come on out 'n' we'll have us a friendly little chat, Southern-style. Since you seem to know so much about us poor

Southern folks, I'm sure y'all know what I mean. Mebbe you can write a story about how ol' Sonny Lee Smith whupped your behind."

K.C. put his hand on the door handle.

Jill gave Jimmy a desperate look, but Jimmy was happy to let the fool go to his fate and have her all to himself.

Then K.C. took another long look at the wrench. He didn't have a gun, just an old Boy Scout pocket knife that he hadn't sharpened since he was 11. K.C. started the car, gunned the engine, and before screeching away, said, "Fuck you, Gomer!"

Sonny ran after them angrily brandishing the wrench. The Falcon coughed a couple of times, and K.C. nearly fainted at the wheel. Then it caught, and he was all bluster and bravado.

So was Jill.

They drove the remaining miles to Biloxi with Jill wanting them both, separately or together, and K.C. and Jimmy each wanting her all for himself.

K.C. cruised the coast and found a drive-through liquor store in the shape of a red barn.

There being no beach houses, K.C. found a seaside seafood restaurant and said, "Go put your suit on in there, sweety. Me an' Jimmy'll just change in the car."

"Oh, darn," Jill said, rummaging through her overnight bag. "You know, I don't think I brought a bathing suit. You never said we were going to the beach. I didn't even think Mississippi had a beach."

K.C. pounded his fist against the steering wheel. Then he got an idea.

"You got a safety pin in that saddle bag of yours?"

"Yeah."

"Well, get one." She found two, and K.C. took off his T-shirt. "Here's your bathing suit. Pin it together in the crotch, and you're all set. Come on, surf's up."

While she went to change in the ladies' room, Jimmy and K.C. slithered out of their pants and into their cut-offs. Tourists gawked at the twosome, but they were too drunk to care.

The restaurant stopped functioning when Jill emerged from the ladies room. The T-shirt stretched tightly over her tits and clove to her crotch. The manager thought to say something managerial, but couldn't manage his tongue. Old tourists with angina clutched their chests and told their wives it was the mounds of crayfish they were eating.

The Gulf of Mexico was milky brown and warmer than baby piss. But they went in anyway and frolicked for a while in the knee-deep water. Jimmy said it was too shallow for sharks, but K.C. said sharks always attacked in shallow water.

Jill didn't like the idea of standing in murky water waiting for some unseen predator to chew her off at the knee caps, so she headed for her towel.

"Hey, K.C." Jimmy said, watching her wonderful backside. "Tell me about this Tracy Lynne Montgomery who called. Sounded like a sweet little lady."

K.C. was watching a container ship slip slowly into a nearby dock. "Nice piece of ass, why?"

"You fuckin' her?"

"What's it to you?"

"Well, in case you didn't know, Jill thinks you're burnin' the torch for her down here."

"How do you know what she thinks?" K.C. said.

"What do you mean, how do I know what she thinks? I'm her friend, that's how. And I'm your friend, too, in case you forgot."

"You fucked her when we were up in Wisconsin, didn't you?"

"I don't know what you're . . ."

"Oh bullshit. You thought I was passed out, but I wasn't."

Jimmy's fingers instinctively coiled into fists.

The confrontation had finally come, and Jimmy welcomed it. K.C. tackled Jimmy and grabbed his neck.

K.C. pushed Jimmy under and tried with all his might to drown him. Jimmy swallowed a mouthful of the brackish sea water and felt his strength ebb.

Then the will to live surged through his body, and he broke K.C.'s grip with a series of sharp blows to the neck. Jimmy scrambled to his feet and moved closer to shore where he found better footing.

Jimmy hadn't been in a real fight since he was 11 and took on a 13-year-old who had stolen his hockey puck. His bravado had earned him a profusely bleeding broken nose. After undergoing painful surgery to set the septum straight, he had vowed to stay away from fights. But Jill WAS worth fighting for, broken nose or not.

K.C. closed and put up his dukes. Though neither combatant had had any formal training in the ring, they had watched enough Friday night fights with their fathers to know the basics.

So they clung close and traded a bruising battery of head and body blows. Jimmy was so enraged when K.C. landed a hard left next to his nose that he tried to kick his foe in the balls.

K.C. caught Jimmy's foot and toppled him on the hot sand. He tried to kick Jimmy while he was down, but Jimmy rolled, scrambled to his feet, and resumed the boxing match.

"No kickin', man," K.C. said between labored breaths.

Jimmy nodded and threw a right at K.C.'s head. He cuffed his ear but took a blow to the belly that forced the air out of his lungs.

Both boys were soon bloodied and bruised, but neither would quit.

They cursed one another and threw punch after punch. Their inexperience and three burly lifeguards saved them from serious injury.

When it was over, and the rivals could not lift their aching arms, Jimmy looked at Jill and said, "All right, you decide. Him or me?"

K.C. caught his breath and shook his head. "Yeah, him or me?"

Jill wanted them both.

But she chose K.C. with a kiss on the cheek.

Jimmy wiped off the wet sand, gathered up his things, and walked out of their lives. He didn't cry until the bus was well beyond Jackson.

Chapter Thirty-Nine

"Hi. Claire, it's me, Jimmy Clarke. I know. It's been a long time. I know. It's been a hectic summer for me too. Well, the reason I'm calling is . . ."

"You want to talk to Jennifer."

"How'd you guess?"

"A mother's intuition. I'll go wake her. It's about time that young lady got her fanny out of bed. I swear, she must have some kind of sleeping sickness," Claire said.

"Look, Claire, I can call back. Please don't . . ."

"Nonsense. Life is going to pass that young lady by if she doesn't start getting up earlier. It's good to hear you again, Jimmy. It's been entirely too long. We'll have to have you over for dinner before the summer's through."

"That'd be nice."

"Yes. Hold on."

"Okay."

There was a fumbling with the phone. Then a sleepy female voice said, "Hullo."

"Hi, Jennifer, it's me – Jimmy Clarke."

"Oh, hi. What time is it?" Jennifer yawned loudly into the phone.

"Nine o'clock. Actually, it's more like 8:30. I wanted to . . ."

"Eight thirty! You're calling me at 8:30 on a Saturday morning?? What, are you crazy? Did my mother put you up to this?"

"No, of course not. I figured you got up early for classes and all."

"Not on weekends. God, are you crazy? What do you want, anyway?"

"To go out with you. There's a play downtown at the Schubert I'd like to see, and I thought . . ."

"Play? What play?"

"Well, I don't know about you, but I still haven't seen HAIR. I was going to see it when it was on Broadway at the Biltmore, but I couldn't afford it. Anyway, I think I can swing the ticket prices here, and it's pretty much the original cast. If you've already seen it, we could . . ."

"No, I haven't seen it either. I was going to go when it was in New York, but we couldn't get tickets."

"So, what do you say? We could have dinner somewhere, maybe in Greektown or Chinatown, go to the play, and have a terrific time."

"You know the play's full name is 'The American Tribal Love-Rock Musical.'"

"Does that mean you want to go?"

"I can't believe you called me at 8:30 on a Saturday morning. Were you born on a farm or something?"

"No, I'm a suburban kid just like you. I was on the swim team in high school—we worked out at 6 every morning, including Saturday."

"God, you must be a fish or something."

"I guess. Well, would you like to see HAIR with me?"

Jennifer yawned into the phone again. Got to make him think I'm not excited, she thought, feeling her pulse quicken.

"All right," she said, at last. "But when do you want to go? I'm very busy this summer."

"Well, how about tonight? There's an 8 o'clock show, and they just happen to . . ."

"You mean you . . ."

". . . went and ordered tickets. Actually, we have to be there by 7:30 to pick them up. So I'm an optimist."

"I'll say," Jennifer said. "What if I had other plans tonight? What if . . ."

"Do you?"

"No, but . . ."

"So how about seeing a terrific play we both want to see and having dinner at the restaurant of your choice?"

"You don't have a car, do you?"

"No, but . . ."

"Daddy'll let us use his."

"Great. If he doesn't mind."

"Of course he doesn't mind."

"Okay, so I'll see you at quarter to seven."

Jennifer yawned again and said: "Yeah. You know how you'll be able to recognize me?"

"How?"

"I'll be the one with the bags under my eyes because some jerk woke me up at 8:30 on a Saturday morning."

Chapter Forty

Jennifer wore a flowing purple cotton dress and put Jimmy's white rose in her hair.

Jimmy wore a blue button-down Oxford shirt with the sleeves rolled up, tan chinos, and penny loafers without socks.

The dean was in a meeting, so Claire saw them off.

"I'm jealous," she declared. "I've been after George for months to take me to see HAIR. Maybe that nude scene has him spooked. I don't know. Well, you two flower children have a marvellous time."

She escorted them to the door humming "The Age of Aquarius."

When they were heading south on Sheridan Road in the dean's big, black Mercury, Jimmy said, "Your mother's terrific. You're lucky to have such terrific parents, Jennifer."

Jennifer sat at the far end of the wide seat. "Yeah," she said distractedly, "they're okay."

She was brooding over the last man she let herself love, Dan Richards. They were the talk of Parker High School. She was the brainy sophomore who always had her nose in a book, and he was the equally brainy senior who threw precision passes every Saturday afternoon at Parker Field. Dan was Jennifer's first and only love, and despite her parents' suggestions, she refused to date anyone else when Dan went off to Williams College on a full scholarship.

He promised he would love her forever, but he gradually stopped responding to her daily letters. Soon, he stopped writing all together and never seemed able to get home for a weekend.

Finally, he admitted he had met someone else and thought it would be best if Jennifer started dating again too.

"You're young." he said. "You have your whole life ahead of you. Go out with lots of guys. Have fun. You'll get over it."

But Jennifer didn't get over it, and she didn't go out with lots of guys. She was crushed and refused to go to homecoming or the prom that year and the next. She buried herself deeper in her books and was one of the first at Parker to protest the war in Vietnam and espouse feminism. Men, specially Dan Richards, had betrayed her, and she was damned if she was ever going to fall into another of their traps. Ever.

While she finally began accepting an occasional date, she carefully kept her emotional distance, and never ever went out with someone twice. Especially the ones she liked. Soon, she wasn't bothered with any offers.

In college, she fell in with the misfits and alienated intellectuals. They travelled in big loose packs, smoked lots of dope, and stayed mainly on their own planes. But though it all, she longed for a relationship with a decent man.

Jennifer glanced at this boy, this man, this whatever, driving her father's car. He certainly was good looking, and she liked his sensible driving. Dan had always driven like a maniac.

But what about THAT night in my room, she thought, fretting. God, he probably thinks I'm a retard or something, the way I acted.

"Jeez," she gasped.

"Beg your pardon?" Jimmy said, turning left on Lake Shore Drive.

"Nothing," Jennifer said. "Just talking to myself. I think I have some loose screws."

Jimmy laughed. "I doubt it."

Jennifer blushed and looked at the expanse of green parkway and blue lake was unfolding before them. In the distance, the setting sun bathed the skyline in soft shades of orange and amber.

"Pretty, isn't it?" Jimmy said.

"Yeah," Jennifer said.

They were serenely silent with one another for a few miles, then Jennifer got the courage to say, "Look, about that night in my room. I, ah . . ."

"Forget it. I'm the one who should apologize for acting like some kind of sex maniac, or maybe Joni Mitchell should apologize for casting a weird spell on us."

"I just don't want you to think I'm some kind of weirdo."

"Don't worry."

Jennifer smiled and had a wonderful time that night. HAIR was heavy, and they joined the cast at the end in singing "Let The Sun Shine In."

They went to a Greek restaurant on Halsted Street that reminded Jennifer of the sensual feasts her paternal grandparents had hosted in her childhood.

"Opa!" she said, as the waiter ignited their brandy-soaked Saganaki cheese dish.

Jimmy clinked her glass with his. "Great, isn't it?"

Jennifer chugged her wine.

Jimmy did likewise and refilled their glasses.

Assuming that Jennifer was a lovely Greek princess, the owner appeared with a complimentary bottle of retsina. It tasted of pine and went down quite well with the sumptuous feast of braised lamb, eggplant, egg lemon soup, moussaka, stuffed grape leaves, and other delights.

They finished their meal with honey-sweetened baklava and gooey Greek coffee.

Jennifer, who had hungrily cleaned every plate, dumped Jimmy's cup on the saucer.

"Hmmmm" she said, thoughtfully examining the grounds.

"What do you see, Jennifer?"

"My grandmother taught me how to read coffee grounds when I was a little girl," she said.

"So what do you see?"

Jennifer bit her lip and looked at Jimmy. Then she ran to the restroom where she stayed for a long time. She was her old, safety-sealed self when she returned to the table.

"Jennifer, what's wrong? Are you all right?"

"Nothing's wrong. I'm just tired, that's all. Can we go?"

"Sure," Jimmy said. "I'll pay up as soon as I can get the waiter's attention."

"No," Jennifer said, opening her shoulder bag. "Daddy gave me money for dinner. You paid for the tickets, let Daddy pay for dinner. He insisted."

"All right. That's really nice of him."

Jimmy finally got the waiter's attention. While they were waiting for him to tally the bill, he asked, "What did you see in my coffee grounds? Must have been . . ."

"It's just a lot of silly old junk my grandmother believed in. She was an old Armenian peasant. I shouldn't have bothered."

She handed the waiter a crisp $50 bill and told him to keep the change.

"Come on," she said, I'm tired, and it's a long drive back to Evanston."

"If you say so."

Jennifer pretended to fall asleep on the way back, and Jimmy fiddled with the radio until he found a black station that played mellow jazz. He lost himself in the meandering melodies and glanced wistfully at the sleeping beauty.

"You don't have to walk me to the door," Jennifer said when they returned to the seminary compound.

But I'd like to. And I'd like to know why you got so freaked out by those coffee grounds."

"I told you," Jennifer said, walking as fast as she could, "it's just some silly peasant thing my grandmother taught me. It doesn't mean anything."

They got to the deanery door, and Jimmy grabbed her shoulder. "But you believe it, and you saw something that upset you. Didn't you?"

Jennifer shook loose and tried not to look at the man the grounds foretold for her. When he asked her if she would like to go out again, she burst through the door and slammed it in his face.

Chapter Forty-One

Jimmy clicked his blue, Parker T-Ball Jotter and tried again. But he crumpled the paper when he found himself writing:

"Dear Bishop Hamilton,

"Send money fast, or I'll blow up the seminary.

"Your servant in Satan,

"Jimmy C."

Jimmy rubbed his temples and looked out the window. Some seminary brats were outside playing a game based entirely on yelling. Jimmy went to the window and shouted, "Keep it down out there! Some people have work to do around here."

The kids glanced warily at the strange man and moved their yelling a few yards down the block. Didn't this guy know it was 7 o'clock at night — kid time? Besides, they had been warned by their parents to stay away from the single students.

Jimmy turned away from the window wishing he could be a kid again.

"Being an adult sucks," he said.

"Hey, that's it," he answered. "Dear Bishop Hamilton, being an adult sucks. I hereby request your episcopal permission to fully regress to a permanent state of blissful childhood."

Realizing a passing senior had heard him talking to himself, Jimmy blushed and backed into his room. Bruce was off doing his house-sitting thing, so he was all alone now, and it was driving him batty.

Especially the business with Jennifer. He had gotten up the nerve to call her three times since the night of the fallen coffee grounds, but she had refused to come to the phone. Claire had been more than sympathetic and had even offered to force Jennifer to the phone, but Jimmy declined.

He was crushed by this inexplicable rejection. And try as he might, he just couldn't get her off his mind.

Jimmy ground his teeth and primed his Parker.

"Ember Letter Trinity Season

"Dear Bishop Hamilton,

"It's been a pretty good summer.

"I've been getting to church every Sunday as part of my duties at St. Augustine's, and Father Swann lets me administer the chalice. It's a good experience.

"The clinical thing at St. Mark's Medical Center is going as good as can be expected, but I don't think I'm cut out to be a hospital chaplain. I just don't know what to tell a lot of those people, especially the ones who don't get any better.

"I've been swimming in Lake Michigan most mornings before I go to the hospital, so I'm in pretty good physical shape.

"I haven't been doing much lately. In fact, the way things have been going, I wouldn't object if the Episcopal Church required its priests to take a vow of celibacy.

"Well, that's about it for now, other than I'm kind of thinking about taking a leave of absence. You know, maybe work off campus for a while or something and kind of think this whole thing through.

"Have a good summer—what's left of it—and give my regards to Miss Worden.

Respectfully,

Jimmy Clarke"

Bishop Hamilton's reply came by return mail, and, as always, was perfectly typed by Miss Worden. It read:

"Dear Jimmy,

"I was disturbed by the negative tone of your letter and encourage you to pay strict adherence to the Rule of Life. A morning swim is all well and good, but I think you'd do much better attending morning prayer instead.

"As for the leave of absence you propose, I advise against it. I have yet to see a seminarian come back from one. Plus, isn't there the matter of the draft? If we were to grant your request, you would lose your student status and therefore your deferment.

"Sounds to me like you've got a normal case of the post junior blues. Please stick with it, and bring your troubles to the altar of the Lord.

"Miss Worden sends her regards.

"Yours in Christ,

"Charles Francis Hamilton + Bishop of Philadelphia"

Jimmy crushed the bishop's letter and threw it against the wall.

"I know where to take my troubles," he said, facing Philadelphia, "I know exactly where to take them."

Chapter Forty-Two

Jimmy was settled on the sofa watching afternoon re-runs when Sharyn Craig came home. He took another swig of beer and went to kiss her.

She resisted his amorous advance and went to the kitchen to inspect the refrigerator. He tried to cut her off, but she hadn't been drinking beer all afternoon.

"I thought you were going to buy some groceries today," she said, surveying the neat rows of beer cans.

"They had a sale on Old Style. I figured maybe we could go out for dinner. There's that new Mexican place on Belmont, and we could . . ."

"Translation: I can take you out to dinner on the money you saved me by buying two cases of beer for the price of one." She slammed the refrigerator and faced him. "How long do you think this is going to last?"

"What do you mean?"

"You know damn well what I mean. The free ride I've been giving you for the last two weeks. You've eaten all my food, used up all my laundry soap, and you've bummed at least five bucks off me for carfare and lunch every day you've been here."

"Look, Sharyn, that cafeteria at the hospital isn't cheap, and you know what my skin was starting to look like after all those potato chips. Besides, you said you'd do anything to help. And it's not like you're not getting anything in return."

"I'd be better off buying it on the street," she said.

Jimmy followed her into the bathroom. She was his last hope before the recruiter's office.

"You know I give you good loving," Jimmy said, watching her pee.

"Oh, Jimmy," she said, wiping herself, "what am I going to do with you?"

Jimmy just unzipped his pants and grinned.

* * *

At CPE, McGann and Patton were practicing the good cop/bad cop routine on Jimmy, but it wasn't working.

"Gee," McGann said, all sweetness and life, "everything must be just great in your life now. You seem so calm, Jim."

Jimmy shrugged and looked at the one-way window. He was sitting closer than he normally did and realized that by looking a little sideways at it, he could see the figure on the other side. Gabi Volter clearly didn't realize this, because she was masturbating with a practiced hand.

Jimmy smiled at McGann. "I am calm, Mark. Real calm."

"Yeah, but you weren't calm a couple of weeks ago," Bryon Patton said, leaning forward and fixing Jimmy with one of his penetrating looks. "All you could talk about was your financial problems. Then you come back from another one of your crazy long weekends looking like the Hell's Angels worked you over. You were obviously sitting on a lot, but you wouldn't share any of it with us. I think you're just leading us on. You're not part of this group. Don't you agree, Paul?"

Paul Jordan nodded, spilling burning tobacco out of his pipe.

Jimmy watched the Teuton twiddle her twat. She was coming to a quiet, but intense, climax. He crossed his legs to hide his sympathetic reaction.

"I don't think I'm leading anybody on. I'm just not worried about money any more, that's all."

"What do you mean, you're not worried about money anymore?" McGann said. "You get a job? Somebody give you money—like your minister at home? What? We've got a right to know."

"No, you don't," Jimmy said, smiling.

And so it went for the rest of the hour.

Jimmy rushed out when it was finally over and collided with Gabi Volter. She was neat as a pin now in her white coat, clipboard, and khaki skirt.

"Good hour, eh Doctor Volter?" he said.

She nodded impassively. "Vhy do you say dat?"

"I don't know. Just seemed like everybody was rubbing the wrong way today." He winked. "Well, maybe not everybody."

Her rock jaw came loose and she hurried off to have another look at the one-way window.

Jimmy was still chuckling when he breezed into Sharyn's apartment three hours later. He was heading for the refrigerator and a cold beer when he realized Sharyn was seated on the couch with a beer in her hand.

The re-runs were rerunning, but she wasn't watching. Instead, she was staring fixedly at the dutch elm dying outside her window.

"Sharyn? Are you okay? What are you doing home so early? You usually don't . . ."

"We usually don't lose the Wrigley account. I got fired, along with about ten other people in the creative department. Gilkenson said to stay in touch—in case they get another big account, but I'm not gonna hold my breath."

Jimmy got a beer and held her. She was lively as linoleum.

"Hey, you'll get another job. You hated that Gilkenson guy anyway. Look on the bright side. Maybe this will turn out . . ."

"What the hell do you know?" she said, moving away. "You've never been fired."

"I got canned by that bitch at the library."

"That's not the same. That wasn't a real job. You've never had a real job. You've never really been on your own. I've had this job for three years—ever since I quit school. They were going to pay half my tuition at Roosevelt so I could finish. It was a real job, Jimmy, with a real paycheck. Not some bullshit like you had at the library or you have at St. Augustine's."

They sat in silence for a long time, listening to the Puerto Rican kids playing in Spanish. When he stopped beating himself, Jimmy realized he was going to have to do something about money for the first time in his life.

"Why don't I take you to dinner to that Mexican joint on Belmont?" he said.

Sharyn laughed. "That's great—you're going to take me to dinner with MY money to celebrate ME getting fired."

"Well, what do you want to do?"

"Cry." She did, and when she was finished, she said, "Let's fuck. At least that's still free."

"You want to get high first?"

"If you want," she said woodenly. "There's some aluminum foil in my jewelry box. Should be two hits of windowpane in there. Unless you already ripped it off."

"No," Jimmy said. "I don't go through your stuff."

They each took a full hit.

Sharyn put some Moody Blues on the box and peeled quickly out of her clothes. "Come on, let's do it."

They did — for two hours and five minutes.

Exhausted, Sharyn collapsed on Jimmy and cried herself to sleep.

When he was sure she would not wake, Jimmy gently extricated himself, gathered up his things, and walked out on her.

Chapter Forty-Three

Jimmy was still strung out on Sharyn's acid when he walked into the navy recruiting office in downtown Evanston.

It was the "Pride Runs Deep" poster showing a squadron of F-4 Phantoms streaking over a surfacing submarine that did it.

"Money," Jimmy muttered, pushing eagerly into the battleship gray office.

"Came to the right place for that, bub," Boatswain's Mate First Class John Polazar said, glancing up from a pile of paperwork. He wore a telephone in the crook of his neck. His neatly rolled sleeves exposed a perfectly executed anchor on his left forearm.

"Have a seat, bub. Be with you in half a sec. Just gotta get one of your future shipmates squared away, and we'll get you aboard. Here, have a smoke."

Jimmy popped a Pall Mall out of the petty officer's pack. He sucked the unfiltered cigarette and peered through the smoke at this guy in the service dress blues.

Polazar was born to wear a set of tailor-mades — the bell-bottomed blue trousers with the 13-button fly or "marine dinner plate," and the blue jumper trimmed with white piping. He enhanced the classic look with a trim, black moustache; a clean, dry haircut; and an air of supreme self-assurance. Jimmy could just see this guy on liberty in Hong Kong kicking the shit out of about 30 marines, and then wading into a whorehouse and taking names later.

"Welcome to the navy, bub," Polazar said, when he finished with the phone call. "Bo's'n First Polazar at your service. Call me John." He extended his hand.

"Pleased to meet you, John. Jim Clarke."

"So how long can I sign you up for, Clarke?" Polazar said, rolling a fresh form into his Remington. "Why not go all the way and do a 20-year hitch? Hell, I'm more than half way there myself. I'll get out when I'm 40 — a full retirement, medical benefits, exchange privileges for life — the works. Man, you can't beat it. Gonna get me a resort down in the Ozarks and be a rich, lazy fisherman for the rest of my life. You like to fish?"

"Yeah, in fact I was just up in northern Wisconsin not too long ago. You shoulda seen the muskie I almost caught with my bare hands."

Polazar sniffed suspiciously. No booze, but then this one looked like one of those draft-dodgin' hippies who wanted a nice cushy place in the reserves.

Probably under the influence of some mind-alterin' chemical bullshit. Don't mean nothin', Polazar thought, 'cause his ass is as good as the next one, and I've got my bonus in the bag if I get him.

"With your bare hands, huh, Clarke? Well, I guess that's one way to get 'em, but I prefer a good 12-pound test line myself," Polazar said, lighting another smoke.

"Yeah, but I could have caught him if I had a spear gun. That sucker was too fast. And he was as big as a shark. I thought he was gonna turn on me and have me for dinner."

"Yeah, well. Hey, how about a jug of java?"

"Huh?"

"Coffee."

"Yeah, sure. I'm kinda tired."

"You work nights?" Polazar said, winking slyly.

"Yeah, you could say that," Jimmy said, playing along.

"On the old pussy patrol, huh, Clarke?"

"Yeah, you can say that again," Jimmy said, still feeling the lurch of Sharyn's lovemaking.

"You know what Daniel Boone said."

"No, what's that?"

"You shoot a beaver; you gotta eat it."

Polazar clapped Jimmy's back, and they shared a good, sea-going guffaw. Jimmy took his coffee black and told the recruiter he wanted what was on the poster in the window.

"You wanna be a shit-tube sailor or an airdale? You can't be both, Clarke," Polazar said, rummaging through his literature.

Jimmy thought about it. The acid wasn't letting him down very easy, and the only images he could conjure up came straight from hell. He was strapped in the cockpit of a stricken Phantom and was about to crash into a hospital full of crippled Vietnamese kids. Then he was aboard a sub that had just been torpedoed by the Russkies and was heading for the bottom where they would all burst from the pressure. Jimmy put his hand to his throat and mumbled, "God, what a choice."

"Hey, no problem," Polazar said, "you got plenty of time to decide."

"I'd like to check out submarines," Jimmy said.

"Submarines it'll be, Clarke."

"I wanna be one of them shit-tub sailors you talked about," Jimmy said, slurring his words.

"That's the shit-tube, Clarke. Shit-tube." The phone rang, and Polazar tossed Jimmy a glossy brochure with a nuclear-powered attack submarine on the cover. "Here, take a look at this while I field this call. Then we'll run you through the test."

"The test?" Jimmy wondered if there was a shit-tube out back.
"Yeah, you know, multiple choice. I hope you're good at math."

Jimmy nodded grimly and opened the brochure. He hated math.

But his aversion to arithmetic disappeared when he read:

"Submarine duty is different from anything else in the navy; it requires a special temperament which not all men possess. Every man aboard a submarine is highly qualified. Sub crews refer to themselves as the 'Silent Service' and to their submarine as the 'boat.'"

"Silent service — the boat," Jimmy repeated, committing them to memory.

Polazar glanced up from his call and nodded encouragingly. A real live one.

Jimmy continued reading: "Modern submarines are true submersibles; a nuclear-powered boat can remain on station, submerged, for as long as 60 days. Nuclear boats operate at depths greater than 400 feet and speeds faster than 20 knots; how much deeper or faster is classified. Such submarines are, in a sense, the first space vehicles, for while submerged their crews are, in a very real sense, out of this world."

Shit, Jimmy thought, I'm already out of this world.

Polazar finished his phone call and said, "So what do you think, Clarke? You ready to wear the Silver Dolphins?"

"You get to wear something special?"

"Shit yeah, bub. Them shit-tube sailors are the most elite people in the fleet. Except I guess some airdales might argue with that, but you wear them Silver Dolphins, and you get admirals salutin' you.

Nothin' better. And I hear they got the best chow in the navy. Well, why don't I give you the test, and we'll see if you qualify for submarine school. Let's see, you gotta have a GCT/ARI of at least 115, so I hope you're ready. Maybe you might wanna come back when . . ."

"Nah, I'm ready."

"All right. Don't say I didn't warn you. You got any questions before we start?"

"Yeah, can you receive long-distance phone calls on submarines?"

Polazar laughed. "Are you kiddin'? Man, if your old lady croaked while you're on patrol, they don't tell you until you return to port. They don't want anybody geekin' out down there, especially in them missle boats."

"Good," Jimmy said, glad that he would soon be incommunicado. "I'm ready when you are."

Jimmy ripped through the reading comprehension and word skill sections, but fell apart in the math and mechanical areas.

Question:

"For accurate weapons control, it is necessary to know the exact location and speed of the target, plus:

a) its weight;

b) direction of travel;

c) type of power plant."

Jimmy's answer: "Shit!"

Question:

"Navigational methods depend on exact measurements of distance, speed, direction and:

a) depth of water;

b) wind;

c) time."

Jimmy's answer: "This sucks."

The strain on his brain became too great and he made random marks on the rest of the answer sheet.

Polazar placed a master grid over Jimmy's test and quickly scored it. "Sorry, bub, 107. Ain't good enough for submarine school. But it's plenty good for a whole bunch of other ratings. Why don't you take some of these books home and think about it."

"No," Jimmy said, "I wanna join the navy. Now."

Polazar peered at his prospect. "You in trouble with the law or somethin', bub?"

"No. Never have been. Except for two moving violations when I was in high school, but that's it."

"Just askin'. You, ah, knock up some broad?"

Jimmy gasped. God, what if Sharyn wasn't . . . nah, she always took her pill. Always.

"No, man, I just want to join the navy, that's all. Is there any crime against that?"

Polazar shook his head, thinking of that nice fat bonus. "No, there sure ain't no crime against that."

Chapter Forty-Four

"So what do you think?" Jimmy asked.

Bruce MacKenzie turned from the stove and wiped his hands on his apron. "I think it'll do you a lot of good. You need some discipline in your life, and believe me, those chiefs'll kick it into you. I don't know who you think you've been fooling around here, but I've seen through your act from day one. Hand me the oregano, would you, dearsie?"

They were in the Evanston mansion Bruce was house-sitting.

"So you think I should do it, huh?" Jimmy said.

"Yep," Bruce said, tasting his sauce. "Here, tell me what you think."

"It's fine, Bruce. To tell you the truth, I already enlisted, but I just wanted to bounce it off you."

"You tell the dean yet?"

"Not yet."

Jimmy looked around the well-appointed kitchen and pictured his mother here whipping together one of her famous meatloafs. Then he realized he hadn't even thought of telling his parents.

"You ask me, I think the dean'll be relieved. You should hear what people say about you at the seminary," Bruce said.

"You should hear what I say about them. Look, I made a mistake. I didn't belong here in the first place. But it was the only thing I could come up with at the time. I told you that."

"No, you didn't," Bruce said.

"Well, in so many words. Anyway, I'm relieved that it's resolved. I was really getting tired of living with a lie. And no money. Man, I can't tell you how crazy it's been this summer."

Bruce glanced over his shoulder. "How could anything be crazier than our little expedition to the north woods?"

"You shoulda seen my little trip to Mississippi with Jill."

"What happened?"

"Well, K.C. got the girl, and we both got bloody noses. Neither of us won, really, so I asked Jill to decide. Crazy bitch chose K.C. Can you believe it?"

"I can believe it. Broads like her need to be beaten. They love jerks like K.C. Makes life interesting. So, I don't see you all summer, and now you show up at my doorstep to tell me your tale of woe."

"Sorry. What can I say? Hey, look, is there anything I can do to help?" Jimmy said, wanting to make amends.

"Yeah, you can put that new DOORS album on the stereo. And we can both have a good cry."

Jim Morrison, singer, songwriter, poet, and DOORS leader had been found dead that summer in Paris, France. The official cause of death was listed as heart attack. The 27-year-old admiral's son was survived by his wife, Pamela.

"Maybe he would have turned out all right if he had listened to his old man and joined the navy," Jimmy mused.

"Yeah," Bruce said, "at sea with Jim Morrison. God, the possibilities are endless."

Jimmy went to the living room and put "L.A. Woman" on the Magnavox. At least I didn't turn out like him, he thought when the dead rocker's voice boomed through the J. Robert Tuthill family's big Prairie-style house. Designed by a protege of Louis Sullivan, it was nestled at the end of a tree-lined cul de sac off Sheridan Road. Old man Tuthill was the senior partner in a grand old Loop law firm, and Mrs. Tuthill was on the women's board at the seminary. The kids are probably all on drugs, Jimmy thought, returning to the kitchen.

Bruce was playing the air guitar and sobbing. "God," he said during an instrumental, "what a tragedy. What a fuckin' tragedy."

"Yeah," Jimmy said, thinking Morrison probably had it coming. "Maybe we should smoke a joint in his memory or something."

"Good idea," Bruce said. "Have I got the pot for you."

Did he ever. They were soon so stoned they forgot all about the spaghetti and garlic bread and danced around the living room to the driving beat of the dead Door. Although the house was centrally air-conditioned, they were soon sweating like a couple of collegiate wrestlers.

"So what are you gonna do when you're locked up in boot camp with all those hot young studs?" Bruce said, leering at Jimmy.

Jimmy stopped dancing and looked at Bruce. "Nothin', why?"

"That's gonna be a long, long time without pussy for a lover boy like you. Maybe that's why you're really joining the navy. I always figured you were latent. Now I know. You want all that hot meat for yourself. And don't believe that bullshit about salt peter. You'll be so horny in boot camp you'll gladly take the first offer to have your cock sucked."

"I don't think so," Jimmy said, grinding his teeth. "Anyway, the recruiter said sodomy is a violation of the code."

"Penetration, however slight, constitutes sodomy—article 120, Uniform Code of Military Justice. You know how many sailors would be left to man the fleet if they enforced that?"

"No," Jimmy said, staring sullenly at Bruce.

"None," Bruce said, winking. "So why don't you 'fess up to old Father Bruce, admit you're a queer boy at heart, and you're joining the navy because you want to be locked up with all that hard meat out in the middle of the ocean."

"It's been real, Bruce," he said, extending his hand.

"What? You can't leave. I've got a whole pot of spaghetti in there. Besides, the evening was just starting to get interesting."

"Sorry to disappoint you, Bruce. But I'm not joining the navy because I'm homosexual. I'm joining because I don't belong here, and I don't have anywhere else to go. I know it's probably not the ideal solution, but at this point, it's the only one that makes sense to me. I came here because I wanted your advice as a friend, and I think I got it. Sorry I can't stay for dinner."

"You're sorry?" Bruce said. "What am I going to do with all this spaghetti?"

"Freeze it," Jimmy said, walking out the front door.

Chapter Forty-Five

It was the end of a three-week binge, and Jimmy wasn't sure where he had been or how he got home.

Just a fuzzy image of stopping by a pizza joint for a few slices and a pitcher or two, and some fool honking at him after that.

Anyway, he was home in bed, but he had to keep one foot planted firmly on the floor to keep the room from spinning. Finally, he knew there was no way he could sleep without throwing up, so he went to the john and made a clean job of it, proof positive that he wasn't powerless over alcohol.

He was stumbling back to bed when the phone rang, shattering what live nerve endings he had left.

It was Sharyn Craig, and she was hysterical. "I've been trying to get a hold of you for three days," she said between wracking sobs.

Jimmy rubbed his face. His heart and lungs were out of synch, and he had to sit in the dust to keep from fainting.

"I was at the hospital. I'm always at the hospital on weekdays; you know that. What's wrong?"

"You've got to come over. Now!"

"Now?!? It's the middle of the night!"

"It's only 12:30. I don't care what time it is. You've got to come over right away. I'm bleeding to death."

"What?!?"

"I'm bleeding to death."

"Have you called an ambulance? Did somebody attack you? What happened? Are you all right?"

"Of course I'm not all right. Otherwise why would I be calling you in the middle of the night? Look, I'll tell you about it when you get here. But hurry. Goddamn it, hurry!" She hung up, but she picked up the phone again before Jimmy clicked off. "And get me a box of Kotex Supers."

"What?"

"Just get 'em, and get your ass over here. You got me into this, you fuckin' asshole. Where were you all night?"

"I was out with some friends," Jimmy said. Me, myself, and I.

"What's her name?"

"It was a guy. Another student. Look, I'll be right over. Okay?"

"All right, but hurry. And don't forget the Kotexes."

Jimmy sat in the dark listening to the dial tone. When his lungs synchronized with his racing heart, he padded back to his room, found enough change for the elevated, and headed south to God knows what.

He stopped at an all-night pharmacy on Belmont and bought a big blue box of Kotex Supers. He knew what she needed them for, but he didn't want to know.

Sharyn was in her bathrobe when she answered the door. She grabbed the Kotexes and rushed into the bathroom. She was in there a long time, so Jimmy snooped around.The ashtrays were piled with cigarette butts, and her bed was a mess of bloody towels. I should have bought two boxes Jimmy thought.

Jimmy went to bathroom and knocked softly on the door. "Sharyn, you all right?"

She was sobbing softly. "I'll be right out." When she came out, she whispered, "It was yours, you know. From when . . ."

" . . . we did that windowpane."

"I wanted you to come with me. I wanted you to be there. I thought I'd be the one woman who brought the creep who knocked her up, but I ended up alone like all the rest. All alone on that table, while they stuck that thing in me. 'Won't hurt a bit,' the fuckin' doctor said. Yeah, it didn't hurt that asshole a bit, because he's a goddamn man, and he'll never know what it's like."

Jimmy took her in his arms and guided her to the couch. Then he cradled her while she cried it all out.

Sharyn fell asleep with her head on his shoulder, and he held her for a long time.

Finally, he lay Sharyn on the couch, put a pillow under her head, and covered her with fresh sheets and blankets against the unseasonable coolness. Then he settled on the floor beside her and kept watch through the night.

She was still sleeping when he was ready to go to the hospital, so rather than leaving her to awaken to an empty apartment, he called in sick.

The Reverend Paul Jordan answered. "You don't sound sick, Jim. You didn't look as though you were coming down with anything yesterday. What I'm hearing is . . ."

"What you're hearing is — go fuck yourself, you pompous jagoff!" Jimmy nearly broke the phone.

Seething with anger, frustration, and resentment, he took a long walk. He felt calmer after five blocks and went back and cooked a big batch of the only thing he knew how — scrambled eggs with onions and cheese.

Sharyn had been in the bathroom and was now sitting straight-legged on the couch staring at the dying dutch elm.

"The bleeding seems to have slowed down," she said.

"Good. That's real good. But don't you think you should go see your doctor? I'll take you."

"In what? You don't have a car."

"In a cab."

"With my money?"

"Well, yeah, but . . ."

She saw the eggs and made a happy sound. "Oh, who cares if you're a poverty case. I'm glad you're here. I just wish you were with me yesterday."

"I would have been if I had known. You know that, don't you?"

She looked at him for a long time. Finally, she decided he probably would have gone. "You know, the baby would have been retarded or deformed."

"Yeah," Jimmy said, setting the steaming plates on the coffee table. "I know. Acid messes up your genes pretty bad. Hey, I hope you're hungry."

She was ravenous.

While she ate, he made a pot of coffee and some orange juice.

They sipped their coffee and listened to the neighborhood go to work. The elm tree diffused the morning sunlight, and soon it was quiet save for the occasional elevated train and the birds.

Jimmy sat on the floor and held Sharyn's hand.

"What would you have said if I had reached you? Would you have wanted me to have the abortion?" Sharyn asked.

"It's your body, isn't it?"

"I knew you'd say that. You sound like some Zero Population Growth pamphlet. But it was OUR baby. Our baby, Jimmy."

"Yeah," Jimmy said. "But you couldn't have been pregnant very long. We've only been making love . . ."

". . . for three months, two weeks and five days," Sharyn said. "The doctor said I had been pregnant less than a month. So I figure it was that time we were doing windowpane."

"So it didn't look like much more than a tadpole, did it?"

"That's what they say," Sharyn said, staring woodenly out the window.

Jimmy exhaled. Whatever it looked like, it was theirs.

"It's just as well, isn't it, Sharyn? I mean, chances are it would have been deformed or retarded. All that acid we did — it didn't have a chance in hell of having one normal gene. But you're sure . . ."

"I'm sure," she said, dropping his hand. "I forgot to take my pill. I forgot to take my goddamn pill."

"Oh well."

"Oh well," she repeated, gazing out the window. "Oh well."

They stared at the dying elm for a long time. Finally she said, "Jimmy?"

"Yeah."

"Jimmy, I love you."

She pulled him up on the couch and kissed him so hard he thought his teeth would break. Her salty tears dripped into his mouth, and he had to break away for breath.

"It wouldn't have been right, having the baby now," she said, stroking his forehead. "I think we should wait until you've got your church and we're settled in the rectory. Then the curate's wife can get herself in the family way and . . ."

"Sharyn, hold on. You're goin' too fast," Jimmy said, pulling away. "There's something I've got to tell you."

"What?"

The phone rang.

"It's probably Leslie," she said. "He's been calling off and on to see how I'm doing."

"Leslie — you mean Father Swann. You told Father Swann?"

"Of course I told him. He's my priest. What good are priests if you can't share your disasters with them?"

"I don't know. But that's what I want to talk to you about. See . . ."

"I'm going to get the phone. Stay right there, all right?"

"But Sharyn, I want to . . ."

"Jimmy, I'm going to answer the phone. All right?"

He nodded.

She went to the phone and said, "Hello, Leslie. Um huh. Yeah. Better. Yeah. Right. Yeah, he's here. Want to talk to him? Okay, hang on. Jimmy, he wants to talk to you."

"Shit. All right," he said, getting up. "Just a minute."

Jimmy took the phone and grimaced. "Hello, Father Swann."

The Reverend Leslie Swann sat up straighter and made no attempt to hide his righteous indignation as he said, "I knew I should have issued chastity belts when you showed up. Are you satisfied? Or are you looking to carve another notch on your belt this week?"

Jimmy bit his lip and said, "Look, I'm really sorry. I really am."

Sharyn wrapped her arms around herself and leaned against the door jamb.

"A little late for that, isn't it?" Father Swann said. "And where, might I ask, were you while that poor young woman was going through that awful ordeal? At least you could have been with her when she needed you."

"I said I'm sorry. I would have been there with her if I had known. Believe me, I would have."

"That's just it — I don't believe you," Father Swann said. "I don't believe anything you say because you can't be trusted. You assume everyone and everything exists for your pleasure. Well, let me tell you something, young man, that's not the way it works. Not at all. You are one of the most undisciplined people I have ever met. Ever. As to why the seminary admitted you in the first place I don't know, but I'm going to personally see that . . ."

"Don't bother," Jimmy said.

"I beg your pardon?" Father Swann said.

Sharyn unfolded her arms and looked at Jimmy.

He looked at her as he said, "I said don't bother, because I'm leaving the seminary. I joined the navy, Father Swann."

"What?" Sharyn said, alarmed.

Jimmy nodded.

Father Swann said: "Well, it's about time if you ask me. Maybe they'll force some discipline into that willful mind of yours. Maybe you'll finally learn something about living with others. Maybe . . ."

"Father Swann?"

"Yes?"

"Fuck off."

Jimmy turned to Sharyn.

She was crying too hard to talk, so he ushered her back to the couch and put his arms around her. The phone rang, and they ignored it.

Jimmy dried Sharyn's tears with his sleeve and said, "I'm sorry I had to break the news to you like this. I was trying to tell you when he called. But I guess there wouldn't have been any good time to tell you. I guess . . ."

"When did you do it?"

"After I left here last time. I couldn't go to sleep—that acid had me so wired—so I wandered around Evanston for a while, and I just ended up at the navy recruiter's office. Sharyn, I don't have to tell you what a mess I've made of things. God, I feel like such a jerk."

Finally, Jimmy cried.

Sharyn cradled him against her breast and let him cry it all out. When was finished, she asked, "Did you ever love me?"

"No, Sharyn," he said softly. "I never loved you."

"That's what I thought," she said. "My mother always told me my eternal optimism would get me in trouble. Maybe I should start listening to her."

"I guess you should. Sharyn?"

"What?"

"Will you forgive me?"

She looked at him for a long time. "About this time yesterday, I wanted to kill you. I wanted to stick that vacuum thing up your ass and suck your brains out sideways. But, you know, I don't feel that way now. I don't know what I feel, but I know I don't hate you."

Jimmy stayed for a week nursing Sharyn back to health. He cooked and cleaned and made Kotex runs and told her how sorry he was.

When she was better and wanted to make love, he let himself out while she was in the bathroom taking her pill.

Chapter Forty-Six

Jimmy had finally gotten the nerve to call his parents when there was a sharp rap on the door.

"Just a minute, Mom, there's someone at the door," Jimmy said.

Louise Clarke was still in shock. "What's this about the navy, dear? You spoke so fast."

"I said I'm joining the navy, Mom. Not joining, joined. I report to boot camp in two weeks. Look, there's somebody knocking at the door. Why don't I call you back when Dad's home. Okay?"

"Well, all right," Louise said, knowing her husband was having one of his long, liquid lunches and would be in no shape to discuss anything with his son when he came home. "Call us tonight."

"Okay. Talk to you tonight. Bye."

Jimmy sighed and shuffled to the door. He was afraid to open it until he looked out the window and saw a phone company truck parked in the drive.

A phone company truck, he thought, I don't have any problems with my phone. Then he remembered that there were two, maybe more, unopened phone bills somewhere in that mess on his desk.

The phone guy had a beer belly and a bad attitude. "You Clarke? James G?"

"Yeah, that's me," Jimmy said.

"The 'G' stand for — God?" the phone guy said, eyeballing the churchly digs.

"Very funny. I don't remember making a service call."

"You got number 555-8684, right?"

"Yeah, but . . ."

"Yeah, well then I'm here to take your phone."

He flashed a picture ID.

"You gonna let me in, or do I have to climb through the window?"

"There must be some mistake. I . . ."

The phone guy flashed a keypunched card. "Ma Bell don't make no mistakes. You is what we call a deadbeat. Now do I gotta get de cops, or is you gonna let me in like a nice little altar boy?"

"Look, I was going to have it disconnected in a week anyway. Just let me have it one more week so I can wrap up some things, and I'll pay my bills. Honest."

"The check's in the mail, we'd love to have you for dinner, and I won't come in your mouth. Tell me another one. Where's the phone, pal? I got a lotta calls today."

Jimmy was too tired to argue.

"This way," he said.

The phone guy was about to snip the line when the phone rang.

"Just to show you what a nice guy I am," he said, smiling, "I'll let the condemned man have one last phone call. As long as it ain't collect."

"Go ahead and cut it."

"You sure? Could be yer girlfriend. Oh that's right, yose guys ain't allowed to have girlfriends. Is ya?"

"This isn't a Catholic seminary," Jimmy said.

"It ain't? You mean dere is some udder kind?"

"Yeah. Hey, look. I've got lots to do today. Do you mind?"

"Hell no." he said. "My pleasure." He snipped the line, silencing the phone in mid-ring. Then he artfully wrapped the cord around the phone and tucked it under his arm.

"Here," he said, handing Jimmy a form. "Sign this – here and here. Good. If I were you, Rev, I wouldn't go askin' Ma Bell for another phone for a while. And I wouldn't let no health inspectors in here until I took a flame t'rower to this joint. Well, Rev, it's been a slice. Light a candle for me or somethin'."

"We don't do that here," Jimmy said.

"Oh, dat's right. Youse is Publics."

"Publics?"

"Yeah, youse is either Cadlic or Public. Yose goes to a Cadlic school or a Public school. Yose goes to a Cadlic church or a Public church. Yose is Cadlic or yose is Public. Take care, Rev, and don't touch nothin'. You might get some unmentionable disease."

When the smirking gomer was gone, Jimmy went to the bathroom sink and tried to remove the brown crud with the butt of his hand. He couldn't look at the toilet where there was something green and growing.

He opened some windows and shuffled through the dust, wondering what to do next. He wished he was reporting to boot camp today. Jimmy decided to tell the dean about the navy as soon as he cleaned up the rooms and paid the phone bill with what little money he had left in his checkbook.

The work felt good, and Jimmy threw himself into it. He swept and scrubbed and wiped and scoured until he felt he was washing his sins away.

He tore down the rock posters he had taped to the wall and didn't think twice about stuffing Jim Morrison in the garbage. He took inventory of his possessions and realized he didn't have much beyond a few changes of clothes. He resolved to give his clerical shirts to Mike Harper and the rest to Episcopal Charities.

Jimmy paid his phone bill and winced when he realized he would have to make it until book camp on $29.95.

Then he went to the pay phone and called Paul Jordan at St. Mark's Medical Center. Jordan was doing one of his tedious one-on-ones with another member of the group, so Jimmy told the secretary, "Just tell him that Jimmy Clarke slammed the last door. I'm through with CPE. I'm leaving the seminary, so I won't be back."

"Wait, wait," the secretary said. "He'll want to talk to you about this. Where can you be reached?"

Jimmy smiled. "I can't."

Next, he went to the dean's office, ready and eager to have a long morning's talk.

Jimmy rapped his knuckles on the thick oak door, but there was no answer.

Funny, he thought, it's Tuesday—he should be in there. Especially with the new quarter about to start. Maybe he took the day off and went for a bike ride.

Jimmy went to the deanery and rang the buzzer.

"Morning, Claire—oh, uh, hi." Jimmy said, unable to remember the woman's name. She was a faculty wife; that's all he knew.

She didn't know his name either. She only knew he was that junior they called the "Phantom."

"May I help you?" she said.

Jimmy looked past her and saw that the living room was full of Gatesbury women. Claire must be having a little do for the wives or something.

"Look, I didn't mean to interrupt your tea; I just wanted to have a word with Dean Manoogian. Is he here? I tried his office, and he wasn't there."

The woman stepped forward and closed the door behind herself.

"Dean Manoogian is dead," she recited woodenly. "He died in the middle of the night of a heart attack. We tried to find you, but you weren't in, or you weren't answering your door, and when Miriam Blake tried to call you this morning, your phone was disconnected. Anyway, visitation is in the Guthbertson Chapel and begins this evening at seven. Bishop Franklin will celebrate the requiem mass on Thursday at 11 at St. Luke's. Contributions should be sent in lieu of flowers to the American . . ."

As she recited the long list of worthy causes and organizations, Jimmy felt the sidewalk slipping out from under him.

When she was finished, he said, "I'd like to see Jennifer. Is she here?"

"Yes. I mean no," the woman said rigidly. "I don't think this would be a good time. As you can well imagine, Jennifer is quite upset. Well, I do hope you'll find time to attend the funeral. We'd like to have 100 percent representation."

Jimmy nodded. "I'll be there. Don't worry."

Without thinking, he went back to the dean's office and rapped on the door.

That bitch was just pulling his chain. They were out to get him for being such a deadbeat, like the phone guy said.

Jimmy pounded and pounded. He bruised his hands and continued pounding. Finally, it hit him, and he collapsed against George Manoogian's door and sobbed uncontrollably.

Chapter Forty-Seven

As promised, Jimmy called home that night. Collect, of course.

His father, who had had a long, liquid lunch, took the call in the den.

"Yes, operator, I'll accept the charges," he slurred, "but it's the last goddamn time."

"Hi, Dad. I guess Mom told you about . . ."

"'Bout time you did something worthwhile with your life." He paused to freshen his drink and to tell his wife to get off the other phone. "The navy sure as hell didn't do your old man any harm, and it won't do you any either. You hear me? You listen to those chiefs. They're the backbone of the navy."

"Sure, Dad," Jimmy said.

"So when do you report to Newport?" Jim said, taking a gulp of good scotch.

"Newport?"

"Yeah, Newport. Where the hell else are you gonna become a ninety-day wonder?"

"Dad, actually I'm not going to be an officer. You see, I'm going to Great Lakes and . . ."

"You're gonna be a goddamn swab jockey?!?"

"Yeah, but . . ."

"A goddamn swab jockey! I bust my ass to send you to college, we go broke sending you to that goddamn seminary, and now you tell me you're gonna be a goddamn swab jockey? Well, it figures. You and your goddamn generation are nothin' but a bunch of stupid, lazy punks. Goddamn worthless punks. You hear me??!"

"Dad?" he said after a long pause.

"What?"

"Good bye."

Jimmy returned to his room and looked across the drive at the dean's darkened office. How come I couldn't have had a father like him, he thought.

Feeling numb and nasty, Jimmy wrote his farewell letter to the bishop. It read:

"Dear Bishop Hamilton:

"By the time you get this letter, you'll probably already know that Dean Manoogian died of a heart attack. I can't tell you how sorry I am that he's gone. He was a wonderful man."

Jimmy bit his lip.

"Anyway, I'm writing to tell you that I am leaving the seminary in two weeks to join the navy. You may recall from my last letter that I wanted to take a leave of absence. Well, to be honest with you, Bishop Hamilton, I made a mistake coming here. I'm sorry. Anyway, I'm broke and pretty confused right now, and I figure the navy will do me some good on both of those fronts.

"Thanks for your patience. Please give my regards to Miss Worden.

"Sincerely,

"Jimmy Clarke."

Jimmy looked at the letter and parked his Parker.

He walked to the mailbox at Orrington and Noyes and thought of how he and Dean Manoogian had strolled along this street.

As he walked, Jimmy realized that he had not prayed for the repose of the dean's soul.

With his eyes wide open he prayed: "God, all I can say is you'd better treat him right, because he sure as hell treated me right. Hope you're having a good time up there, Dean Manoogian. Amen."

Chapter Forty-Eight

Chief among the multitude of mourners crowding St. Luke's Episcopal Church, Evanston, was the Right Reverend Charles P. Franklin, Bishop of Chicago.

As celebrant of the requiem mass honoring the dearly departed dean, he stood in front of George Manoogian's closed casket and said, "I am the resurrection and the life, saith the Lord: he that believeth in me, though he were dead, yet shall he live: and whosoever liveth and believeth in me, shall never die. I know that my redeemer liveth, and that he shall stand at the latter day upon the earth: and though this body be destroyed, yet shall I see God: whom I shall see for myself, and mine eyes shall behold, and not as a stranger. We brought nothing into this world, and it is certain we can carry nothing out. The Lord gave, and the Lord hath taken away; blessed be the name . . ."

Jimmy wondered why church architects never thought to install ceiling fans. He closed his eyes and watched George Manoogian careen along Orrington Avenue on his daughter's bicycle. He heard his rich laugh and rubbed his eyes.

The nearest Armenian lady handed Jimmy her embroidered hanky and patted his shoulder. Pam Millar shifted uneasily in her seat. Despite all her talk about wanting men to be free with their feelings, it made her extremely nervous to hear a man cry.

While the bishop and his boys did their high church hocus-pocus, the Gatesbury choir sang the Kyrie Eleison.

Then Lance Gordon read an overwritten tribute from the student body.

Jimmy gazed around the great vaulted space and realized he wasn't going to miss it. He doubted he would have much if anything to do with it when he left, and that didn't bother him.

Jimmy closed his eyes and felt the dean's warm presence.

Old Vicar Marshfield was next. He read Tennyson's "Crossing the Bar," and there wasn't a dry eye in God's house when he finished. Jimmy wondered if he was going to do a little Churchill number for an encore.

Jimmy was hurt that Claire Manoogian hadn't asked him to read something. Maybe I wasn't the most visible student on the block, but she knew how much I liked her husband. Jimmy lowered his eyes and sobbed quietly. The Armenian lady patted his hand and told him to keep her hankie.

Jimmy dried his eyes and knelt when Bishop Franklin turned to the congregation and said: "Let us pray for the whole state of Christ's Church. Almighty and everlasting God, who by thy holy Apostle hast taught us to make prayers and supplications, and to give thanks for all men: We humbly beseech thee most mercifully to accept our alms and oblations, and to receive these our prayers, which we offer unto thy Divine Majesty; beseeching thee to . . ."

Jimmy had a clear view now of Claire and her three daughters in the first pew on the Gospel side. Jennifer was wedged between her older sisters who handed her endless tissues and whispered consolingly in her ears. Still, she shook and sobbed uncontrollably.

Oh Jennifer, he thought, I do love you. Even if you don't love me.

Jimmy wrung his hands and asked God to make a comfortable place for the dean. Let him smoke all the Luckies he wants, Lord. Then he asked for a word with the deceased.

"Mr. Dean, I'm really sorry for the mess I've made at the seminary. I'm sorry you died before I could tell you how sorry I am. I really wanted to talk to you about joining the navy. I think it's the right thing to do considering what a mess I've made here. I knew you'd agree. Take care."

When it was his turn to file by the closed casket, Jimmy touched the polished wood and looked lovingly at the dean's photograph. George Manoogian stared forthrightly into the camera, a hint of mischief twinkling in his eyes.

Jimmy sighed. Others were waiting their turn. He ran his fingers along the casket and bit his lip. Unashamed, he let the tears roll down his cheeks.

When he turned to offer his condolences to the family, he realized with alarm that Jennifer wasn't there. He hadn't seen her leave, but then there had been a lot of foot traffic. Claire pointed helpfully to the sacristy, off to the left.

Jennifer's sisters and the Reverend Godfrey J. Wiltwright had protectively encircled the inconsolable young woman. But their best blandishments could not stop Jennifer's keening.

Jimmy stepped across the threshold and said in a breaking voice, "Jennifer, it's me, Jimmy."

"You can't come in here," Wiltwright said, blocking Jimmy's path.

Jimmy tried to get Jennifer's attention, but she was beyond seeing anyone.

So he mouthed "I love you" and returned to his pew, knowing he would never see her again.

Chapter Forty-Nine

Jimmy stood at the entrance to the Recruit Training Command at the Great Lakes Naval Training Facility and saw long rows of battleship gray barracks and drill halls. Companies of blue-clad boys marched in practiced cadence as men wearing red aiguillettes shepherded them toward manhood.

Jimmy was about to knock on the blue sentry box when an officious young recruit in a white helmet ordered him to halt and present his papers.

"Well, Clarke," the recruit petty officer said, "welcome to the navy. It's not too late to change your mind, you know. You can turn around right now and walk out that gate, and I'll just say I never saw you. You wouldn't be the first. Otherwise, you're in for some big surprises."

"Like what?"

"Like you ain't gonna get no booze or pussy for at least eight weeks. And no cigarettes for the first two weeks. And that's just the beginning. Well, what do you say, Clarke?"

"I'm ready," Jimmy said.

"You're gonna be sorry, boy, real sorry."

"I guess. Hey, do I have to go to church here?"

"No, that's one thing they don't . . ."

"Then what the hell are you waiting for? Let me in!"

The End